Days of Deception

Murder, mystery, intrigue, suspense, love, Yankees and Southerners on a post-Civil-War train—all the ingredients of a first class thriller as only Lee Roddy can tell it.
Jack Cavanaugh
author of *An American Family Portrait* series

The Pinkerton *Lady* Chronicles

Days of Deception

LEE RODDY

Chariot VICTOR
PUBLISHING
A DIVISION OF COOK COMMUNICATIONS

Victor books is an imprint of Chariot Victor Publishing,
a division of Cook Communications, Colorado Springs, Colorado 80918
Cook Communications, Paris, Ontario
Kingsway Communications, Eastbourne, England

DAYS OF DECEPTION
© 1998 by Lee Roddy. All rights reserved. Printed in Canada.

Editor: Susan Reck
Design: Bill Gray
Cover Illustration: Matthew Archambault

1 2 3 4 5 6 7 8 9 10 Printing/Year 02 01 00 99 98

**Published in association with the literary agency of Alive Communications,
Inc. 1465 Kelly Johnson Blvd., Suite 320, Colorado Springs, Colorado 80920**

Library of Congress Cataloging-in-Publication Data

Roddy, Lee.
    Days of deception/by Lee Roddy.
        P.   cm. — (Pinkerton lady chronicles ; bk. 1)
    ISBN 1-56476-635-7
    I. Title. II. Series: Roddy, Lee, Pinkerton lady
    chronicles ; bk. 1.
    PS3568.0344D38 1998
    813' .54—dc21   97-35531
                                                              CIP

To Cicely

with all my love on our
very special anniversary
October 17

The lone man with the saber scar across the bridge of his nose and right cheek had braced himself for what he might see, but he wasn't prepared for this.

Blackened and unidentifiable stacks of rubble lay like unburied dead between the two great chimneys. They were all that stood upright, like gravestones at both ends of what had been his childhood home. What little had escaped the burning house had been carried off by invading Yankees to feed their campfires, now dead and cold in the September morning.

Slowly shifting his six-foot body and favoring the wounded left leg, Ridgely Granger let his blue eyes skim the trampled green lawns and gardens that had been his late mother's special pride. She rested beside her husband in the family plot overlooking the river.

Ridge's gaze lingered there before he continued his visual inventory. The slave quarters under the great oaks had been razed, along with all the outbuildings. The stables were gone. So were the blooded horses that had whinnied in welcome each morning until he rode off to join the Confederate cavalry.

The tobacco fields were abandoned and silent. There was an eerie quiet, broken only by the rising autumn wind in the grand old trees. They were all that remained of what had been one of the most beautiful small plantations in northern Virginia.

The wind tugged at his tattered dress jacket where the three bars of a captain had faded on the collar, as had the entwined sleeve insignia. The frayed pants with yellow piping along the seam were tucked into scuffed knee-length boots.

Ridge threw back his head and cried out the great agony of his soul. Some startled crows in the ruined garden took wing, but he did not notice.

His gaze shifted beyond the river to the nearest house. Smoke from a tall chimney testified that Varina Owens, now married, was in her new home. She had promised to wait, but hadn't.

Ridge closed his eyes tightly, but her image floated in his memory. So did the beautiful little church with its stained glass windows where he had been baptized and planned to be married. The Yankees had destroyed that, too. Everything was gone now, even his faith.

With an effort, he turned away and opened his eyes to the ruins before him. Slowly, as if forever burning the scene into his memory, he took one final look at the stark remains of what he had fought for the last four years—and lost.

Nothing was left except a deep emotional wound and a nagging question: should he forget this place and go away forever, or try to reclaim it from the Northern carpetbaggers who had seized it under Union Confiscation Acts?

Before he made that decision, however, he had to deliver a letter. It had been given to him by a teenage Union soldier whom he found dying the morning after a battle. The infantryman had made Ridge promise to hand carry the letter addressed to Charley Bartlett, Elm Street, Chicago, Illinois.

The Confederacy was short of weapons, so in the early morning light after a battle the previous afternoon, Ridge had been searching for usable Federal arms. That's when he heard a moan.

At first, Ridge thought the kid was dead, along with all the other somewhat older Federals. But the youth had begged for water as Ridge approached. He was about sixteen, Ridge decided, as he shared his canteen. That's when the Northern infantryman pleaded with Ridge to deliver the letter. Ridge had resisted, but the silent imploring look in the young eyes had made him give his word. He had slipped the letter inside his jacket pocket and carried it for the rest of the war.

He had often berated himself for his rash promise to the boy in the blue uniform. In an earlier skirmish, Ridge had suffered a saber cut to the face. Later, grown Union soldiers had put a minié ball into Ridge's leg and killed his only brother.

But it was a matter of honor to keep a promise. With a shuddering sigh, Ridge turned from the plantation ruins and limped purposefully back the way he had come.

He would first go to Chicago to deliver the letter. Then he would face the decision of whether to return to Virginia and fight to rebuild, or turn his back on all that had been his, and drift wherever the wind blew.

Chapter 1

The crisp autumn wind whipped across Lake Michigan and prowled Chicago's streets, making Ridge glad that he had worn his Confederate overcoat with the long cape favored by cavalrymen. In accordance with official ordinance, it had neither officer's insignia nor sleeve braid, but he wore the top open so that his yellow-trimmed Confederate cavalry jacket showed.

There was a reminder in the proud and defiant way Ridge wore his jacket that strong emotions still ran close to the surface, even five months after official cessation of hostilities. For some, the war was *not* over. Ridge's bearing suggested he was such a man, a person to be left alone with his internal wars.

He was only vaguely aware that men and women stepped aside as he approached, but he did not care when they surreptitiously glanced at him. Subconsciously, he tried to minimize his limp, as though it might suggest a weakness. He focused on delivering the letter so that he could get on with his life.

He saw two young factory workers approach and stopped in front of them. "Pardon me," Ridge said with a hint of Southern accent, "Can you tell me how to get to Elm Street?"

The shorter of the two men started to answer, bringing his hand up to point, but his heavier companion spoke first. "What's the matter with you, Reb? Don't you know you're not welcome up North?"

Ridge's cold blue eyes locked onto the speaker's brown ones. Ridge shifted his weight to brace his feet and eased his hands slightly forward of his waist. He said nothing, but continued to give the heavier man a cold, hard stare.

His companion nervously clutched at his sleeve. "Come on, Ed," he urged, taking a step. "Let's go."

Ed suddenly dropped his eyes, nodded, and stepped aside to go around Ridge. His companion hesitated long enough to say, "It's over by the lake, Mister."

Ridge thanked him and glanced toward Lake Michigan, where the cold wind had been whipping leaves off of trees and chasing them down the street.

Pulling his coat tighter about himself, Ridge started to cross the street when he observed a pretty young woman in a buggy easing her horse toward a hitching post.

A heavier carriage driven by a gray-haired man suddenly cut the corner, putting the rig on a collision course with the light buggy.

"Look out!" Ridge shouted as the man pulled sharply on the left rein.

The horse veered left, but the passing vehicle's rear wheel caught the back corner of the buggy. Instantly, it tipped sharply, throwing the lone woman occupant free. She landed ingloriously in the street, her hoopskirt flaring high.

Ridge rushed across the street while the other driver brought his horse to a halt. They reached the victim at the same time.

The driver apologized, "I'm so sorry, Miss! I was late for an appointment—"

Ridge interrupted, "Are you hurt, Miss?" he asked, kneeling beside the woman. She was trying to recover her dignity by pressing the recalcitrant hoopskirt down around her legs.

She was petite, Ridge noticed, not much over five feet tall, but what there was of her was all woman.

She replied, "I think so. I've had harder falls from my horse."

Both men reached down and helped her regain her feet. The older man asked with great concern, "Are you sure? Perhaps we should consult a doctor."

She gave him a reassuring smile. Her entire face lit up with the practiced skill of a young woman who knows how to flatter. "My hands are only a little scratched. . . ." She broke off her thought when her violet eyes met Ridge's. They were pale blue ,she noticed, yet with a mysterious darkness in their depths. He wasn't quite handsome, but he was certainly good looking, standing about six feet tall. The only defect on his sun-browned skin was a slight scar across the bridge of his nose and right cheekbone. She guessed that was from a war wound.

"Thank you," she said, her eyes crinkling as her smile widened. "It all happened so fast. . . ."

She left her sentence dangling when she became aware of Ridge's Confederate jacket.

He didn't mind. He had been stared at a lot since getting off the train cars in Chicago. Instead, he used her momentary pause to let his gaze sweep over her.

Her tiny nose and small mouth were offset by flawless skin. It contrasted with very dark hair which was arranged so that curls bounced on either side of her throat.

The smile slid from her face and her eyes narrowed disapprovingly. She declared haughtily, "I can take care of myself! I certainly don't need any help from a Rebel!"

Ridge didn't answer for a moment, but let his eyes slide down to her dirty skirt and the street where she had been thrown. "Yes," he said quietly, "I have just seen a demonstration of how you do that."

He turned and walked on, hearing her sputter behind him. He tried to minimize the limp, then chided himself for doing that. He had suffered enough at the hands of a woman to care about impressing another, especially this ungrateful and saucy one.

Ridge walked a discreet distance, then cautiously turned and looked back.

He saw her pause under a sign with an all-seeing eye and the words, *The Eye That Never Sleeps.*

Ridge recognized the symbol for Allan Pinkerton's Detective Agency. He frowned, recalling that Pinkerton had formed the North's Secret Service for spying on the South early in the war.

After the woman entered the building, Ridge continued toward the lake, anxious to unburden himself of the letter. But he found himself wondering why that woman had gone to a detective agency.

In Pinkerton's office, Laurel Bartlett was her usual charming self. She felt confident in what she had come to do: deceive one of the Union's most shrewd men. Allan Pinkerton did not take missing person cases, but she wanted desperately to find her missing fiancé.

Claude Duncan was alive, Laurel knew, but he had not returned home or contacted her since the war ended. She needed to support herself while searching for him. For that, it was necessary to convince Pinkerton to hire her as an operative without letting him guess her real motive.

After accepting his invitation to sit down, she apologized for her slightly soiled skirt by briefly telling him about the carriage accident.

Pinkerton regarded her thoughtfully from across his desk. He was a bearded, powerfully built man in his mid-forties who was known to like the ladies. He listened to Laurel, waiting for her to say why she had come to him again.

Straightening her skirt and clearing her throat, Laurel moved toward her goal. "I appreciated the way you let me become an operative working behind Confederate lines when I was barely eighteen."

He nodded. "You did a good job, especially in obtaining intelligence about the planned Rebel cavalry raid at Bethel Crossing. Our forces cut them to pieces."

She gave him a grateful smile. "Thank you."

"Unlike some other operatives, like Pauline Cushman, the Confederates never caught you."

"I'm thankful for that," she replied, recalling that Cushman had been sentenced to hang, but had been spared when Union General Rosecrans attacked the area where she was held.

Laurel opened the drawstring on her reticule and produced some newspaper clippings. "I've been following your recent railroad investigations. There seems to be a number of employees who are stealing from the company, especially conductors."

"It's easy for them to do," Pinkerton said as Laurel spread the clippings across his desk. "People don't buy a ticket in advance because some communities have no depot. It's common practice for any passenger to simply board a train and pay the conductor directly. About half the money collected is stolen."

"That's what I read." Hesitating only slightly, Laurel suppressed her real motive in coming to offer a reason she thought Pinkerton would accept. "The papers say you 'test' railroad employees by having operatives secretly observe their honesty."

"Spying on them," he said bluntly.

Laurel flinched. She hated the word "spy" and had always thought of herself as a courier or an operative during the war. "Whatever it's called," she admitted, "it seems to work. Arrests prove that."

"It works," he agreed.

"Except," Laurel said, carefully watching his face to see how her proposal would be received, "on the Great Central Railroad operating out of Chicago and heading toward New Orleans."

"No railroad goes directly from here to there," he replied, realizing what she was trying to get him to do.

"I know you have to change trains and take other lines, but someday the Great Central will probably go all the way through. Maybe one of George Pullman's new sleeper hotel cars will be part of that line."

"Not until they straighten some curves and do some other work. That car's too long." Pinkerton leaned forward, sure of his ground. "Let's get to the point, Laurel. You want me to hire you to test the conductors on that line, but the answer is no."

She had expected that. Without being at all concerned, she leaned toward him and spoke firmly. "You have had men operatives riding that train for some time now, without success. Oh, they suspect that a conductor named Hannibal Schramm is stealing fares, but he's too smart for them to catch."

"And you can?"

"A woman would be less likely to be suspected, especially by Schramm. He pays lots of attention to young pretty ladies in his cars, even though he's been married twice. He won't suspect me of testing him."

"You think you know a lot about this, don't you?"

"I do," she agreed, smiling confidently. "You need to put me back on as a paid operative."

"Hold on! You probably read about railroad thievery in the newspaper, but what you don't know is that Schramm is also suspected of being involved with one of those new gangs of former soldiers and border ruffians. They're mostly angry ex-rebels, but some are former Union soldiers. They're now robbing towns and killing people."

"That doesn't change my mind." Her quick agreement was meant to soften any idea that Pinkerton might think her answer was impertinent. "I've taken lots worse risks behind Confederate lines, so how about it? Put me on the case."

The detective asked bluntly, "What's your real reason for wanting this assignment?"

A little startled at how perceptive Pinkerton had been, Laurel hesitated only a fraction of a second before smiling confidently. "Why, money, of course. In the war, it was my patriotic duty to do what I could." A hint of frown touched her forehead. "Especially after my only brother was killed by Rebels. But now, it's money."

Brightening again, she added, "The sooner I start, the sooner you'll have the facts you need to arrest Schramm."

"Not so fast! If he is guilty of all charges, as suspected, he might harm you if he discovers you're an operative."

She flared, "You sent me on missions behind enemy lines during the war when danger lurked on every side! I handled myself well then, and I can certainly do it with a train conductor!"

"It was different then." Pinkerton pushed back his chair and stood up, indicating the interview was over. "Everyone was involved for the good of the cause. This time, it would only be one woman against a man clever enough that he's outsmarted some of my best operatives. But thanks for coming in, Laurel."

"I won't fail!"

"I've lost good men who shouldn't have failed, but did. Things sometimes happen that nobody can anticipate. Besides, once a train leaves a community, it has no effective lawful protection until it reaches the next station. You, now just nineteen, want to venture alone into that environment where you might be suspected and murdered. I needed you in the war, but not this time."

Laurel did not move even though he walked to the door and opened it. "I recognize those dangers, but I can handle it. Schramm won't suspect a woman, especially me. Think about it!"

Her voice had risen with her determination because she needed this assignment to achieve her real objective.

For several seconds, Pinkerton studied her chin, now tilted defiantly. "You proved yourself in the war," he said thoughtfully, "so it seems you've earned the right to a peacetime project. All right, but on my conditions."

Laurel had the feeling that he had been testing her to learn how much she wanted this assignment. But she was so relieved she simply asked, "Which are?"

"As with all the operatives in this agency, you will be entirely on your own. You work alone, as in the war. Next, you must not make contact with any other person who might work for this agency. You are to communicate only with me, and that directly through coded telegraph messages."

Trying not to show her relief, Laurel nodded. "Agreed."

"There's more. You must find a female traveling companion."

"Why?" Surprise made Laurel's voice rise indignantly. "I was alone every time I slipped through Confederate pickets to do my job. Besides, you just said I was to work alone."

"You will. Neither your companion nor anybody else is to know that you're an operative, or what your mission is. The companion is for appearances. A comely young woman traveling alone on trains would arouse unwanted curiosity."

Reluctantly, Laurel agreed. "All right, but I'll need advance payment for our tickets, plus some pocket money."

Pinkerton's eyes narrowed in understanding. "Still not getting along with your father?"

"He disapproves of what he calls my 'mysterious absences' the last year or so. He claims I ruined my reputation on those trips I took during the war."

"Too bad." Pinkerton shrugged, then concluded, "You meet my conditions, and you'll have the money. Oh, there is one more thing. You have one week."

"One week?" Laurel rankled under the unexpectedly harsh terms. Her hidden reason for wanting the job made her control her temper. "How about six weeks?" she countered.

"Seven days. Now, are you in or out?"

Resigned to the inevitable, she nodded. "I'm in."

"Good! Come back when you have the traveling companion, and I'll fill in other details you'll need."

Laurel walked out with conflicting feelings. She chafed under Pinkerton's conditions, but she was grateful that at last she could start searching for answers that had eluded her these five months since the war ended.

Why had Claude not sent word to her or come home? Laurel intended to find out.

Laurel hitched her horse outside of the small frame home where Sarah Perkins lived alone in one of Chicago's poorer districts. The house was a legacy from Sarah's late parents. Laurel hurried up the tidy path where fallen leaves had been neatly raked from lawns on either side. Sarah dried her hands on a cheerful yellow apron when she opened the door. "Laurel!" she exclaimed, her gray eyes lighting with pleasure. "I'm so glad to see you! I just made a pot of tea. Come in! Come in."

Laurel regarded her buxom friend with curiosity. Laurel was always the bubbly one, not Sarah. But now she positively glowed, in spite of her dark hair being parted in the middle and pulled back to a knot that made her look much older than twenty-one.

"Rejoice with me, Laurel!" Sarah urged, taking her visitor by both hands and giving them a squeeze. "I'm betrothed!"

Laurel cocked her head in disbelief, for Sarah was not known to have many male suitors. However, the radiant face confirmed her statement.

Laurel recovered from her surprise. "You are? To whom?"

"John Skillens. Remember him?" Sarah gushed on without waiting for a reply. "He used to work at the funeral parlor before he went away to fight the Rebels. He came back and got a job on a ship sailing the lake."

Laurel remained silent, sensing that Sarah was not going to be her traveling companion.

Sarah didn't seem to notice, but rushed on. "He said that he thought about me all the time he was away, and last night he came over and proposed!"

"I'm so happy for you!" Laurel forced herself to say as cheerfully as she could at the moment. "When is the wedding?"

"We haven't set a date, but probably next June. Oh! Forgive my manners! I'm talking a blue streak and haven't allowed you to say a word. Any news about Claude?"

"Yes. That's what I came to see you about."

"Wonderful! Let's go into the kitchen so you can tell me everything."

Laurel followed down the uncarpeted hallway, past a massive framed picture of Sarah's late parents. Laurel hid her concern that persuading Sarah to go with her might be a problem.

Preparing her case, Laurel explained, "As you know, I hadn't heard a word from Claude even though Ambrose Nevers told me they walked out of that Andersonville prisoner-of-war camp together. Then yesterday Ambrose returned from a train trip down south. He said he saw Claude working on a branch rail line near the Kentucky-Missouri border."

"If Ambrose has seen Claude and he's all right, why hasn't he contacted you?"

"That's what I intend to find out."

"Good!" Sarah exclaimed, entering the spacious old kitchen with two embroidered Scripture verses on the wall next to her cupboard. She motioned for her guest to take a chair at the table. "So you're going to find him?"

"I certainly am."

"Where are you going to get the money? Or have you and your father patched things up?"

"I got the money, never mind how. I came to you because I need a traveling companion. Since you're not going to be married for a while, I'll buy your ticket so you can come with me."

Sarah set rose-patterned cups and saucers on the table before replying. "Ordinarily, Laurel, I would love to go, but I can't."

"Of course you can! You said John works on ships sailing the lake, so he'll be gone quite a bit. Why should you sit home alone when you can see parts of our country that you have never seen before? Besides, it'll only be seven days at the most."

Sarah paused, lifting the steaming teakettle from the stove. "It sounds wonderful—"

Laurel interrupted, "Then it's settled! Can you be ready to travel with me in a few days?"

Sarah poured the tea, then looked wistfully out the window at the leaves blowing from the maple trees. "I've always envied your sense of adventure, and courage. Most of all, I longed to have men flock around me as they did you, like Claude."

Turning to face Laurel, Sarah said firmly, "But I've waited too long for a good husband. I don't want to risk losing John, so I plan to be near him as much as possible from now on."

"But this would only be a few days out of a lifetime!"

"I know, but I just can't. You'll have to get someone else."

"Like whom? All the girls we grew up with are married except you and me!"

"Exactly my point! When you find Claude, then that would leave only me unmarried. So how about asking your Aunt Agnes?"

"Too much like her brother. I don't get along much better with her than I do with him."

Laurel's natural tendency was to push to get what she wanted, but her strongest arguments with Sarah were fruitless. Finally, knowing how much marriage meant to Sarah, Laurel nodded in rare defeat. "I understand. I'll find someone else."

On the slow drive back, Laurel vainly tried to think of whom she could ask besides her aunt. Laurel had lived in the same affluent neighborhood all her life, but most of her girlfriends had married hastily during the war or right after it ended. No matter how many names came to mind, Laurel reluctantly found herself thinking that the only possible candidate was her spinster aunt.

Then an idea flickered across Laurel's mind: maybe her twenty-two-year-old sister Harriet would have a suggestion. Laurel could not tell anyone about the Pinkerton assignment, but she could admit to looking for her fiancé. Laurel turned her rig toward Harriet's modest home.

There Laurel was dismayed to find that their oldest sister, Emma, and her five preteen children were visiting. Emma never approved of anything Laurel did. Reluctantly, Laurel led up to the subject of a traveling companion by updating her sisters on Ambrose Nevers' recent sighting of Claude.

With dark eyes snapping indignantly, the oldest sister whirled from yelling at two of her children to glare at Laurel. "You have taken leave of your senses!" Emma exclaimed. "I told Harriet that when you got engaged to that worthless Claude Duncan! You don't love him! You never loved any man even though they swarm around you like brainless flies!"

"Wait!" Laurel interrupted, her anger rising, "I didn't come here to hear your opinion about my fiancé!"

"You're going to hear it anyway," Emma shot back.

"I'm horrified at the idea! It was bad enough that you repeatedly ran off with who knows how many soldiers during the war."

Harriet ventured a cautious comment. "Now, Emma, we don't know that's what—"

"What else could it have been?" Emma broke in. She scowled disapprovingly at Laurel. "You put us through all kinds of misery—never knowing where you were, or when you were coming back, if ever. Now you want to go on a wild goose chase after a man who doesn't care enough about you to come back to you, or even write."

Laurel flared, "You don't know what you're talking about!"

"Don't I?" Emma countered. "You've become such a little liar that our poor mother would turn over in her grave if she knew how you're behaving."

"I'm not going to stand here and listen to your tirade," Laurel said, her voice high and angry. "Just tell me if you can suggest a traveling companion, and I'll be out of your life."

Emma opened her mouth to answer, but suddenly threw up her hands and turned away in disgust. "I give up. Harriet, maybe you can talk some sense into her."

Harriet began quietly, "Laurel, I understand how you feel about wanting to find Claude—"

"He's a bounty jumper!" Emma interrupted. "He and that no-good friend of his, Ambrose Nevers, both enlisted to collect the money and then deserted. They did it twice!"

She rushed on, the venomous words spewing out. "They're a

pair, they are! It served them right that the last time they tried that trick, they were rushed off to battle right away! They deserved to be taken prisoner. I hear that Andersonville is the worst prisoner-of-war camp there ever was!"

Emma took a quick breath as though to continue, then said more quietly, "Harriet, tell her about the danger on railroads and what all those lawless former soldiers are doing. Tell her."

Laurel spoke quickly. "You don't need to tell me. I already know. Things are so bad that there is talk of forming vigilante groups in Indiana and Missouri to cope with the growing danger. But nobody has yet robbed a train, in spite of the rumors that it might happen. So I'm going to make that trip and find Claude."

"Stubborn!" Emma cried. "Foolish and stubborn! I'm glad our poor mother isn't here to see what a disgrace you are to all the Bartletts!"

"Good-bye," Laurel said, turning toward the door. "I'm sorry I bothered you."

Harriet followed. "Wait." She quickly hugged Laurel and whispered, "Don't let her upset you too much. I hope you find Claude."

"Thanks. I will." Laurel opened the door and looked toward Emma, who turned her back on Laurel. Laurel took a slow breath and left, deeply distressed in spite of knowing that Emma was always belittling her. She tilted her chin defiantly, thinking, *I'm going to find him, even if I have to put up with Aunt Agnes!*

Ridge headed up the long tree-lined driveway on Elm Street. The two-story red brick home was solid and respectable, indicating a very affluent owner. At Ridge's knock, a matronly woman in servant's black dress and a white apron opened the door.

"Is Charley home?" Ridge asked politely.

The servant studied his Confederate jacket through brown eyes that narrowed suspiciously under her graying brown hair. Partially closing the door, she parried, "Who wants to know?"

Ignoring the impertinence, Ridge said evenly, "I have a letter for Charley Bartlett."

"I'll take it."

"No." Ridge shook his head. "I promised to deliver it personally. Now, is he home?"

"No!" The servant followed her sharp retort by starting to close the door.

"Wait!" The authority in Ridge's word stopped the servant. "When will he be back?"

"Can't say. So give me the letter."

"I told you," Ridge replied with an effort to remain calm, "I will give it only to this Charley. Tell him I'll be back."

"I'm not going to waste my time talking to no Johnny Reb!" she snapped. "Get out of here before I set the dogs on you."

Rankling, but controlling his temper, Ridge replied quietly, "Tell Charley that I'll be back when I can."

He turned and stalked away, wishing more than ever that he had not promised that dying kid that he would deliver his letter.

Chapter 2

After his unpleasant encounter with the servant, Ridge walked aimlessly, vainly trying to convince himself that he should have just left the letter. If he had done that, he could have been on his way back to Virginia by now. However, Ridge had given his word to the dying Yankee boy who wrote the letter.

It was a matter of honor for Ridge to complete his mission, even though he had crucial personal matters that required proper decisions. He didn't want to make any mistakes, though, so he determined to take his time and carefully think them through.

He had silently struggled with those problems on the cars from Virginia while staring moodily out the windows. He had not really noticed any of the landscape as the train followed a circuitous route up to Pennsylvania, then across Ohio and Indiana into Illinois.

Ridge drifted toward the railroad depot and the cars that would take him back home. . .or to what was left of it. But he wasn't sure that's what he wanted to do. He wasn't sure of anything, and that galled him. He was used to being in command, to making decisions, and to executing plans.

No matter what assurances the North gave about binding up the reunited nation's wounds, Ridge was a realist. Union locusts with iron jaws were already descending on the prostrate South and, under smooth-sounding phrases and new laws, were seizing what little was left of it.

Ridge probably would have to fight to keep even the ravaged land that had been his ancestral home for three generations. He was tired of fighting, but four years of war had sharpened his skills in that area. It was the uncertainty of what he really wanted that troubled him. That uncertainty was made the more vivid because Varina Owens had broken her promise to wait for him. He shook the bitter memory of their final parting from his mind. Whatever he did, she would not be a part of it.

He was aroused from his reveries when he slowed to pass some men lined up outside the Great Central Railroad depot. His eyes lifted to a sign above the door, "Now hiring."

As he passed, a heavyset man suddenly reached out from the line and grabbed Ridge's overcoat.

"Well, now," the man called to the others in line, "lookee here! We got ourselves a traitor." He turned to Ridge. "We licked you Rebs proper. So what're you doing up North? Trying to take jobs from honest men?"

Ridge said quietly, "Let go of my coat."

Instead of obeying, the man jerked hard.

Ridge struck fast. His hard left-hand blow to the pit of the man's stomach was followed by a right that smashed into his nose. The man staggered backward, moaning in pain.

Ridge gave him a casual glance, then turned cold eyes upon the half-dozen other men. When no one moved, Ridge turned slowly and started walking.

"Hey, Mister! Wait!"

Ridge spun, bracing himself and dropping to a slight crouch

as a uniformed trainman stepped out of the office. He held up both hands, palms forward.

"Easy, Mister! Easy!" he said. "You handle yourself pretty good."

"Had some practice," Ridge answered softly.

"I wouldn't be surprised. You as good with a gun as you are with your fists?"

"I can shoot."

The trainman glanced at the faded bars on Ridge's collar before asking, "You were a captain?"

"Yes. Cavalry."

"You want a job? Short term only, guarding an express car on a run down Missouri way. Good pay, a place to eat and sleep when you're not working."

"No, thanks. I'm just passing through."

"Only be a few days, starting right now," the trainman persisted, his eyes skimming Ridge's well-worn clothes. "We'll show you what to do so you can leave tomorrow and be back the end of the week and get paid."

Ridge had not been aware that his absence of funds was so obvious. He declared, "I don't need your money."

"Didn't say you did. Anyway, it's not my money, it's the railroad's. How about it?"

"How do you know you can trust me?"

"I'd take a chance on a man who is honest and brave enough to wear part of a Confederate uniform this far north."

Ridge smiled at the compliment and thought about the letter. He started to decline the job offer, then hesitated. The letter could wait until he earned a few of the new greenback dollars. He could also catch up on some missed meals. He asked, "These clothes of mine make any difference to you?"

"You'll wear a railroad uniform. I'm looking for an express messenger to guard a car. There's some risk involved."

Ridge admitted, "I've heard rumors about gangs planning to rob a train."

"It's never been done, but who knows what could be tried? There are an awful lot of unhappy former soldiers out there with no law to stop them. It's not likely to happen, but the railroad pays good wages to guard what it carries. So how about it?"

Ridge slowly nodded. "Let's get started."

❧

Outwardly, Laurel was her usual smiling, bubbling self when she accepted Agnes Bartlett's invitation to sit in the parlor filled with early Victorian furniture. Inwardly, Laurel felt overwhelmed by the ponderous rosewood pieces that reflected her aunt's taste.

She had not offered tea, which didn't surprise Laurel. Aunt Agnes was a frugal woman.

"So," Agnes interrupted her guest's breezy comments about the falling leaves and the smell of autumn, "what rare occasion brings you to visit me?"

Laurel had rehearsed how she should approach the subject, but the faint hint of suspicion on her aunt's thin face made Laurel falter. "I have learned that my fiancé has been seen near the Kentucky-Missouri border. I want to find him, and I need a proper chaperon."

Agnes shook her head. "Don't try that on me, Laurel. You've run all around the country by yourself, doing who knows what unspeakable things, so don't expect me to believe you're now concerned about your reputation."

Laurel did not flinch under the blunt comment. "It's the truth. I need a traveling companion. I'll pay your ticket."

"With what?" Agnes snapped. "Money paid by some soldier who dallied with you?"

It was hard to reply quietly, but Laurel forced herself to do so. "It's money I earned in honest work."

"What kind of honest work can a young woman do?"

Laurel said the first thing that came to mind. "I will be a correspondent for the *Chicago Globe*."

Aunt Agnes considered her niece through suspicious eyes. "I find that hard to believe."

Rankled, Laurel replied, "Believe what you want."

"I believe you've become such a little liar that you wouldn't know the truth if it bit you on the nose."

Laurel jumped up, fighting for control. "Aunt Agnes, I didn't come here to hear you preach!" She hurried toward the front door.

The older woman raised her voice. "I'll pray for you. Your Heavenly Father loves you, and so do I."

Laurel whirled, her hand on the knob. "Just like your brother does, I suppose?"

"Your father loves you very much, Laurel. He grieves at how far you've strayed from the faith you professed until a few years ago."

"He loves me?" Laurel flared. "The only thing that concerns him is that he can't control me as he once did!"

"Wait!" Agnes said firmly as Laurel jerked the door open. "I think you've rebelled against both your father and God because you want your own way. That's not right, Laurel!"

"Think what you want," Laurel replied, and left.

Laurel was still seething, but she was determined to meet Pinkerton's condition about a traveling companion when she returned to her father's home. She entered the back door in hopes of avoiding an encounter with her father while she packed a trunk and small carpet bag.

"'Evening, Miss Laurel," the woman servant said from where she was setting the table. "Your father's in the parlor."

"I don't want to disturb him, Maggie. I'll just go up to my old room to get some things I need."

"Suit yourself. By the way, there was somebody here awhile ago who claimed he had a letter for Charley."

Laurel had started out the kitchen door into the dining room, but stopped at the mention of the name. "You sure he said it was for Charley?"

"Positive. The man wouldn't give the letter to anyone else. He said he would come back later, but . . ."

Maggie left her thought hanging when Laurel's father entered the room.

"I thought I heard your voice, Laurel," he said, fixing her with shrewd blue eyes. They were shielded by a wide forehead left bald by gray hair that had retreated to the middle of his scalp. At sixty, he stood just under six feet tall and carried no excess weight.

"Hello, Papa," she said, smiling with a warmth she did not feel. "I didn't mean to disturb you. I just came by to pick up a few personal belongings."

"I see." Her father's clean-shaven square chin and tight, grim lips suggested disapproval. "Off on one of your infamous dalliances again?"

"Please, Papa! Don't start!" Laurel stepped past him and started toward the stairs leading up to her bedchamber.

"Do you know what the neighbors think?" he asked, following her. "Do you know what you're putting your sisters and me through with your escapades?"

Laurel didn't answer, but took the stairs two at a time. She knew there was no use trying to reason with him. He had refused to believe her back during the war when she attempted to explain that she would periodically have to be gone, but for good and honorable reasons. As when Laurel was growing up, Hiram Bartlett remained an uncompromising man. He still tried to dominate his grown children in the same stern way he ran the company he had founded years before. Manufacturing iron wheels and other parts for the Union railroad's rolling stock had made him wealthy.

Her father called after her, "Don't walk out on me, young woman!"

Laurel pretended not to hear. She burst into the room she had occupied when growing up. She stalked angrily past the early Victorian mahogany bed with the flowered chamber pot underneath. She crossed in front of the matching basin and large-mouthed pitcher on the marble-topped table to the deep closet. The sweet fragrance of cedar swirled around her as she pulled a large carpetbag from a far back corner.

"Laurel!" Her father's voice slapped at her from the door she had left open. "Don't be like this!"

She straightened up with the bag in her hand. "I'm not your little girl anymore. I'm of age. So why don't you treat me that way?"

He strode across the room toward her and lowered his voice.

"I love you, Laurel!"

"Then why don't you act like it?" She circled around him and headed for the hallway door. "Why must you always believe the worst of me when you don't have a shred of evidence to think that way?"

"I'm trying not to," he said softly. "I'm really trying, but you won't tell me anything about what's going on."

She paused at the door and answered patiently, "I have told you that I can't. Never mind the reason! But I have done nothing to dishonor this family."

He regarded her without speaking as the doorbell sounded in the downstairs front hallway. "I'd like to believe that, Laurel," he said. "But you must tell me something to help me do that."

"I told you, Papa! I can't!" She headed down the hallway toward the top of the stairs, hearing Maggie open the front door.

Laurel recognized Sarah's voice. "I was on my way to Laurel's place when I saw her rig outside. Is she here?"

"Coming," Laurel called, hurrying down the stairs, glad to end the uncomfortable conversation with Papa. As she approached, Laurel noticed that Sarah's nose was red and her eyes swollen. "What's the matter?" Laurel asked anxiously, dropping the carpetbag and taking her friend by both hands.

Sarah glanced at Hiram Bartlett standing at the top of the stairs while Maggie retreated toward the kitchen. "Can we talk outside?"

"Of course," Laurel replied, stepping out onto the wide covered wooden porch and closing the door.

"It's John," Sarah said, her voice quivering. "We had a terrible fight. Our marriage is off."

"Oh, I'm sorry," Laurel exclaimed sympathetically. But this

news gave her hope that Sarah might change her mind about going with her on the train.

Sarah sniffed, then took a deep breath. "It's all right," she said firmly. "I'll make John regret this. There are still plenty of other fish in the sea."

Suppressing a smile, Laurel reflected briefly on how brave Sarah was trying to sound. Her record of finding other beaus did not warrant her statement, but Laurel didn't want to mention that. "What are you going to do?"

"Is that offer still good to be your traveling companion?"

Smiling with relief, Laurel threw her arms around Sarah. "Of course! But are you sure you want to do this?"

"I'm sure. When do we leave?"

"As soon as I take care of something tomorrow morning."

Outside Allan Pinkerton's office, Laurel paused to straighten her hoop skirt. The door opened from the inside, and a tall, slender man with a full black beard stepped into the hallway so quickly that Laurel had to move aside to avoid being bumped.

"Sorry, Miss," he said, using his right hand to touch his cap respectfully. "Guess I was in too big a hurry."

"It's all right." Laurel smiled reassuringly at him.

She watched him bob his head in acknowledgment and scurry down the hall.

In his left hand, he carried something Laurel recognized. . .a telegrapher's black box. When a train broke down or was derailed, a telegrapher on board could climb one of the telegraph poles that paralleled the tracks, attach the unit to the wire, and send a Morse code message for help.

Laurel entered the detective agency's office and greeted Allan Pinkerton with her best smile. "I've arranged for my traveling companion," she announced cheerfully.

He did not return the smile. "I'm withdrawing my offer," he said coolly.

"What?" Her voice shot up in surprise.

He leaned across the desk to look her squarely in the eyes. "Why did you lie to me?"

Startled, she stalled by asking, "Lie to you?"

"You know very well what I mean!" His tone was harsh. "Did you think I wouldn't find out?"

Seeing her opportunity to find Claude slipping away, Laurel hesitated while rapidly trying to think what she should say to salvage her plan.

The detective continued, "When you came in here with your proposal to 'test' that conductor on the Great Central States Railroad, I knew you had done some investigating. Since then, I've done mine. I know your real reason for wanting to be reinstated as an operative. But I'm not going to pay you to find your fiancé!"

Laurel realized her only hope was to be honest and show Pinkerton how he would benefit by what she had in mind. "You're right," she confessed, "but I can do both jobs at the same time, and do it better than any male operative you have."

"You're mighty sure of yourself, aren't you?"

"I'm determined, just as I was when I volunteered to be a courier for you during the war."

"You didn't do that until after your brother was killed," Pinkerton reminded her.

"And I turned eighteen," she quickly pointed out. "Up until then, my father would never have permitted me to do any such thing. In fact, he probably would be furious today if he knew the truth about why I was gone so often back then."

The detective said nothing, so Laurel added ruefully, "Not that he isn't upset enough even now, but that's because he thinks my virtue has been for sale to various military men."

Pinkerton regarded Laurel with narrowed eyes. "You are convincing," he admitted grudgingly. "But I don't like my operatives lying to me."

"The very nature of this work requires deceit, as you well know. You've done it yourself, like when you got into uniform and passed yourself off as Major E.J. Allen during the late unpleasantness. But you were a civilian."

"You're sure a saucy one." His tone had softened and carried a hint of admiration.

"So I've been told. Now, you want a job done. I can do it and also look for my fiancé at the same time."

When he hesitated, she asked, "You want to know the whole story?"

He nodded, leaning back but watching her face intently.

Laurel had known Pinkerton long enough to know he would not volunteer information. Rather, it was his nature to listen, gathering bits of intelligence to augment what he already knew.

"As you probably know, I grew up with Claude Duncan and Ambrose Nevers. They joined the army together and were taken prisoner by the Rebels just before the war ended. Before that, one time when Claude was home, he and I became engaged. My father and sisters disapproved of him, claiming it was only a wartime romance."

"Was it?" Pinkerton asked quietly.

Laurel shifted uncomfortably in her chair before answering. "What difference does it make? We're engaged, and he's missing, so I'm going to find him."

"From what I hear, you always had lots of beaus, but you chose to become betrothed to this Claude. Your family dislikes him as much as they do Ambrose Nevers."

Laurel observed, "Some of my friends talk too much. But that's none of their business. You wanted to know the whole story, so I'm telling you."

Pinkerton nodded. "Go on."

"Shortly after the Confederacy surrendered, Ambrose came home. He told me that he and Claude had walked out of Andersonville prisoner-of-war camp together. The last time Ambrose saw Claude was when Ambrose was waiting for a ride here to Chicago."

She paused, debating whether to mention that both men had collected bounty for enlisting, then deserted and rejoined another unit. She decided that Pinkerton probably already knew that.

She continued, "Both men had only been prisoners a short time, so they hadn't suffered like most of the Union troops. Anyway, Claude didn't come home. I didn't have any idea of what happened to him, until a few days ago. Ambrose returned from a trip to Missouri where he said he saw Claude. Ambrose said he told Claude that I was anxiously waiting for him, but he refused to talk about it. So I decided to go find him, but I needed money to travel. That's why I came to you."

"Did you think I wouldn't learn the truth?"

"I had to take that risk. My father long ago cut off my financial support. So I thought of a way that your agency could pay me while I searched. I admit I was wrong to try fooling you, but I'm desperate. I can test that conductor and search for Claude at the same time." Hesitating, she finished, "So how about it?"

Pinkerton leaned across the desk to ask, "What's your real motive for finding Claude?"

Laurel couldn't imagine why the famous detective would ask such a question. But since he had, she had to reply. "I told you."

"I didn't hear you say you loved him."

Laurel considered that impertinent, but she had to remain unruffled with Pinkerton. She said, "I didn't think it was necessary."

"Perhaps you were just enamored with the romantic notion of being engaged to a soldier. All your friends were doing that, or getting married. But when Claude didn't come home to you, your pride was hurt. Maybe that's the reason you want to find him."

Laurel felt her face flush. "That's not true!"

"It doesn't matter to me. All I want is proof that Schramm is guilty of stealing railroad money. In spite of your lying to me, I believe you can get that proof."

"I certainly can," she replied with rising hope.

"I was impressed with you when you were only seventeen and approached me about working behind enemy lines. You were too young, but when you were a year older and reapplied, I appreciated your fervent patriotism, self-confidence, and charming manner. I was also influenced to hire you because you had done your own investigation about me before you came here."

Laurel nodded, recalling what she had told Pinkerton at their first meeting. She knew that he had formed and headed up the Secret Service for General George McClellan. There were countless spies on both sides during those days. Many were caught, but not Laurel.

She asked, "So am I again an operative?"

Puckering his lips, Pinkerton regarded her thoughtfully for several seconds. "If you were, how would you handle this?"

"I'll say I'm looking for my fiancé, who hasn't returned after the war. To protect my family, I'll use the name of Laurel Wilson and say it's the name I write under as a correspondent for the *Chicago Globe*. If I'm asked, I'll say I'm working on an assignment about the future of railroads. That's logical because serious work has begun on the transcontinental railroad from Omaha to Sacramento. So, am I hired?"

For a long moment, the detective sat without moving. Then, abruptly, he reached into his desk drawer and pulled out a package. "There's a photograph of this conductor, Hannibal Schramm, in here, along with other information you'll need. I also have for you the name of an editor at the newspaper and some press credentials."

He slid the envelope toward her. "Schramm is scheduled to leave tomorrow morning on his regular run. Can you and your traveling companion be on that train?"

Laurel's smile lit up the room. "We'll be on board."

"Remember, you've got a week; that's all."

That night, having been briefed on what his duties would be in guarding the express car, Ridge made another fruitless attempt to deliver the letter. He fumed on the way back to the railroad. Honor required him to keep trying, but now that would have to wait until he completed his short-term job on the railroad.

Laurel met Sarah at her home to brief her on the trip. "In addition to looking for Claude, I'm going to write something for the *Chicago Globe*," Laurel explained. "I'll use the pen name of Laurel Wilson, so please don't ever mention 'Bartlett' on this trip."

Sarah's eyes narrowed suspiciously. "This sounds like you're still in the spy business. Are you working for Pinkerton again?"

"I told you what I'm doing. Let's leave it at that."

Sarah nodded. "All right, but this isn't like in the war. I helped you, but then I stayed safely at home while you slipped across enemy lines. I hope that you're not doing anything now that will get us in trouble."

Laurel silently hoped so, too.

L aurel and Sarah stepped out of the depot waiting room onto the platform and shivered slightly in the crisp morning air. They each carried a drawstring reticule and small carpetbag in preparation for boarding the Great Central States' wooden cars. Laurel's carpetbag contained personal items, plus a novel and writing materials.

Trains had come a long way in the last thirty-plus years since South Carolina boasted a line of 136 miles, then the longest railroad in the world. The late war had changed that, just as railroads had changed the war.

The engineer and firemen were already in the cab. The remaining five crewmen included the conductor, a trainman/flagman (who also helped the conductor with the passengers), two express messengers or guards, and the combination baggage man and brakeman.

The baggage man pulled a wheeled cart with a final load of trunks, barrels, and boxes past the women, heading toward the rear baggage car. Laurel glimpsed her small gray trunk and Sarah's larger green one.

Laurel and Sarah were the only female passengers. The others waiting on the platform were men wearing whiskers, sideburns, or mustaches. The men politely stepped back so the women could be first in line.

This gave them an unobstructed view of the locomotive and tender with the five wooden cars behind. The mustard-yellow express car was first, followed by two forty-five-foot-long passenger coaches, a smoking car, and the baggage car at the back end.

Laurel glanced appreciatively at the small wood-burning engine with the gold lettering *R.W. Wentworth* on the cab's side. Under the Wentworth's polished brass exterior fixtures and silver bell, the locomotive panted as if impatiently waiting to leave the busy city and attack the open prairie. The kerosene-burning headlight, the wooden cowcatcher, and the drive wheels were all painted bright red, contrasting with the glistening black boiler accented with gold stripes.

The equally black smokestack or spark arrester flared upward like a giant cone. A thin column of dark smoke would soon turn to a puffing cloud mixed with flying cinders. These cinders had been known to blow into open windows and burn holes in passengers' clothes.

In spite of its faults, there was a romance to the railroad that generated excitement in Laurel's breast. In less than a week, she would know the answer to a question that had nibbled at her heart for months.

At the conductor's call of "'board," the women headed for the first passenger car.

Sarah asked, "You have the tickets handy?"

"No. I'm going to buy them after we board."

"You should have bought them before we got on."

Laurel ignored the hint of reproof in her friend's remarks. "It's a common practice to pay the conductor," Laurel replied. She had no intention of explaining her plans to prove if the conductor was stealing ticket money.

Sarah shifted the heavier carpetbag to her stronger right hand. "I was talking to one of my friends from church last night. She says it's dangerous to be riding the cars through all that open country where we could be robbed."

"Nobody's ever robbed a train," Laurel assured her, fearful that Sarah might be having second thoughts about making the trip. "Besides," Laurel continued, "with all these men aboard, who's going to risk it?"

"We don't know that any of them are armed," Sarah protested. "But we do know that there have been a lot of night riders and killings going on just about everywhere outside of this city."

Laurel laughed lightly, hoping to dispel Sarah's concerns. "You fret too much. There's not going to be any trouble on this trip."

Approaching the end of the first passenger car, Laurel recognized Hannibal Schramm from the photograph Pinkerton had given her. Schramm made a striking figure in his dark blue railroad uniform with the silver word "Conductor" on the front of his small-billed matching cap. Laurel slowed a half step so Sarah would have to be first to enter the car.

She turned and whispered, "Say, he's rather handsome, isn't he?" Without waiting for an answer, she added softly, "I wonder if he's married."

Laurel didn't reply, but she knew the answer to that, and a lot more. She had learned much from the confidential information packet that Pinkerton had given her. Schramm sported a black mustache, was twenty-seven, stood five-eleven, weighed 190 pounds, and had been twice divorced. He was known to be proud of his good looks and easy way with women. He had boasted of personally killing two Johnny Rebs in the war.

"Ladies," Schramm said pleasantly, offering his hand to Sarah. "Watch your step, please."

Laurel saw that Sarah was wasting no time grieving over the loss of her beau. She gazed warmly at Schramm as he helped her onto the open platform leading into the car.

When he turned to assist Laurel, she gave him a bright smile. He returned it, saying, "I hope you have a pleasant trip, Miss."

"Thank you. I'm sure I will," she assured him, letting her eyes suggest an invitation to help her make it so. He would be less suspicious of her if he later initiated a conversation and she asked seemingly innocent questions.

Inside the car, the two young women walked past the wood-burning stove in the corner with a protective metal screen around it. The door was locked to prevent fire from escaping should there be an accident. A brass spittoon was strategically placed near the stove.

Sarah said under her breath, "He really is good looking, don't you think?"

"He'll do." Laurel glanced ahead into the car with the aisle down the middle dividing twin rows of maroon velour seats with brocaded back covers. Coal oil lamps were fixed in the seven-foot ceiling above the aisle.

Laurel asked Sarah, "Do you have a preference about which side to sit on?"

"No, because going south, we'll either have the sun in our eyes in the morning or the afternoon."

"Then let's sit near the back, closer to the stove, but not too close. That way, we won't freeze or get too warm." Laurel stopped at the third seat from the rear on the right, nearest the depot. "How about this?"

"Fine." Sarah looked up at the decorations running the length of the wooden car above the luggage racks.

She pointed to the neat rows of multicolored birds that had been meticulously hand-painted above the seats. "Aren't those pretty?"

Laurel casually glanced out the window at some of the train crew walking from the depot toward the cars in front of the passenger coach. She stared at a tall man in railroad uniform carrying a heavy knapsack, an overcoat, a rifle, and a shotgun. He seemed to have a slight limp.

Sarah repeated, "Aren't they?"

"What?" Laurel asked as the man passed out of sight below the cars.

"The birds." Sarah set her reticule on the seat and pointed to the decorations.

"Beautiful." Laurel replied absently, easing into her seat as male passengers streamed past, taking some of the remaining forty-six seats. She frowned, trying to think why that man outside had seemed somehow familiar. And why was he so heavily armed?

Through the express car's open sliding side door, Ridge reversed the Henry rifle and the sawed-off shotgun to hand them up butt first to his burly fellow guard, George Aiken. The men had met yesterday when Aiken was assigned to teach the new employee what was expected of him.

Aiken had protested, making it clear that he was not pleased to have his former partner replaced by a Rebel. A brief warning from the station agent had stopped Aiken's grumbling, but Ridge still sensed the hostility.

Ridge carefully placed his Confederate overcoat and soft knapsack on the floor. The knapsack contained all his personal belongings, including a Richmond arsenal belt and holster with a Confederate-made Leech & Rigdon .36-caliber six-shot percussion pistol.

As Ridge hoisted himself into the car, Aiken leaned the Henry and shotgun against one of several heavy metal strong boxes. "You know what to do with these guns?"

Ridge nodded. He recalled when the Federals first started using the sixteen-shot repeating Henry. Confederate soldiers, mostly equipped with old single shot rifles or muskets, had said that the Yankees loaded up a Henry in the morning and shot all day without reloading.

Reclaiming his weapons, Ridge faced the other man. His chest was nearly as wide as the heating stove in the corner by the cane-bottom chair. Dark brown eyes peered from under heavy black eyebrows that looked as though they were about to fly off his square head.

"I been riding these rails since I got back from the Rebellion, and never even needed this." He patted the holstered revolver at his belt. "But if the railroad wants to pay us to ride along and carry these, who are we to kick, huh?"

"No complaints here," Ridge's eyes sought the dark recesses of the car. He could discern the bottoms of several strongboxes that had been stacked against the back wall and partially covered with heavy canvas. A padlock showed on one box where the cover had slipped. Ridge guessed the boxes held gold or silver coins.

His gaze swept the rest of the express car, which had four doors. There were two sliding ones, back and front, on the length of the car. Cargo could be loaded or unloaded through these doors. At either end of the car, there was a small door big enough only to admit only one person at a time. This is where someone coming from the passenger car behind it would enter.

Aiken slid the front door shut and slipped a heavy wooden bar across it. When that was in place, matching the door across from it, he inserted a heavy padlock at the end of the bar.

"We don't open this door for nobody unless I recognize the voice," he explained, snapping the lock shut. "It's an easy place to defend because the only other way in or out is through the back end of this coach into the first passenger car. The small door in front opens against the tender."

Aiken picked up a second shotgun and checked the load before adding, "If the train gets robbed, they'll have to come through those little doors, one at a time. These scatterguns say they won't make it."

"Fine with me," Ridge said in the semidarkness the closed door had caused. The only light was a small coal oil lamp with a brass reflector attached to the wall by the chair.

Aiken lowered his considerable mass into the chair and laid a shotgun across his knees. "Hey, Johnny, you curious about what we're carrying?"

"Not particularly." Ridge looked around but didn't see another chair. "Like I told you before, my name's Ridge." He eased down against the front end of the car where he could see all four entrances.

He heard the engineer sound two short blasts from the whistle, signaling that the train was ready to roll.

Aiken ignored the name preference. "You may as well know that I was infantry, myself. Federal. I didn't much like your kind of Johnny Rebs, riding horses when we had to walk through mud up to our belts."

Ridge didn't answer. He felt the car jerk as the engine began moving forward. He had an uneasy feeling it was going to be a long ride. He didn't really mind, though, because he would have time to puzzle out what he should do about his plantation after he delivered that letter.

The train had reached its maximum speed of forty miles an hour before Laurel heard the conductor enter the car from behind her.

"Tickets!" he called, "tickets, gentlemen. . .and ladies." He made his way down the aisle, swaying with the car's motion until his eyes rested on the two young women. "Glad to have you aboard."

He raised his voice to address the male passengers. "I'm sure you men will respect the young ladies' rights, and do your chewing and such in the smoking car. It's behind the second passenger coach. The newsboy got sick at the last minute, but we have a supply of newspapers to read in the smoking car."

As the conductor stopped by the seat she and Sarah shared, Laurel opened the drawstrings on her reticule, a small lozenge-shaped handbag made of velvet. She said, "I was told it was permissible to pay you direct," as she handed the conductor some of the new Federal greenbacks. "Is that enough for both of us?"

"More than enough," he said, accepting the bills while his

eyes swept approvingly over her. "You've got change coming. And you were correctly informed that it's permissible to pay the conductor." He inserted Laurel's bills into a holder at his waist and handed a gold coin back to her. "If there's any way I can be of assistance to you. . .either of you. . .please let me know."

Laurel had not seen any evidence that Schramm was doing anything improper with the cash handed him. He was too shrewd for that, she guessed. He must have an office space of some kind. She would have to find that and try to figure out how he stole the money, but she must not get caught or even arouse Schramm's suspicions.

She said, "I'm on assignment for the *Chicago Globe*. As you know, there aren't many women correspondents, so I'm a little anxious because this is my first big opportunity to write about peacetime railroad travel."

Sarah declared, "She's looking for her fiancé."

Laurel felt a flicker of annoyance at the unnecessary announcement, but she understood that Sarah was trying to verbally cut her out of any possible competition.

"That's true," she said, opening the drawstring on her reticule and dropping the coin inside. "He didn't return after the war, but I've heard he's working on a railroad in the Missouri-Kentucky-Tennessee area. I hope to find him on this trip."

"I'll be glad to help you in any way I can," Schramm assured her. "Perhaps we can talk later?"

"Thank you," Laurel replied.

When he had walked out of hearing range behind them, Sarah declared a little tartly, "That's not fair!"

"What isn't?"

"Flirting like that! You've got a beau. I don't. . . not anymore.

So give me a chance."

Laurel was a little surprised at Sarah's outburst, but decided that she was probably just overly sensitive about breaking up with John Skillens. "I didn't mean to give that impression," Laurel said. "But the conductor might be in a position to help me find Claude. After all, railroad men must know each other, don't you think?"

"I suppose. But just give me a chance. All right?"

Laurel couldn't think how to warn Sarah about Schramm's suspected activities without giving away her assignment. She shrugged. "It didn't take you long to get over breaking up with John, but I'm not romantically interested in the conductor or any other man in these cars. So you can have your pick of any of them, for all I care. I just want to find Claude."

Sarah asked softly, "Do you, really?"

"What does that mean?"

"Never mind."

Laurel persisted. "I want to know."

Sarah shrugged. "Very well. Everyone except you knows that Claude doesn't have any redeeming features. So why should you really risk so much searching for him?"

"Because we're going to be married, that's why!"

"I notice that you didn't say you love him. So why don't you admit what you're hiding, even from yourself?"

Laurel didn't answer, but a forbidden thought flickered through her mind. It was one she had not allowed herself to consider. Had she deliberately chosen Claude *because* of his lack of redeeming qualities? She had known that her engagement to him would further enrage her unloving father and self-righteous sisters. Did she want to get even with them that much?

Laurel squirmed, knowing those were not logical reasons to search for Claude, but the validity of that possibility made her speak coolly to Sarah. "I think you've said quite enough!"

Sarah suddenly wrapped both arms across her body. "I think you're right. And you know what? I'm a little cool." She stood up. "I think I'll get my cloak from my trunk. I wonder if I can get to the baggage car from here."

"Probably," Laurel guessed, retrieving her book. "Just be careful stepping from the open platform of each car to the next."

"I'll go find out."

Laurel stared thoughtfully after Sarah, wondering when she had changed from the quiet, subservient girl whom Laurel had grown up with to the more outspoken woman riding the cars today. It was only after Sarah exited the car that Laurel realized she had gone forward toward the express car instead of back toward the baggage car.

"Where's your friend?"

The question jerked Laurel from her thoughts. She looked up to see the conductor smiling down at her. "Oh, she went to the baggage car to get her cloak." Thinking quickly, Laurel added, "She and her beau just broke up."

Schramm grinned knowingly. "The cars are a good place to see and be seen." His face sobered. "I've been thinking about your newspaper work and attempting to find your fiancé. I'll be busy for a while, but after we make our next stop, I will have some free time. If you would care to let me help you? . . ."

Laurel said brightly, "That's very kind of you, Mr. Conductor."

"It's Schramm," he said with obvious pleasure at her answer. "Hannibal Schramm."

"I'm Laurel . . . Laurel Wilson," she said, offering her right hand.

He took her hand and held it a trifle longer than necessary. "It's my pleasure to know you, Miss Wilson." He glanced beyond her and out the window where the black smoke from the locomotive whipped by. "Well, time to announce the next stop." He paused to look at Laurel before adding, "I'll look forward to seeing you later."

Nobody got off the cars at the tiny depot, but Laurel watched a short, powerfully built man with a full beard tinged with gray hurry toward her car. He carried a battered handbag and a Federal sky-blue wool kersey overcoat with a short cape and stand-up collar. He wore informal Kentucky jeans, heavy work brogans, and a formal new bowler hat with brown crown. The combination represented such contrasts that Laurel figured he didn't care how he dressed. When his coat blew open, she glimpsed a big revolver stuck in his belt.

Moments later, she heard him enter the car behind her, then pause in the aisle beside her. Hastily, she exclaimed, "This seat's taken."

"Sorry, Miss." He indicated the one across the aisle from her. "How about this one?"

Reluctantly, she admitted, "Nobody's sitting there."

"Good!" He dropped his hat on the seat, shoved his bag into the overhead rack, and sat down. "I'm heading south to see my daughter. She's about your age, but expecting her first baby. My wife's dead, so I'm going to be with my little girl instead."

Laurel nodded, trying to avoid a conversation, but the new passenger didn't seem to notice.

"My name's Lucas," he said. "Jacob Lucas."

"How do you do?" Laurel replied formally without revealing her name. She was relieved when he didn't ask.

He was only about five-three, she guessed, but obviously possessed great physical strength. His nose had a noticeable tilt to one side, as though it had been broken and not reset properly. She had the feeling that he was a man used to brawling. When he shifted the pistol at his belt, Laurel unintentionally stared.

His sharp blue eyes caught her reaction. He explained, "Some wild country up ahead. Outlaws and vigilantes, as I guess you've heard. I figure it's a good idea to come prepared."

Laurel was relieved to see Sarah hurrying down the aisle toward her, swaying with the car's motion. Her eyes were bright with excitement. Laurel said, "You went the wrong way to get your cloak."

Sarah glanced briefly at Lucas, who nodded politely to her before she dropped into the seat beside Laurel. "I found that out when I ended up in the express car. I want you to go back there with me."

"Why?"

Dropping her voice, Sarah explained. "A couple of men from the train crew are in there. One is very attractive. Come with me so I can start a conversation with him."

"You can do that alone."

"It wouldn't look proper." Sarah tugged at Laurel's arm. "You don't have to say much, just be there."

"I'm not interested."

Sarah frowned. "That's no reason to deny me a chance to meet this man."

After taking a slow breath, Laurel agreed. As the two women walked forward in the car, Laurel quickly told Sarah what little she had learned about the passenger who had taken the seat across from them. "He's got a gun," Laurel concluded.

Sarah didn't seem to care. Instead, she softly explained about the train crewman she wanted to meet. "Wait until you hear this man talk. He's got some kind of an accent. Maybe he's a Rebel. That's kind of intriguing, isn't it? I mean, now that the war's over, it's proper to at least talk to one of them, isn't it?"

Laurel sensed that this possibility somehow gave Sarah a feeling of doing something rather exciting and forbidden. She had never risked much in her life, but the loss of her betrothed seemed to have opened a streak of daring in her that she had never permitted to exist before.

"I suppose," Laurel replied without enthusiasm. She followed Sarah down the length of the passenger car, aware that the men were watching their passing.

The entrance to the express car was barely wide enough for a broad-shouldered man to enter, but there was plenty of room for two young women.

The two uniformed crewmen stopped their conversation and looked up questioningly at the women who stepped uncertainly into the semidarkened car.

"Excuse me," Sarah said, "I want to get my cloak. It's in my trunk. Is that all right?"

"The baggage car is at the opposite end of this train," the shorter man replied. "I'm both the brakeman and the baggage man. If you'll go with me to point out which one is yours, I'll get it out where you can open it."

"Thank you, Mister? . . . " Sarah said brightly, approaching the two men.

"Harkins, Miss. Frederick Harkins, at your service."

"She's Laurel . . . uh . . . Wilson," Sarah glanced at Laurel to indicate she had almost forgotten and said "Bartlett." She added quickly, "I'm Sarah Perkins." She hesitated, glancing expectantly at the other, taller man.

"Oh," Harkins said hastily. "We just met. This is his first trip. Uh . . . what was your name again, Mister?"

"Granger. Ridge Granger." There was a hint of Southern accent.

For a moment, Laurel frowned, thinking she had seen him before, but she couldn't think when or where.

Harkins said, "I was just visiting Ridge here while his fellow express messenger had to leave for a few minutes. If you'll come with me, Miss Perkins, I'll help find your cloak."

Laurel caught a look of disappointment in Sarah's eyes as they lingered on Ridge's face, but she had no choice except to politely follow the brakeman out the door.

When they had gone, Ridge said, "Please excuse me, Miss Wilson." He turned away and took a couple of steps.

Laurel noticed the slight limp and gave a small, involuntarily gasp of recognition.

He heard and turned back to face her. "I see you're still taking care of yourself," he said softly. There was a hint of mockery in the words.

That annoyed her. "And I am still capable of doing that!" she snapped.

A slow grin spread across his face. "You're still just as saucy. Or do all you Yankee girls grow up being disrespectful and ungrateful?"

The bold words seared through Laurel. Her voice rose without her noticing. "You have no right to talk to me like that!"

"Don't I?" he asked. "The way I see it, I have just as much right as you had to bite my head off in Chicago when I tried to help you after you were thrown from your carriage!"

He was right, Laurel knew, but she wasn't going to admit that. "You're rude, Sir!" she exclaimed, thinking she should stalk off. She wasn't sure why, but she did not want to do that, not just yet, anyway.

"And you could use some manners." His voice was quiet but firm. "Then maybe you could be considered a lady!"

No man had ever spoken to her that way, and Laurel opened her mouth to verbally slash at him. Before she could, however, she heard somebody stop in the narrow doorway behind her. She did not turn, but glared at Ridge.

A man's voice from behind her asked, "What's going on here?"

Laurel twisted her head to see the conductor looking suspiciously at her and Ridge. "Uh . . . nothing," she stammered. "I accompanied my friend to find her cloak, but we obviously ended up in the wrong car."

Schramm said suspiciously, "I heard angry voices." His eyes lifted beyond Laurel to Ridge. He asked, "Is this Rebel bothering you, Miss Wilson?"

"No," Laurel said, forcing a quick smile so that both Schramm and the upstart express messenger could see it. Then she gave Ridge a haughty look of dismissal and turned back to the conductor. "Thank you for looking out for me."

"It's my pleasure. If you don't mind, I'll walk you back to your seat."

"I'd like that," Laurel replied. As she stepped through the narrow door, she turned to give Ridge a triumphant look. She was disappointed to see that he had turned his back on her and was headed toward the other end of the car. Laurel felt rebuffed, and flounced after the conductor, her cheeks warm with indignation. She wished there were some way she could take that Rebel down from his high horse.

Ridge mentally chided himself for even wasting time talking to her. Yet he couldn't resist stealing a quick look back at the petite woman smiling at the conductor. Ridge was surprised to realize he didn't like that.

Chapter 4

Schramm returned Laurel to her seat and continued on his duties. She was relieved that Jacob Lucas was not there. She guessed that he was in the smoking car. That suited her fine because she wanted to be alone to think, but she had barely rested her head on the back of the seat and closed her eyes when Sarah returned.

"I'm sorry for what I said awhile ago," Sarah told Laurel when she opened her eyes. "You and I have been friends since we were little girls. I should not have sounded doubtful when you said you just wanted to find Claude."

Sitting up straight, Laurel admitted, "It did upset me when you said it, but I've been thinking about it. I mean, why I really want to find him."

"How about letting me sit next to the window?" Sarah asked.

Wordlessly, Laurel moved out and stood in the aisle. When Sarah had slid into the seat nearest the window, Laurel sat down on the aisle side.

Sarah prompted, "Why do you think you are trying to find Claude?"

Laurel hesitated, struggling with the question. "I'm still trying to figure it out," she finally answered, and again rested her head on the back of the seat. With her eyes closed, the rhythmic clicking of the wheels helped her drift back to how she had become engaged.

Claude was home on leave, at least, that's what he had said. She wasn't quite sure she believed him. Perhaps he had been absent without leave, or had even deserted again. She didn't really want to know. She was content to go for a buggy ride with him along the shores of Lake Michigan.

He said, "You're mighty quiet."

"Am I?" She absently gazed across the water.

"Had another fight with your old man?"

The question unleashed memories of the night before. "He is so unreasonable!"

"I'll bet you told him you were going out with me, didn't you?"

"I didn't have to tell him that."

"No, I think you did because you know how much he dislikes me. Always has." Claude grinned mischievously. "I think you like to stir him up."

"That's ridiculous! I just want him to act like a real father."

"Isn't he acting like a father when he objects to some of your suitors, especially me? And when he wants to know where you've been going the past few months?"

"What does that mean?" she demanded rather sharply, wondering if somehow Claude had heard about her secret courier missions. But that wasn't possible because only she, Allan Pinkerton, and Sarah knew about that.

Laurel reflected briefly on the fact that the very nature of spying required lying or deceiving. Laurel's success and even her life depended on acting alone, but in preparing for her first wartime spying venture, Laurel had realized that she needed assistance in finding ways to hide written military intelligence, and with a couple of disguises she wore.

She didn't tell Pinkerton or anyone else, but she had turned to Sarah, who aided her in devising ways to conceal sensitive information under her hoopskirts, in her shoes, and even in her hair.

Throughout the war, Laurel always had a private fear that another agent would somehow uncover her wartime activities. That was possible, even though Pinkerton thrived on intrigue and prohibited his agents from knowing or talking to each other. It was also a possibility because it was in a spy's nature to discover others' secrets. Self-preservation precluded bragging or calling attention to oneself. Instead, fear required anonymity and long-term secrecy, even after the war.

Laurel's reflections were interrupted by Claude. He said, "I found out that you've been going off somewhere for days or even weeks at a time. Even Sarah Perkins claims she doesn't know where you've been."

Laurel teased, "Does that bother you?"

She met Claude's gaze, but his gray eyes were always partially hidden by heavy reddish eyebrows that matched his beard but not his light blond hair. She could not see into him the way she could with most men.

"You're of age," he countered, reining in the horse and turning to slide his arm around her.

She was disappointed by his casual attitude toward her possibly going off with other men. She saw the desire in Claude's eyes, but she did not yield. Instead, she sat stiffly looking up at him.

At just over six feet in height, with broad shoulders and a trim waist, he was easily the handsomest man in her circle of friends. He was also the most wild, even more than his longtime friend Ambrose Nevers. That wildness had intrigued Laurel because other men fell all over her, but she was never sure of how she stood with Claude. He alone was a challenge. She had never surrendered herself to him because she was sure that he would then leave in triumph.

He leaned over to kiss her. She allowed that, but without enthusiasm. He pulled back in surprise.

"You can do better than that," he complained.

"I was thinking of what you said about my father."

"I don't like you thinking about anyone except me when I'm kissing you, not even him."

"I can't help it. Papa makes me so mad sometimes! He's estranged from all of us children, except my older sister. She's so much like him that he leaves her alone. But I never would buc-kle in to him, and neither would my brother. We were both rebels."

"I always suspected that's why Dorian ran away and enlist-ed, even though he was just a kid."

"He was fifteen, but he looked eighteen." Laurel's voice soft-ened, remembering. "Since no proof of age was required, the army accepted him. In a way, I blame Papa for causing Dorian's death."

Claude tried to pull Laurel close to him, saying, "The Rebels killed him, not your father."

Laurel again stiffened, resisting Claude's amorous efforts. "I still blame him. I want to hurt him the way he hurt me."

Claude chuckled. "If you really want to do that, tell him you're engaged to me."

"Is that a proposal?" she teased.

He shrugged. "Why not?"

Laurel hesitated, knowing it was a noncommittal remark, devoid of any romance. However, Claude and she were both rebellious and nonconformists, and they had grown up together. These were the bonds that drew them to each other. Besides, betrothal to Claude would punish her father and judgmental sisters.

Laurel nodded. "I accept," she said, half-jokingly.

"Then kiss me properly," he said, and claimed her lips. This time, she did not resist.

❦

The express car swayed and bucked on the tracks, but Ridge paid no attention. His focus was on George Aiken. He sat in the wicker-bottom chair and scowled at Ridge leaning against the coach wall.

"You were gone a mighty long time," Aiken said.

Ridge locked eyes with Aiken, wondering if he disliked him so much because he had fought on the opposite side during the war, or if the resentment was because the railroad had suddenly replaced a former fellow guard with a stranger.

"You said I could stretch my legs," Ridge answered mildly. "That's what I did."

"Listen, Johnny, your job is here with me, guarding this gold."

Ridge's eyes flickered to the strongboxes stacked against the wall and partly covered with a large sheet of canvas. He doubted that Aiken had made an accidental slip. Rather, Ridge suspected he was deliberately confirming the boxes' contents and tempting him to think about stealing some of the gold.

Aiken seemed to read his thoughts. "Don't even think about it. If you make any suspicious moves, I'll blast you into kingdom come, then tell the company it was self-defense when you tried to steal this shipment!"

There had been several very brief stops at small rural stations before the afternoon sun slanted through the western car windows and made Laurel sleepy. She rested the novel on her lap, but resisted the temptation to doze off as Sarah had done.

Laurel's mind had strayed from Claude to her paid assignment. She tinkered with ideas of how she could prove Schramm was stealing part of the passengers' fares. When the conductor had walked her back from the express car, she had acted the part of a naive young woman asking innocent questions.

When she asked where he went when not collecting tickets, he showed her a back section of the second passenger car that served as his tiny office. There was a green shade over the small window so nobody could see in. That seemed a logical place for him to divert part of the ticket money from the railroad for his personal use. But how did he do that? She needed proof.

Somehow, Laurel had to find an opportunity to slip in there without being seen and search for answers. But with only one way in or out, and people frequently passing down the narrow corridor, she ran a big risk of being seen. She would have to find a time when that risk was minimal.

In the war, no single person had threatened her life, although discovery meant she would be hanged by the Confederate military. Here on the train, she had one specific man to fear. Pinkerton had warned her that Schramm was suspected of involvement with gangs of former soldiers and ruffians who had been attacking towns and killing people. Her heart speeded up at the possibility that the conductor might harm her if he caught her rummaging through his office.

She forced those thoughts aside to think about finding Claude and to her paid assignment. But before she could focus on either, she recognized Lucas' heavy footsteps. To discourage him from engaging in conversation, she closed her eyes as though asleep. She heard him slide into his seat directly across the aisle where he rustled a newspaper and muttered to himself.

She heard the paper fall into the aisle and his soft exclamation as he reached for it. His head bumped her elbow. Her eyes flew open.

"Sorry, Miss," he said, retrieving the scattered pages. "Didn't mean to wake you."

Laurel didn't believe that. She was sure that bump had been intentional, but she said sleepily, "It's all right."

"You read this?" he asked, shoving a page toward her.

"No," she replied with a hint of annoyance at being forced into a conversation. She let her eyelids droop in an obvious hint to be left alone.

Lucas didn't seem to notice. "I found it in the smoking car. The newsboy must have put some copies on at one of our stops. Crying shame the way the law is falling apart once you leave the cities. Look at this."

Left with no choice, Laurel sat up and scanned the headlines he held out for her. In the popular style of the day, the top bold headline proclaimed, *Three Killed in Robbery*. Underneath, instead of starting the story, two other headlines, each in smaller type than the one above, summarized the piece. *Armed Guerrillas Attack Sleeping Town. Vigilantes Rumored Forming to Stop Rampages.*

When Laurel shifted her gaze from the paper to Lucas' eyes, he shook his head vehemently.

"Had to happen, you know. It's rumored that the border ruffians were mostly Southerners or border state malcontents. However, there probably are some former Union soldiers who want to pillage and profit against those who can't fight back, including women and children. Of course, Rebels who belong to the new gangs are still so mad at losing that they're now terrorizing innocent civilians. Missouri and Kansas had their share of this kind of thing before and during the war, but it hasn't stopped."

Laurel was interested. "I didn't notice where this latest event took place."

"On the Missouri and Kentucky border. Our cars stop there later, so we'll get a chance to learn more about everything." Again shaking his head, Lucas added, "Those gangs are getting bolder all the time. Wouldn't surprise me if eventually they tried to stop a train."

Laurel's eyebrows lifted in surprise. "Really?"

"Oh, yes, but don't worry, Miss. As long as I'm here, you and your friend will have my protection."

"Thank you." Laurel decided that Lucas was kind of a strange little man, but he was charming and gallant in a rough sort of way. She asked, "May I see that paper, please?"

She had absorbed most of the details when Sarah stirred and sat up. Laurel handed the paper to her, urging her to read it. Almost at once, Laurel realized she had made a mistake. Sarah's eyes opened wide in fright.

"Maybe we shouldn't have come," she said. "Maybe we should get off at the next stop and go back home."

Alarmed at the possibility of losing her required traveling companion, Laurel declared, "That's silly! We'll be all right. Besides, I can't go home without knowing what happened to Claude and finishing the story for the newspaper."

Glancing out the window at the lengthening shadows, Sarah suggested, "Well, then at least let's stay on the cars when they stop. We won't be attacked here, will we?"

It was hard for Laurel to accept the fact that Sarah had never been an adventurer. She had always been a homebody, caring for her aging parents and avoiding any kind of risk. Sometimes Laurel thought that she and Sarah got along so well because they were total opposites.

"I expect to be safe anywhere," Laurel replied. "So when we stop for supper, I'm going to get off and ask around to see if anyone has seen Claude, or anyone resembling him."

The conductor entered the car from the front and raised his voice. "Brookeville next stop. Thirty minutes for supper."

As Schramm passed Laurel and Sarah's seat, he smiled at them. "Food's not very good," he whispered, "but it's better than starving."

Sarah leaned toward him. "Is it safe?" She patted the open newspaper on her lap. "I mean, I just read about what happened, and Laurel and I are concerned. . . ."

Laurel frowned at the unwarranted inclusion of her name in Sarah's statement, but Schramm didn't seem to notice.

"There will be plenty of men all around, ladies. Nothing unpleasant can happen, so enjoy your meal in safety." He walked on, again calling out the next stop.

Lucas leaned into the aisle. "Ladies, stick close to me, and you won't have a thing to worry about."

Sarah smiled gratefully, but Laurel shook her head. She needed to be alone so she could try looking in the conductor's office. "Thank you, but we'll be fine."

He shrugged and leaned back in his seat.

Sarah whispered fiercely, "Why did you do that? It wouldn't hurt to have someone around us who's armed."

"You go with him if you want," Laurel whispered back to Sarah, her tone brittle. "I told you that I've first got to ask around about Claude. Then I'll join you and Mr. Lucas if he's still with you."

As the train slowed at sundown, Aiken stood up and leaned his shotgun against the express wall. "You want to go eat first?"

"Makes no difference to me."

"Me, either. So why don't you go first? I'll stand guard."

Ridge rose from his uncomfortable position of sitting on the wooden floor with his back against the wall. The movement caused the corner of the letter inside his shirt pocket to poke into his ribs. He forced his thoughts away from all the trouble he was having in delivering that.

He warned Aiken, "Suits me, but don't go blasting away with

that scattergun when you hear me coming back."

"Don't worry, Johnny. Just come through the rear door, slow-like, so I can see you. Anyway, if I shoot at you, it won't be an accident."

When the train halted in front of the depot, Ridge exited the express car through the small side door. From the open platform, he stepped down onto the gravel bed beside the tracks. He stretched while his eyes swept the passenger coaches behind. He was disappointed that Laurel and her friend were not among the passengers getting off.

"Hey, there!" a man's voice called, making Ridge turn around. He recognized Frederick Harkins, the brakeman, jumping to the ground. "You want company?"

"I hate to eat alone," Ridge replied.

"And I hate being a brakeman," Harkins said. He quickly glanced around and lowered his voice. "Of course, I wouldn't want the company to know that. Jobs are too hard to find, even dangerous ones."

The two men fell into step, heading toward the small restaurant adjoining the depot. Ridge said, "I heard being a brakeman is the riskiest job on the line."

"That's not the half of it! You see, the engine has no brakes, so the engineer has to put the thing in reverse to slow it down and stop. He also signals with the whistle when he's going to do that so that the brakeman can climb outside to his stations and apply the brakes on the tender. Makes no difference if it's rain or shine, sleet, snow. . . ."

He broke off his thought and lightly jabbed Ridge in the ribs. "Look who just got off the cars."

Ridge glanced back, surprised that he felt an emotional

response to seeing the brash Yankee woman and her rather plain friend. A short man with a bowler hat trailed them.

Harkins joked, "I wouldn't mind finding her shoes under my bed."

Ridge said softly, "I would appreciate it if you didn't speak that way."

The brakeman glanced sharply at him. "Something personal?" he asked. "Or just that Southern chivalry I've heard about?"

"I don't like such remarks about any woman."

"Sorry, Ridge. I didn't mean to get you riled up."

"No offense taken."

Harkins nodded. "Good! Maybe we can sit near them at supper and get better acquainted."

"You can if you want. I'm not in the mood."

"Trouble with your girl back home, Ridge?"

"There's nobody back home." He angrily quickened his pace and left the brakeman behind. "Nobody at all," he repeated softly to himself.

Laurel pretended not to notice Ridge, although her gaze had been drawn to him even before the conductor helped her step down from the car.

"Oh," she said, pointing past where Ridge walked with the brakeman, "I see the telegraph office. You get us a table, Sarah. I'll ask about Claude, then join you."

"There's not much time. . . ." Sarah began, but Laurel had already changed course and headed toward the telegraph office. Laurel glanced back as Lucas increased his tempo and fell into step beside Sarah. She would like having an armed protector close.

Laurel next located the conductor. He was still standing by the car, watching the last straggling men step down. Maybe he would join the others in the diner, giving her an opportunity to search his office. She tried to keep an eye on him, but when she opened the squeaking door to the six-by-six-foot telegrapher's office, she lost sight of Schramm.

The telegrapher's vest was draped over the back of an old hickory chair. He leaned forward, his back to her while he lightly tapped on the key located on his tiny desk. A small clock and a kerosene lamp were located on the wall directly above a shelf. The shelf held two jars of what appeared to be water with some electrical wires leading in and out. Laurel had no idea how telegraphy worked.

"Yes?" The man finished sending the message and twisted in his chair. "Oh!" He was very tall and skinny, and obviously very surprised to see a pretty young woman in his office. He leaped up so fast his elbow hit the table, almost knocking over his double inkwell with its quill pen. He snatched up his vest and struggled into it as though she had caught him improperly dressed. "What can I do for you, Miss?"

"I'm looking for my fiancé," she began, noting the look of disappointment shadow his bearded face. Briefly, she gave Claude's name, his military rank, and explained that he had not returned home after the war.

She concluded, "I heard he was working on the railroad somewhere down in this general area. I thought perhaps you might have seen him?"

"Sorry, Miss. Nobody around here like that. But you might

ask the agent. He sees more people than I do."

Laurel thanked the telegrapher and headed for the door marked Agent, but her eyes swept the abandoned train. She wondered if Schramm had stayed aboard or if he had gone to supper. She chided herself for not making sure. Well, she could peer into the restaurant after she saw the agent.

If Schramm was eating, she could skip her meal and try to slip back aboard the train to examine the conductor's office. This was perhaps her best opportunity to do that, although she might lose enough time that she would get no supper.

The agent was older, with a sagging waistline that he sucked in when Laurel approached him. She had to hide her smile as he held in his stomach while she repeated her inquiry about Claude. The agent could not help her. As she walked away, she heard his breath rush out in relief when he let his stomach droop back over his belt.

Laurel had not really expected to easily find a lead to Claude's whereabouts. She walked toward the restaurant door as though about to enter, then stopped, letting her gaze skim the diners inside. Sarah and Lucas were sitting at a table with a vacant chair held for Laurel. Back in the corner she spotted Ridge, the brakeman, and other crew members. Schramm was not with them.

With a disappointed sigh, she decided he must still be aboard the train. Searching his office would have to wait. She put her hand on the doorknob, then stopped at the sight of the conductor entering the restaurant from a back door. She thought he had probably gone to wash his hands.

Now! she told herself, and turned toward the train.

No! She checked herself. *I can't go directly there because somebody might see me.* She glanced around, trying to think of the best way to enter the car unobserved.

She casually walked down the station platform, past the empty baggage carts. Lengthening shadows would protect her when she cut across to the second passenger coach. The coal oil lamps in the cars had not yet been lit, so she would not make a silhouette when she entered the car.

She was grateful that no one was in sight, yet there was always an element of surprise and risk. Her pulse quickened at the thought of what she was about to do.

Laurel approached a small building at the far end of the platform. She stopped to look back and was satisfied that she seemed to have the evening to herself. She turned toward the tracks, but stopped suddenly at the sound of someone inside the building.

She waited, barely breathing. But there was only a stillness. She strained to see into the open door, which was barely visible in a strange, reddish light. In the twilight, she could discern a large trunk. It stuck part way out of the open door, suggesting this might be a baggage storage area.

Laurel pressed against the side of the building, not wanting to be seen and yet reluctant to give up an opportunity to rummage through Schramm's office. Just as she was about ready to move on, she heard faint sounds of movement from the open door. There was something about them that suggested stealth, alarming Laurel enough that she waited silently.

In a back corner of the restaurant, Ridge ate without really tasting his food. He absently listened to Harkins, but Ridge's eyes kept swiveling toward Sarah and the short older man with a huge chest. An empty chair showed that they were expecting Sarah's petite companion.

As Ridge watched, the wide-chested man stood up, dropped some coins on the table, and headed out the door.

Ridge finished his meal, but the little man did not return. "Excuse me," Ridge said to Harkins and the other crew members. "I've got to get back and relieve the other guard so he can eat."

Darkness was settling fast, and the weak kerosene lanterns hanging outside on the platform showed no one moving about. Ridge glanced around. Where had the little man gone? Why had he left Sarah alone, and where was Laurel? Ridge headed for the door with the word *Agent* painted above it.

The room was silent and empty. Ridge called, "Anybody here?" but there was no answer. Shaking his head, Ridge left and approached the telegrapher's office.

Ridge asked, "Did you see a young woman come by here in the last few minutes?"

The telegrapher grinned. "Sure did. And I can sure see why everybody's asking about her. She's a purty one."

"Everybody?" Ridge repeated in surprise.

"Sure. You're the third one."

Ridge's forehead wrinkled thoughtfully. "Was one a little man, but stout looking?"

"Yep, he just left."

"What about the other man?"

The telegrapher hesitated. "Why do you want to know?"

Ridge parried, "What did they want?"

"Why, to know if she sent a telegram. But she didn't. She just asked about her missing beau. Say, what's this all about?"

Ridge didn't answer, but stepped outside onto the platform again. Who was the first man to ask about Laurel? Why did they care if she sent a telegram?

"And where is she?" he whispered to himself.

Down at the end of the platform, Laurel had stood motionless for at least a minute. Then, slowly, she relaxed and gathered her skirts about her. As she passed the open door, she heard a low moan.

She froze, her eyes sweeping the room's interior. The reddish glow came from a bull's-eye railroad lantern sitting on a trunk toward the rear. There were scattered barrels, crates, and boxes, with a large partly open door in the back of the room. But there was no sign of life until she heard another moan.

All thought of her mission vanished. She took a cautious step inside the open door. "Hello?" she called softly. "Anybody in here?"

There was no answer, but the sound of someone moving in the back of the building made her look that way. She caught a fleeting glimpse of a man's shadow slipping through the partly open back door and into the night.

Alarmed, she started to back out, but stumbled over something. She regained her balance and looked down to see that she had tripped over a man's leg. It stuck out from behind a barrel a few feet inside the door. Hearing another moan, and controlling her alarm, she bent to look behind the barrel.

In the shadows cast by the railroad signal lantern, she discerned the form of a man lying face down between the barrel and a couple of trunks. A knife handle protruded from his back.

With a startled gasp, she straightened up and hurried back toward the door. She bumped into somebody behind her.

Instantly, she screamed.

Chapter 5

Laurel struggled to pull back, but strong fingers gripped her arms. She screamed again, striking out blindly against the shadowy figure in the doorway.

"Laurel! Stop!"

The quiet voice sliced through her sudden terror. She stopped her flailing and looked up into Ridge's face.

"Oh!" she exclaimed in immense relief, and collapsed against his chest, but instantly pushed herself back. "There's somebody there!" She pointed behind the barrel. "I heard him moan and . . ." Ridge gently moved her aside and knelt beside the victim.

She heard excited voices down the platform as diners spilled out of the restaurant in response to her screams.

She fearfully asked Ridge, "Is he? . . ."

"There's no heartbeat."

"But I heard him. . ."

"Probably did," Ridge interrupted, "but he's dead now." He stood up and stepped close to Laurel. "Are you all right?"

"Yes! That is, except for being surprised and frightened."

"What happened?"

"I was walking outside when I heard something in here, like somebody moving."

"Maybe a scuffle?"

"I don't know."

The sound of running feet echoed loudly on the board platform, coming closer as she continued. "When I looked inside, somebody was just going out the back door."

She indicated the rear exit beyond the red railroad lantern. "At first, I didn't see . . ." She glanced down at the body, then turned to the open front doorway as the conductor, Lucas, and some other men dashed into the room.

Schramm glanced at Laurel, then glared suspiciously at Ridge. "What's going on here?" the conductor demanded.

"Somebody's been killed, over there." Laurel waved in the direction of the leg sticking out from behind the barrel.

The conductor quickly examined the victim by the eerie red glow of the signal lamp, then swore softly. "He's one of our passengers."

One of the other men standing around agreed. "I seen him in our car. Don't know his name, though."

"I don't either," Schramm replied.

The other passenger added, "I didn't see him talking to anybody on the whole trip. Kept to himself, he did."

Sarah arrived breathlessly and pushed her way through the men. "Laurel! What on earth? . . ." She broke off at the sight of others staring down at the victim. Sarah gasped, covered her mouth with her hand and quickly turned away.

Lucas asked Laurel, "Did you see it happen?"

Schramm said gruffly, "This is railroad business. I'll handle it." He turned to the skinny telegrapher standing nearest the door. "Sam, run get the sheriff. Until he gets here, I'm in charge."

He reached into his uniform coat and removed a small pad

and pencil. "Now, the rest of you stand where you are, and don't touch anything. I've got some questions."

He turned to where Sarah clung to Laurel in shocked disbelief, with Ridge nearby. "Miss Wilson," Schramm began, "let's start with you two ladies and this Reb . . . uh . . . gentleman. Tell me what happened."

The train's departure was delayed until the heavyset local law enforcement official arrived and introduced himself as Sheriff Rodgers. By then, two regular lanterns had been brought from the depot. Their pale yellow light mingled with the red glow from the railroad signal lamp. Setting one lantern on the floor by the body, Rodgers crouched to examine it. "Anybody know who he is?"

"I already asked everyone," Schramm replied. "He was a passenger on my train, but nobody knows his name."

Sheriff Rodgers carefully continued his examination, then spoke almost as if talking to himself. "From the looks of his hands and right forearm, he tried to defend himself, but it didn't do much good. He has multiple stab wounds to the chest and abdomen. He must have tried to run away when the fatal blow was struck."

Using his booted foot, the officer shoved the lantern closer to view the victim's face.

Laurel caught her first good look at his features and gasped.

Sarah whispered, "What's the matter?"

"I think I've seen him before," Laurel replied so softly that not even Ridge could hear her from where he stood closer than any of the other men.

Sarah nodded. "Probably have. The conductor said he was a passenger on our train."

"No, I think it was someplace else."

Ridge tried to shut out all sounds except what the two women were saying, but he only caught enough to surmise that Laurel seemed to know the victim.

Rodgers went through the victim's pockets. "He wasn't robbed," he reported. "He's carrying twelve dollars in greenbacks, but no identification."

Ridge noticed that Sarah seemed more upset and frightened than Laurel. After her first startled scream, she had regained her self-control and answered the conductor's questions quietly and directly.

Laurel sensed Ridge's eyes were on her. She glanced away from the sheriff and the victim just as Ridge swiveled his gaze away from her. She frowned slightly to indicate that she did not need his concern. At the same time, she recalled the strength she felt in his arms during the brief moment he had held her.

The sheriff picked up the lantern and straightened up. "Well, whoever he was, he sure as blazes got hisself knifed to death."

For the first time since Schramm had cut Lucas off, the small man spoke up. "I would guess he was surprised, so it must have happened fast."

The sheriff glanced disapprovingly at him. "You think so, huh? You a Pinkerton or something?" The detective agency was so well known that it was common practice to identify a suspected or known detective as a Pinkerton.

Ridge caught the sarcasm in the sheriff's voice, and apparently Lucas did, too. He lowered his eyes but didn't answer.

The conductor cleared his throat. "Sheriff, I interviewed

most of the other people here, so I can save you some time by giving you what I've got."

"You may as well," Rodgers said resignedly, as though he had to humor these nonprofessionals. "I only been doing this for twenty years. Tell me who found the body, and then let's go to the depot or restaurant where it's warmer."

"She found him," one of the other passengers declared, indicating Laurel. "She and him." The eyes shifted to Ridge.

Schramm scowled at the uninvited participation. "That's true." With a jerk of his chin toward Ridge, the conductor added, "The rest of us were having supper when we heard her scream. We came running out and found her with him, and the victim lying there. I've written down what each person said. . ."

"Tell me inside," Rodgers interrupted gruffly. He started out the door, then spoke over his shoulder to the station agent. "Henry, you'd better stay here and see that nobody bothers anything until I can come back and go over the whole place with a fine-tooth comb."

Inside the depot waiting room, Laurel stood close to the pot-bellied stove with the ever-present spittoon beside it. She confirmed her story as Schramm repeated it from his notes, then she started shivering. Even borrowing Sarah's cloak did not help. Laurel realized the shaking was nerves, and not a reaction to the night's creeping coolness.

During the war, she had often slipped between pickets to mingle freely with Confederate officers or their troops, glean bits of military intelligence of use to the North, then creep back through the pickets.

That had been challenging and exhilarating, especially when a nervous sentry called out in the night or fired a shot in her direction. She knew that the secrets she passed on had caused the death of men in gray uniforms, but she had never seen a single person who had died violently.

Schramm finished reading the statement she had given him before the sheriff arrived. When he looked questioningly at her, she nodded.

"Yes, that's right. I got cold and decided to go to the baggage car to get my cloak from the trunk. You know the rest."

The sheriff asked, "You're sure that you didn't see who went out the back door?"

"As I said, it was really just a shadow."

Rodgers turned to Ridge. "You got anything to add to what the conductor says you told him before I got here?"

"No. I ate fast and left early so I could go back and relieve George Aiken, the other express guard. I stuck my head in the agent's door, but he wasn't in. Then I spoke to the telegrapher."

Schramm seemed dubious. "For a man who was going to relieve his partner, you sure took your time getting there. And how do we know you stopped at the agent's office?"

"A better question," Rodgers said tartly, indicating he did not approve of the conductor's participation in the inquiry, "is why you asked the telegrapher if this young woman had been in?"

Laurel had been startled when the skinny telegraph operator told the conductor before the sheriff arrived that Ridge had been asking about her. In his statement to Schramm, Ridge had not mentioned it.

She had glanced at him, but he didn't meet her eyes. Instead, he had told the conductor that he didn't discuss women with other men. After the sheriff's question to Ridge, she again glanced at him.

"Well, Mr. Granger," Rodgers said. "We're waiting to hear your answer."

All eyes focused on Ridge, but he didn't reply.

Harkins, the brakeman laughed. "Sheriff, if you was younger, you'd know why."

The other men snickered, but Ridge gave them a cold stare that plunged them into silence.

Ridge regretted that he had made that impromptu inquiry. He didn't want this saucy Yankee girl to think he had any interest in her. He avoided her eyes, but countered Rodger's question with his own.

"Don't you find it more curious that both Mr. Lucas here, and the conductor, had already asked if she had sent a telegram?" Ridge fastened his eyes on the telegrapher. "You did confirm that the other man was the conductor. Right?"

Sam, the telegrapher whom Schramm had earlier told to get the sheriff, bobbed his head and pointed to the two men. "Yes, both of them."

Laurel was intrigued but unable to think of why either of those men would care if she sent a telegram. There was no way Schramm could know of her assignment, and she had just met Lucas, so she was puzzled.

Rodgers lifted a hand to stop the discussion. "I'll come back to the reason you gentlemen did that." His pale blue eyes flickered over the combined railroad crew and passengers. "Now, Mr. Schramm, tell me again who was not present when Miss Wilson screamed?"

The conductor checked his notes. "Mr. Lucas suddenly left the table where he had been sitting with Miss Perkins, waiting for Miss Wilson."

Lucas snapped, "I already told you; I went out back for personal needs."

"But," the sheriff mused, "you went to the telegraph office instead."

"I did both!" the little man replied hotly.

Rodgers lifted an eyebrow. "Why would you want to know if Miss Wilson sent a telegram?"

A dark flush showed on Lucas' face. "That has nothing to do with this murder!"

The sheriff motioned to Schramm. "Go on with the list of who was not present at the time of the scream."

"According to Miss Perkins, Mr. Harkins, back there, left the table right after the express guard Granger did. And according to what Harkins said when I questioned him awhile ago, he went out the restaurant's back door, also to use the facilities."

All eyes turned to the brakeman, who simply nodded.

Rodgers said, "What about you, Mr. Conductor? You admitted already that you were late for supper."

"I told you," Schramm answered. "I was delayed with duties on the train, and then I went out back here to wash up before coming in for supper."

The sheriff commented, "It's curious that not one of you gentlemen mentioned seeing the other out there."

"I was here eating when she screamed," Schramm pointed out, his tone showing annoyance. "Everyone knows that! I was first out the door when she cut loose, too. Besides, what reason would I have to kill the man? I don't even know his name."

Rodgers nodded. "So you said. But so far, we don't know who had a motive for murder. All we know now is that a man is dead, and someone killed him."

Lucas demanded, "Does that mean you consider us all suspects?"

The sheriff replied, "I don't have any reason to eliminate anyone yet."

He continued his interrogations until he had talked to every one of the passengers and crew present. Then he allowed everyone to return to the train while he interviewed the engineer, firemen, and other crewmen who had not yet left the train.

The usual reserve among passengers had been destroyed by the murder. Those who had originally boarded the train as strangers now clustered in the stopped cars to speculate and offer opinions. Ridge returned to the express car, leaving Laurel as the center of interest.

Lucas pushed past half a dozen other men to stand in front of her and Sarah. "Are you sure that you told the conductor and the sheriff everything you remember?"

Laurel rankled at the short man's question. "I'm sure," she replied curtly.

Sarah said, "You didn't tell them that you thought you had seen that dead man someplace before."

Laurel shot a disapproving look at her friend, but it was too late to stop new interest.

Lucas exclaimed, "Is that right, Miss? You've seen him before? Where?"

"I don't know. Maybe I was mistaken."

Lucas pushed for more information. "Then what made you think you'd seen him?"

"He just looked sort of familiar," Laurel replied evasively, regretting that Sarah had brought up the subject. To end the matter, she said, "The conductor said he was in the other coach. Maybe that's where I saw him."

Sarah reminded her, "You weren't in that coach."

"Then maybe it was when we were boarding." To control her annoyance, she turned to the short man with the bowler hat.

"Mr. Lucas," Laurel continued, her tone frosty, "I didn't hear your answer to the conductor's and sheriff's question about why you asked the telegrapher if I had sent a telegram."

He shrugged. "It was just idle curiosity."

Laurel's eyes showed that she did not believe that.

Lucas asked, "Why don't you ask the conductor the same question, Miss Wilson?"

"Maybe I will." Turning to Sarah, Laurel said, "I would like to return to our seats." Then to the rest of the passengers, she said, "This whole experience has been very trying, so I would appreciate it if all of you left us alone."

Laurel led the way down the aisle between the seats but turned her head and spoke softly so that only Sarah could hear. "Why did you say anything to them? What I told you about thinking the man looked familiar was meant to be in confidence."

"Why? What difference does it make?"

"Probably none, but I'm tired of being the center of attention. I want to find my fiancé, and yet here we are, stuck way out by some little prairie railroad station while my time is getting short."

"Maybe you'd like to be alone for a while?"

Laurel realized she had been speaking too harshly. "No, I'm just upset and frustrated. Besides, there's no way I can be left alone. Anybody who walks by will stop to talk."

"I'll tell the others you've gone to wash your face. You can lock yourself in the little room where nobody will bother you."

Nodding, Laurel said, "That might work. But what about you?"

"I'll go talk to some of the other passengers."

The women parted, each going her own way.

When Ridge reentered the express car through the small rear door, the other guard was angry.

"What in the blazes is going on, Johnny?" he demanded, setting his sawed-off shotgun against the wall and standing up in front of his cane-bottom chair. "You was supposed to be back long ago. And why ain't this train moving?"

Ridge picked up the shotgun and sat down in the just-vacated chair. "Somebody got stabbed to death outside the depot."

"Yeah? Who?"

"Nobody seems to know."

George Aiken's tone softened. "How did it happen?"

Ridge ignored the question to avoid getting into a discussion. "I expect the sheriff will want to tell you when he finishes talking to the engineer and firemen."

Aiken swore fervently. "My belly is rubbing against my backbone, so I'm not going to sit here and starve to death waiting on no sheriff. I'll get the whole story from the people in the restaurant. You keep an eye on things here."

Ridge heaved a sigh of relief as the other guard exited through the small door. Countless questions and thoughts twisted and tumbled through Ridge's mind. He settled back in the chair to sort them out.

A stranger was dead. Laurel had found him just before he died. Ridge was sure that part of her story was true because he had arrived just as she straightened up from examining the body. He had left the telegrapher's office in time to see Laurel stop outside the baggage storage area. She could not have killed the man.

But who had, and why? What was Laurel doing in that area? He doubted her claim that she was going for her cloak, because the baggage car was on a nearly direct line from the station platform. But why had she lied? And why had both Jacob Lucas and Hannibal Schramm asked the telegrapher if she had sent a telegram?

Ridge shook his head in bewilderment just as Frederick Harkins stuck his head in the rear door. "You mind company, Ridge? There's no work for a brakeman until these cars roll again."

Ridge wanted to think more about the murder, but that was no reason to be unsociable. "Come on in."

Harkins approached Ridge asking, "What do you make of all this?"

Ridge shrugged. "You know as much about it as I do."

He recalled that Sarah had told both the conductor and the sheriff that Harkins had left the table right after Ridge did. Had Harkins gone out back as he claimed? Or could he have run down the back side of the storage area and killed the man just before Laurel arrived on the scene?

"Terrible thing, Ridge," the brakeman said, easing down so his back rested against the car wall. "I've been thinking on it. Since it had to be someone who wasn't at supper, that narrows the field down to less than half a dozen." He shook his head. "That includes you and me."

Ridge slowly fixed Harkins with a cold stare.

"Oh, not that I think you did it!" he exclaimed. "I know you're new on this run, being your first time and all. But I don't think you'd have a reason. Not that you would kill a man in cold blood. Maybe you did in the war; we all had our chance at that."

He paused as though to give Ridge an opportunity to confirm or deny that he had killed in combat, but Ridge didn't reply.

"So," Harkins continued, "you didn't do it. I didn't do it, and neither did the girl. Apparently, the conductor couldn't have. So that leaves only that short little man, Jacob Lucas, unaccounted for."

"Not quite." Ridge stretched his legs straight out in front of him. "Henry, the agent, wasn't in his office seconds before when I stopped by."

"I forgot about him."

"What about the people who were still on the train?" Ridge continued. "Or what if it was someone who wasn't on the train, but maybe lives around here?"

"You're right, Ridge. I sure hadn't figured on all those possibilities. Let's see, instead of Lucas being the only possible suspect, we've now got the station agent, plus those who were still on the train, like the engineer, firemen, and your fellow guard. Five or six, at least."

"Well, with all the excitement this murder has stirred up, we'll probably soon hear where everyone was, and who had the opportunity to knife that man. But motives will be harder to come by."

Harkins said, "You're good at this."

"Just thinking out loud," Ridge remarked. He wondered if the brakeman was sincere or if he was trying to flatter Ridge.

A shadow appeared at the small doorway at the end of the car, causing both men to look that direction.

Sarah asked, "Am I interrupting?"

"No, of course not," Harkins replied heartily. "Come on in."

The express car was Ridge's responsibility, but he overlooked the other man's breach of etiquette and stood, offering Sarah the only chair.

"Where's your friend?" Harkins asked.

Sarah answered him but looked at Ridge. "She needed to wash her face and be alone for a little while. I didn't want to be out there by myself with all those men asking questions I can't answer. You're sure you don't mind my stopping here for a few minutes?"

Harkins smiled broadly. "You're welcome anytime, Miss Sarah." He caught himself and quickly turned to Ridge. "Isn't that right?"

"Of course."

The conductor and the sheriff appeared at the small door. Schramm called out, "Careful with that scattergun. Mr. Rodgers wants to talk to George."

"He went to supper," Ridge said. "Should be back soon."

The sheriff nodded. "I'll go find him." He looked at Sarah. "I want to talk to your friend again, but neither the conductor nor I can find her."

"She's indisposed," Sarah said delicately.

"Well, undispose her. Mr. Schramm here will show me your seats as soon as I finish with the other guard. Please be so kind as to have Miss Wilson available then."

Sarah stood, but her manner indicated she plainly was not ready to leave. "All right," she said, and exited the express car just ahead of the sheriff and conductor.

Ridge followed them with his eyes, wondering what the sheriff wanted to ask Laurel now.

Several minutes later Schramm and Rodgers approached the seat where Laurel and Sarah sat expectantly. Lucas still had not returned to his place opposite them.

"Sorry to inconvenience you again, Miss Wilson," the sheriff began, "but before I let all of you go on your way, I need to ask you another couple of questions."

"Of course."

Rodgers smiled at her, then turned to the conductor. "I'm sure you've got things to do to get the cars ready to move again."

Schramm took the hint and left, his face showing some displeasure at being dismissed without hearing what else the sheriff wanted to know from Laurel.

When the conductor was out of earshot, Rodgers sat down in the seat usually occupied by Lucas.

"Miss Wilson," the sheriff began, "you said that you saw the shadow of someone slip out the back door, leaving the victim still alive, or, just barely, and not for long. So the conductor couldn't have been the one you saw."

Laurel said, "I didn't really see. . ."

"The question is," Rodgers broke in, turning his penetrating gaze on her, "did he see you?"

"What?" she asked in surprise.

"You heard him, or maybe the victim and the killer," the sheriff pointed out gently, "so maybe the killer heard you coming. Maybe he got a look at you, enough to make him think you might identify him."

"No!" Laurel cried in alarm. "I didn't see anybody, just what I told you! A shadow. That's all."

"I see." Rodgers stood up. "Well, I hate to release these cars, but if I don't, the railroad and all your passengers will be after my hide. So I'll have to let everyone go, subject to being called back if it's necessary."

Sarah exclaimed, "Oh, thank you! I can't wait to leave this unpleasant place!"

"I can understand that, Miss Perkins." The sheriff partially closed his eyes to regard Laurel thoughtfully. "But it's only fair to warn you that there's a possibility that the killer is on this train."

Sarah gasped. "Oh! I hadn't thought of that."

Laurel admitted in a hoarse whisper, "Neither had I."

"The reason I mention it," Rodgers continued in a kindly tone, "is because if that's true, then the killer either was present tonight during my interrogation, or he'll get word of what happened."

Laurel realized where the sheriff's words were leading. "You mean he might not believe that I didn't get a good look at him?"

"Miss Wilson, in my job, you have to think of all kinds of possibilities. So I suggest you be on your guard just in case he decides to keep you from ever possibly identifying him."

Chapter 6

The train continued south from Brookeville, but the coal oil–burning headlight provided only thirty feet of visibility, so the miles passed slowly. Laurel stared out the window at the unseen prairie, glad that the conductor had turned down the coach lamps so passengers could sleep. But Laurel and Sarah were very much awake.

Across the aisle, Jacob Lucas' short body was sprawled across the seat. His head and left shoulder rested between the end of the seat and the window. The bowler was perched precariously over his face.

Sarah whispered to Laurel, "You think he's really asleep?"

Laurel watched the slow but measured rise and fall of Lucas' big chest before answering. "I hope so."

Her thoughts tumbled over each other, momentarily displacing the murder with her twin reasons for being on the cars.

Sarah said, "He asked a lot of questions, even after he got away from the sheriff and the conductor. And why should he want to know if you had sent a telegram?"

Laurel was troubled by that. She had rejected the possibility that Schramm might somehow have learned of her real reason for being on the cars. No one except Allan Pinkerton and herself knew that.

She told Sarah, "I don't have the faintest idea."

"I can't figure that out, either. The conductor and Ridge are young enough to be interested in you, but Lucas is old enough to be your father. Why would he ask the telegrapher about you?"

"I don't know. What I do know is that this delay is keeping me from finding Claude." *And getting a chance to look through the conductor's little office without being seen.*

"I think Lucas talked to as many people about the murder as Mr. Rodgers did." Sarah shook her head. "Lucas is a curious little man."

"If you don't mind," Laurel said, her thoughts still tumbling, "I want to sit quietly and think."

Sarah lifted her shoulders in a resigned shrug while the wooden coach swayed and creaked, and the wheels clicked over the connected rails. Finally Sarah asked softly, "One more question: Are you frightened about what the sheriff said?"

"Not really, especially since the conductor came through afterward and reported that the firemen, engineer, and other crew members all seemed to have good alibis."

"So you don't think the killer is on this train?"

"That's two questions, but to satisfy your curiosity, no, I don't. I believe it was someone who lived somewhere near that depot."

"If that's true, how did he know when and where to find the victim alone after he got off these cars?"

"That's the sheriff's job to find out, not mine."

"Even if the murderer thinks you could identify him?"

"That's enough!" Laurel's voice rose so sharply that Lucas stirred in his sleep. Concern about the possible ramifications of the murder caused Laurel to be unduly upset with her friend. She added softly, "You'll frighten both of us with that kind of speculation!"

Rebuffed, Sarah again fell silent and looked away.

Laurel's musings drifted back to her meetings with Pinkerton. She had no doubt that he would not give her an extension at the end of a week if she hadn't proven that Schramm was stealing. More importantly, it meant that she would not be able to continue searching for her missing fiancé.

Sarah leaned forward, peering through Lucas' window on the left side of the aisle. "I think we're slowing up, but we're in the middle of nowhere. There's not a single light showing anywhere out there."

"There's probably a water station or a woodshed coming up."

"That's logical," Sarah agreed. "We periodically have to take on wood and water. When the wood burns in the engine's boiler, it turns water into steam to power the locomotive."

Laurel wasn't interested. The murder had delayed her attempts to find Claude. The murder had also kept her from fulfilling her business objective to surreptitiously search the conductor's office for evidence that he was stealing from the railroad.

But her basic drive concerned Claude. She again heard her older sister berate him. *Worthless. Twice a bountyjumper. He and his friend Ambrose Nevers deserved to be taken Confederate prisoners before they could desert a third time.*

Laurel flinched at the recollection, but she felt defensive at Emma's declaration that she didn't love Claude. *You never loved any man even though they swarm around you like brainless flies! Now you're going off on a wild goose chase after a man who doesn't care enough about you to come back to you, or even write.*

Laurel wondered, *Why do people say I don't love Claude?* Even Sarah had questioned Laurel about that after they boarded the train. *Why else would I go on this trip if I didn't love him? Am I hurt because he didn't come home, sort of rejecting me? No man has ever done that. Has he stopped loving me. . .if he ever did? Or am I mystified and just want to know the truth about our real feelings for each other?*

The train squeaked to a stop and the swaying motion ceased. Through the left window beyond Lucas, Laurel saw lanterns and men's legs moving in the pale yellow lights. She glimpsed the wooden supports of a water tower and a telegraph pole holding up the ever-present wires that ran beside the rails.

Laurel snapped upright in her seat, startling Sarah.

"What's the matter?" Sarah asked anxiously.

"I just remembered where I first saw that man!"

"The dead man?"

"Yes!" In the excitement of remembering, Laurel had forgotten to whisper. She saw Lucas' breathing change. Fearful that he was awake, she gently pushed against Sarah's shoulder. "Let's go where I can tell you in private."

❦

Ridge had become used to the lurching of the express car, so when it ceased, he immediately sat upright on the blankets that served as his bed on the wooden floor. He started to reach for the shotgun but stopped when he heard George Aiken's chuckle.

"Johnny, you sleep real light."

Ridge had forced himself to accept the fact that the other guard was going to continue goading him with the hated name of

Johnny Reb. "Why are we stopping?" Ridge asked.

"To take on water." Aiken had tilted the chair back so the front legs were in the air. "You still got an hour to sleep before it's my turn."

Nodding, Ridge yawned and lay back down.

Aiken asked, "You changed your mind about not telling me what you was really doing out there with that purty gal when she found the dead body?"

"I told you all you need to know." Ridge hadn't meant to speak so bluntly, but there was something very irksome about Aiken.

"You take offense real easy, don't you?"

"Where I come from, a man doesn't talk about women to other men." Ridge kept his voice even, although it was an effort. But he had told himself he could stand this man for one trip.

Aiken's tone hardened. "Why are you defending her, Johnny? All women are alike under their chemises."

"I don't like crude remarks about any woman."

The front legs of the chair came down hard. "You saying I'm crude?" Aiken stood up and walked heavily across the floor toward Ridge. "By ol' Nick," Aiken growled, "I don't have to take that from no Rebel!"

Quickly standing upright, Ridge said quietly, "You sure you want to push this conversation any farther?"

The other guard stopped as though he had run into an invisible stone wall. Then, apparently concerned that his action might be misconstrued as cowardice, he spoke through clenched teeth. "Not here, not now, but when we finish this run, I'll mop the floor with you."

"Are you calling me out, Aiken?"

When the guard hesitated, Ridge continued in the same quiet, confident voice. "If you are, that gives me choice of weapons. How are you with a cavalry saber?"

"I'll use my bare fists and boots. . ."

"No!" Ridge broke in. "The one challenged chooses the weapons. You challenged; I choose cold steel." He gently touched the scar on the bridge of his nose and right cheek. "I got this from a saber, but I'm here and my opponent is dead."

Slowly, Aiken relaxed. "No need to get all het up about it, Johnny. . ."

"The name is Ridge."

"Right. Ridge."

Two short signals from the engineer warned that the train was about to move again.

Aiken backed up to his chair and sat down with the sawed-off shotgun in his hands. "No offense, Ridge. You can go back to sleep now."

With a brief bob of his head, Ridge lay back down. He lowered his eyelids to slits to watch Aiken while the train gathered momentum and creaked on across the dark prairie.

❧

In the back of the second coach by the stove, too far away from the seats for anyone to overhear, Sarah's eyes opened wide at what Laurel had told her.

"You're sure?" Sarah asked. "Absolutely sure?"

"Yes! I don't know his name, but the man lying dead back there is the same one I recently passed coming out of Allan Pinkerton's office."

"What were you doing there?"

"That's not important."

Sarah vigorously shook her head. "I think it is! I asked you earlier if you were working for Pinkerton again, and you hedged in answering. I've been concerned about that ever since, but I went along with your request. I've also introduced you as Wilson instead of Bartlett. I've wondered why you're claiming to be a newspaper correspondent."

"I am going to write for the *Globe*. So far, I've been gathering story material."

Slowly shaking her head, Sarah declared, "I wish I could believe that. Anyway, things have changed. A man is dead, and you obviously know more than you're saying! That scares me! So what are you keeping from me?"

"What I'm trying to do is figure out why anybody would kill that man."

"You didn't answer my question."

"I'm telling you what you need to know, Sarah. At the time I saw that man leaving the agency's office, he was carrying a little portable telegraph box."

Sarah sighed, reluctantly realizing that Laurel wasn't going to tell her much. Sarah snatched at the straw of information Laurel had offered. "You think he was killed for that?"

"No, that's not what I'm saying. But he must have been a telegrapher, although Schramm said he was a passenger, not a crew member."

"Did you see that box when we all went with the sheriff to search around the dead man's seat?"

"I wasn't looking for it, but now I'd like to take another look. Maybe it's in the overhead luggage rack by his seat."

"You want to go right now?"

"It can wait until there are fewer people around to wonder what I'm doing. Maybe at the breakfast stop."

"You be careful! Maybe the murderer had an accomplice. You know, one killed that man while the other took the box from his seat."

"I think you've got a lot of imagination. Besides, we don't even know if he had it with him in the cars. He could have stored it as baggage."

"It's not likely, if that's why he was killed."

"Maybe that wasn't the reason at all."

Sarah wanted to learn all she could about what Laurel knew. "Is it possible that the dead man had gone to Pinkerton's office to hire a detective to protect himself from someone?"

"They agency doesn't do that kind of work."

Sarah challenged, "How do you know that?"

"Pinkerton mentioned it back once when I was still crossing Confederate lines."

Sarah was momentarily stumped. Then she exclaimed, "Maybe he was a Pinkerton agent!"

Laurel's eyebrows shot up in surprise.

Sarah frowned. "If he was, what was he doing on this train?"

Instantly, Laurel thought she knew the answer. It was well known that Pinkerton assigned agents to check on the work of other operatives. The dead man could have been sent to spy on her.

She resented Pinkerton doing that. In her previous wartime service, she had never done anything to make him distrust her. *Well,* she reluctantly admitted to herself, *maybe this time I have.* She had tried to hide her true motive from Pinkerton. That could have been his reason for assigning an operative to spy on her.

Sarah asked, "What are you thinking?"

"Nothing special."

There was suspicion in Sarah's next question. "You really are keeping something from me. I know it. You're not looking for Claude at all!"

"I am! I certainly am!"

"You don't need to lie to me. I know there's more to it than what you've said. Are you working for Pinkerton now?"

Sidestepping a direct answer, Laurel mused on a new thought. "If the dead man was a Pinkerton, then somebody might have known that and killed him. But why? What did somebody have to hide that was so important it cost a life?"

It was obvious to Sarah that she wasn't going to get an honest reply. She shrugged in defeat, then admitted, "I don't know, but it's frightening. We've got to tell somebody! The conductor! He'll know what to do!"

"Wait!" Shaking her head vigorously, Laurel declared, "I don't trust him because he asked back there if I had sent a telegram. It's none of his business whether I did or didn't."

"The same is true of Jacob Lucas. So whom can we trust? How about Ridge Granger? He didn't ask if you'd sent a telegram, so I think that means he was just interested in you."

Laurel made an impatient gesture. "Not him, either."

"Why not? If the murderer is on this train, he might come after you! He might think you told me something, so I could be in danger, too! I think we should tell Ridge. He would protect us."

"You just want an excuse to be near him."

"What's wrong with that?"

"I just don't want to tell anyone, including him," Laurel said firmly. "I'll look out for both of us."

"You're used to taking risks, but I'm not! I don't like this!" Fright showed in Sarah's eyes. "Oh, I wish I had never come with you on this trip!"

Laurel didn't reply. Except for being careful, there was nothing she could do about the murderer. But she could continue her search for Claude, and she could get proof of the conductor's thievery. Maybe at the breakfast stop, if she hurried, she could look for the dead man's black box plus slip unseen into the conductor's office.

❧

At Aiken's urging, Ridge left the express car as soon as the train made its breakfast stop at Hickory Corners. The sun was rising when he seated himself at the end of the nearest of two long tables.

Sarah led the crew and other passengers through the door. She waved cheerfully and walked directly toward Ridge. "Good morning," she said with a smile. "Would it be too rude of me to ask if I might sit here?"

"Glad to have your company." He looked past the other passengers hastily taking seats. Most crew members seated themselves at the far end of the second table. Ridge did not see the conductor or Frederick Harkins, the brakeman.

Ridge's gaze lifted to take in the train standing on the tracks. There was no sign of Laurel. It was a temptation for Ridge to ask about her, but he resisted.

Sarah followed his eyes. "She'll be along shortly. She said she had something to do first."

Ridge nodded but said nothing while the older man who ran the place with his wife sleepily poured coffee for everyone from a large, blue-enameled pot.

"I didn't sleep much last night," Sarah said in hopes of returning Ridge's interest from Laurel to herself. "It's bad enough that a man got killed, but to think his murderer might still be on the train with us is most frightening."

Ridge halted the coffee cup at his mouth. "What makes you think he's on the cars?"

Leaning forward and lowering her voice, she asked, "Didn't you hear?"

"Hear what?"

Sarah glanced around. Everyone was engaged in his own conversations with nobody looking at her, not even Jacob Lucas. "Maybe the sheriff didn't tell everyone," Sarah said in a confidential tone, "but he told Laurel and me that it was only fair to warn us that there was a possibility the killer was still on the train."

"That's news to me," Ridge admitted.

"Then please don't tell anyone I mentioned it to you."

"I won't."

She gave him a grateful smile. "The sheriff told us something else," she continued, keeping her voice down. "He says that there is a possibility the killer might not believe Laurel didn't get a good look at him. He might be afraid she could identify him, so the sheriff warned us to be on our guard."

Frowning, Ridge asked, "Does the conductor know all this?"

"I suppose the sheriff told him, but Laurel doesn't trust the conductor. She doesn't like the fact that he asked the telegrapher about her. She doesn't trust Mr. Lucas for the same reason."

"Mr. Lucas?"

"Jacob Lucas, the short man down at the far end of the table. I think he's watching us." She blinked, then exclaimed in embarrassment, "Oh! I didn't mean that because you asked the telegrapher about her that she doesn't trust you. But they wanted to know if she had sent a telegram, and you didn't ask that."

Ridge offered no excuse for inquiring about Laurel. Instead, he told Sarah, "A person can't be too careful around strangers."

Sarah looked out toward the train, with the omnipresent telegraph poles and wire along the right-of-way. "I wonder what's keeping Laurel."

"I'm sure she'll be along." He hesitated before asking, "You known her long?"

"We grew up together." Sarah saw an opportunity to diminish Ridge's obvious interest in Laurel. "She's looking for her fiancé, you know."

For a couple of heartbeats, Ridge didn't answer. Finally he said, "No, I hadn't heard that either. We don't hear much back there in the express car."

"He didn't come home after the war." Sarah hurried to make her point. "She knows from another friend who was with Claude that they were released together from a prisoner-of-war camp. But it's been nearly six months now, and Claude hasn't written or anything. So she's trying to locate him."

"I see."

Sarah sensed the disappointment in his words and tried to press her advantage. "Her father doesn't like Claude or his friend, Ambrose. We all grew up together, so I know both men well. I tend to agree with Laurel's father, but Laurel always was headstrong."

Ridge didn't answer but leaned back as the man reached down to set a high stack of pale brown pancakes on the long table. Ridge motioned for Sarah to help herself.

She thanked him and lifted two of the poorly cooked cakes onto her plate. "Laurel's going to miss breakfast if she doesn't hurry."

"There will be time. George Aiken, the other express guard, sent me to eat first with the passengers. He says that fewer people eat after that. So don't worry."

"I'm not really." Sarah smeared butter onto her cakes. "Laurel's used to taking care of herself."

Ridge smiled. "So she said."

Sarah's eyes opened in surprise. "Did she tell you that?"

He took a bite of food and chewed slowly, avoiding her eyes.

Sarah realized that he wasn't going to answer her.

She decided to try learning more about him. "Seeing that dead man last night was probably nothing new to you. I mean, I guess you got used to it in the war."

"Not really."

She sensed that he also didn't want to talk about that, but she had to know more about this man. She tried an indirect approach. "I lost some friends." His questioning glance made her quickly add, "Not beaus. My parents used to say I was too picky. Maybe that's why I am still unattached."

She watched for his reaction, but he didn't give any or even reply. Sensing that she had been too forward, she returned to the war. "I suppose you lost friends?"

He did not want to tell her that he had lost everyone and everything except the bare ground of what had been his family's tobacco plantation. Finally he said quietly, "A brother."

"Oh, I'm sorry! I didn't have any brothers or sisters, but Laurel's only brother was killed."

The moment she said it, Sarah regretted bringing Laurel back into the conversation. Yet, now that she had said that much, she felt obligated to explain.

"He lied about his age and enlisted when he was only fifteen. He was killed a year later. Just a boy."

Ridge's fork stopped halfway to his mouth, but he did not speak. Instead, Sarah saw something in his eyes, a flash of something like remembered pain. It was gone so quickly she couldn't be sure why he had reacted that way.

Confused and concerned, she blurted, "Laurel and he were very close. Very much so. She took his death hard."

Still without speaking, Ridge placed the fork on his plate. His fingers went to the letter in his shirt pocket, then he stood abruptly. "Excuse me. I've got to get back to relieve Aiken."

"But you haven't finished your breakfast."

He didn't seem to hear, but quickly left. Sarah watched him stride out, unable to understand his sudden departure. Sighing, she lifted her eyes toward the cars, wondering, *what's keeping Laurel?*

Laurel had exited the train on the side away from the depot and little restaurant. Shielded from view by the wooden cars and their shadows from the rising sun, she picked her way along the tracks and climbed onto the front of the other passenger coach. She was relieved to see it was empty.

It had only taken a few seconds to search around the seat where the dead man had ridden yesterday. Whatever belongings he had brought on board were gone. She assumed that the sheriff had taken them for a more leisurely examination, perhaps to seek some clue to his identity.

She exited the car, grateful that she had not seen anyone on board. She hurried along in the train's shadow to the end of that car where the conductor had his office. Lifting her skirt, she started to climb aboard, but stopped when she heard a low murmur of male voices.

One swore softly. "So he was a Pinkerton?"

"Yes. His name was Edmond Woods. The telegraph operator handed me the message a couple of minutes ago when I stepped into his office here."

Laurel recognized the second speaker's voice as that of Hannibal Schramm! She couldn't identify the first voice when she heard it again, but she overheard him say, "I remember that name! He's the same Pinkerton who caught that conductor stealing on the Central Illinois three months ago. So Woods must have been closing in on you."

Schramm snapped, "He probably was, but you should have waited and pushed him off the end of a car while we were moving. If it looked like an accident, that blasted sheriff wouldn't have come poking around."

Laurel's heart speeded up. *They're talking about that murdered man!*

The unknown male voice protested, "I intended to, but I saw him watching me. He was suspicious, so when I saw him take his little box and head toward a telegraph pole, I figured I had better not wait until later."

"You were a fool!"

"Watch your mouth!"

Schramm snapped, "Don't tell me what to do! You've jeopardized the big plans."

"This has nothing to do with those!"

"The blazes it doesn't!" Schramm shot back angrily. "What if she saw more than she says?"

He means me! Laurel thought.

The other man was thoughtfully silent before saying quietly, "Then we'll have to do something about it."

"Don't do anything that messes up what we came to do. Do you understand that?"

She couldn't hear the unknown man's reply, but the conductor's next words were clear. "Because you didn't follow orders, the law may suspect something big is up."

"They got no reason to think that."

"Haven't they?" Schramm asked scornfully. "They will figure out that the Pinkerton was not killed because he was checking on whether or not I am pocketing railroad money. They'll know it was something more than that. A federal marshal could be . . . Sh! Someone's coming!"

Laurel heard footsteps on the board platform, but the car where she stood blocked her view.

Schramm said, "It's that Rebel returning from breakfast. You get back where you belong, fast! Bend low and go through the cars and hope nobody sees you!"

Laurel remained motionless, barely breathing, wanting to risk a peek at the unknown man with Schramm, but not daring to do so for fear they might see her.

That must not happen, she told herself. *They admitted murdering that man. . .Woods. They're now planning something big, and they'll probably kill me if I get in their way.*

Laurel felt the same surge of excitement she had often experienced after gaining important military intelligence behind enemy lines. She had to get that information back to the Union side without being caught. But this was different because she could not leave until she had accomplished her double goals for coming on this trip.

With that realization, she cautiously raised up enough to see that both the conductor and the unknown second man were nowhere in sight.

Sighing with relief, she climbed back into the car, knowing that she had to be confined to a train where an unknown killer and suspicious conductor were watching her. She ardently hoped to quickly locate Claude, plus get proof of Schramm's thievery, without losing her life.

Chapter 7

By the time Sarah returned to the car, Laurel had sorted through her thoughts and come to a decision. Her life was in danger from the unknown man who had killed the Pinkerton operative, but she wasn't going to just sit and take a chance on being murdered. She had to discover the identity of the man she had overheard talking with the conductor.

Sarah slid into her seat and began scolding. "What's the matter with you, Laurel? You're missing breakfast!"

"I'm not that hungry." She looked out the window at the people drifting out of the restaurant. "Who all was in there with you?"

Sarah smiled knowingly. "Oh, so you are interested in him?"

"What?"

"Don't play the innocent with me. You know who."

"If you mean Mr. Granger, you're sadly mistaken. I wasn't thinking of him."

"You weren't?" Sarah sounded relieved.

"No. Which of the train crew did you see in there?"

"Why do you want to know that?"

"Because it's important!"

"All right! All right! Don't sound so impatient. Let's see . . .

almost everyone was there. Ridge, of course. We sat together and talked—"

"Who else? No, maybe it'll be faster to tell me who wasn't there."

"What's the hurry?"

"Please! Just tell me."

Closing her eyes as though to better see the restaurant's interior in her mind, Sarah began. "Well, the engineer was there, but not the firemen or the guard who works with Ridge in the express car. I didn't see the brakeman."

Brakeman! Of course! Laurel's thoughts leaped at that possibility. *A brakeman could throw somebody from the train and under the wheels. It would seem like a perfectly logical accident.*

Sarah continued, "We met the brakeman named Harkins. You remember him, don't you? We met him and Ridge Granger when we went to get my cloak."

"I remember. Did you see Harkins last night at dinner just before the murder?"

"I don't recall. Laurel, you're scaring me! What's going on?"

"Think back! I've got to know."

"I'm trying. Well, let's see. Jacob Lucas and I were sitting together, holding a place for you, but you didn't show."

Pausing, Sarah added, "Ridge might know. I think I saw him and Harkins talking together before supper, but so much has happened since then, I can't be sure. We could ask Ridge."

"Good idea!" Laurel exclaimed. "Let's ask him before the train starts again."

Alone in the express car, Ridge held the sawed-off shotgun in

the crook of his arm and absently fingered the letter in his pocket. Hearing about Laurel's sixteen-year-old brother had punched
a hole in his own walled-off memories of another death.

The images returned, vivid and strong. Ridge's cavalry had
charged into a cornfield to attack Yankee infantrymen. The
standing stalks were cut down by musket fire or trampled by
plunging horses. In the great scope of the war, this was a minor
skirmish. That is, for all except the dead and wounded.

When the battle was over, Ridge had ridden his weary, lath-
ered horse away to rest. On the way, he noticed the number of
dropped but still serviceable Yankee weapons that could be recovered tomorrow and used by the Confederates, who were very
short of arms. Ridge also spotted an abandoned drum. At various
battlefields where he had previously fought, Ridge had seen
drummer boys or heard them valiantly thumping away in the
midst of incredible carnage. They were aged twelve or so, going
where they were not required to go by conscription until they
were eighteen. But in four years of war, Ridge had never before
seen an abandoned drum.

Too weary to care at the moment, Ridge had gone on to rejoin
his detachment and try to sleep through the crisp autumn night.
Yet there was something so compelling and tragic about the silent
drum that Ridge rose the next morning before dawn to look for it.

He remembered exactly where he had seen it, and in the
strange half-light of a new day, he had walked toward it, bypass-
ing some abandoned Federal weapons and being careful to avoid
stepping on the dead sprawled in every direction. Some fell so
close together that blue and gray uniforms seemed almost to be
one mixed with red. Ridge had been hardened to such gruesome
sights, yet he mentally steeled himself against the possibility of

what he might see. In the grim silence, Ridge hurriedly relocated the drum. He inspected it and found it to be in good condition. Brushing off some corn leaves, he picked it up and started back toward camp.

That's when he heard the groan.

He froze, glancing about in fear that one of the blue-coated infantryman might be able to aim his rifle and fire point blank. Ridge completed his rapid 360-degreevisual sweep without seeing any sign of life.

Then a whispered word came from behind him. "Water."

Ridge spun, reaching for his pistol, but the wounded infantryman weakly lifted a bloody arm and repeated the word.

It was the face that held Ridge's attention. Black with powder, it was still a child's face. *A boy*, Ridge realized. Not a drummer boy, but a tall, gangly teenager in blue. He would not have been more than fifteen or sixteen, barely two or three years younger than his own brother.

By then, Ridge had reason to hate all those who wore the uniform of the North. But this boyish face and the obvious bayonet wound in the chest hit Ridge emotionally.

Ridge lowered the drum and shared his canteen.

"Thank you, Sir." The weak reply was barely a whisper. "In . . . my shirt." He tried to raise his good hand, but it fell back onto the cornstalks. "Letter."

Ridge gently removed the envelope from above the gaping wound. It was strange, he thought, but there was no blood on it. "You want to hold it?" he asked, offering it to the boy.

"No." The faced grimaced in pain. "After the war . . . take it . . . to name on . . ."

He had not finished the sentence, but Ridge glanced down

and read: Charley Bartlett, Elm Street, Chicago, Illinois.

"Please, Mister," the boy pleaded, his voice weaker. "Promise me . . . you'll deliver it."

It was an impossible request. Ridge knew that, and silently berated himself for even considering the idea. He started to explain, forcing himself to look again at the youthful face, and the envelope.

"Please! Promise?"

Ridge didn't mean to nod, but he did. "I promise," he repeated softly.

Through the powder-blackened face, a hint of a smile touched the boy's lips. "Thanks."

It was the last word he ever uttered.

Ridge never forgot that strange little smile. It haunted him, driving him to attempt delivery of that letter when he wanted to forget the entire incident.

Yet he could not, not even when sitting in the express car, waiting for George Aiken to return from breakfast. Ridge regretted the promise, yet he was honor bound to again try to make the delivery when he returned to Chicago.

He was startled by a woman's voice from the narrow doorway at the end of the car.

"Anybody home?"

He recognized Sarah with Laurel just behind her, so he called for them to come in.

Sarah entered first as he stood. She asked, "Are we intruding?"

Ridge leaned the shotgun against the wall and shook his head. "Not on me. I'm not sure what Aiken would say. I take my orders from him, but he's having breakfast, so I guess it's all right to invite you in."

He grinned, saying, "I don't expect we'll have any robbery attempts in a busy place like this. So won't you ladies have a seat?" He motioned to the single chair and added, "Or at least one of you?"

"No thanks," Laurel said. "We can't stay."

"She's got some questions for you," Sarah explained.

"Oh?" He turned to Laurel. "I don't know that I can be much help, but I'll try."

She was entirely too uppity for his taste, yet he felt a little surge of interest. It wasn't just that she was pretty, he decided, although she certainly was that. She had a smile that warmed him clear down inside where he had felt only coldness since returning home from the war.

"As you may have heard, Mr. Granger, I'm a correspondent for the *Chicago Globe*."

He raised both eyebrows in surprise. "I hadn't heard that, Miss Wilson."

She resisted a temptation to frown. "You don't approve of women working, Mr. Granger?"

Shrugging, he replied, "I'm not familiar with any who do, but then, I've had very little contact with them for the last four years."

Laurel asked archly, "Do I detect a note of sarcasm in that remark?"

He said sharply, "Detect what you will. I was busy defending my home from some invaders. I believe they came from up your way, Miss Wilson."

Laurel felt the conversation running wild, away from what she wanted to know. She avoided making the tart reply that sprang to her lips. With an effort, she said, "Perhaps I should begin again."

Ridge waited, stealing a glance at Sarah. He had a feeling that she was pleased with the sparks that had been struck by the few words spoken.

"In my work," Laurel said, choosing her words carefully, "it's required that I be a good observer of what goes on around me. Sarah and I were discussing which members of the crew were at supper at the same time you were last night."

Ridge was suspicious of that explanation. "Miss Sarah, I'm surprised that you didn't remember. You said you told both the conductor and the sheriff that Harkins had left the table right after I did."

"Of course!" Sarah exclaimed. "I forgot! Oh, this terrible murder has got us all mixed up!"

"Yes, it has," Laurel agreed. "But Mr. Granger, do you remember who else was taking supper the same time you were?"

He recalled Harkins later speculating on who might have committed the murder. Schramm, the conductor, had come in late, so Harkins had ruled him out as a suspect. That had left Jacob Lucas, Henry the station agent, George Aiken, the train engineer, and the firemen.

Ridge concluded, "This is my first trip ever as a railroad employee, so naturally I haven't met many of the other crew members. There may be some I don't know about."

"Earlier," Laurel said, "I saw you talking with the brakeman. Harkins, I believe his name is."

It wasn't a question, but Ridge understood her meaning. He asked, "Does your work as a newspaper correspondent mean you want to help solve a murder?"

She flashed the same charming smile she had used to disarm young Confederate officers when she had infiltrated their lines. "Oh, certainly not! I am merely interested, as is almost every person in these cars."

Ridge didn't believe that, not at all. "Of course," he replied, then added, "but if I can be of any assistance—"

George Aiken interrupted by calling from the side entrance, "What's going on in here?"

Both women jumped, but Ridge spoke quietly. "I guess that means he thinks I should be standing guard alone." He raised his voice to the other guard. "These ladies just stopped by for a moment."

Sarah exclaimed, "We were just leaving."

Laurel said nothing, but stood for a moment with a slight frown before agreeing. "Yes, we were. Sorry to have bothered you gentlemen."

When they had gone, Aiken strode across the express car floor, his heavy boots clumping loudly. "You're supposed to be guarding this car, not entertaining women!"

"We haven't been robbed."

"That's not the point! You can't be alert if you're distracted!"

"I'll remember that."

Unable to rile Ridge, Aiken dropped heavily into his chair and picked up the shotgun. "What were they asking about?"

"Nothing special."

"The murder last night?" Aiken asked suspiciously.

"Everybody's going to be talking about it until we reach the end of the line."

"What did they want to know?"

"Why don't you ask them?"

"I'm asking you!"

Ridge's tone went flat and hard. "I'll answer questions about my job, but that's all. I'm not obligated to do more."

Aiken took a deep breath, then slowly let it out just as the engineer's familiar two-note whistle sounded, alerting the crew that the train was going to move on.

As the cars gathered speed out of Hickory Corners, Laurel nudged Sarah and motioned to the empty seat across the aisle from them. "I wonder where Mr. Lucas is."

"Probably asking questions somewhere."

"He's a mighty interesting man," Laurel said.

"Not as interesting as Ridge Granger. Why did you light into him a few minutes ago?"

"He rankles me, that's why."

"How so?"

"I don't know; he just does."

"I think he's fascinating." Sarah slumped lower in the seat so the back of her head rested on the cushion.

"He's annoying."

"I think I know what's bothering you, Laurel. He's about the only man who doesn't fall all over himself in trying to impress you."

"I have no interest in anyone except Claude."

"I hear you, but I don't believe you."

"I don't want to talk about it."

"Suits me. When I compare Ridge to John, you know how John comes out? He is a good man, but, well, so ordinary, like every man I ever knew. Now, on the other hand, Ridge is . . . well, different."

Laurel didn't answer but watched the telegraph poles slipping by. *Who was that man I heard talking to the conductor? I've got to find out before he decides that I might identify him.*

She barely heard Sarah who seemed to be almost talking to herself. "John's going to be an undertaker. If I had married him, do you realize what kind of crude humor I would have had to put up with the rest of my life?"

She waited for an answer that didn't come. "But Ridge is different from anyone I know."

"I agree with that," Laurel said sharply. "He's arrogant, cold, and so sure of himself."

"He looks a little bit dangerous to me, sort of an unpredictable man. I find that exciting."

Laurel was intrigued by Sarah's paradoxical nature. One moment she was fearful and playing it safe, the next she wanted to flirt with a man like Ridge. Laurel blamed that on Sarah's having led a sheltered life and having been infrequently courted by very ordinary men. Perhaps that was why she was also intrigued by male strength and the mysterious quality in Ridge.

Shaking off her reflections, Laurel reproved Sarah. "He's a Rebel! His kind killed my brother!"

Sarah sighed. "And our kind killed his."

Laurel's eyebrows rose in surprise. "He lost a brother in the war?"

"That's what Ridge told me."

Sighing, Laurel observed, "It seems almost everyone lost someone. More than 600,000 were killed on both sides, and I'm sure Ridge had a hand in taking many lives of our boys. I tell you,

Sarah, this is a man to stay away from."

A slight shiver of excitement gripped Sarah. "I'm not afraid of him." She sat up and turned to look into Laurel's eyes. "I want to know this man better. Please help me do that."

"I don't think that's such a good idea."

"That's not the point. I'm of age. Even if I never see him again after this trip, I want to enjoy whatever little relationship there can be. Please! Say a good word to him about me!"

Laurel made an impatient movement, anxious to return to her thoughts of how to deal with the threat to her life, prove the conductor was stealing, and most of all, find Claude, all against Allan Pinkerton's deadline.

"All right, Sarah. I'll see what I can do. But remember this: something big is about to happen, but I don't yet know what it is. However, I'm sure it's dangerous."

"What is it?" Sarah's voice tightened in concern. "Tell me!"

"I can't yet because I don't have all the details. But I will speak to Mr. Granger about you. Now, please let me think without interruption."

Ridge regretted the tension between his fellow guard and himself. It had not bothered him when their verbal clash had ended short of a duel. Dueling had been outlawed, but gentlemen still surreptitiously met on the so-called field of honor. Ridge had correctly guessed that Aiken could be bluffed about such a personal encounter.

But there was something different about his reaction to finding that Ridge had been talking to the two women about the murder. Aiken was one of several men who might be considered suspects, including Ridge himself. But he didn't want to mention the subject again in hopes of avoiding any further tensions until the trip was over.

Aiken, sitting in his chair with the front legs tilted up, suddenly leaned forward. The legs came down sharply, rousing Ridge from his musings.

"We're slowing down," Aiken announced.

Ridge hadn't noticed it before, but he listened and noticed from both the creaking of the wooden car and the rapidity with which the iron wheels clicked over the rail connections, that speed was slacking off.

"Are we going to take on more water or wood?" Ridge asked.

"No." Aiken stood, cradling the shotgun. "Listen! Hear that?"

Ridge heard only the faint whistle from the locomotive.

Aiken explained, "The engineer's signaling for the brakeman to get to his post. We're stopping, but we're not supposed to be. Something's wrong! Grab your gun!"

Laurel was aware that the telegraph poles were going by much more slowly. She eased her face against the window and tried to see down the track. It was straight, so she could see nothing except the side of the express car ahead. The engine's usual black smoke and showers of cinders had trailed off. The prairie still stretched endlessly on both sides of the tracks.

Hearing rapid footsteps behind, Laurel turned to see the conductor striding purposefully toward the front of the car. "Mr.

Schramm," she called as he passed, "why are we stopping?"

"That's what I'm going to find out," he replied and quickly passed out of sight.

Sarah asked in alarm, "What do you suppose is happening?"

"I don't have any idea." Laurel stood up in the aisle and peered out the windows beyond where Jacob Lucas had been seated earlier. "I don't see any water station; in fact, I don't see anything except the side of the car ahead. There's not a house nor a building in sight."

"Maybe we're being robbed!" Sarah's voice rose in alarm. "All those stories we've heard about guerrilla bands from the war turning into outlaw bands–"

"Stop it!" Laurel interrupted, glancing ahead at the other passengers. They were craning their necks to see out the windows beside them or standing in the aisles to peer through the glass on the other side. "Remember, there's never been a train robbery, ever."

"But there could be, couldn't there? I mean, there is no law between towns. We both know that. So–"

"So what?" Laurel snapped impatiently. "We've got a car full of men, and some of them must be armed, so even if there was an attack, we have nothing to fear."

"I wish I hadn't let you talk me into coming on this trip!"

A smile tugged at the corner of Laurel's mouth. "Then you would never have met Ridge Granger."

"Oh," Sarah said thoughtfully as the train came to a jerking halt.

When the express car stopped moving, Ridge pushed himself

from the wall and faced the sliding front door with the shotgun leveled.

"Stand at ease," Aiken said from where he stood in front of his chair, sawed-off scattergun in the crook of his arm. "If anyone wants in here, they'll try to talk us out first."

Easing the gun barrel down, Ridge turned to face the other guard. "When that doesn't work, then what?"

"Nobody's ever tried it, but my guess is that then they'd place some black powder around the doors."

"But if they touched that off, they might blow up the whole car."

"My thoughts exactly, Ridge. You, me, and all the gold back there." With his free hand, he motioned toward the padlocked strongboxes stacked against the back wall.

"Now," he continued, "anybody in his right mind who wants those boxes is not going to blow up this car if he can help it."

Ridge nodded and listened for voices outside the closed sliding door.

❧

About five minutes passed while the male passengers clustered around the only two women on board, and everyone tried to guess the reason for the unscheduled stop. Jacob Lucas entered the front of the coach, bringing every eye to focus on him. A chorus of questions greeted him.

"Something's wrong with the locomotive," he announced. "I got close enough to hear the engineer telling the conductor. Something about the boiler losing steam."

Laurel stifled a disappointed groan at another delay.

Lucas caught her eye and spoke reassuringly. "There's nothing to worry about. They'll send a telegram to the next station so they'll know what's happening."

Sarah asked, "How can they do that from way out here?"

Laurel recalled seeing the bearded man leave Pinkerton's office with a little box, and so she knew the answer to Sarah's question. However, she said nothing while Lucas explained importantly.

"See those poles and wires running along the railroad right-of-way?" When passengers nodded or called out affirmations, Lucas continued.

"There's a crewman on board to handle such emergencies. In a few minutes, you'll see him climb a pole with a portable telegraph key and a way to hook up to the wire. He'll send the message, and then we'll just have to wait until he gets a reply."

"What then?" Sarah asked nervously.

"The railroad company could send another locomotive," Lucas replied, "or maybe tell us to limp on in with what steam is left in the boiler."

A heavyset man asked skeptically, "How come you know so much, Mister?"

"I told you. I overheard the engineer and conductor talking."

Sarah asked, "Are we in any danger? I mean, there are stories about possible robberies–"

"Never fear," Lucas interrupted. "We'll be safe, just a little late. Look!" He pointed out the window. "There goes the telegrapher now."

A uniformed crew member approached the nearest telegraph pole carrying a black box in his hand.

Most passengers returned to their seats, including Laurel

and Sarah, although a few men stood and watched the telegrapher climbing the pole.

The conductor returned, briefly confirmed what Lucas had reported, and gave Laurel a friendly smile.

She forced herself to return it.

When Schramm continued on out the back of the car, Sarah whispered, "He's sure got his eye on you."

"I noticed," Laurel answered, remembering that she had to find a way to go through his tiny office without being seen. She looked past Lucas who had returned to his seat and was watching the telegrapher.

Laurel's gaze lifted to the black box that the man on the pole had opened in preparation to hook up to the wire. Suddenly, she frowned and leaned across the aisle.

Sarah asked, "What's the matter?"

"Just a second." Laurel studied the telegrapher's equipment container before leaning back and lowering her voice so only Sarah could hear. "Come with me."

"Where are we going?" Sarah asked, standing up to follow Laurel who had already started down the aisle toward the heating stove.

She didn't answer until they were too far away from Lucas or anyone else to overhear.

"See that black box?" Laurel asked, pointing through the window toward the man on the pole.

"Of course. What about it?"

"I wonder if the dead man had brought his along so he could send messages to Pinkerton that nobody knew about."

"Why would he do that?"

"He was spying on someone, and whoever it was found out."

Laurel's right hand flew to her temple as though to capture a thought that eluded her brain. "Of course! That's it! He must have gone down the tracks a little way where nobody could see him when he climbed the pole."

"Why wouldn't he just use the regular telegraph office?"

"Because he didn't want anyone to know. Of course, he could have used a code, but apparently this was so important that he didn't want to even risk that."

"How do you know about telegraph codes?" Sarah asked with a hint of doubt.

"That's not important. The poor man was murdered, and nobody knows why. But it must have something to do with . . ." Laurel checked herself in midsentence.

"With what?" Sarah prompted.

"Never mind. I don't want you involved in this."

"You're frightening me again! What's going on? What aren't you telling me?"

"You're better off not knowing."

The women fell silent while watching the telegrapher disconnect his equipment from the overhead wire and ease down the pole.

Sarah asked with a quiver in her voice, "You've changed your mind about the killer not being on board these cars, haven't you?"

Laurel didn't answer.

"I knew it!" Sarah exclaimed. "He is, and you know something about it! You know who he is, don't you?"

Again, there was no answer.

"You could get killed!" Sarah's tone held an edge of panic. "Me, too! You're going to get us both murdered!"

"Sh! Get a hold of yourself. Nothing's going to happen to you or me. Come on, let's go back to our seats and see if we can find out what the railroad company plans to do about our broken-down train."

Sarah was visibly upset, twisting and turning in her seat so much that Lucas leaned over and asked if she was all right.

Laurel replied for her. "She's just a little anxious about all this. But she'll be fine."

Lucas nodded in understanding as the conductor left the train to meet the returning telegrapher.

Chapter 8

Everyone watched as the conductor met the returning telegrapher. They spoke briefly, then hurried together toward the cars. Those watching from inside speculated on what the railroad company had decided to do about R.W. Wentworth's faulty steam boiler.

Sarah whispered, "If there's a chance to get off this train and go back home, I'm going to take it."

"You can't!" Laurel said firmly under her breath.

"Why can't I? I'll pay you back for my ticket."

"It's not that," Laurel replied, knowing she could not reveal that Allan Pinkerton required her to have a female traveling companion.

"Then what is it?" Sarah's voice rose.

"Sh! Keep your voice down and I'll try to tell you."

"That sounds fine, Laurel, but you've just more or less admitted that you think the killer is on this train, yet you won't tell me anything specific. The sheriff seemed to think your life might be in danger from whoever the killer is, so how do I know that I'm not, too?"

"Everything will be all right," Laurel replied, turning with the male passengers to face the conductor as he boarded the car.

He raised his voice. "May I please have your attention? The telegrapher contacted the railroad officials about our locomotive losing steam. We're instructed to proceed slowly to our next station, Trinity, which is only a few miles from here."

Laurel's pulse quickened. *Trinity? That's where Ambrose had reported seeing Claude!*

Sarah spoke up, her voice unsteady. "Is that safe? I've heard about boilers exploding and killing the engineer and—"

"It's safe! Quite safe!" Schramm broke in with a confident smile. "You'll only be aboard here another few minutes, and then we'll disembark at Trinity."

"Good!" Sarah declared. She lowered her voice so only Laurel could hear. "When we get there, I'm taking the first northbound train home, no matter what you say!"

This was no time to discuss that, so Laurel waited for Schramm to continue. He explained, "There are no facilities to make repairs at Trinity, so you'll all have to leave the cars and take rooms at the hotel—"

A chorus of disappointed groans interrupted him.

He continued, "A new engine will be sent north to meet us. Then we'll switch locomotives and go on to our final destination."

Lucas called, "When will the other engine get here?"

"Sometime tomorrow." The conductor's words brought more groans. He added some details, but Laurel was no longer listening. Her attention shifted inward as her thoughts tumbled over each other.

The delay would cut into the seven-day deadline that Pinkerton had given her to accomplish her two goals. But surely he would learn about the reason and grant her an extra day if she needed it.

On the positive side, Laurel saw special benefits in the delay at Trinity. She would have more time to search for clues as to Claude's whereabouts, and it would be easier to privately examine the conductor's small office if the train was empty of most people.

If she could get proof that Schramm was stealing from the railroad, her job would be half done. If she found Claude, her entire mission would be a triumph. It would be even better if she could discover the identity of the man who had plotted with the conductor to kill the Pinkerton agent. Then at least she would know whom to stay away from.

Finally, she would seek an opportunity to find Ridge alone and say a good word about Sarah, as she had requested. Laurel began to look forward to the prolonged stop.

❦

The Trinity Hotel was an unpainted two-story frame structure located just to the west of the railroad tracks. Laurel asked the clerk for a room farthest away from the tracks where it would be quieter. He explained that wasn't possible. Another set of tracks belonging to the Mississippi and Gulf Railroad paralleled the Trinity Hotel on the west. The M and G was a misnomer because it only had lines in Missouri, Tennessee, and Mississippi, but someday planned to reach Louisiana, ending up at the Gulf of Mexico.

Unpacking in their sparsely furnished second-story room, Sarah remarked, "It's too bad that railroad companies don't let other lines use their rails."

Lifting a dress from her carpetbag, Laurel explained, "They

can't because not all railroads have the same size tracks, or what they call gauge: narrow and standard gauge. Before the Rebellion, that was especially true in the South."

"I never understood that."

"The railroad companies were all independent of each other," Laurel continued. She used her free hand to move a chemise to cover an extra pair of shoes at the bottom of her bag. One shoe held a pair of pliers. The other hid a screwdriver. The shoes had been wrapped separately so the tools wouldn't make any noise.

"Even in the South's dire emergency," Laurel added, moving to hang the dress in a huge oak armoire, "when one railroad reached the end of its line, everything had to be unloaded and taken by mules or horses to the second train. Sometimes that was clear across town. That second line then reloaded the goods to carry them to their final destination. Unless, of course, there was a third line involved with still a different size set of tracks."

Sarah commented, "I heard that all the South's railroads were ruined. Mostly destroyed by cavalry raids." Sarah straightened up from where she had laid a fresh dress on the bed. "I wonder what branch of the military Ridge was in."

"Cavalry."

"You sound mighty sure of yourself."

Laurel nodded, recalling the yellow piping on Ridge's Confederate jacket and pants when he had tried to help her when she was thrown from her carriage.

Sarah looked enviously at Laurel just as there was a knock at the door. She opened it to the conductor.

He smiled broadly. "Pardon the intrusion. I want to make sure your accommodations are satisfactory."

"They're adequate," Sarah said. "At least we won't have to

sit up all night and wake up with a stiff neck in the morning."

Laurel remained quiet, feeling confident that Schramm had another reason for checking on them. Maybe it had something to do with the conversation she had overheard between him and the unknown man who had knifed the Pinkerton agent.

Schramm hesitated, looking from Sarah to Laurel. "I . . . uh . . . the railroad and I would like to make partial amends for this inconvenience by escorting you to dinner tonight."

Sarah bristled at the man's glance lingering on Laurel before coming back to her. "Thank you, no," Sarah replied coolly.

Laurel saw an opportunity to use this invitation to her advantage. "Oh, Sarah," she said quickly, "just because I have this previous commitment doesn't mean you shouldn't enjoy Mr. Schramm's hospitality."

Sarah stared at Laurel without understanding. Laurel said pointedly, "You remember you asked me to do something for you?"

For a few seconds, Sarah didn't reply, then she smiled. "Oh, of course!" Turning to the conductor, she asked, "Is that agreeable with you, Mr. Schramm?"

A momentary flicker of disappointment showed in his eyes, but he nodded vigorously. "Of course! It would be nice if both of you were available, but I'm delighted to have your charming company, Miss Perkins."

When he had gone after arranging the time and place to meet, Sarah said to Laurel, "I hope you meant you're going to say a good word about me to Ridge."

"That's exactly what I'm going to do."

I'm also going to search Mr. Schramm's office when I know I won't be disturbed.

That evening, from the top of the stairs, Laurel watched Sarah and Schramm enter the hotel's restaurant.

He had changed from his conductor's uniform to civilian clothes. When they were seated at a table for two in the back corner, Laurel slipped out the hotel's back entrance and strolled casually toward the silent train.

I should be asking about Claude, she told herself, double-checking to make sure that no one was around, *but I'd better take the opportunity to search that office while I know he won't disturb me.*

From the outside, the cars seemed empty. With no interior lamps burning, she couldn't be sure, but when she was satisfied that no one was watching, she climbed into the wooden coach. She listened, holding her breath, but when all remained quiet, she started down the aisle toward the conductor's small office.

It would be locked, she knew, but that was not a problem. She had slipped the pliers and screwdriver into separate coat pockets.

Her heart speeded up, just as it had every time she had slipped behind enemy lines during the war. But this was different, for whoever had killed the Pinkerton agent might be waiting for an opportunity to catch her alone.

Outside Schramm's office door, she paused to listen. Satisfied that no one was there, she felt for the lock in the semidarkness of the coach's interior. Her fingers closed on it when she heard voices. She jerked her hand back so suddenly that she accidentally knocked the heavier pliers against the door jamb. This made so much noise that her pulse leaped into a rapid beat.

She hesitated, unwilling to leave unless it was necessary to avoid detection. The voices were outside the cars, coming closer. One is Ridge, she realized. *But who's the other man?*

Laurel waited for them to pass, their feet crunching on the gravel beside the tracks. *He sounds like the same one who was talking to Schramm about the murder.* The temptation to identify him was so great that Laurel eased away from the conductor's door. She took a few quick steps and leaned over an empty seat cushion to peer through the window.

She confirmed Ridge Granger's identity from the slightly rolling gait caused by his wounded leg. But in the unsteady light from the barrel of burning pitch outside the hotel, she could not be certain who the other man was.

I've got to know who that is! She held both hands against her pockets to prevent the tools from making any sound. Then she crouched low, slid across the seat, and slowly raised her head so that only her forehead and eyes showed above the windowsill.

Both men had moved away from the car. Laurel quickly spotted one silhouetted against the fluttering light given by the burning barrel of tar. The same source also cast the shadow of a second man walking toward the locomotive.

Disappointed at failing to see who had been with Ridge, Laurel removed the screwdriver from her pocket and returned to the conductor's office door.

❧

Hannibal Schramm's considerable experience with women had helped him develop an act that always worked. He lavished his full attention on Sarah, giving her some doubts that he really had preferred Laurel's company for dinner. Sarah had never tasted wine, and at first declined to even touch the golden beverage he ordered before dinner. He was persuasive, so she finally agreed to take one sip from the bit he poured in her glass.

She sipped gingerly, then smiled at him. "It's good!" she exclaimed, happy at having discovered something new in her sheltered life. "I expected it would be bitter, but it's sweet."

"You'll enjoy your meal much more with this," he said, and poured the glass half-full in spite of her protests.

He lifted his glass and lightly touched hers, making a faint ringing sound. "To a lovely and gracious lady." Sarah struggled to keep a girlish giggle from escaping. She felt herself flush as the sweet beverage hit her empty stomach, warming her all over.

He leaned closer, his eyes half-closing. "I want to know all about you," he said, his voice low. "So let's have another toast and then tell me everything."

Sarah warned herself, *Whatever you do, don't talk about Laurel! And remember what other women have always said: make a man talk about himself.* Aloud, she said, "That's very flattering, but I'd rather hear about you."

Reaching across the table, he lightly touched her hand. "I am honored, but I prefer that you go first."

His warm touch added to the glow spreading with the wine throughout her body. Flattered, she lowered her eyes and said softly, "Well, if you insist."

❧

Laurel fervently wished she had more light, because no matter where she placed the point of the screwdriver, it would not spring the lock. Twice the instrument slipped, hitting the wooden door frame. She hoped there wouldn't be marks that would be noticeable in the daylight.

She concentrated so hard that she forgot to keep glancing around and listening. When she heard a footstep outside of the car, she froze, her heart thudding.

The conductor's office was at the rear of the coach, less than ten feet from where someone was climbing aboard. It was about another thirty feet to the far end of the car and the other exit, but there was no way she could run the length of the aisle between the seats without being seen. Quickly pocketing the screwdriver, she walked purposefully toward the end of the nearby car.

"Oh!" she exclaimed, as a male figure appeared at the door. "You startled me!"

"Laurel? What are you doing here?"

She almost cried out with relief upon recognizing the faint Southern accent. "Ridge! I mean, Mr. Granger!"

"You were right the first time, Miss Wilson." There was a hint of smile in his voice. "Did you lose something?"

She thought quickly. "I had misplaced the book I was reading. I thought I might have left it in the car."

"Are you going to spend the evening reading in your hotel room?"

"Well, yes, after I inquire around about a missing friend. . . ."

"I heard your fiancé didn't come home after the war."

"That's true."

"I hope you find him."

"Thank you." She quickly tried to think of ways to talk to him alone without appearing to be too forward. She added casually, "After I finish asking around town, I plan to have some supper." Laurel started to ease by him, heading for the end of the car.

"Please allow me to help you down." He turned before she

could protest, climbed down from the car to the ground, and reached his right hand up to her.

She felt a tingle of pleasure as their hands met. She gave him a smile that was more than grateful. She asked, "Do you know of any suitable restaurant where an unescorted lady might go?"

He released her hand with some reluctance, wondering if she were dropping a subtle feminine hint. "No, I'm sorry, this is my first time in these parts."

"Thank you anyway." She turned toward the hotel.

"You shouldn't be out here alone, Miss Wilson. It's not safe. Allow me to see you safely inside."

As he fell into step beside her, she said, "That's very kind of you."

He remembered the haughty way she had rejected his offer of assistance when thrown from her carriage in Chicago. "Of course, I remember a time you said you could take care of yourself, but since the sheriff said there is a possibility a murderer is among us. . . ."

She stopped abruptly and looked up at him in sudden anger. But she quickly controlled that emotion. "Perhaps I was a little frosty in Chicago," she conceded. "I appreciate your concern now."

They reached the barrel of burning tar where the flames illuminated their faces clearly. After the way Varina had mistreated him, he had no intention of paying attention to another woman, especially a saucy Yankee. Yet there was something very appealing about this woman.

He said, "I hope you locate your fiancé."

"I'm confident I will." Laurel turned toward the hotel's front entrance. "He was reportedly seen working here, on the other railroad, to be exact."

"Are you going to walk around town alone and ask about him?"

"I have no choice."

They stopped at the hotel entrance. "Perhaps you might permit a suggestion, Miss Wilson?"

She tried not to hold her breath, although her opportunity to say a good word for Sarah was slipping away, and she had yet to find out to whom he had been talking awhile ago. "Of course, Mr. Granger."

"I could be your escort for dinner and also while you make inquiries about your fiancé."

She hesitated in order not to show how pleased she was at that suggestion. "Well," she said, "I suppose."

He smiled and reached for the door. "Dinner first?"

Laurel didn't want to be anywhere near Sarah and Schramm. "That sounds delightful, but first, I really need to make some inquiries about Claude. Besides, I detest hotel food. Do you suppose we could ask around about him and get a recommendation for a good restaurant at the same time?"

"I'm sure we can find one." He offered his arm.

She started to slip hers through his, then changed her mind. No matter which side she would have close to him, there was a chance he might feel the weight of either the pliers or screwdriver still in her pockets. She had to get rid of them. She asked, "Would you excuse me a moment first?"

"Don't be long."

"I won't," she promised, and stepped through the hotel door, which he held open for her. *So far, so good,* she thought, turning to give him a quick smile.

Out of the corner of her eye, she glimpsed someone step back into the shadows, away from the barrel light. Laurel could only make out a bowler hat, but that was enough. *How long has Jacob Lucas been watching me?*

Sarah Perkins had never experienced anything as warm and pleasant as the feeling given her by the sweet white wine. She felt as though she were floating on a cloud of pleasure when Hannibal Schramm deftly shifted the conversation from himself to her.

"After that terrible murder," he began, "are you and your friend concerned about your safety?"

"She's not; I am."

"Oh? Why is that?"

Careful! Sarah warned herself. She shrugged. "That's just the way it is."

"You don't think she actually saw the person who killed that poor man back there?"

"She doesn't tell me much."

Schramm seemed to sense Sarah's reticence to discuss that topic. He reached for the wine bottle. "Have you and Miss Wilson been friends long?"

"Wilson?" Sarah blinked, then repeated, "Miss Wilson? Oh, yes, we have."

The flash of interest in Schramm's eyes made Sarah hastily place her hand across the top of the glass. "No more, thanks," she said, surprised that there seemed to be a slight slurring of the simple words.

Watch out! she warned herself. *That was a bad slip!* The

knowledge that Schramm was really more interested in Laurel seeped through Sarah's pleasant warm feeling and alerted her.

She spoke carefully, making sure the words came out distinctly. "I would like to order dinner now."

"Of course." The conductor picked up the bill of fare. "What would you like?"

Grateful that he had not really pursued her verbal slip, Sarah tried to focus on the menu. The words were a little hazy, alarming her that she had imbibed more than was wise.

She lowered the menu and reached for the bread, recalling hearing somewhere that food helped dissipate the effects of alcohol. "You order for me, please."

"Do you have a preference of entrées?"

She waved an indifferent hand and kept her answer short. "No." She fervently wished that she had not failed to instantly recognize the surname Laurel was using.

❧

Rejoining Ridge in the lobby, Laurel vainly sought information about Claude Duncan from the hotel clerk. She had no better success at the telegrapher's and station agent's offices at both the Great Central and the nearby Mississippi and Gulf depot.

"This town has closed up tight for the night," she told Ridge as they sauntered toward the restaurant recommended by the M and G station agent. "I wish I could stay over tomorrow and continue my search when I can talk to merchants and rooming house operators."

"I would like to stay and help you, but when our replacement engine arrives, I'll have to be back in the express car."

"Of course. I will have to be on the train again, too." She quickly scanned the outside of the restaurant and decided it looked respectable. "Does that place look all right to you?"

He grinned. "It's a palace compared to some places I've eaten in recent years."

They entered the front door where Laurel fussed with her cloak for a moment as an excuse to casually look back. There was no sign of Jacob Lucas, but she felt confident that he was somewhere nearby, watching. But why?

Seated in the nearly empty restaurant, Laurel picked up the bill of fare but didn't look at it. "I hope I didn't distress you back there on the train when you startled me."

"Not at all."

"I thought I heard your voice earlier outside the car."

"You probably did. I was talking with Frederick Harkins."

Laurel forced herself to sound casual. "The brakeman?"

"Yes. I believe you met him when he and I were talking on the cars the first day out of Chicago."

Of course! No wonder his voice sounded familiar when I heard him telling Schramm about killing that poor detective.

Ridge observed, "Does that upset you?"

Chiding herself for having let her thoughts show in her face, Laurel shook her head. "No, not at all. It's not important."

She glanced at the menu, then quickly added, "I want to apologize for the conductor's rudeness in calling you a Rebel."

His grin returned. "It's not the first time I've recently been called that."

Laurel felt herself flush. "Oh! I guess I should first apologize for my own rudeness back in Chicago."

"No apology necessary."

She found herself warming to him. "I don't want you to think Sarah is anything like me. I've known her since we were little girls. She's a very warm, caring person."

"I'm sure she is." Ridge regarded Laurel with thoughtful eyes. "I'm sure she says the same about you."

Having achieved her dual purpose in talking with Ridge, Laurel told herself that she really shouldn't have circuitously managed to have dinner together. She should have other concerns, like how to deal with the possible threat on her life from Schramm and Harkins. Yet Laurel sat across from Ridge, wanting to know more about him.

She mentally searched for the right way to do that. "What did you do before the war?"

"I helped my parents on their plantation."

"What kind? Cotton?"

"No, tobacco. In Virginia."

His tone became flat, lifeless, alerting Laurel that this was a painful subject. She promptly shied away from that. "What brought you to Chicago?"

"A promise I made."

Laurel debated whether to ask more, but again, she felt this was a sensitive area to be avoided. She asked, "When you finish this trip, will you remain in Chicago or go back to Virginia?"

"Depends."

He had no intention of telling her about his indecision on whether to return and fight for what was left of his world, or to forget it and drift west. But unless he gained control of the discussion, she would continue to probe into areas of great pain.

He asked, "What about you? After you find your fiancé, then what?"

"As a newspaper correspondent, I've thought of what it would be like to be the first woman reporter to travel the new transcontinental railroad when it's completed."

Ridge's eyebrows raised in surprise. "What about your fiancé? I mean, after you find him and are married?"

"That, Mr. Granger, is none of your business!"

The words flashed across the table, striking him so forcibly that he recoiled slightly as from a blow.

"You're right. I apologize." He pushed his chair back. "I'm afraid I've overstepped my welcome. Please excuse me."

She blinked in surprise as he stalked stiffly away.

Suppressing an urge to call out for him to wait, she silently scolded herself for the outburst. *I came here on behalf of Sarah, so why should I care that he's walking out on me—again—just as he did that first time in Chicago?*

As the door slammed after him, she shook her head.

They were recent enemies from two different worlds, cultures, and beliefs. They had nothing in common, so it was just as well that it had ended before anything started.

Then why am I sitting here feeling as though I've lost something special?

Chapter 9

To hide her embarrassment, Laurel also left without eating. Her mood changed to anger against Ridge, but their conversation had given her valuable information about who had killed the detective. She crossed to the telegrapher's office.

He said that he would be leaving shortly, but the relief man would come on duty, and she could send a message any time during the night. She thanked him and returned to the hotel for privacy to compose a coded message to Allan Pinkerton.

Then, if she could force herself to concentrate on the murder, she planned to make notes for her story. She was sure this would be more interesting to the *Chicago Globe's* editor than the dry facts she had gathered about the transcontinental railroad. Murder and mystery always made good copy, even if she couldn't write down everything she knew; at least, not yet. But maybe by the time she reached the end of her trip, she might even be able to add that to the finished story.

Opening the hotel room door, she saw that the coal oil lamp was lit and Sarah was sprawled on her bed, fully clothed. She had a wet cloth on her forehead.

Laurel's mood softened in concern. She hurried toward the high bed. "What's the matter?"

Sarah tried to sit up, but fell back with a low moan. "I did a terrible thing."

Laurel bent anxiously over Sarah, then drew back and turned her face aside. "You've been drinking!"

"Just a little white wine."

"What happened?"

"I think I made the conductor suspicious of you," Sarah said. She told Laurel about failing to recognize the name when Schramm asked how long she had known "Miss Wilson."

Sarah concluded, "I tried to cover it up, but I could see by his face that he didn't believe me."

Alarmed that Sarah's inexperience might have caused her to tell about Laurel's wartime activities, she asked, "What else did you tell him?"

"Nothing. I was very careful after that, and I came here right after I ate. I wouldn't have even waited that long, but I was afraid I might make a spectacle of myself if I tried to walk out, feeling unsteady as I did."

Laurel, still angry with Ridge, was tempted to lash out verbally at Sarah. But she had threatened to return home instead of continuing the trip. Laurel had to stop that. She removed the cloth from Sarah's forehead, saying, "I'll freshen this up for you."

Laurel's thoughts leaped while she wet the cloth in a flowered ceramic bowl on the washstand. How would Schramm react to Sarah's slip? He would know that Laurel had lied about her surname. He might also believe she had lied about not seeing the killer attack the victim. If so, she could be in great danger.

Laurel wrung most of the water from the cloth and returned to the bed. Fortunately, she had not told Sarah about the Pinkerton assignment, or of overhearing Harkins and Schramm talking about killing the Pinkerton agent.

Sarah pleaded, "Can you forgive me?"

Laurel didn't really feel very forgiving because both her reasons for coming on this trip were now in real jeopardy. But what else could she say to a lifetime friend who was obviously in mental anguish?

"Of course," Laurel said, replacing the cloth on Sarah's forehead.

"Thank you. That feels good." Sarah hesitated. "Did you have a chance to say something nice about me to Ridge?"

Under the circumstances, the question was ridiculous, but Laurel hid her displeasure. "Yes, I did."

"What did he say?"

Laurel's anger toward Ridge returned. She didn't want to talk or even think about him. "I'll tell you in the morning when you're feeling better."

"No, please tell me now."

Laurel paused, then nodded. "Very well. I told you before that he is arrogant and cold. Now I can say he's also rude and impertinent."

Sarah demanded, "So tell me what he said."

Hesitating, Laurel realized that in retrospect, Ridge had only asked her a logical question: what would she do after she found her fiancé and was married? Instead, she had snapped that it was none of his business. She wondered why she had reacted that way, especially after he apologized. She should have stopped him before he walked out. But now it was too late, and she didn't want to admit her error to Sarah.

Laurel answered evasively. "It's not that important! Let's forget it!"

Sarah asked suspiciously, "Why are you raising your voice? Did you two have a fight?"

Laurel headed for the door, knowing that she would not be able to code a telegram with Sarah's incessant questions. "I don't care to discuss it!"

"Where are you going?"

"I'll be back shortly."

"Please don't leave me now!"

Laurel left the room without replying.

As the door closed behind her, a slow smile crept across Sarah's face. Maybe Ridge would now be more interested in her.

Laurel turned toward the stairs at the end of the hallway but glimpsed a man's foot, and the brim of a bowler hat suddenly withdraw around the corner to her right. She quickened her pace and called out to the retreating figure. "Mr. Lucas! Wait, if you please!"

The controlled fury in her voice stopped him. "Ah, Miss Wilson," he said, his tone charming and pleasant.

Now she had a target to strike without concern. She demanded sternly, "Why are you following me?"

"Following you?"

"I'm in no mood for any pretenses. What's going on?"

He sucked air into his massive chest and let it out slowly, as though wounded by her manner. "As I told you and your companion on the train, we're traveling through areas that are dangerous for nice young women. As a father, I'm giving you the protection I would my own—"

"Stop it!" Laurel snapped. Nothing was going right, and she knew she was taking out her frustrations by verbally assaulting Lucas. She continued hotly, "I don't believe you. Even if I did, I don't need your help! Now, either leave us alone, or I'll speak to the conductor!"

"Miss Wilson, I have no desire to—"

"Which is it going to be, Mr. Lucas?"

"I wish you would reconsider."

"Which is it going to be?"

He shrugged. "Very well. Have it your way." He turned and hurried down the stairs.

Laurel waited until she thought he had time to cross the lobby, then she descended and asked the desk clerk for a pad and pencil. She took them to a corner chair under a reflecting wall lamp and composed her message. She used the same Confederate cryptology they had used throughout the late war. Called the Vicksburg Square, the system used a variable code word so that the message seemed innocuous to a casual reader. The system was so simple that little material was needed by the cipher clerk. Only Allan Pinkerton and his trusted clerk would know that the operative, Woods, had been murdered, Laurel had overheard two suspects plotting something big, and she was still trying to get evidence on her assignment. She did not mention her own sense of danger for fear Pinkerton might wire ahead and pull her off the case.

Satisfied, she left the lobby and crossed the street to the telegrapher's office. The one-legged relief operator in his middle twenties reached for crutches to stand when she walked in. She motioned for him to stay seated while noticing his red hair and ruddy complexion.

She handed him the paper. "I would like to send a telegram, please."

He accepted the innocent-looking message, skimmed it, and said, "I'll do it right away, Miss Wilson. Will you wait for a reply?"

"No, thank you." He had noticed her correspondent's code name from the signed message. She added, "But while I'm here, I want to ask if you've seen a man named Claude Duncan. I heard he's working somewhere on this railroad."

"Sorry, I don't recognize the name. What does he look like?"

"He's very handsome. Tall, just over six feet, wide shoulders, slim waist. . . ."

"Your beau?" the telegrapher asked with an understanding grin.

"Fiancé." She continued with the same description she had given wherever she had inquired about him on this trip. "His eyes are gray. He's got reddish eyebrows and beard but light blond hair."

"He sounds like quite a catch, Miss Wilson, but I haven't seen him."

"If you do, please send word to the hotel. I'm staying there until a replacement locomotive arrives for our cars." She opened the drawstring on her reticule and produced a greenback. "How much do I owe you?"

When she paid what he asked, she added, "Oh, should anyone ask if I sent a telegram, I would appreciate it if you told them no."

"Don't worry, Miss Wilson. Telegrams are private." He glanced at her message again. "Only you and I know that you contacted the great detective himself."

Laurel froze. "What?"

"The recipient, Major E.J. Allen." He tapped the paper with a forefinger. "I get a few of these now and then from people traveling the railroad. Always been men before. You're the first lady Pinkerton I ever met."

"You think I'm a detective?"

He gave her a knowing wink. "Not if you don't want to be."

She demanded, "What makes you think I could be?"

"It's all right, Miss Wilson. Before the Rebs caught me in a telegraph wagon and cost me this," he tapped the stump of his left leg, "we had a Union man called himself Major E.J. Allen. I recognized him as Allan Pinkerton."

Shaking his head, the telegrapher continued, "I'm sure you know that he formed the Secret Service for General McClellan. Well, the 'major' may have been a great detective before the war, but he gave 'Little Mac' lots of bad intelligence, always overestimating the Rebel forces. I heard Pinkerton had some lady agents, but I never saw one before."

Laurel saw only one recourse. She gave the telegrapher the most disarming smile she could, asking softly, "Sir, what is your name?"

"Zimmerman, Jedediah Zimmerman, at your service."

She looked at him with innocent eyes and gently touched his hand. "Mr. Zimmerman, my life is in your hands. I trust you not to betray my little secret."

His faced reddened even more than its natural shade. "I gave a leg for my country. I'd as soon lose my life as make you sorry about anything, Miss."

"Thank you, Mr. Zimmerman." She let her smile linger. "Now I can sleep peacefully tonight." When he squirmed awkwardly, she added, "Oh, if anyone asks if I sent a telegram, or if you hear news of my fiancé, is there some way you could get word to me over at the hotel?"

"There's a colored man named Hector who helps around the depot. He could do that."

"Very well, only please don't tell him anything more than that you have a message for me. I'll come to you as soon as I receive word. And please give me a description of anyone who asks about me."

"You have my word, Miss Wilson."

On the way back to the hotel, Laurel reflected on Ridge's humiliating exit at the restaurant. She had so many unanswered questions. What promise had he made that had taken him to Chicago? What was he really like under that sensitive and explosive exterior?

She sternly checked her thoughts. She should let her anger toward him linger. Yet she wished that she could talk to him without either of their emotions blowing up so easily. But at the moment, she had more pressing concerns. What would Schramm and Harkins do about her now?

After the conductor's suspicions were aroused by the slip about Laurel's surname, he escorted Sarah back to her hotel, then hurried to the coach to check his office. He inserted his key in the door, but the lock didn't turn freely. He tried again, standing to one side so the faint light from the coal oil lamp mounted on the coach wall fell directly on the lock.

When the key again seemed to hang up, he stooped to search for the cause and saw fresh gouge marks in the wood. Swearing under his breath, he gently ran his fingers along the telltale marks.

Satisfied, he stood up. *It had to have been her. That's why she didn't go to dinner with us! Well, she didn't get in, but that won't stop her from trying again.*

Schramm headed for the express car to discuss the problem with George Aiken.

Ridge was tired of his fellow guard's complaining.

From the time Ridge had returned from abruptly leaving Laurel at dinner, Aiken had been complaining. This time, however, he avoided any personal remarks about Ridge. Instead, seated in his usual chair with the front legs tipped up, Aiken grumbled about the job.

"It wouldn't hurt the company a bit to unload this stuff someplace safe in the depot so we could get a good night's sleep in a real bed. But no, we have to stay here and sleep on the floor. It's as bad as during the war."

It was Ridge's turn to sleep, so he had stretched out on a straw pallet by the tarpaulin-covered express cargo. He was so preoccupied with thoughts of Laurel that he did not really hear Aiken's remarks.

I don't know why I let her bother me, Ridge told himself. *She is too independent and self-willed. Sure, she's pretty and she's got a smile that could melt an icehouse, but she's got a tongue that cuts like a whip. Besides, she's engaged. She's not worth my time to even think about.*

But he couldn't forget her.

He was aware that Aiken was still criticizing the railroad's policy when the conductor stuck his head in the narrow door at the end of the car.

Schramm glanced at Ridge, then turned to Aiken, "All quiet in here, men?"

"All quiet," Aiken answered.

"Good," the conductor nodded. "Have you both had supper?" When they nodded, he said to Ridge, "Can you hold things down here while I borrow Aiken for a while?"

"Sure can," Ridge assured him. He stood up and reached for the double-barreled shotgun. "I'm not sleepy anyway."

Aiken followed Schramm through the narrow rear door. "What's up?"

"Trouble," the conductor replied when they were beyond Ridge's hearing. "Her name's not Wilson, and she got me in such an awkward situation that I had to take her friend to dinner. While I was there, I'm pretty sure our Miss Wilson, or whoever she is, tried to break into my office."

After briefly filling in the details, Schramm concluded, "She's onto something, or she wouldn't be using a false name. There's no way any ordinary woman would take those kinds of risks, so she must be working for someone."

"You mean Pinkerton?"

"Who else? Almost everyone working on a railroad knows that the companies hire Pinkertons to check on employees suspected of stealing."

"I thought that Woods was the agent?"

"He was," Schramm agreed, "but Allan Pinkerton probably sent two of them, including our charming Miss Wilson. She lied about her name, and I'm sure she also lied when she said she didn't see you knife Woods."

"If she did, and testifies against me . . ."

"Relax! She's not going to! Still, it's a shame to eliminate anyone as pretty as her, but it's got to be done."

The express guard said doubtfully, "I don't know about that. Doing in that Pinkerton man isn't the same as doing it to her."

"You want to risk getting hung?"

"No, of course not! But there should be some other way to stop her. Maybe just scare her off?"

The conductor shook his head. "We can't risk it, not with what we've got coming up."

Aiken paused for several seconds, making Schramm demand, "Well, are you up to this job or not?"

"Me? Why me?"

"Because you like to hurt people, that's why."

"I never hurt a woman! Besides, why should I listen to you now? I told you before this trip that you were getting greedy by dipping too deep into the ticket money! Now this could cost us all the big plans for—"

Schramm broke in, "Nothing is going to stop us from pulling that off!"

"If she knows about the murder and your stealing, she probably also knows about our other plans. Maybe Pinkerton got word of it, so he sent two agents."

"There's no way he could have heard."

"I'm not so sure. Anyway, this is too important for us to handle alone. I think we should contact the leader for instructions."

"We can't right now. You know that. We'll just have to do what's best."

"I'm still against it."

"You're a fool, Aiken!"

The guard angrily sucked in his breath. "Don't you ever say that again!"

"All right! All right! But if I'm correct, we can get rid of all our problems at the same time, including her. Only this time, it will look like an accident."

Sleep eluded Laurel while she mentally examined her problems and tried to decide on the best solution.

Her brother, Dorian, had been killed in early April 1863, barely ninety days after Laurel turned seventeen. Deeply stirred, she wanted to do something to avenge his death. Hearing rumors that there were women spies, she had approached Pinkerton, but he wouldn't even talk to her about becoming an operative because of her age.

After she became eighteen in January of '64, she returned to Pinkerton and persisted until he gave her an opportunity to try one minor mission behind enemy lines. Her success led to other assignments.

Usually Laurel worked alone, but when she needed assistance in finding creative ways to hide sensitive Confederate military data she had gathered, she turned to Sarah.

In spite of Pinkerton's edict forbidding anyone to know that Laurel was a spy, she first swore Sarah to secrecy, then revealed her clandestine role. It wasn't in Sarah's nature to take risks, but Laurel convinced her that she would not be in peril, and that it was Sarah's patriotic duty to help the North win the war by aiding Laurel in her missions.

Once convinced, Sarah vicariously thrived on helping Laurel with disguises or creating places in her hair, bustles, and shoe soles to secretly smuggle military intelligence from behind Rebel lines.

On one such trip, Laurel had borrowed a minstrel wig from one of her friends who performed in the very popular blackface shows. From another friend in a hospital, she obtained silver nitrate. Mixed with water and applied to her face, hands, and arms, she had passed as a slave.

Laurel's trips into the Confederacy had shown her that white Southerners generally spoke as freely in front of their slaves as if they were furniture, so she gathered military details that she wrote in a milk mixture that acted as invisible ink. Still in her disguise, she escaped through Confederate pickets. This material ended up in Union officers' hands.

Usually, Laurel had posed as a Southern belle with whom unsuspecting young Confederate officers shared confidential information. To impress her, some had even shown her military defenses or plans for coming attacks. Her most successful mission had resulted in the ambush of a Confederate cavalry unit. After the war, this feat, along with her other spying successes, came to General Grant's attention. He had presented her with a commendation.

Rousing herself from such memories, Laurel told herself, *But that was relatively easy because nobody suspected me of being a courier. Now, the conductor and the brakeman know I'm not who I said I was. They must believe I saw that Pinkerton man knifed. They won't dare risk letting me testify against them. I can't leave with Sarah when she goes home tomorrow because this is where I should find Claude. I've got to find a way out of this–and fast!*

For a while, Laurel seriously considered disobeying Pinkerton and telling Sarah, if she could be persuaded to stay on for the remainder of the trip as Pinkerton required. If Laurel did tell Sarah, however, it was possible that her life might be in danger as much as Laurel's was.

Laurel was still awake when there was a gentle tapping on the hotel room door. She sat up in bed, instantly feeling the lack of sleep and the start of a headache. In the other bed, Sarah's damp cloth had fallen off her forehead onto the pillow, but she did not move.

Whoever was at the door began to be more insistent. The knocking caused Sarah to stir but not awaken.

"Yes?" Laurel called softly. "Who it is?"

"Hector. That man at the telegraph office done sent me to git Miss Wilson. You her, aine you?"

"Yes." Hope for news about Claude drove the sleep from her fogged brain. "Just a minute and I'll give you a little something for your trouble."

"That aine necessary, but thankee anyhow. You gonna go right over to see him?"

"Yes, thank you, Hector. I'll be there as soon as I can dress."

Jedediah Zimmerman reached for his crutches and struggled to his feet when Laurel opened the door to his telegraph office. "I didn't want to disturb you, Miss Wilson, but you said . . ."

She made an impatient gesture. "It's all right. Thank you for your thoughtfulness. What happened?"

"Just a few minutes ago, a man came in and asked if you had

sent a telegram."

"What did he look like?"

"Short kind of a fellow, big chest, away bigger than most men his size."

Jacob Lucas! "What did you tell him?"

"Nothing, 'cept that such information was confidential. Then he offered to pay me, but I told him to get out. He did."

A scowl crept over Laurel's brow. *I guess my little talk with him didn't do any good.* "Thank you." She reached for the drawstring on her reticule.

"There's more." Zimmerman shifted his weight on the crutches and lowered his eyes.

"I can guess," she said. "The conductor also asked if I had sent a telegram."

Zimmerman shook his head. "No, just the one asked, but there's something else. I'm not sure I should even mention it. . . ." He didn't finish the sentence.

"Why not?"

"Well, something else came over the wire awhile ago about a man who sounded a little like the one you're looking for."

"Claude Duncan?" she asked in sudden hope. "There was something about him?"

"There was no name, and it's probably not the same man, but the description sort of matches."

"What happened?"

The telegrapher raised his eyes to meet hers. She saw a pleading look in them. "Miss Wilson, I pray to God I'm wrong. Last night, at a town south of here, there was another of those robberies and killings that have been going on for some time. Three men, a woman, and a little boy—"

"Claude! He was killed?"

"No, not him."

"Oh, thank goodness."

Zimmerman dropped his eyes again. "What it said on the wire was that a man answering that description, well, uh . . . he led the raid."

She exclaimed, "It wasn't Claude!"

"That's what I figured, Miss Wilson, but the description was so close that I thought you should know."

Laurel sank into the telegrapher's chair and gripped the edge of the little desk to control a trembling she felt in her fingers. "How . . . how did it happen?"

"I told you all that's come over the wire so far, except that this good-looking man got away on horseback. Him and some others. Took a sack of gold coins and some other banknotes and negotiable bonds."

Laurel regained her feet. "That wasn't Claude. But thank you for letting me know."

She produced a greenback, which the telegrapher refused. She thanked him again and headed for the door as the telegraph key began clicking. Zimmerman turned and tapped an acknowledgment. She heard the instrument begin sending a message as she walked outside.

Claude was always wild, just like Ambrose. But he would never do anything like that. She shuddered. *A woman and a little boy. No, that couldn't have been Claude!*

Laurel stood uncertainly in the empty waiting room, her thoughts tumbling over each other. *It can't be Claude, but the only way I can prove it is to find him.*

"Oh, Miss Wilson!"

She turned around as the telegrapher's door opened and Zimmerman propped it there with a crutch. "Another message just came in."

"Oh?" She tensed, fearful that Pinkerton was ordering her off the case.

"That replacement locomotive will be delayed until tomorrow afternoon, so you'll have more time to look for your beau."

Chapter 10

As the autumn's evening cold seeped through the express car, Ridge leaned his shotgun against the tarp-covered strongboxes. He opened the door on the heating stove and added more wood. After walking out on Laurel, he had vainly tried to focus on what he should do about his family plantation. Instead, Laurel's face and words crowded out everything else.

Aiken watched him in thoughtful silence before pulling a plug of chewing tobacco from his pocket. "Chaw?" he asked Ridge.

He shook his head but didn't reply. He could not understand why Laurel should disturb him, yet she had somehow gotten inside his mind and stirred him up.

The other express messenger bit off a piece of tobacco. "What's on your mind?"

Ridge didn't feel like talking. He picked up his weapon without answering.

Aiken complained, "You going to talk or not?"

"I have nothing to say."

"Well, something sure as blazes is gnawing on you, and that makes me nervous."

"No reason to be. This doesn't concern you."

"That's what a sojer told me once when we was going on picket duty, then he up and shot at me in the night. Claimed he thought I was a Reb."

Ridge's annoyance with Laurel was easily directed against Aiken. "I have personal things to think about."

"Me, too, but that don't stop me from being sociable."

Ridge snapped, "Right now, I have some things to sort out in my mind. So I'd prefer to be left alone."

"When a man talks like that, it usually means he's got woman trouble."

Ridge chose not to answer. He glanced absently at the two cargo doors on each side of the car's length. These sliding doors were bolted from the inside. Ridge's eyes shifted to the narrow open door at the front of the express car. That door was closed, but he knew that just beyond it, smoke and sparks from the loco-motive's diamond stack flowed back over the tender to which the express coach was connected.

Ridge turned around as the conductor stuck his head through the narrow open door at the rear of the car.

"Word just came over the wire," he said. "The other engine won't be here until sometime tomorrow afternoon. Until then, the railroad wants the contents of this car transferred to where they think it'll be safer."

Aiken spat against the hot stove. "Suits me. Where are we going to move this stuff?"

"The local bank is going to open up for us. George, you come with me to stand guard outside while the station agent rounds up some hands to help." Schramm turned to Ridge. "You stay here and watch from inside."

On the swaying open platform outside the express car's narrow back door, the conductor and Aiken could not be overheard. Schramm said, "I just came from the telegraph office. That woman sent a message last night, but the telegrapher wouldn't tell me what it said or who she sent it to."

Aiken swore softly. "You think she sent word about what she saw me do to that Pinkerton?"

"That's my guess. But the telegrapher did say that I'm not the only one who was asking."

Aiken guessed, "That short little man again?"

"Exactly. I can't figure out why he's so interested."

"You think he knows something?"

"How could he?" Schramm slowly shook his head. "But we know what that woman's up to. So meet me again after the transfer and we'll work out something to eliminate her as a problem."

Laurel returned to her bed, relieved that Sarah was asleep. Laurel didn't try to sleep, but kept thinking about Schramm and Harkins. She had heard enough from the conductor to know he was involved in the Pinkerton operative's murder, although the brakeman had implicated himself as the actual killer.

If there was some way I could get proof beyond what I overheard them say. . . .

A knock at the door made her jump nervously. She slid down from the high bed and padded barefooted to the door. "Who is it?" she asked softly.

"Hector."

Feeling suspicious, Laurel opened the door a crack and confirmed that the black man was alone. He whispered that the telegrapher wanted to see her a second time.

Laurel had guessed the reason for the second message even before she dressed and again entered Zimmerman's cramped office.

He apologized, "I hated bothering you again, Miss Wilson, but there was another inquiry."

"A tall man?"

"Yes. The conductor. How did you know?"

She ignored the question to ask, "What did he say?"

"Same as the other man: who did you send a message to, and could he see a copy. When I said no, he said it was railroad business, but I didn't believe him."

"Thank you." Laurel reached for the drawstring on her reticule, but he stopped her.

"I can't take money for helping a lady, but if you're in some kind of trouble, maybe I could help?"

"You're very kind, but I'll be fine."

She turned to leave, but stopped at the sight of four men pushing iron-wheeled luggage carts toward the train.

Zimmerman explained, "The railroad must be moving the treasure chests from the express car to the bank. Happened once before when a train broke down."

Laurel thought of Ridge guarding the strongboxes. She asked, "Are they expecting trouble?"

"I don't know. There's been nothing on the wire about it, but who knows? There have been so many robberies lately that the company may be nervous."

"I thought that once this terrible war was over, we would have no more of that kind of thing."

"For some, the war's not over."

"I suppose," Laurel mused, wondering if that were true of Ridge. *Maybe that's why he is so short-tempered.*

"Just last week," Zimmerman continued, "a gang hit the county treasurer's office, killed two people. The bandits filled saddle bags with nearly fifteen thousand dollars in gold coins, but left silver and securities."

He hesitated before continuing, "If you don't mind a suggestion, Miss Wilson, you should stay close to your hotel room, and I'll pray I don't have to send Hector after you again."

She thanked him and returned to her room. Sarah, not used to alcohol, still slept. Laurel walked to the window and realized that it faced the bank. She crossed the room, blew out the lamp, and returned in darkness to stand by the window.

Knowing she could not be seen, she watched by the unsteady flare of the burning tar barrels that lined the street, while the strongboxes were transferred from the express car to the bank. George Aiken and his shotgun accompanied each load, but there was no sign of Ridge.

When she finally saw him emerge from the car and follow the cart, she realized that she had become tense. With a relieved sigh, she decided that the last load had been moved. Still, she remained at the window while the four workmen dispersed. Ridge, Aiken, and the conductor remained talking for a minute or so. When the latter two walked off together, Ridge alone stayed where he was.

Sensing that he was looking up toward her, she quickly drew back from the window. At once, she chided herself. *He can't see me. He doesn't even know which room we're in. Besides, what dif-*

ference does it make?

She peeked again, but Ridge was gone. Instead, several men crossed from the adjacent railroad line, heading toward the restaurant. A train must have just pulled in over there, she realized. She started to turn away from the window, then stopped.

She recognized Ridge's slight limping walk as he also headed toward the restaurant. *Probably going for some coffee.* It sounded like a good idea.

Sarah's voice broke into Laurel's meditations. "Why are you standing there in the dark?"

"I couldn't sleep." She headed for her bed. "But you've been out like a light."

"I've been awake a few minutes. What's going on outside that you watched so intently?"

"I think they moved those chests from the express car to the local bank."

"Why would they do that?" Sarah wondered.

"It's not our concern, so go back to sleep."

"I'm not sleepy anymore. You're obviously not, either. So light the lamp again and let's talk."

"I can't. I've got to work some things out."

"Did something happen while I was asleep?"

"Nothing I can't handle."

Sarah exclaimed, "You say that one more time and I'm going back to Chicago on the next northbound train!"

"I thought you had already decided to do that."

"I thought I had, too, but I don't want to leave you alone when your life is in danger."

"I'm used to it."

"This is different." Sarah threw back the covers and lit the lamp. "I've seen you before and after going on one of your secret trips during the war. It was like a game to you. You were excited and bubbling with patriotism. But somehow, you're not enjoying this." She pulled a blanket off the bed, covered her shoulders and stood up. "It's getting cold in here."

She put some small pieces of wood in the stove to build up the fire. Then she walked to the window, hid most of her body from any outside view, and peered out. "You were watching him, weren't you?"

Laurel sat with her feet dangling over the edge of the high bed. "Watching who?"

"Don't try to fool me." Sarah left the window and crossed to stand in front of Laurel. "Why are you interested in Ridge when you're betrothed to Claude?"

"I'm not interested in Ridge."

"Aren't you?" Sarah studied Laurel's face. "He's in the restaurant, isn't he?" When there was no reply, Sarah nodded. "I think I'll get dressed and go have some coffee."

"You shouldn't be out there alone! Especially after having had something to drink awhile ago."

"Is that what's bothering you? Would you like to come along with me?"

It was a temptation, but the memory of Ridge walking out on her again roused Laurel's embarrassment. "I'll stay here."

She sat in thoughtful silence until Sarah had gone out the door. Then slowly, Laurel's head dropped forward, loose hair spilling down to cover her face.

Ridge sat alone in a far corner of the restaurant, well away from the noisy Mississippi and Gulf railroaders who had just arrived on the other set of tracks. With great effort, Ridge put aside his personal emotions to sip coffee and think practically.

After leaving Virginia to deliver the dead Yankee soldier's letter, nothing had gone the way he expected.

He had been frustrated by failing to locate Charley Bartlett to whom the letter was addressed. Ridge had taken this short-term railroad messenger job on the assumption that it would give him time to reach a conclusion about the family plantation.

Instead, he had met a sharp-tongued young Yankee woman who kept intruding on his mental processes. No matter how he tried, he could not get her out of his mind. But he didn't want to even think about another woman—not now, not after Varina.

Before the war, his parents and friends all assumed that he and Varina would marry. They had grown up on adjacent plantations and began courting just before the Yankees invaded Virginia. Before the young men went off to war, there had been lots of hasty weddings, but he and Varina had waited.

Through four long bloody years, he had planned on what they would do with the Granger plantation. She had been his reason for plotting a future. But when he returned home after General Lee surrendered to General Grant at Appomattox, everything had changed.

Varina had married another. His mother, father, and brother were dead. Nothing remained of their plantation except the land, and even that had been worked too long and hard without giving it proper expert care. General Lee and President Lincoln had talked of reconciliation and binding up the nation's wounds. But with Lincoln dead, the Black Republicans in Congress had set out to punish the Confederacy with the noble-sounding word, Reconstruction. To Ridge, that was another name for reaping and pillaging a broken and destitute people. Southern lands were being seized under the legal power of the victorious Union. Unless Ridge fought wisely and hard, he would never win back his land, poor as it was. But what reason did he have for even returning to Virginia, let alone fighting?

Four years of war had given Ridge enough fighting to last a lifetime. Yet that was the only way he could regain control of land that had been in his family for three generations. That was the least appealing choice, but emotionally, it tugged at him because it was the only home he had ever known. He had risked his life for what it represented when he rode off to war. What remained when he returned were only painful memories and indescribable loneliness.

Unable to make up his mind regarding this new struggle, he had considered two alternatives. The one he had most often considered around the mess camp fires had been to have a part in the planned transcontinental railroad. It was an incredible undertaking: running rails from Omaha to the Pacific. Instead of tearing up tracks, there was a romantic appeal to building them toward the sunset.

The second alternative had been suggested by a Texas cavalryman who had ridden with Ridge in the war. In one of the rare letters from his Texas home, he learned of postwar plans to round up a herd of wild longhorns and drive them north. People in the East were tired of pork. They wanted beef, so all the drovers had to do was have herds on hand when rails were laid to Kansas, then the cattle would be shipped east from there.

It wasn't exactly a new concept, but driving millions of head of cattle was such a grand dream that his fellow cavalryman had invited Ridge to join him. It was a temptation, but by then, neither man had a horse, so Ridge declined. The other man had stolen a Yankee mount to ride back to Texas and become part of this new beginning.

Ridge took another sip of coffee and wondered if he should have gone with his friend. It would be good to have no responsibilities for a while except to keep some cattle moving.

He was so deep in thought that he didn't notice Sarah until she spoke.

"Mr. Granger! I didn't expect to see you here at this time of night."

He glanced up and smiled. "I could say the same thing about you, Miss Perkins."

"Sarah," she said. "My friends call me Sarah."

"I'm Ridge." He didn't want company, but there was no choice. "Won't you sit down?"

"I believe I will, thank you." She eased down opposite him. "I couldn't sleep, so I thought I would get a cup of coffee."

Ridge suppressed annoyance at the interruption and signaled for the older woman who had served him.

After Sarah's cup was filled, she commented, "I understand that the contents of your express car were moved to the local bank."

Ridge raised an eyebrow. "Who told you that?"

Not wanting to inject Laurel's name into the conversation, Sarah evaded the question. She asked, "Why was that done?"

"Haven't you heard? The replacement locomotive won't be here until sometime tomorrow afternoon."

"Really?" Sarah made an impatient gesture. "We'll all be

stuck out here with nothing to do."

"I'm sure you'll find something."

Sarah stirred her coffee. "Tomorrow is the Lord's Day. I suppose there is a church here. I could attend services."

"I'm sure you and Miss Wilson will be able to find a house of worship to meet your needs."

Sarah ignored the reference to Laurel. "I attend regularly when I'm home." She waited for Ridge to volunteer something about his religious background, but he didn't. She said, "I've heard that toward the end of the war a revival swept through General Lee's troops."

"That's true."

Sensing an opening, Sarah asked, "Did you see any of that?"

"Some."

"You know General Lee?"

"I've seen him, but I don't really know him. I was only a captain."

It was difficult to get more than a brief, polite response, but Sarah was determined. "Tell me about the revival, what you saw of it."

"There's not much to tell. Times were desperate. Some infantrymen had no shoes, no overcoat, not even a blanket. Foraging for food was difficult because both armies had swept back and forth across Virginia so many times that nothing edible was left."

"How awful."

"It was beyond description. I heard that one of your Union generals said things were so bad that if a crow flew over, it had to carry its own food."

"So you're saying that the Confederate soldiers had nothing

left except their faith, and they turned to that in their final desperate days?"

"No, I'm not saying that. I'm just telling what it was like."

"I take it that you're not religious?"

"My parents reared me as a Christian, but I saw so many terrible things during the war that I began to doubt. After all, both sides had the same God, the same language, and sometimes the same blood, as when father fought against sons, or sons battled each other.

"We had everything in common, it seems, until the North decided that we in the South could not live the way we wanted, but insisted we live the way they wanted. When we objected, Lincoln held the Union together with the point of a bayonet."

He did not raise his voice, but the words spewed out in a hard, cold torrent of pain. "They invaded our land, blockaded us to the point of starvation, and left us destitute. Now the Black Republicans are talking Reconstruction, but they really mean to punish the South and make things worse, if possible."

Sarah considered how to tactfully say what she felt. "I've never talked to anyone who thinks like you."

"Sorry if I distress you, but that's how I feel."

"And you blame God for all that's happened?"

"I don't think 'blame' is the right word. But I know that both sides prayed to the same God, asking for victory, believing each was right, and the other wrong. My parents and my brother prayed, as did my . . . uh . . . a young woman I knew. I didn't, not after awhile, anyway."

Sarah asked, "What happened to her . . . uh . . . them?"

He took a deep breath before answering quietly. "She's married. The others are all dead, except me."

"I'm sorry, really sorry, but I wish you wouldn't lay that all on the Lord."

"As I said before, I don't blame Him. I just lost something in that realm, along with everything else."

"Your home, too?"

"Burned to the ground. Crops ruined." Ridge's words were short, clipped, hard. "Now the carpetbaggers and scalawags are picking over what little is left."

He took another long, deep breath and let it out with a shudder that shook his whole body. "You must pardon me, Sarah. I had no intention of burdening you with my problems."

"It's no burden. Besides, I asked."

He stirred restlessly, glancing around as though about to make an excuse for leaving.

Sarah didn't want that. Impulsively, she blurted, "Perhaps if you went to church tomorrow? . . ."

"Thanks, no," he interrupted, starting to stand. "You and your friend should go and refresh your souls."

"Laurel doesn't go to church anymore."

Ridge stopped halfway to his feet. "She doesn't?"

"She's a little bit like you. Her family was always a strong, churchgoing one. So was she until she began drifting away about the time the war started. I always blamed Claude and his friend—"

"Claude?" Ridge interrupted, sitting down again. "Her missing fiancé?"

"Yes. He and Ambrose Nevers. Laurel and I grew up with them, but they were wild, not at all like either Laurel or me. Her father is very strong-willed and rules with an iron hand. When she got into her early teens, she started to rebel against him. I think knowing Claude and Ambrose made it worse. Anyway, when her brother was killed . . ."

Sarah left the sentence hanging in midair, regretting that she had said so much about Laurel. This time she had no excuse for loose talk.

Slowly, Ridge regained his feet. "I have very much enjoyed your company, Sarah, but you must excuse me."

She had also enjoyed getting to know more about him and didn't want him to leave. She desperately searched for a way to delay him. The solution occurred so rapidly that she blurted it out without thinking. "She thinks we're in danger!"

Ridge bent down over her. "What kind of danger?"

Sarah saw no alternative but to say more than she knew was prudent. "It's because of that murdered man."

"What about him?"

"I . . . ," checking herself, Sarah exclaimed, "I really can't say any more. I've already said too much."

"You can't stop now." He sat down quickly and took her hands in his. "You're both in danger because you know something about that murder?"

She could barely breathe, excited by the firm grip on her hands. "Yes. The killer is on the train, and–"

"Do you know that for sure?" he interrupted. "I thought the sheriff just said there was a possibility he might be on the train."

"I . . . I can't tell you, but it's true. I'm concerned, but Laurel says she can take care of things herself."

Ridge's jaw muscles twitched. He had no doubt that's what Laurel had said. "I'll ask her about this."

"Oh, no, please! If she finds out that I betrayed her confidence . . ."

For a long moment, he didn't say anything. Then, as though aware for the first time that he had taken her hands, he let go and quickly stood again. Reaching into his pocket, he dropped a greenback on the table. "Very well. I won't say anything to her."

Also rising to her feet, Sarah asked, "What are you thinking?"

"I'm thinking that two young women should not have to be worrying about their lives. Come on, I'll walk you back to your hotel."

"Thank you." She fell into step beside him, wondering if she had done the wrong thing in trusting him while betraying Laurel's confidence.

Chapter 11

Laurel stood by the window in the darkened hotel room until Ridge and Sarah left the restaurant together. Satisfied that they were heading for the lobby, Laurel hurriedly undressed and climbed into bed.

It seemed to her that a lot of time passed before she heard Sarah's key in the lock. When the door opened, a quick glance showed Laurel that Sarah was alone.

She tiptoed across the room in the darkness, but stopped abruptly at Laurel's voice.

"You don't need to be so quiet. I'm not asleep."

Sarah eased around the end of her bed, feeling her way in the darkness. "Anything happen while I was gone?"

"No. It was all very quiet." Laurel sat up. "You may as well light the lamp while you get ready for bed."

When the glass chimney was settled over the new flame, Sarah sat on the bed to silently remove her shoes. Laurel asked, "Did you enjoy the coffee?"

Sarah detected an edge to the query. "Yes, I did."

"What did you two talk about?"

Sarah replied evasively. "Oh, the usual things."

"Such as?"

Sarah began slowly undressing and hanging her clothing in the armoire before replying. "Well, his parents and brother are dead, and his family home in Virginia burned down. He apparently had a lady friend who married somebody else while he was off fighting the war."

Laurel frowned. *Why didn't he tell me such things? At least, he didn't have to share such personal matters with Sarah. I guess that's because he and I are always fighting, drawing more sparks than conversation when we're together. But then, why should I care?*

Aloud, she asked, "Is that all, or didn't the coffee loosen your tongue as much as the conductor's wine did?"

Sarah gritted her teeth but resisted striking back at Laurel's criticism. "Well, he grew up as a Christian, only he doesn't go to church anymore. So many terrible things happened that he said he lost his faith during the war." She added hastily, "But he doesn't blame God."

Laurel asked suspiciously, "Did you talk about me?"

"I tried not to do that."

"That doesn't answer my question."

"All right, if you must know," Sarah replied sharply, "I told him you used to be a believer, but you had changed, and I blame Claude and Ambrose."

"You had no right to say that!" Laurel leaped from her bed and hurried across to stand in front of Sarah.

"Maybe not, but it just seemed like the right thing to do. He was being so honest and open with me—"

"Then you could have been the same about yourself, but left me out of it!"

Sarah squirmed uncomfortably under the verbal slashing. "I

tried, but he thinks so differently from me. He says Lincoln held the South in the Union with a bayonet, and now the Black Republicans are hiding under the name of Reconstruction to further pillage the South."

Laurel resented Sarah having reached a personal part of Ridge that she had been unable to even approach. "Is there anything you two didn't talk about?"

Sarah dropped her eyes, unwilling to admit that she had told Ridge that Laurel's and her life could be at risk. "Isn't that enough?" she parried.

Laurel hesitated, eager to know if there was anything more, but aggravated over what had already been disclosed. She said, "Let's get some sleep."

Sarah turned her back on Laurel and heaved a controlled sigh of relief. She was secretly pleased that she had told Ridge about her fear of the murderer. Sarah found it comforting to have Ridge aware of her concerns. Somehow, she didn't feel as alone as when only Laurel knew that a killer was on the train they would have to ride again tomorrow. She blew out the lamp, said a silent prayer of gratitude, and slipped off to restful sleep.

Ridge had no money for a hotel room, so after he said good-night to Sarah in the lobby, he returned to the express car. He lit the wall lamp, relieved that Aiken was not there. Ridge built up the fire in the heating stove before stretching out on the pallet. But he did not sleep.

I believe Sarah was telling the truth, he thought, staring at the car's ceiling nearly seven feet above. *She was obviously frightened that she—and especially Laurel—are in danger from the killer won our train. But who is he? Why did he kill that man?*

There was no answer to the last two questions, but Ridge felt confident about the reason Sarah feared for her life. *Laurel claims she didn't see the killer, but he probably doesn't believe that. He thinks he'll be found out if she talks. Whoever he is, he probably suspects Laurel told Sarah, so now they're both in jeopardy.*

Ridge felt that he had to do something, yet he was very limited in what that could be. When the new engine arrived and the trip continued, he would be stuck in the express car and couldn't help the women in the coach if the murderer acted while the train was moving.

Ridge was disturbed by that because he didn't know when or where the killer might try to strike. But if the killer felt that Laurel could cause his arrest, he could surely try to murder her and perhaps Sarah as well. However, Ridge was reasonably sure that Laurel was too independent to tell him anything, or even to ask for help.

I must have more information, he decided. *Sarah is the only one who might provide that. But how can I talk to her alone again before that engine gets here?*

After mulling it around, he decided there was one possible way. It wasn't his preference, but it was the only way he could speak privately to Sarah.

He arose and dressed again. He started to reach for the sawed-off shotgun, then changed his mind. From the soft knapsack containing all his personal belongings, he removed a Richmond arsenal belt and holster. It held a Confederate-made Leech & Rigdon .36-caliber six-shot percussion pistol. He checked the cylinder, stuck the dragoon-type barrel into the holster, strapped on the belt, and headed for the hotel.

Laurel had nearly dozed off when she was aroused by a light tapping at the door. She sat up. "Who's there?"

The answer was muted. "Ridge."

"Who?" she demanded, unwilling to believe what she had heard.

"Ridge. Ridge Granger. From the train."

Recognizing the voice, she frowned, wondering why he was calling at such a late hour. "Just a minute, please."

She flipped back the covers and extended her short legs, which didn't reach the floor. She pulled a blanket from the bed, wrapped it around her, and padded barefooted across the cold floor.

When she turned the key and opened the door a crack, Ridge quickly spoke the words he had mentally rehearsed. "I'm sorry to bother you, but I wanted to ask you ladies a question, and I was afraid that if I waited until morning, I might miss you."

Laurel sensed that wasn't his reason at all. "Yes?"

"Are Sarah and you comfortable?"

"She's fine, thank you!" Laurel hadn't meant to be so short, but hearing him mention Sarah first gave her the impression that was why he had called. He was interested in her. Laurel started to close the door, but he spoke again.

"Is she asleep?"

"Of course! Do you realize what time it is?"

Sarah said sleepily from behind her, "No, I just woke up. What's going on?"

"It's your friend, Mr. Granger," Laurel replied coldly. "He wants to know if you're all right."

"Oh, Ridge!" Sarah exclaimed from her bed. "How thoughtful of you to check on us."

He shifted his position slightly as if to peer into the darkened room beyond Laurel. "Miss Perkins, I came to say I'd changed my mind about tomorrow. That is, if it's all right with you."

"Changed your mind?" Sarah repeated.

"About going to church." He hesitated, taking a quick, short breath. He knew what he must say, yet he hoped that Laurel would decline. "If you ladies don't mind, I would be glad to escort you both—"

Laurel exploded, "You came here to say that?"

"I know it's late," he began, "but—"

"Thank you, Ridge!" Sarah called happily. "We would be glad to—"

"Speak for yourself, Sarah!" Laurel exclaimed.

"Fine!" Sarah said. "I'd be delighted."

Laurel said coolly, "Good night, Mr. Granger!" She closed the door hard, aware that her blood suddenly surged through her body so fast she felt flushed.

Sarah complained, "Why did you do that? He was being thoughtful—"

"He was being nosy, you mean!" Laurel's voice slapped through the darkened room. She hurried to the bed, threw the blanket off her shoulder, and reached for the lamp. "He didn't come here for that reason at all!"

"No? What other reason would he have?"

Laurel lit the lamp and resettled the fragile glass chimney before answering. She said accusingly, "Because you told him about the men I heard talking about killing that Pinkerton agent. But you left that out awhile ago when I asked what you two had talked about. Right?"

"So what if I did?" Sarah demanded defensively. "You're not afraid, but I am. Two women alone with a couple of men on board who might kill us–well, I think we need help, and I trust Ridge."

Laurel lost her struggle for control. "You don't know him! You never saw him before we got on that train! For all you know, he could be in on that murder!"

"You don't believe that any more than I do! Now, I'm sorry if I did something you don't approve of, but I think I did the right thing. I'm going to church with him tomorrow, too! It wouldn't hurt you to come along instead of staying by yourself where those men could attack you."

"You go." Laurel's voice dropped to a cool, assured level. "I've got things to do."

Down the quiet hallway from the women's hotel room, around the corner where Laurel had earlier accosted Jacob Lucas, Ridge pulled an upholstered chair from the wall. He placed it where he could see anyone coming or going in either hall. He settled into the chair, shifted the holstered pistol to a more comfortable position, then stretched out his long legs. He felt a little foolish, but he wasn't going to take any chances. He waited.

He was gone early the next morning when Sarah arose and

Laurel was still sleeping. Sarah hurried to her trunk in the baggage car and returned with her best dress. She was fully clothed and fussing with her hair when Laurel awakened.

Promptly as the community church bells chimed their Sabbath invitation, Ridge arrived. His eyes widened in appreciation at Sarah's appearance. She greeted him warmly, her eyes admiringly sweeping his trim figure. Laurel barely nodded to him, then turned away.

However, she noticed that he looked sleepy and that he had changed out of his dark blue railroad uniform. Except for the overcoat, he again wore the same faded uniform he had had on when she first saw him in Chicago.

The regulation Confederate cavalry jacket and dark trousers with the narrow yellow piping along the seam were aged, yet he wore them so proudly and defiantly that he presented a handsome figure.

After he and Sarah left, Laurel stood at the hotel room window and looked across the street. She counted three churches within walking distance. She dropped her gaze to the street where Ridge took Sarah's arm. Sarah smiled up at him while they waited for a carriage to pass. Sarah didn't have a pretty face, but as she started across the street with Ridge, Laurel noticed that Sarah looked very attractive. Laurel silently admitted that Sarah looked good with Ridge. In fact, Laurel thought they made a striking couple. That caused Laurel to have mixed emotions.

She wondered if Sarah would feel embarrassed by Ridge's apparel. *No, I don't think so,* Laurel admitted. *Sarah looks so happy, even proud. A Yankee woman captures a Rebel.* An unbidden thought flickered through Laurel's mind: *I wouldn't be humiliated to be seen with him.* Instantly, she commanded herself,

Stop that! I'm not going anywhere with him, especially to church.

Abruptly, she turned away from the window and forced herself to concentrate on her two original tasks. During the night, she had decided that these must be completed before the new engine arrived and their journey continued south.

Ridge was conscious that Sarah still had her arm linked with his even as they sauntered along the boardwalk where there was no danger from passing horses or carriages.

He asked, "Do you have a preference as to which church you'd like to attend?"

"Well, I was reared Methodist. How about you?"

"Episcopalian." He grinned at her. "But today I think I'll attend the Methodist church, if there is one in this town."

"There is. I found that out when I stopped at the desk early this morning. I understand it's right down the street." She pointed. "Probably that white building with the spire and cross on top."

They walked slowly toward their destination while carriages and teams moved by in both directions and a locomotive shunted cars onto a siding on the M and G Railroad. From one of the churches, a bell pealed belatedly.

"Listen to that," Sarah urged, stopping. "I love that sound. It's like an angelic voice of invitation to come to worship."

Ridge didn't answer until the final chimes faded into the distance. He resumed walking with her arm in his before he admitted, "It takes me back."

"Good memories?"

"Very good ones. My parents, brother, and I always rode together in the carriage behind two matched horses. At church, we sat together while my brother and I watched the sun shining through the stained glass windows with all their Bible scenes. It was very peaceful, and God was so real and close. . . ."

He left the sentence incomplete, adding quietly, "That was a long time ago."

"Have you been there since the war?"

His jaw muscles twitched briefly. "The Yankees burned the church, along with everything else from my childhood. Only ashes remain." He sighed before adding in a hoarse whisper, "Ashes."

Sarah let a thoughtful silence settle over them before observing, "People rebuild from ashes."

"Some people do. Some don't."

She looked up at him to say quietly, "I think you're the kind of man who will rebuild."

He shook his head. "I'm not so sure."

They walked on while Sarah reflected on that. Finally she said calmly, "I am. You'll rebuild."

A pained smile tugged at his lips. "Thank you, but I'm still debating."

"About what?"

"I have some other alternatives," he confessed quietly. He hesitated, then spoke with firmness. "But that's enough about me. I've been thinking about what you said last night, about being in danger. I want to help, but I need more information, the details."

"I've already said too much."

"I disagree. I can't help unless you tell me everything you know."

"I'm sorry, Ridge, I really am, but I can't say more."

"Can't? Or won't?"

"It doesn't matter. Besides, this isn't your concern."

"Oh, but it is! Now, start from the beginning. . . ."

"No!" Stopping abruptly, Sarah shook her head. "I have already made Laurel upset by telling the conductor some things that I shouldn't have, and then I told you."

"Schramm? What's he got to do with this?"

"I don't know. Maybe nothing, but Laurel got upset with me for . . . for something I let slip to him."

"About her?"

Sarah nodded.

Ridge persisted. "Something serious?"

"I didn't think so, but she sure did. Then I made things worse by talking to you. I can't say any more."

They stopped across the street from the church.

Ridge asked, "Are you willing to risk your life–and hers–rather than let me try to help?"

"I want to trust you, but Laurel reminded me that I don't know you, not really. Just a few months ago you Southerners were killing my people from the North, just as we were doing to your people. The wounds are too fresh, too deep, too painful to really trust just yet."

"I see." He took her hand firmly in his and stepped into the street as a buggy passed. "Let's hope that we can both find something comforting about the service."

Laurel dressed and exited the hotel lobby, then stood in front as though trying to decide which way to go. She was really searching for Jacob Lucas, Hannibal Schramm, or Frederick Harkins, but none of them was in sight.

Laurel wanted very much to again try breaking into the conductor's office, but that was risky in daylight. Still, she was willing to chance it if she knew for sure that the trio was someplace where they would not be likely to surprise her. She casually checked out the restaurant, but they weren't there.

Laurel's second task was to try learning more about Claude's possible whereabouts. That search had to begin at the telegraph office.

She told herself that there was no way Claude Duncan could have led the raid where even a little boy had been killed. Yet the description on the wire last night matched Claude's, and Ambrose Nevers had told her in Chicago that he had seen Claude in this area. Laurel had to prove that it was a coincidence and that the outlaw leader was not her fiancé.

The telegrapher had just crossed the Mississippi and Gulf Railroad tracks on his crutches, his left pants leg pinned up above the stump, when Laurel spotted him. Her call stopped him. He waited, leaning on his crutches until she caught up with him.

"Mr. Zimmerman," she began, "I want to thank you again for all your kindnesses to me last night."

"No thanks is needed, and please call me Jedediah."

She gave him a friendly smile. "Very well, Jedediah. Did you have a quiet night after the last time I saw you?"

He smiled. "Yes, which was probably good news for you, but frankly, it was a long night for me. I mean, I sort of wished you could have come back over." A faint flush tinged his cheeks. "Please don't be offended."

"On the contrary, Jedediah. I am flattered." She was fairly certain that he had probably been rather glib around young women before losing his leg. Now she sensed that he was embarrassed. She added, "Very flattered."

He dropped his eyes and the flush deepened.

Laurel spoke quickly to ease his embarrassment. "I would appreciate it if you told me again about the description of the man who led the raid that killed those people, including the child."

"A little more came in over the wire later." He shifted his weight on the crutches. "Let's see what I can remember that you don't already know."

"I'd appreciate that, but let's not stand out here."

He nodded, swung around on his crutches, and led the way toward an unoccupied bench in the shade of the nearby Mississippi and Gulf Railroad depot.

"This is the same band of outlaws that's been terrorizing the country for the last two months or so. There's talk of a vigilante movement to stop them because the law–or what little there is of it–can't do it."

"Do they have a name?"

"Not that I know of. But whoever they are, they're just like Quantrill's Confederate guerrillas were in the war. They killed about 150 civilians."

"Is this new gang made up of Confederates?"

"Nobody knows, except at least a couple of them seem to have no Southern accent. Some members may be Yankees who've gone bad. Anyway, they're all using Quantrill's tactics." As they reached the bench, the telegrapher stopped and waited until Laurel sat down before joining her, his crutches placed on the wooden platform beside him.

"They've killed more than a dozen people," he added, "including a child. Just like Quantrill did."

With a disapproving shake of his head, Zimmerman concluded, "Each time this gang gets more daring, hitting bigger places and taking more loot."

"Their leader," Laurel began, reluctant to ask what she knew she must, "has anyone ever heard one of the gang call him by name?"

"If they did, it's not been on the wire."

"But you're sure of the description you gave me last night?"

"Yes. He's tall, nice looking, with light blond hair but kind of reddish eyebrows and matching beard."

Laurel licked her lips which seemed suddenly dry. "You said his eyes were gray?"

"Yes, cold and gray. That's exactly how one of the wounded people described him after this last raid."

Laurel still didn't believe it was Claude, but there might be a way to further clarify that. She asked, "Were there descriptions of other gang members on the wire?"

"Just one. A man about average height who is sometimes with the gang, but not always. He was on this last one. He was clean-shaven except for a mustache. His slouch hat fell off during the raid, showing he had very black wavy hair."

Abruptly, Laurel stood, deeply disturbed at the strong similarities to both her fiancé and his wild friend, Ambrose Nevers. "Thank you, Jedediah," Laurel said. "You've been a big help."

She walked rapidly, trying to burn off some of the fearful emotion that clutched at her heart. *It can't be Claude!* she told herself with as much conviction as she could muster. *Can't be! But it sounds like him—and even Ambrose.*

She shook her head vigorously at something Sarah had once said: "Why do you even speak to such a man as Ambrose Nevers? Everyone knows he's the most notorious liar in Chicago."

A fragment of thought crossed Laurel's mind: Could he have lied to her about being in that Georgia prisoner-of-war camp with Claude?

"Miss Wilson! Oh, Miss Wilson!"

It took a moment for the voice to penetrate her thoughts. Laurel turned and recognized the brakeman, Frederick Harkins. She jerked in a subconscious reaction to seeing the man she thought had killed the Pinkerton detective. Then she gained control of herself, aware that he would not make an attempt on her life out here in the street.

He hurried up to her. He said, "I've been calling you since you crossed the tracks. Are you all right?"

"I'm fine, thank you." She kept her voice cool but firm, then continued walking toward the hotel.

"Mind if I accompany you?" he asked with a friendly smile. "I've been wanting to talk with you."

Laurel did not want to be anywhere near this man, but she didn't want to create a scene in public. She merely shrugged as he fell into step with her.

"Miss Wilson, I know it's an imposition and a bit bold on my part, but I wonder if you—"

"No!" The word exploded from her. "Please don't ask!"

He blinked and stopped. "Oh!" He shrugged, lowering his eyes. "Excuse me, but I thought it wouldn't do any harm to—"

She interrupted angrily. "Absolutely not!" She gave him a hard look to augment her stern words. "Now, please leave me alone!"

As she turned away, he said contritely, "I didn't mean to upset you. It's just that she's such a nice-looking woman, and I thought you . . ."

"She?" Laurel whirled around in surprise. "She?"

"Yes, your friend. I didn't think there would be any harm in asking you if it would seem improper for me to try getting better acquainted with her."

Startled, Laurel stood in uncertain confusion for a moment. *Sarah? He wants to . . .* She caught herself. This was the man she believed had killed the Pinkerton agent. "Stay away from her and me. Is that clear, Mr. Harkins?"

Without waiting for an answer, Laurel turned and hurried toward the hotel.

In the conductor's small office on the train, Schramm and the other express messenger watched Laurel leave the brakeman standing forlornly on the street.

Aiken said thoughtfully, "Looks like they had an argument."

"It's an act," the conductor replied. "She's probably mad at him for speaking to her in public."

"You think so?"

"Yes, I do. I also think he's another Pinkerton. Anyway, we've seen enough. We have too much at stake to take a chance on letting him live, especially if he's a Pinkerton. Now that he's talked to her, we must act. When that other engine gets here, you'd better watch your chance to get him. But this time, make sure it looks like an accident."

"I'll wait for him until he's setting the brakes. Lots of brakemen have fallen under the wheels doing that. But what about that woman?"

Schramm considered that question for a moment before answering. "I've decided that right now we must concentrate on carrying out the big plans. So I think we can wait awhile before deciding for sure what to do with Miss Wilson, or whatever her real name is. But if it's necessary to keep her from testifying against us, then we'll do what has to be done–whenever that might be."

After church, Ridge and Sarah walked back toward the hotel. She commented, "I think your uniform helped the preacher make his point about the need to forgive others if God is to forgive us."

A hint of smile touched Ridge's lips. "I think some of those men in the pews were struggling with that concept. A few would have liked to take a swing at me."

"In church?"

"This uniform represents a lot of bad memories for some who fought in the war and older folks who lost a son or husband."

"I've seen many men with a military jacket or part of a uniform, but not wearing a full outfit. So is that why you wore it–to start a fight?"

"No, that's not the reason."

"Then what is?"

He didn't want to tell her that they were the only clothes he owned. The express messenger uniform was loaned by the railroad. He said, "I'd rather talk about how I might help you and Laurel in your situation."

"I'm sorry, Ridge. As I said earlier, I can't tell you anything about that."

"Even if your life is in danger?"

"I want to tell you, but Laurel would be angry."

"So pleasing her is more important than your life?"

Sarah stopped and glared at him, her face flushing. "That was a mean thing to say!" She hadn't intended to strike back, but his remark stung.

He was a little surprised at the sudden display of temper, but he pushed ahead. "Words can't kill, but—"

"Don't try to frighten me any more than I am!" Her voice rose, making other pedestrians turn to look.

A male voice came from a bench in front of a closed store. "Hey, Reb! You heard the lady. Stop scaring her!"

Ridge turned cold eyes in that direction and recognized George Aiken holding a bottle. Without answering, Ridge shifted his attention back to Sarah. "I'm just trying to help. . . ."

Aiken yelled, "Don't you hear good? Leave her alone!"

Ridge pivoted at the sound of the express messenger heaving his considerable bulk from the bench and the demijohn falling to the boardwalk. "This doesn't concern you, George."

Aiken didn't seem to hear. He lowered his head and charged across the few feet of boardwalk, his big arms spread wide, and his head aimed like a battering ram at Ridge's stomach.

"Stop, George!" Ridge commanded, stepping away from Sarah whose hands had flown to her face. "It's me, Ridge, from the cars!"

For a man of such bulk, Aiken was agile. He spun to follow Ridge's short retreat. "I don't care who you are. You can't insult a lady and wear that Rebel uniform in front of me!" With an animal-like roar, he followed his adversary.

In spite of his bad leg, Ridge shifted his weight enough so that he avoided being butted, but Aiken's right arm circled

Ridge's slender waist and propelled him toward the other grasping arm.

Ridge avoided being caught in a crushing bear hug by spinning away on his good leg. He heard Sarah shriek as Aiken stumbled and fell hard on the boardwalk.

"George!" Ridge yelled, stepping close. "Stop it!"

Sarah pleaded, "Oh, yes, please stop!"

Cursing loudly, Aiken rolled on his side and kicked at Ridge. His foot shot out from under him and he crashed to the boardwalk.

With a triumphant yell, Aiken grabbed the front of the hated Confederate cavalry jacket with one hand and brought his huge fist back with the other.

Ridge ducked, feeling the wind from the near miss. He had learned earlier that his leg required any fight to be brief. He defended himself, using all the skills he had developed in four years of war. He no longer felt anything except hot blood scalding through his body and the satisfying power of his shoulders and arms as he relentlessly drove his fists at their target.

He was aware that he yelled, matching Aiken's roaring threats, while from what seemed like a great distance Sarah screamed.

The noisy struggle seemed unreal and distant, as though his mind had retreated from this reality to another, much more terrifying fight.

It had started quietly, like many other raids. At dawn, he and his brother, Second Lieutenant Harvey Granger, rode stirrup-to-stirrup into the shelter of some woods on their very secret mission. The small cavalry detachment following the two young officers quietly reined in their mounts for a final look at their intended target. It was a new Federal railroad bridge over the shallow stream called Bethel Crossing.

Ridge stood in the stirrups to make a final visual scrutiny of the surroundings. Except for some new rails crisscrossed over the ties on the near shore, everything seemed exactly as it had been a week before when he and Harvey had scouted the area in preparation for the surprise strike.

Subconsciously, Ridge looked in vain for the jaunty yellow feather worn by his thirty-one-year-old long time leader, Major General J.E.B. Stuart. Ridge had ridden with the dashing officer since July 21, 1861, when the South won the war's first major victory at what they called Manassas, but the Federals knew as Bull Run.

When Ridge's brother joined the cavalry, it had been arranged so that they both rode with Stuart. They had been with him in May 1864, when he was fatally wounded at Yellow Knife, just a few miles from the Confederate capital at Richmond.

Now, five months later at Bethel Crossing, Ridge glanced at Harvey in the crisp October air. He grinned as if they were going to play a game the way they had when they were children.

Ridge, leading the cavalry detachment, drew his saber to signal that the attack was to begin.

Only token resistance was expected from the few Federal infantrymen who had been detailed to guard the bridge. But something went terribly wrong.

From behind newly made and disguised breastworks, blue-coated Federal infantry rose as one man to pour deadly musket fire into the unsuspecting Confederate horsemen. Their onrushing front line toppled the way standing wheat fell before a scythe. The infantrymen dropped out of sight to reload as Union cavalrymen charged out from behind the low hill and across the short expanse of open ground.

In the swirling masses of frightened, neighing horses and cries of desperately wounded men, Ridge saw a Yankee cavalryman charge upon his brother from behind. Ridge shouted a warning, but it was impossible for Harvey to hear above the din. The first saber thrust caught him in the left shoulder. He started to collapse over his horse's neck, but valiantly raised his blade in his right hand to block the Yankee's second thrust.

Ridge yelled like a madman and spurred toward the Federal cavalryman, who followed up his initial slashing saber stroke by knocking Harvey's defensive blade aside. The Northern man thrust his steel through Harvey's chest. Harvey clutched at his fatal wound, vainly tried to stay in the saddle, then slid to the ground.

With an anguished shout that pained his throat, Ridge spurred close to the bluecoat, ready to strike with his saber. The Yankee twisted in the saddle to meet Ridge's charge. Ridge ducked the slashing blade, leaned forward, and drove his own point home. The man fell beside Ridge's brother, Harvey. His plunging horse, mortally wounded by a bullet that smashed into his chest, trampled over both of them on the ground.

Ridge's mount suddenly screamed and stumbled. Ridge tried to leap clear, but a minié ball smashed into his leg. He felt the shock but no pain before his horse fell across him, and he slid into blackness.

A different kind of blackness closed about Ridge as he continued to defend himself against George Aiken. The realization that his bum leg would not allow a long struggle made him desperate for a quick finish. He felt the other man start to weaken, to sag, but Ridge could not stop his attack. Deep down in his mind, he knew he should stop, but he kept on.

It was only when he felt Sarah tugging at him, and he sensed rather than heard her sobbing pleas, that Ridge was able to draw back and look at what he had done. Both of Aiken's dark brown eyes were puffy and starting to close. His heavy black eyebrows were matted and no longer looked as if they were about to fly off his square head.

"George," Ridge puffed, his voice hoarse, "I'm sorry."

Aiken groaned but did not answer, not even when Ridge bent over him and repeated his words.

Only when the dark cloud of blind rage had retreated from Ridge's eyes did he see that a crowd had gathered, and hostile eyes focused on him.

He turned to Sarah whose face was pale, her eyes bright with tears. "I really regret this," he told her through swelling lips that made his words difficult to form. "Are you ashamed to walk with me back to your hotel? If you are, I'll understand."

Ridge's words touched her because no man had ever fought for her before. Her face puckered as though she were about to break into fresh weeping. "I would be honored to walk with you. When we get to the hotel, I'll help you clean up."

Aiken dragged himself back to the train, found the conductor, and told him about the encounter. Aiken roared threats of what he would do to Ridge while Schramm filled a basin with water.

"I want him off this train!" Aiken thundered, gingerly washing his facial wounds. "I want him off before I kill him!"

"To do that," the conductor observed dryly, "seems to me you'll need more luck than you've had so far."

"If he hadn't taken me by surprise, he'd still be stretched out in the street."

Sarcasm dripped from Schramm's comment. "I thought you said you jumped him."

"I come at him right enough when he wouldn't leave that woman alone, but I'd been drinking!"

"You weren't drunk then, because you're not now. So why don't you stop trying to lie to yourself and making excuses to me? He bested you, plain and simple." Schramm shook his head in mock sympathy. "A Rebel with a game leg against your bulk."

"I'm warning you, Hannibal!" Aiken turned to glare, his lips curling menacingly. "That's enough!"

The conductor nodded. "Maybe it's a good thing this happened, because it shows that when the attack comes, you'd better get him fast. Otherwise, he could get you, then blaze away at the riders. If he's as good with a shotgun and Henry rifle as he is with his fists—"

Aiken interrupted. "I don't want to wait that long!"

"It doesn't matter what you want!" Schramm's tone turned hard. He thrust his face close. "Too much planning went into this!

We follow those plans to the letter, except now you know to get him fast when it starts."

The express messenger growled. "You can be blasted sure of that. I'll also make sure an 'accident' gets rid of Harkins, the other Pinkerton. But what about the women?"

"You let me worry about them. Now, finish getting cleaned up. The telegraph just brought word that the relief engine passed the next station."

"Has this delay changed the attack time?"

"No. It comes off tomorrow exactly as scheduled."

"Good! I can't wait to get even with that Rebel."

In the hotel room, Sarah finally stood back and examined Ridge. He had removed his jacket and draped it over one of the walnut posters at the foot of the bed where he was propped up with pillows.

"What do you think, Laurel?" she asked, replacing a wash-cloth in the ceramic basin of water.

"I think he'll live," she replied with a teasing smile. "But he won't win any prizes for looks."

Ridge looked past Sarah to where Laurel sat on the other bed, swinging her legs above the floor, which was several inches below her feet. "You're always saucy, aren't you?"

She flashed a knowing smile at him. "You should see me when I'm in a bad mood."

"Like when you were thrown from your carriage in Chicago?" he asked, trying to return the smile, but stopping, wincing at the effort.

Sarah glanced from Ridge to Laurel. "What's this? You two knew each other before and never let on to me?"

Ridge commented, "We just barely met."

"Our meeting was short," Laurel replied, her eyes teasing. "And I think it was like tinder striking flint. Very brief, but enough to make sparks."

Sarah caught the look that passed between Laurel and Ridge. With a hint of suspicion, Sarah asked, "What happened?"

"Nothing," Laurel said.

Ridge nodded, his eyes still on her. "I think that about sums it up, except for your remark when I tried to help you up from the street that you could take care of yourself."

Sarah was bewildered. "I don't understand at all."

"Apparently Mr. Granger doesn't either." Laurel turned thoughtful eyes on him. "Or is it simply that you don't believe I can do that?"

"Oh, I believe that you think you can take care of yourself," he assured her.

"But you don't *think* I can?" Laurel questioned. When he shrugged, she asked quietly, "Is that why you slept in the hallway last night with a pistol?"

"What?" Sarah cried in exasperation. "Would somebody please tell me what you two are talking about?"

"From one of the Negro men who works here," Laurel explained, "I learned that a man answering Mr. Granger's description seemed to be guarding our door last night."

Sarah's eyes opened wide in understanding. She said to Ridge, "I thought you looked sleepy this morning when you came to take me to church."

He was annoyed at being found out, but shrugged and offered

an explanation. "I was tired of sleeping in that express car, that's all."

Light laughter bubbled from Laurel, but Sarah said with deep feeling, "That was a noble thing to do, Ridge."

He grinned, wincing at the pain of his cut lip. "You should see some of the places I've slept the last four years."

"Don't be modest!" Sarah exclaimed. "You might have saved our lives."

"We weren't in danger," Laurel declared.

"Maybe not," Ridge told her, "but I couldn't be sure, and since Sarah wouldn't tell me anything because you told her not to, I decided not to take any chances."

He reached toward his jacket at the foot of the bed. "Now, if you'll hand that to me, I'll get out of your way."

"Not yet," Sarah said. "You'd better rest—"

"Thanks," he interrupted, "but it's time for me to go. Laurel, if you please?"

She picked up the jacket, touching the paper in the pocket. She knew that it was a letter and wondered if it were from a sweetheart. She felt a twinge of pain that surprised her.

When Ridge had gone, Laurel mused, "He's giving you a lot of attention in taking you to church, defending you in the street, and fretting about your safety."

Sarah straightened up from pouring the basin of dirty water into the chamber pot. She shoved it back under the high bed, out of sight. "He's been very nice, a real gentleman, but I'm no fool."

"I don't understand."

Sarah came to face Laurel. "That's because you don't want to. When the three of us are together, he can't keep his eyes off you."

"Nonsense!" Laurel exclaimed without conviction. "He's just concerned for our safety."

"Yes, he is concerned about that, but I see things you don't–or won't. He makes me feel good about myself." Sarah turned to the looking glass and examined her reflection. "This morning when he came to take me to church, he complimented me. He made me feel attractive. He talked easily with me, and made me feel important."

Her eyes shifted from her own image in the glass to Laurel's. "I am getting fond of him, but I can see clearly that he's more interested in you than in me."

Laurel shrugged off the thought, but she turned away so Sarah couldn't see her face in the mirror. "Well, then, it's a one-way street. I'm not interested in him."

Sarah asked softly, "Aren't you?"

"Of course not. We have nothing in common. We're from different worlds, and he is so very arrogant!"

"You mean you can't push him around as you do all other men?"

"I don't push men around!"

"You're right. You lead them around like puppies on a leash, and then you walk away and leave them. This man is different, Laurel. Don't let your stubbornness drive him away."

"Even if what you said was true, which it isn't, Ridge and I don't really know each other."

"Make all the excuses you want, Laurel, but when this trip is over, you may never see him again unless you open your eyes, and your heart."

Laurel picked up her cloak and fastened it around her body like a cape. "Think what you want. I'm going out and try to find out if anyone has seen Claude." She left the room, but she was surprised to realize she wasn't thinking about her fiancé.

Instead, she asked herself, *Why does my heart beat faster when I think of Ridge Granger?*

Ridge was reluctant to lose sight of the two women and whatever danger they faced. *Especially Laurel,* he thought, then he gently upbraided himself for that selectivity, but realized it was true. After Varina, he had no intention of becoming interested in another woman, and certainly not a Yankee with Laurel's disposition. Still, he felt warm inside thinking about her while he decided how to pass the time until the new engine arrived. He didn't want to return to the train where he might encounter Aiken. After their fight, it would be difficult enough being confined in the same express car for the rest of the trip. That left few choices. He could walk around town, but the autumn wind with a sharp nip to it had come up. He preferred the warmth of the restaurant or the waiting rooms of the two railroad stations.

Ridge chose the restaurant. There he could watch the hotel and have lunch to help pass the time. Except for a couple of uniformed Missouri and Gulf railroad men sitting at a back table, the place was empty. Ridge sat at the counter and picked up the bill of fare, but glanced toward the hotel just in time to see Laurel walk outside. She headed toward the Mississippi and Gulf depot.

She's probably going to ask about her fiancé he thought. He stood up quickly, realizing that after she spoke to the station agent and telegrapher there, she would probably return to the Great Central depot and repeat her questions. Whistling, he headed there in hopes of seeing her again.

The waiting room was empty except for the agent looking through his grillwork.

Ridge explained, "I'm with the cars waiting for an engine to come up from the south. Is it all right if I sit here where it's warm?"

"Sure thing, but I'd be obliged if you stuck another stick of wood in that stove."

Nodding, Ridge passed in front of the long line of sturdy benches. There was a faint smell of stale cigar smoke and the fragrance of strong coffee in a battered pot left too long on the top of the tall heating stove. He fed the stove and picked up the remnants of a newspaper someone had abandoned. He didn't read it, but followed Laurel's small figure until she entered the telegrapher's office at the M and G depot.

It seemed she was out of sight a long time. Ridge idly watched what little activity was visible in Trinity. Churchgoers had returned to their homes. Except for an M and G switch engine shunting cars, and an occasional team passing in the street, the town was quiet.

The agent said, "I'll be right back in case somebody wants to buy a ticket."

Ridge nodded without looking around, but his eyes never left the telegrapher's office Laurel had entered. Behind him, Ridge heard the agent close a door. Then there was only the sound of the metal stove expanding with the heat.

When Laurel reappeared across the tracks, Ridge followed her with his eyes, longing to know her better.

As he expected, she headed for the depot. He watched as she glanced around, then lifted her hoopskirt, showing a scarlet petticoat beneath. A gust of wind caught the skirt and flipped it up. Ridge sucked in his breath at the sight of a trim ankle.

He was still having trouble with irregular breathing when she entered the depot, her hair slightly windblown. Without seeing him, she walked up to the grilled window. Ridge said, "The agent will be back–"

He broke off when she gasped and whirled around, her eyes wide. "Oh!" she exclaimed softly. "It's you! You startled me."

He stood. "Didn't mean to." He grinned, adding, "but I knew you wouldn't be frightened because you can take such good care of yourself."

A pink flush showed in her cheeks, but she didn't reply.

His grin widened in surprise. "I didn't think you could blush."

She pivoted back to the agent's window and called, "Anybody back there?"

"He said he'd be right back. Any news of your fiancé?"

"No, not that it's any of your business."

Taking a deep breath, Ridge changed his tone. "You know what I'd like?"

"What?" she asked over her shoulder.

"I'd like to have a nice, polite conversation with you."

She turned. "Then why do you torment me?"

"I haven't really meant to. But I would like to talk to you seriously."

"What about?"

"Oh, lots of things. Everything, in fact. If nothing else, I would like to hear your voice. It's . . . it's, well. . . soft and warm and . . ." He stopped, shrugging. "I didn't mean to say that."

She took a couple of steps toward him. Her knees felt just a tiny bit weak. "It's all right, I guess."

With a smile, he invited her to sit. When she did, their shoulders lightly touched. He twisted sideways to look into her eyes. "They're beautiful, like all of you."

She jumped up, flustered. "What did you want to talk about?"

"You," he said honestly, softly, but when she stiffened, he took her hand and gently pulled her back to the bench. "Relax. I promise I won't bite."

"You're impertinent!" She jerked her hand free.

He seemed unaffected. "I'd like to know why you won't let me help in whatever trouble you're having."

There was something so sincere in his words and look that Laurel softened toward him. "I had no choice," she said. "My father . . ." She hesitated, then continued, "He is a very strict, stern man who ruled his children with an iron hand. My sisters didn't seem to mind, but I . . ."

She frowned, surprised that she was telling this Rebel stranger such things.

Ridge guessed, "So you rebelled and went out on your own, taking care of yourself?"

"Well, yes. And my brother was like me, except he could join the army by lying about his age. There wasn't much I could do except, well, do what I thought best."

"Did you help nurse the wounded?"

"No." She closed her mouth firmly so that she didn't somehow let slip anything that might indicate her wartime courier activities. She stood up. "Where *is* that agent?"

"He'll be right back." Ridge gently pulled her back down beside him. "What about your fiancé?"

Laurel recognized it as a question with much deeper meaning than the few words might indicate. "I've got to find him."

"Because you love him?"

"That's none of your business!" She sprang to her feet and faced Ridge. "You are the most impertinent, arrogant man I have ever known!"

Ridge's eyebrows shot up. "Why are you so defensive? Most girls would have a simple answer: yes or no."

"Oh!" she cried in exasperation and took an agitated step toward the ticket window.

Ridge seized her hand. "I apologize. Please, sit down again. I'll quit prying."

She stood looking up at him uncertainly. In spite of herself, she enjoyed feeling the warmth of his hand. She recalled the power in his arms when she had accidentally bumped into him after finding the dead man's body.

Ridge did not let go of her hand, and she made no effort to free it. With his other hand, he touched a stray strand of her hair. "Since your fiancé isn't here, why don't you let me help look out for you?"

In spite of her inclination to jerk her head away, she held still while he pushed the hair back into place.

Then, very gently, he released her hand and placed both of his on her face. She felt herself tremble.

A door slammed behind them and she pulled back, her heart beating rapidly. Ridge's hands slid along her shoulders and down her arms to her hands. He did not let go, but held them, looking at her with a tenderness she had never seen in any man's eyes.

The agent called from his window, "I'm back. Miss, you want to buy a ticket?"

No, she thought, *that's not what I want.* She pulled her hands free and turned, feeling her face glowing with a pleasant warmth. "No, thanks," she replied. "I'm waiting for the replacement locomotive."

"The telegrapher just now told me that it should be close enough to hear the whistle any minute. You will be on your way again, and your trip will be over tomorrow."

Tomorrow? Laurel repeated silently. *Will I ever see him again after that? She shook her head. What difference does it make? I'll find Claude and then forget I ever met Ridge.* But she wasn't quite sure she believed that.

Chapter 13

Laurel and Sarah dressed against the rising wind and threatening clouds that arrived along with the replacement locomotive and tender. The wood-burning engine was a twin of the faulty R.W. Wentworth except that the new cab carried only a single surname: Jennings.

The women left the hotel to watch while the engine and tender were connected to the express car and the other coaches.

Laurel watched as Frederick Harkins scrambled agilely upon the tender to apply the brakes. She had not seen him kill the Pinkerton agent, but from what she had overheard Schramm and him say, they thought she had.

She still needed to prove that Schramm was stealing from the railroad. She didn't think he was a killer, but he was certainly involved in the murder. As for Harkins, as long as he was on the train, Laurel felt her life was in danger.

She casually glanced over the stranded male passengers waiting to board. She didn't see Ridge. She assumed he had returned to guard duty when the strongboxes were taken from the bank's safe and she was in the hotel room. Now, she thought, Ridge would be inside the express car, guarding the boxes with the man he had fought in defense of Sarah.

The only two women passengers were allowed to board first. Laurel and Sarah entered the first of the passenger coaches connected to the express car. Sarah returned to the same seat she had occupied earlier, next to the window. Laurel took the aisle seat. The male passengers began to return to their previous seats, except for Jacob Lucas, who had sat alone directly opposite the women.

"Wonder where he is?" Sarah mused. She lowered her voice. "If that killer you suspect is still on the train, it would be good to have Lucas and his pistol nearby."

Laurel didn't reply, but moodily stared out the window at Trinity. She was lost in thought about Ridge Granger, and why she even wasted time thinking about him.

Sarah broke into her reverie. "Oh, here comes Lucas." Her voice dropped to a whisper, "He's terribly nosy, but since Ridge is in the express car and can't protect us, at least Mr. Lucas can."

Laurel wasn't sure how much protection he would want to give her after she had warned him in Trinity to stop following her.

The short man with the unusually big chest slid into his seat across from them. "Ladies," he said with a smile, "I trust you both enjoyed our enforced delay in Trinity." He gave no indication that Laurel had confronted him at the Trinity hotel and ordered him to stop following her.

Sarah played up to him. "It was a nice break from riding so many hours on this swaying old coach, and I also got to go to church. Did you enjoy Trinity?"

"I had work to do," he said, adjusting his clothing.

Sarah smiled at glimpsing the big pistol under his coat. "What kind of work, Mr. Lucas?"

"Nothing that would interest you, I'm afraid."

Laurel made an annoyed sound under her breath that caused Sarah to turn to her. "What's the matter?"

"Nothing," she said under her breath.

Sarah's eyes narrowed thoughtfully. "Are you thinking about what I said about Ridge and you?"

"I was thinking about your friend across the aisle," Laurel whispered. "There's something about him that doesn't seem right."

"Such as?"

"I don't know. Now, you visit with him. I've got my own things to think about, like finding Claude."

"Don't take too long. Tomorrow we reach the end of the line. You've got to find Claude by then or return to Chicago without knowing any more than when you started. But more importantly, if Ridge doesn't go back on the cars, you may never see him again."

"I don't care."

"Really, Laurel!" Sarah's voice rose in agitation. "I can't believe you're so stubborn."

Schramm entered the car ahead of them calling, "Tickets, tickets, please." He came down the aisle in his conductor's uniform, checking each of the previous passengers. He stopped to collect a ticket from one of two new passengers who had boarded at Trinity.

Out of the corner of her eye, Laurel noticed the second new passenger paid Schramm in cash. Laurel sighed, knowing Allan Pinkerton was paying her to find out how Schramm was stealing from the railroad.

That wasn't as important to Laurel, however, as knowing he was involved in murder, and that she could possibly be the next victim. Still, she wanted to earn her money, so she had to prove the conductor's thievery before the end of the trip tomorrow.

When Schramm reached the women, he gave them both friendly smiles. Unsuspecting Sarah smiled back, but Laurel's secret fears made it hard for her to do the same. However, she managed to be charming and totally disarming so Schramm couldn't guess what she knew about his involvement in the Pinkerton agent's murder. The conductor nodded politely and continued out the back of the car into the next one, calling for tickets.

"Back to what I was saying about Ridge," Sarah said, "There's another thing. You had better pray that Aiken doesn't try to do him any harm."

"What?"

"There's just the two of them up there all alone," Sarah explained. "If Aiken wants revenge for the beating he got, he can do what he wants to Ridge, then claim it was an accident. There would be no witnesses to say differently. Ridge could even be dead."

Two short whistles sounded from the locomotive. The train jerked into motion. Black smoke and hot cinders rushed by the window. Laurel didn't see them. Her mind jumped into the express car ahead with Ridge and Aiken.

Ridge had expected Aiken to be surly over losing their physical encounter that morning. Instead, Aiken sat in his usual place, his chair tipped back against the coach wall. He was cordial, seeming to have no hard feelings in spite of his swollen eyes and lacerated face. Ridge was cautious, eyeing the other man's vicious-looking shotgun as the kerosene lamp on the wall reflected off of the sawed-off twin barrels. Ridge knew what a mess they could make of a man at close range.

"I'm sorry about this morning, George."

He tried to smile. It was a little crooked because of a cut lip. "You're good, Reb . . . uh . . . Ridge. I don't hold no grudge against a man who stands up for his lady."

"Just the same, I'm sorry it happened."

"Forget it. What're you going to do tomorrow when we finish this run? Go out on the town and have some fun?"

"I don't know." Ridge knew what he wanted to do: court Laurel. He wanted to hear her voice, to touch her hands and again feel their smooth softness. But there might be little chance of that. Suppose she found her fiancé? Besides, was it even right of him to think about her when she was betrothed?

His eyes drifted around the express car, but he didn't really see anything. His thoughts were in the wooden coach directly behind.

Aiken chuckled. "Take a good look. That's as close as you and me will ever get to that kind of riches."

"What?" Ridge said, bringing his attention back to his fellow express messenger.

"I seen you eyeing them strongboxes of gold back there," Aiken replied. "It's enough to make a man willing to take a risk to grab some of them, ain't it?" Without waiting for an answer, he added, "especially if that man was a flat-busted Confederate without two coins to rub together."

"I have some money, and I'm working to earn more on this trip."

"But wouldn't all that much gold tempt you?"

Something in Aiken's tone made Ridge uneasy. He turned from the treasure and shrugged. "If you're asking if I would steal some of this if I had a chance, or fight to keep this for whoever owns it, the answer is simple: I'll do what I'm paid to do."

Aiken slowly nodded. "That's what I thought you'd say."

❧

Laurel made her way down the aisle toward the back of the car, and she swayed with the train as it gathered speed. Her thoughts rolled and tumbled.

I'm in big trouble, she scolded herself. *After the delay in Trinity, I've only got twenty-four hours to do what I came to do. So far, I've not only failed to find Claude and prove that Schramm is stealing from the railroad, but I've also put myself in danger because Harkins and the conductor think I saw that Pinkerton agent murdered.*

There was only one thing she could do on the train besides try to stay alive: again try to learn how the conductor was pocketing part of the cash ticket sales for himself.

Laurel entered the second coach where almost every male passenger looked up at her. She ignored them and kept walking, grabbing the back of a seat to steady herself as the cars started around a curve. A quick glance out the window showed that the train had left the prairie and was entering an area of rolling hills and curves with trees growing along the right-of-way.

Laurel glimpsed the outside of the express car as it followed the engine and tender around the bend. Her mind skipped to one of the express car's occupants.

Why, she asked herself impatiently, *with all I've got to deal with, why should I even think about Ridge Granger?*

She didn't really know much about him. True, he was good-looking, but he was also haughty and strong-willed. Sure, he had shown concern for Sarah and her, but maybe that was just part of his superior attitude toward women. She had heard that Southern men liked their women to be subservient, like their slaves. Well, I'm not like that! Laurel became aware that her pulse had speeded up. Just thinking about him angers me, she fumed. But somewhere in the back of her mind a tiny voice seemed to ask, *Is that really what's making your heart beat faster?*

Approaching the conductor's office at the back of the car, Laurel slowed and casually looked back. *Good!* None of the passengers were looking her direction. Now if the office was empty, unlocked, and she could get inside . . . .

Her thoughts snapped off at the sound of muted male voices from within. Disappointed, Laurel quietly sat down in an empty seat nearest the office. She pretended to be looking out the window at the gathering storm, but her ears were attuned to the conversation sifting through the office partition behind her.

She caught only an occasional word, but recognized the conductor's voice. She could not be sure of the other man's identity, but she was reasonably sure that it was Harkins, the brakeman. Being so close to the men who wanted her dead made Laurel anxious, but she forced herself to stay quiet, hoping to overhear something of value.

A short blast of the engine's whistle sounded, causing the conversation in the cubicle to stop. The door slid open and Schramm exclaimed, "Why in blazes is he whistling for brakes?"

"I don't know, but I'd better get up there and apply them,"

Harkins said. He stepped into the aisle and started rapidly walking forward.

Schramm exited the office and slid the door shut, saying, "Something's wrong. I'd better go check."

Both men passed without noticing Laurel, whose face was turned toward the window.

She remained motionless until she heard the door slide open at the front end of the car. Then, carefully she glanced over the few passengers. Most had not even looked up as the railroad men passed. Nobody looked back toward her.

Casually, Laurel slid out of the seat and stepped in front of the cubicle door. The green shade still hung over the small window, offering privacy within. The hasty departure of both crewmen made Laurel hopeful that the door wasn't locked.

Keeping her back to the passengers so they couldn't see her hands, she watched them out of the corner of her eye in case one turned toward her. Nobody did. Gently, she tried the door. Slowly, noiselessly, it slid open.

A quick glance over her shoulder disclosed that no passengers were looking her way. *Now!* she told herself, and slid the door open just enough to enter.

Sarah watched the conductor and brakeman as they hurried through the coach and out of sight in the express coach. She turned to look behind, past the heating stove and the door to the next passenger coach. There was no sign of Laurel.

Lucas slid to the end of his seat as if he were going to stand up in the aisle. He commented, "They seemed in a hurry."

"A little bit," Sarah admitted, debating whether to go look for Laurel.

Clearing his throat, Lucas asked, "Mind if I ask you something?"

"You can ask. I may not answer."

"Fair enough. Why is your friend so lacking in cordiality toward me?"

"Why don't you ask her?"

"She was rather abrupt with me back at the hotel. She told me to stop following her."

"She's a very independent woman."

"But as I told both you young ladies at the beginning of this trip, I feel a fatherly interest in your safety. Since the war, law and order have been so disrupted that it's not safe for young women to travel alone."

"We've been quite safe, Mr. Lucas."

"I daresay that the man who was found the other night thought he was safe, too."

Sarah wondered if that were a subtle warning. She recalled that Lucas had been talking to her at the restaurant table, but left shortly before the murder. She also remembered that Lucas knew Laurel thought she had seen the dead man someplace before.

Sarah was bothered by an unanswered question: why had Lucas asked the telegrapher if Laurel had sent a telegram the night of the murder?

"If you'll excuse me," Sarah said, "I think I'll go check on my friend."

Lucas nodded. "The train's slowing down, so you'll have an easier time walking." As Sarah slid out of her seat, he placed his face close to the window. "We're on a curve, so I can see all the rest of the train ahead of us. There's no water tower or wood rick, so there must be another reason for stopping."

Sarah bent and quickly verified that there was no indication this was a fuel or water stop. With the hope that they weren't going to be broken down again, Sarah headed into the second coach.

❧

Laurel had quickly opened and searched every drawer in Schramm's small desk. *Nothing. Not a sign!* Sighing in disappointment, she straightened up and scowled. *It's got to be here some . . . wait! What's that?*

She stepped closer to the partition through which she had tried to overhear the conversation between Schramm and Harkins. A photograph of an older man and woman hung there. Barely visible from behind the ornate oval frame, Laurel glimpsed what appeared to be the corner of a thin book.

Gingerly, Laurel reached out, lifted the frame with her left hand, and touched the book with her right. She expected it to fall, but instead, it stayed firmly in place. Quickly but carefully, Laurel lifted the frame enough to see that the book was held in place by four thin strands of wire.

With rising excitement, she saw that one corner of the book had slipped, possibly from being hastily replaced. Removing the item, Laurel realized it was a ledger. Her feelings soared as she opened it and quickly scanned the contents.

"What are you doing?"

The voice behind Laurel made her jump. She whirled around,

trying to hide the book behind her. "Oh! Sarah!" she exclaimed. "You frightened me!"

"And you frighten me! You broke into this office to steal that book? Why?"

"Sh! Keep your voice down!" Laurel urged, darting an anxious eye toward the door with the drawn green shade.

"What for?" Sarah demanded, her voice dropping to a hoarse whisper.

Laurel sighed. She was trapped, leaving no choice but to explain. "It's not what you think. This is a ledger that proves the conductor is stealing from the railroad. See?"

Laurel opened the little flat book and held it out. "It's all here. Here's the name of the depot, the number of passengers paying cash for tickets, and over here, two columns. One's for what he's going to turn into the company, and the other for what he's stealing for himself!"

Sarah shook her head. "Now I understand! You didn't come on this trip to search for Claude, but to get proof that Schramm is a thief. You wouldn't care, but Pinkerton would, so that means you're working for him again!"

Laurel hissed warningly, "This isn't the time or place to talk about this." She thrust the ledger into her reticule where it fitted perfectly, then straightened the picture on the wall. "We've got to get out of here, fast!"

She stepped toward the door, but Sarah, face flushed with anger, blocked her way. "Why didn't you tell me? I never betrayed your wartime activities, so I'm hurt and disappointed that you didn't trust me on this, especially when it's got us both in such danger!"

"Back then, I had to have your help with disguises and places to hide messages. You know a woman can't travel alone, so I needed you to come with me on this trip."

"And got me involved in your danger!" Sarah snapped, her eyes bright with fury. "Have you lost your senses?" Without waiting for an answer, she pointed to Laurel's reticule containing the ledger.

"When Schramm realizes this is gone," she continued, "he's going to question all the passengers. Some of them are going to say that you and I were both headed this way just before the train stopped unexpectedly! Then what happens to us?"

Laurel firmly pushed Sarah out the door and gently closed it. "For one thing," she said, her voice still low, "maybe we weren't noticed because all the men in this car were looking out the windows to see why we stopped unexpectedly. If Schramm questions us, you keep quiet and I'll handle things. At the next depot, I'll telegraph word that I've got what I came for. Come on; let's return to our seats before he comes back."

Sarah followed, moaning softly and saying fiercely under her breath, "You're going to get us both killed!"

⚜

The two women were in their usual seats with the conductor's secret ledger safely tucked into the bottom of Laurel's reticule before the train began moving again and the conductor entered the car in front of them.

"It's all right," he announced calmly when all eyes focused on him. "A small tree had fallen across the tracks. It was no trouble to remove. We'll only be a few minutes late arriving at our dinner stop."

When he came by the women, Laurel was the picture of innocence. She gave him a friendly smile. "I'm glad it wasn't anything serious," she said. "I dislike delays."

She heard Sarah make a strangled sound before the conductor continued out the back door to the next car.

Sarah hissed under her breath. "I can't believe how easily you can tell lies. You weren't like that when we were growing up. What's happened to you?"

"Sh! Lucas will overhear you."

Sarah glanced across the aisle where he was looking out the window as the train again speeded up. "He can't hear, so tell me what's going on."

"I can't tell you, so don't ask."

"I am asking!" Sarah's voice remained low but took on a firm edge. "You've admitted that both our lives are in danger. I want to know from whom, and why."

"Tonight, at supper when we can't be overheard—"

"Now!" Sarah broke in. "Are you looking for Claude, or is that also a lie? What about that book? Did Pinkerton hire you to steal it?"

"Don't get so upset! I'll tell you when it's safe."

"No, now!" Sarah's eyes glittered with emotion. "I've got a right to know if you've been using me to cover up for something that could get me killed."

"Please wait! I can't tell you—"

Sarah stood up suddenly, glaring down at Laurel. "I don't want to believe it," she said through clenched teeth, "but I'm beginning to think you used me just as you did some of those gullible young Rebel soldiers during your times behind the lines."

"That's enough!" Laurel glanced around, aware that Lucas was listening although he still seemed to be looking out the window on his side of the aisle.

"You're right!" Sarah said hoarsely, and stormed down the aisle toward the front of the car.

Lucas said from across the aisle, "Your friend seems very upset."

Resenting the intrusion, Laurel snapped, "It's nothing. She'll be all right."

"I hope it doesn't have anything to do with what the sheriff said, that the person who killed that man might still be on this train."

"Where did you hear something like that?"

"I overheard the sheriff telling you ladies. So if that's true, perhaps your friend should not go off by herself. If you'd like, I could—"

"No, thanks!" Laurel turned to look the direction Sarah had gone. There was only one other car that way, and only two people in that car: Ridge and his fellow guard.

She's very upset, Laurel thought, *but surely she wouldn't talk to Ridge about something like this, certainly not with George Aiken there. . . .*

She interrupted herself as Aiken walked through the front door into the coach. *He and Sarah must have just met each other, so she knows Ridge is alone.*

When Aiken passed, heading out the back of the coach, Laurel clutched her reticule with the ledger in it. She slid out of the seat and hurried toward the express car.

Clutching her bag with Schramm's purloined ledger in it,

Laurel peered into the express car. She saw by the light of the coal oil lamp that Ridge had changed back into his railroad uniform. His Confederate jacket hung on the back of the chair where he sat.

He stood, smiled, and leaned the shotgun against the wall before hurrying toward her. "It's good to see you again so soon."

A vision of their last meeting in the depot flashed through her mind. Remembering the way he had gently tucked a strand of her hair into place made her slightly flustered.

"I'm looking for Sarah."

"Sorry, I haven't seen her since our last stop."

"Thanks. I'll find her." Laurel started to turn away, wondering how she could have missed Sarah, unless she had stopped in the tiny "necessary" room.

"You know she's got to be on the train, so why don't you visit with me for a while?"

It was tempting, but Laurel needed to find Sarah and try to soothe her feelings after their disagreement.

"Thank you, but I can't." Seeking an excuse, she wrapped her arms across her body. "It's too cold in here."

"Come over here by the stove." Before she could protest, he took her free hand and started leading her across the car.

She protested halfheartedly, "I really should go find—"

"Better warm up first," he interrupted, picking up the chair with his free hand and placing it by the stove.

As she somewhat reluctantly started to sit down, he lifted his jacket from the back of the chair. "Here, let me put this around your shoulders."

She almost trembled at the touch of his hands, but quickly gained control of her emotion. "Thank you," she said, "but I can't wear a Confederate jacket." She shrugged her shoulders, causing the jacket to fall to the floor.

Ridge stooped to recover it. As he straightened up again, the letter fell from the pocket, landing at Laurel's feet. "Oh, I'm sorry," she said, bending quickly to pick it up.

Then she froze as light from the wall lamp fell across the front of the envelope. Her heart jumped as she recognized her brother's familiar handwriting: *Charley Bartlett, Elm Street, Chicago, Illinois.*

Gripping the letter tightly, she leaped up and took a step away from Ridge. She stared at him in stunned silence.

He asked anxiously, "What's the matter?"

Too overcome with emotion to reply, she brushed by him and ran across the floor with the letter.

"Laurel, wait!" he called, hurrying after her.

She reached the door just as Sarah entered. "Oh, my!" she exclaimed at the sight of Laurel's face. "What happened?"

Silently, Laurel rushed past her while Ridge called, "Sarah! Stop her!"

It was too late. Laurel plunged through the door, and ran down the aisle of the passenger coach.

Sarah stared in open-mouthed amazement.

Ridge stopped at the doorway, fearfully watching Laurel's trim figure racing through the next car. He exclaimed, "She's got my letter, but I can't leave this car unguarded!"

"What letter?"

"It's one I promised to personally deliver to someone named Charley Bartlett."

Sarah hesitated a moment before saying quietly, "You just did."

Chapter 14

As Sarah turned to follow Laurel, Ridge seized Sarah's hand. "Wait! What do you mean, 'I just did?' "

"I shouldn't have said anything." She pulled her hand away, but he grabbed her shoulders firmly.

"You've got to tell me!"

"I can't, Ridge! Please let me go!"

"Not until you explain."

Sarah made a moaning sound. "She doesn't want anyone to know. Now, let me go so I can be with her."

With a resigned sigh, Ridge released Sarah. "All right, but please tell her I've got to talk to her as soon as possible."

"I will," Sarah replied, and hurried away.

Perplexed, Ridge watched her go. *Why did Laurel run off with that letter, and why can't Sarah tell me?*

Laurel had the answers, but Ridge couldn't leave the car until George Aiken returned. "What's keeping him?" Ridge muttered impatiently.

The express messenger stood in the tiny conductor's cubicle

and examined the wall picture that Schramm had turned around. "You think she took the book, Hannibal?"

"Who else would have?" he replied hotly. "She had to have sneaked in here and rummaged around until she found it."

"So she knows everything?"

"No, not quite. She only has proof that I've been skimming from the railroad, but there's no way she could know about the planned robbery."

"That's good, but she couldn't have just found that ledger by accident."

"Of course she didn't! She was looking for it, and that's because she must be a Pinkerton. That's what the detective agency does: catch conductors stealing and pocketing part of the cash ticket money."

"You really think she's an agent? You said earlier that the brakeman was—"

"He is," Schramm interrupted. "They both are. That's why they were talking together awhile back."

"What are we going to do about them?"

"You already know what has to be done with Harkins."

"I've worked it out in my head so it'll look like an accident tonight. But would the law be suspicious if there were two accidents close together?"

"Three," Schramm corrected, "if you count the Rebel. But nothing will happen to him or her until tomorrow, and then it will look like he got killed defending the gold and a stray ball got her."

"You want her shot during the robbery?"

"What better time? The riders will run by the coaches, shooting at the passengers to make them keep their heads down and not get involved."

Aiken warned, "Watch out for that short man, Lucas. He's carrying a handgun and might try to use it, especially if he's trying to impress those women. I can't be there to help because I'll be in the express car taking out that Rebel."

Schramm smoothly palmed a small, single-shot derringer. "In the confusion, I doubt anyone will notice if a shot comes from inside the coach. Or if Lucas shoots at the riders with that big iron he's carrying, then nobody will hear my little hide-out beauty."

"It should work out right."

"Of course. When it seems the riders force me to ride off with them as a hostage . . ." The conductor grinned, leaving the thought unfinished.

"Just make sure I get my share of the ticket sales."

"That will be a pittance compared to what your share is from those gold coins in the car. Now, you'd better get back there."

"Not just yet. I want to take another walk around to make sure I know exactly where to strike Harkins after he sets the brakes tonight."

"Just make sure you do it right. Tomorrow, when the robbery begins, the first thing you do is kill that Reb."

Laurel was relieved that Jacob Lucas was away from his seat when she returned, clutching the letter that had fallen from Ridge's jacket.

She dropped into her seat and stared again at her brother's familiar handwriting on the envelope. With trembling fingers, she removed the single sheet of crumpled letter and began to read.

Dear Charley, we have been doing some hard march-ing and fighting the last two days, but tonight it is quiet.

I am writing by the light of our campfire in hopes that you will never see this letter, but if anything happens to me, then I pray that somehow this letter does get to you. I don't think this is too much to ask God, even if I didn't walk with Him much until recently.

Hot tears began to seep into her eyes, blurring the words, but she kept reading.

I have seen such fearsome sights that you would not believe. Most of the men I marched with have been killed or wounded, so only a handful of us are left.

I have a bad feeling about tomorrow, which is why I am writing this letter. If I am wrong, then I'll tear it up and you'll never know what I'm thinking tonight.

Laurel caught her breath sharply, and rapidly skimmed the rest of the letter.

Charley, in my mind, I see us the way we were, just the two of us against the rest. You were the only one who ever really loved me, just as you know I love you. It was remembering all this that helped me keep going when so many times I wanted to throw down my rifle and run home.

Laurel had to stop a moment as her tears flowed freely. With an effort, she finally read on.

But tonight I have a strange feeling that I waited too long, and may never get home or see you again. So if you receive this, you'll know what happened. Just remember, you were the best sister any boy could have.

It was signed, *Dorian.*

Closing her eyes, Laurel bent forward and clutched the letter to her breast until Sarah arrived.

She sat down quickly and slid both arms around Laurel. Sarah asked anxiously, "What's this all about?"

Freeing herself from Sarah's arms, Laurel handed her the letter. "It's from my brother. Read it."

Sarah did, then looked up in shock. "Oh, my!"

"He apparently wrote it the night before he was killed. But why did Ridge have it?"

"I have no idea, but he said that you and he had to talk as soon as possible."

"No! I can't face him right now." Her voice began to rise. "There's only one way that he could have come into possession of this letter. He killed Dorian and took it from his body."

"You're jumping to conclusions. There could be another logical explanation."

"Like what?"

"Well, offhand, I don't know. Somebody might have given it to him."

"That doesn't make sense at all, and you know it."

"Well, then, whatever it is, you must find out the truth for yourself."

For a long moment, Laurel remained silent. She glanced out the window, then took a deep breath and turned to face Sarah again. "You're right. I'll lose my mind imagining things until I know. But if he did kill Dorian, I . . . I don't know what I'll do, but I'll not let his death go unpunished!"

"You can decide what to do after you talk to him. He should be here soon, so ask him."

"But I don't want to talk to him in this car where others can overhear us."

"Then go to the express car."

"The other guard might be there, but perhaps Ridge and I can talk privately anyway." Laurel motioned for Sarah to move so she could get up. "I'll wash my face and then go see him."

Laurel was relieved to see that the other express messenger had not returned when she entered the express car. Ridge stood as she approached him and stopped under the kerosene wall lamp.

She had to fight to control her voice. "I have to know: where did you get that letter?"

"And I want to know why you ran off with it."

"Fair enough, but first, answer my question."

"I don't think that's any concern of yours, so please give it back."

Her voice rose in frustration. "Answer my question!"

Ridge regarded her thoughtfully, realizing that she was emotionally ready to explode. "All right."

Briefly, he told about walking through the cornfield the morning after a battle and hearing a moan from among the Federals and Confederates who still lay where they had fallen.

"I found this Union soldier still alive, but just barely." Ridge said quietly. "Actually, he was just a boy, not more than fifteen or sixteen. He asked for water, and I gave him some."

"What . . . what had happened to him?" Laurel's voice was barely a whisper.

"Bayonet wound."

She turned her head away to hide the pain that leaped to her face.

Ridge waited, wanting to comfort her, yet sensing that she would not want him to touch her. His mind leaped with possible reasons she cared about this boy, but there was no logical connection between Laurel Wilson and the letter addressed to Charley Bartlett.

When she had gained control again, Laurel turned to look up at him. "What about the letter?"

"I was coming to that. This soldier asked me to deliver it. There was no way I could do that, but it seemed so important to him that he pleaded with me to deliver it personally. So I promised, planning to do that after the war."

Ridge paused, remembering. He added softly, "Then he smiled a strange little smile I've never forgotten, said 'thanks,' and it was over."

Laurel wasn't sure she should, but she believed Ridge. She shut her eyes, trying to block out the scene of her brother's final moments of life.

The pain in her face touched Ridge. He stood before her, uncertain of what to say or do. He still did not know why she had taken the letter, but there was obviously some close personal reason.

She whirled around and placed her hands and face close to the car wall.

Ridge resisted the temptation to put his arms around her, just as he resisted asking why she had taken the letter. He could only wait.

After awhile, Laurel turned to face him again. She said in a choked voice, "I thank you for doing that for him."

He said accusingly, "You thought I had killed him, didn't you?"

"I thought it was possible."

Ridge's words were tinged with anger. "Do you think I would come across a young boy, not more than a child, and deliberately kill him?"

"I didn't want to. . . ." She began, then stopped.

They were both silent a moment, looking at each other. He wanted to know what connection there was between the letter and Laurel, but before he could ask, she spoke again. "Why do you sound angry with me?"

He took her by the shoulders. "Because I care what you think of me, and I don't want to care." His voice became husky. "I didn't think I could ever let myself have feelings for any woman again, especially when we've only known each other such a very short time."

"I know. I came on this trip determined to find Claude. Now I'm feeling confused and guilty."

"Do you love him?"

"I don't know."

He released her. "All I know is that I feel I've found something valuable, like what's in those strongboxes over there." He motioned toward them, then glanced back at her, adding quickly, "I shouldn't have said that."

"It's obvious that they're full of gold or silver," she replied.

He nodded. "I'm here helping guard them, but I've found something in you that's too precious to lose. At the same time, I'm trapped here and can't protect you when you need help."

She started to reply, but he smiled and spoke first. "I know; you can take care of yourself."

She returned the smile in spite of herself. "It's something I've always had to do."

Slowly, his face sobered. "Now I'd like to hear why you took my letter."

"Because it's intended for me. I'm Charley Bartlett."

"I thought your name was Laurel Wilson."

Her face grew grim. "I'm really Laurel Bartlett. Wilson is the name I use on my newspaper writing. Charley is a nickname, the only one I ever had. It was special to me because of who gave it to me."

"You mean Claude?"

"No, my brother." She dropped her head so that Ridge could not see her face start to contort again in pain.

"Your brother?"

"Yes." She looked up at Ridge. "He's the one who gave you that letter."

Ridge shook his head in bewilderment. "I don't understand . . . ."

"When Dorian was little," Laurel explained, "he couldn't say 'Laurel' correctly, so I tried to get him to call me by middle name of Charlotte. He couldn't say that either, but came up with Sharl, and finally, Charley.

"Seeing that nickname on the letter was so unexpected that I just reacted, grabbing the letter and running off with it. Reading it brought back those remembrances of before Dorian went to war."

A wan smile touched her lips. "You can't imagine what terrible things I was thinking about doing to you when I thought you had killed him."

"Maybe I can," he admitted, thinking of what he would like to do if he could ever learn who betrayed his command, causing his wound and his brother's death at Bethel Crossing.

Ridge continued, "I had some memories about my own brother when I was with Sarah and Aiken got unruly."

Laurel felt a lone tear start down her cheek. "I keep thinking I'll get over it, but it still hurts so much. . . ." Her voice broke.

Ridge instinctively reached out with both hands. "I understand."

She wanted to enter the comfort of his arms, but she checked herself. She avoided his hands, placing both of hers on his chest. She gently pushed him back. "I'm glad you weren't the one who killed him. I don't think I could handle that."

"In that, I think you and I are very much alike."

"Yes, I suppose." Laurel continued softly, "And in death, everyone is pretty much on the same side."

She added quickly, "Tell me something. Did you really go all the way to Chicago to deliver that letter?"

"Yes, I did."

"The war is over, and the postal service is running again, so why didn't you just mail it?"

"Because I promised to deliver it personally. In Chicago, I went to the right address, but was told that Charley Bartlett wasn't home."

"You could have left it with my father or even the servants."

"No, I couldn't. I had to keep my word. I didn't expect this job, but it's only for one trip, so when I returned to Chicago, I planned to try again."

Her eyes widened in wonder. "You would have kept on trying until you delivered it?"

"Yes."

The simple flat statement touched Laurel. "Even though you must have other things to do that are important to you?"

"I had some decisions to make anyway, and I figured that I would work them out in my mind while I was away from Virginia."

"And have you worked them out?"

"No. The fact is, since I met you, I'm more confused than ever."

She hesitated briefly before saying, "There is so much we don't know about each other."

A smile touched the corner of his lips. "Let's change that. Maybe at supper tonight?"

Laurel nodded. "I'd like that."

Sarah was still shaking her head when Laurel finished telling her about her conversation with Ridge.

Sarah glanced around the coach to make sure no one could overhear. "I hope," she mused, dropping her voice to a whisper, "you know what you're going to say when he wants to know about your life."

"That's not a problem."

"One part is. You can't tell him about being a Union spy during the war."

"Sh!" Laurel looked around hurriedly, "Don't ever say that word! I was a courier."

"No, you weren't. You didn't just carry messages back across enemy lines. You were a spy, plain and simple."

Laurel's panic showed in her voice. "Please, don't say that!"

"Why not? The war's over. You were proud of what you did

because you were doing something for our country. So what are you going to do about that? Lie to Ridge?"

Laurel didn't reply. She had never thought of telling anyone about her wartime activities. It was risky enough having Sarah know, but that had been necessary.

She had helped Laurel with disguises, plus creating hidden ways to conceal the information that Laurel discovered behind enemy lines and had to sneak back to the Union side. If that intelligence had been discovered by the Confederates, Laurel could have been hanged.

"Well?" Sarah asked a little impatiently. "How are you going to deal with that?"

The question echoed through Laurel's mind as darkness enveloped the train and she felt the cars begin to slow as the locomotive power eased off.

She looked down the aisle as Frederick Harkins made his way forward to apply the brakes on the tender when the engineer whistled for them. She realized with a start that the incident over her brother's letter had so occupied her thoughts that she had forgotten the danger facing her from the brakeman and the conductor.

I wonder if Schramm realizes his ledger is missing? Anyway, I've got to keep an eye on both of them, she sternly reminded herself. She glanced around but didn't see the conductor. When she faced front again, Harkins had passed out of sight, heading for the tender beyond the express car where Ridge was.

Ridge and Aiken looked up when they heard the engineer's whistle for the brakeman to get to his station. Ridge glanced at

Aiken and caught him watching from under half-closed eyelids. That made Ridge uneasy, because he had noticed this happening a couple of times in the last few hours.

Early in the trip, Aiken had never made any efforts to conceal his anti-South sentiments. There had been grudging respect after Ridge hinted at a possible duel if Aiken continued to call him Reb. Even the fight over Sarah hadn't seemed to make Aiken carry a grudge. Yet something had changed in the last few hours, and Ridge couldn't think why.

Shrugging off the feeling of tension, Ridge reviewed his conversation with Laurel. He tried to tell himself that it was wrong of him to even have a meal with her when she was betrothed and looking for her fiancé. But he found himself eagerly looking forward to their time together. The thought of how soon that would be stirred something warm and pleasant inside him.

He looked up expectantly when he felt the train begin to slow, coasting toward the next depot. He started to put his weapon down when Aiken broke the silence.

"Reckon I'll eat first tonight," he said, standing and placing his shotgun across the seat of his chair. "I'll go stand on the platform so when the train stops, I'll get a running start on those others who'll go rushing in to supper. You keep an eye on things here."

Ridge was surprised, expecting that he would again be first out of the express car so he could join Laurel at the evening meal. Disappointed, but having no choice, he watched Aiken walk across the floor and exit through the small end door leading to the outside platform next to the first passenger car.

But Ridge realized that Aiken would have a better chance of getting to the restaurant first if he were standing outside so he could be first off the train when it stopped rolling.

A late thought made Ridge abruptly hurry toward the small door through which Aiken had just passed. *I can send Laurel a message by him, saying I'll be late.*

Ridge stuck his head out of the small door, but Aiken was not on the small outside platform. Frowning, Ridge looked in all directions. He quietly asked himself, "Where did he go so quickly?"

Shaking his head in bewilderment, Ridge slowly returned to the lone chair. He hoped that the conductor or one of the train crew would come by and he could send a message to Laurel.

George Aiken had climbed the outside ladder to the roof of the adjacent passenger coach just before Ridge stepped onto the express car's platform. Aiken froze, hoping Ridge wouldn't look up. When he didn't, but returned to the express car's interior, Aiken relaxed and looked ahead. With satisfaction, he saw what he expected.

Frederick Harkins was also on the rooftop, carrying a lantern forward prior to scrambling down to the tender. There he would set the brakes when the engineer whistled for them.

Aiken, without a light, moved cautiously across the top of the car toward the unsuspecting brakeman.

Darkness had fallen before the train stopped outside a station called Smartville. Schramm, with a lantern in one hand, smilingly helped Laurel and Sarah step down from their car and said he hoped they enjoyed their supper.

They thanked him and walked together toward the row of lanterns marking the small restaurant and the adjoining depot. Sarah observed, "He seemed to be in a pleasant mood."

"That's good." *That must mean he hasn't found out about the missing ledger,* Laurel told herself. She glanced around for Ridge. She didn't see him and had a momentary feeling of panic that he had changed his mind and might not show up. But she knew in her heart that he would be there as soon as possible.

At the restaurant door, Laurel took a quick look back toward the train. Her pulse quickened at the sight of a man leaving the express car, but even in the weak light of the lanterns she realized it was the other express messenger, Aiken. She sighed in disappointment.

Sarah asked, "What's the matter?"

"Nothing." She tried to sound casual. "Why don't you go on in and order? I'll check with the telegrapher and the station agent about Claude, then I'll join you."

Sarah smiled knowingly. "You mean you're going to stall until it's Ridge's turn to eat, don't you?"

Returning the smile, Laurel replied, "Keep your thoughts to yourself or I'll find Lucas and tell him you want to have dinner with him."

"You wouldn't dare!"

"Try me." Laurel's eyes swept the shadows cast by the lanterns lighting the space between the depot and the train. "Speaking of Lucas, I wonder where he is?"

"I don't know and I don't care." Sarah entered the restaurant and Laurel headed for the agent's office.

She asked her usual questions about Claude, but the agent

said he hadn't seen anyone matching that description. Laurel thanked him and entered the telegrapher's office to query him.

He leaned back in his chair and scratched his head. "Seems to me I recollect something about a man answering that description," he mused. "Maybe it was something on the wire—"

He interrupted himself as the door burst open and the train engineer entered, his face flushed and eyes bright with excitement. He ignored Laurel to tell the telegrapher, "You better notify the superintendent that the brakeman just fell off the cars and got killed!"

"The brakeman?" Laurel repeated. "Harkins?"

"Yes, ma'am. A passenger and me found him."

Laurel closed her eyes. "How awful!" Yet she had a strange sense of relief that at least one of the two men plotting her death was gone.

The engineer waved toward the cars. "The passenger stayed with the body. It must've happened right after—" He stopped in midsentence when Lucas hurried into the room.

The engineer said reprovingly, "I thought you were going to stay with the body."

Lucas nodded to Laurel, then replied to the engineer. "I've got more news for you to telegraph."

"What news?" the engineer repeated. "He must have slipped under the wheels while setting the brakes."

"That's what it looked like," Lucas agreed, "but after you left I took a closer look. He didn't slip. He was murdered!"

Chapter 15

"**M**urdered?" Laurel exclaimed.

"Yes," Lucas replied, "from a blow to the back of the head."

The engineer protested. "That can't be!"

"Grab a lantern and I'll show you," Lucas said.

When they had gone, the telegrapher excused himself, telling Laurel he had better at least notify the superintendent that a brakeman was dead. Laurel nodded absently and stepped outside where she could see the men heading toward the tender.

If Lucas is right, she told herself, *Schramm must have killed Harkins even though they were partners in crime. But why would Schramm do that?*

She searched for possible answers by recalling the conversation overheard earlier between the conductor and the brakeman. They were concerned that she might have seen Woods, the Pinkerton agent, when he was killed.

If so, Harkins had said they would have to do something about her. But Schramm had warned the brakeman not to do anything to mess up their "big plans."

They had quarreled briefly, Laurel remembered, but nothing serious. At least, not enough to kill Harkins.

The night chill forced Laurel into the empty waiting room

where she continued thinking. *They have big plans, but for what?* she wondered. How did those fit in with murdering the brakeman? Whatever the plans were, they involved something so important that they were going to wait until afterward to deal with Laurel, and maybe Sarah, too. But did Harkins' death mean Schramm's strategy had changed? Laurel shook her head, unable to decide.

Word of the second murder had spread. Lanterns showed other crewmen and passengers leaving the buildings and rushing toward the tender. Laurel couldn't see Sarah, but guessed she was alone in the restaurant. Laurel pulled her cape tightly about herself, preparing to join her companion.

As Laurel stepped outside, the engineer and Lucas returned, trailed by other men.

"I was right," Lucas told her.

"Sure was," the engineer agreed, opening the door to the telegrapher's office. "Your friend here tells me that the man was knifed the other night, but someone struck the brakeman from behind, so he fell face first under the wheels. I sure missed that when I first found him."

Laurel wanted to say that Lucas was no friend of hers, but she remained silent. She was puzzled over the unexpected death of her suspected killer.

"There's one difference," Lucas said to Laurel, "this time you weren't anywhere close when it happened."

That was a relief, but Laurel murmured, "It's awful, having two murders on this one trip."

"What's worse," Lucas replied, "is that I don't think it's a coincidence. Until we know what's going on, there could be more murders, so you be careful."

Laurel wasn't sure if that were a veiled threat or a concerned warning. She watched Lucas follow the engineer into the small telegrapher's office and close the door against the other male passengers. She shook her head at the little man's high-handed ways and went to see Sarah.

Sarah looked up expectantly from where she sat alone at a back corner table. "I just heard there was another murder. Everyone went to see, even the cook. Who was it?"

Sliding into the opposite chair, Laurel glanced around to make sure they were alone. "Harkins."

Sarah gasped. "The brakeman?"

"Yes." Laurel briefly explained, adding, "This makes me concerned that the killer might come after me, and maybe you."

"I knew it!" Sarah slammed her palm down on the table, making the silverware clatter. "You're up to something that you won't tell me about, yet you're putting my life in jeopardy, too!"

"That's why I need to talk to you about it." She added quickly, "You already know part of it."

Sarah's face grew pale as Laurel told her about overhearing the conversation between Schramm and another man. "I thought it was Harkins," she concluded, "but now I'm not so sure."

"You're frightening me to death!" Sarah whispered. "If it wasn't Harkins, who was it?"

"I don't know," Laurel admitted. "I know for sure that I heard Schramm plotting with another man. I didn't see him, but I thought I recognized the brakeman's voice. That raises the possibility that either Schramm killed Harkins, or else I was mistaken and it wasn't him I overheard plotting with the conductor."

"What are you saying?" Sarah asked in a low tone.

"If it wasn't the brakeman I overheard, that means someone

else killed that first man, and so both the real killer and Schramm are still on our train."

Sarah gripped both of Laurel's hands. "They're after you, and probably me, too. But I'm innocent!"

"I know. I didn't meant to get you involved in this, but you have a right to know it's dangerous. The one consolation is that they're probably not going to do anything until after whatever this big thing is they've got coming up."

"What do you think that is?"

"I don't know, but our trip ends tomorrow evening, so it's got to happen between now and then."

Sarah moaned softly, "You're used to being in danger, but I'm not. What are you going to do about this?"

"First, I'm going to send a telegram to Allan Pinkerton—"

Sarah interrupted. "So you are working for him!"

Laurel wanted to keep her word to the head of the detective agency. She protested, "I didn't say that."

"No, but I'm beginning to see the whole thing!" Sarah's voice rose angrily. She leaped to her feet, knocking over her chair as Laurel also stood.

Sarah glared across the table. "You wanted to get that ledger from Schramm to prove he was stealing from the railroad. I've read about Pinkerton doing that. But things got out of hand when he and whoever this other man is thought you had seen that detective killed back on Friday night in Brookeville."

She shook her finger in Laurel's face and continued her tirade. "Now they think you told me—which you have—and I could be killed, too. How could you do this?"

"I didn't mean to. Anyway, I'll do my best to keep you safe."

"Oh, sure! You can say that, but you don't have a weapon,

and who can we trust to look out for us?"

Laurel thought of Ridge, but he couldn't help from within the express car. "I'm working on that. Now, let's go join the men at the telegraph office. No matter what I do, you stay right in the middle of them where you'll be safe."

"What are you going to do?"

"First, I'm going to send another telegram."

Ridge heard someone approaching the rear door to the express car. He shifted the shotgun, then relaxed as he recognized the fireman in his dirty overalls.

He asked excitedly, "You heard the news?"

Ridge felt a stab of anxiety. "No. Aiken hasn't returned from supper. What happened?"

"Harkins, the brakeman, got himself killed."

Ridge quickly crossed the coach floor. "How?"

The fireman briefly explained.

"The women?" Ridge asked quickly. "Are they all right?"

"Oh, sure. Last I saw, the pretty one was talking to the telegrapher. The other one was having supper same time I was."

Ridge controlled a quiet sigh of relief. "Is that all you know?"

"That's it. Oh, here comes Aiken. Maybe he knows more than I do."

The burly express guard picked his teeth with a sharpened matchstick while Ridge and the fireman asked what he knew about the murder.

"Nothing," Aiken replied, "except he's dead. I'm lucky I got served before they found the body. Ridge, you may as well go eat, if the cook and the rest of the restaurant staff have had enough looking to return to their duties."

The distraught fireman exclaimed, "How can you expect him to eat at a time like this? A man is dead—"

"Ain't you never seen a dead man before?" Aiken interrupted. "Me and Ridge here, we both seen plenty in the war. Ain't that right?"

Ridge looked at Aiken without responding to his question. "I'm not hungry right now, but I think I'll go look around."

Aiken laughed. "You mean you're going looking for that pretty little woman."

Ridge silently pulled on his Confederate overcoat with the long cape, then hurried out the door.

While the other passengers and some of the crew waited in the restaurant for the sheriff to arrive, Laurel sat alone in the deserted waiting room composing a coded two-line message to Allan Pinkerton.

She reread the first line again: *Good trip so far. Urgent Uncle Homer meet me at end of the line.*

As previously agreed with the head of the detective agency, that would indicate two things: she had found the evidence needed against the crooked railroad conductor, and another agent was to be on hand at the depot so she could quickly transfer the proof to him.

If Schramm suspected her, he could not try to take the proof from her on the train. She wanted to pass it on in case he tried to accost her after the trip was over.

Then she added a straightforward sentence that would alert Pinkerton that she felt some concern: *Train expected to be delayed here while authorities investigate a second murder on the cars.*

Satisfied, she stood up and headed for the door just as Ridge opened it from the outside.

"There you are," he said with a controlled sigh of relief.

She smiled, relieved that he had shown up. "I was just going to send a telegram."

"Mind if I accompany you?"

"I would appreciate it."

He held the door for her while she pulled her cape tighter and stepped into the crisp night air.

"Brr!" she said with a shiver, "winter seems to be coming on fast."

He offered his arm. She took it, aware of the strength concealed under the overcoat. She was reminded of how she had felt when she accidentally backed into his arms after finding the first murder victim.

Stop it! she sternly told herself. Admittedly, she was attracted to Ridge, but she resisted the temptation to let a relationship develop.

I'll forget about him when I find Claude, but I've got to do that fast because this trip is almost over. Even if Pinkerton keeps me on as a detective, he wouldn't be likely to send me this direction again. So concentrate on finding Claude fast, and staying alive!

Ridge broke into her thoughts. "As soon as your message is sent, perhaps you would join me at supper. It'll be warm in the restaurant."

"I should think so. If it's anything like last time, we'll all be delayed there until the local sheriff finishes asking us questions." Laurel didn't want to talk about Harkins because of unanswered questions in her mind. She added, "We'll be very late getting to the end of the line tomorrow."

"I suppose." He slowed at the telegrapher's door to ask her, "What will you do then—go back to Chicago with Sarah?"

"Probably. How about you?"

"I only took this job for one trip. Now that I've delivered that letter, I don't necessarily even have to return to Chicago."

"You're going back to Virginia?" She didn't know why, but she felt a sense of sadness at that thought.

"I still haven't made up my mind." He opened the door, followed her inside, then closed it.

"I'll only be a minute," she said, and handed her message to the telegrapher.

When the transaction was completed, Laurel and Ridge left and headed toward the restaurant. It was full of people milling about in small circles, obviously waiting for the sheriff to arrive.

When Laurel and Ridge were seated at a corner table, he said, "I ran into Sarah while looking for you awhile ago in that crowd. She tells me that she's going back to Chicago and make up with her beau."

"She said that?"

"Yes. Didn't you know?"

"She threatened to do so, but I guess I didn't believe her. She's not used to being around danger."

Ridge asked with a smile, "And you are?"

Laurel thought fast, then smiled. "You've heard about the first battle of Bull Run?"

"In the South, we called it First Manassas. There was a second battle there later. Why do you ask?"

"I was at that first great battle of the war."

Ridge stared in surprise. So were he and his cavalry troop, but he didn't want to say that, not yet, anyway. He exclaimed, "You were?"

She nodded, "I was barely fifteen at the time. Papa had taken me to Washington, D.C., shortly after the war started. So we were there that Sunday, July 21, 1861. Bull Run Creek was only about twenty-five miles out of Washington, D.C.

"It was so close, in fact, that everyone heard there was going to be a battle. But the North was so sure of winning that people thought of it as a kind of holiday. Papa even took me. We joined the crowds headed there on cars, in carriages, or on horseback. People went whatever way they could.

"Looking back, it's hard to imagine such a thing. We were all civilians, including lots of women, about seventy-five newspaper correspondents from both sides, plus a few senators and congressmen. Some people actually brought opera glasses, champagne, and picnic baskets to watch men kill each other."

Ridge remembered that it had not been a picnic for him or his mounted troops, but he wanted Laurel to keep talking so he could learn more about her. He asked, "What happened to you and your father?"

"We only got as far as Centreville, some six miles from Bull Run, but it was close enough so that we could see smoke and hear the cannons. Later, I read that President Lincoln's own private secretary was there, along with six congressmen, some senators—"

"Yes," Ridge interrupted. "I heard that we captured one senator and put him in prison." He hesitated, then added, "that's where the Rebel Yell originated and General Jackson got his nickname of Stonewall."

The waiter interrupted to take their order. When he left, Ridge urged Laurel to continue her story. She took a deep, shuddering breath, recalling that it was about the time of First Bull Run that she had started rebelling against her father.

Laurel said with a slight catch in her voice, "At first, it seemed our Union troops were winning, then it all changed and our boys began running away. They threw away their weapons, their knapsacks, and everything else in their mad scramble to escape. They trampled over us civilians. In that mad scramble, I got separated from my father, and we couldn't find each other."

"What happened? Did you get hurt?"

"No, just a few bruises and scratches. I hid under a stone bridge with dead and wounded men all around me. But those who weren't wounded didn't stop to help. They all kept trying to save their own lives by getting back to Washington. I found a riderless saddle horse with his reins caught on a tree limb. I jumped on him and rode away before the Rebels . . . uh . . . Confederates got there."

"You found your way alone back to Washington?" When Laurel nodded, Ridge shook his head in amazement. "You must have been quite independent and self-reliant, even then."

"It was frightening, especially when it was rumored that the Confederates would just keep going and take Washington. If they had, of course, the war would have been over right then. However, for whatever reason, the Confederates didn't push their advantage."

"Yes, that's true," Ridge replied somberly. He had his own

private opinion about the Southern decision to not cross the Potomac and seize the northern capital. He added, "Some folks say that First Manassas was a great victory for the South. Others say that's when we lost the war—because we didn't finish the job at the time. So it took another three years before that was official."

"Be that as it may, Ridge, that experience not only taught me to control my fear, but I also found a thrill in all the excitement."

He asked with a teasing tone, "So that's what made you so saucy?"

"It made me realize I could take care of myself."

The waiter arrived with their food. The conversation changed until they were finishing dessert when Ridge returned to talking about the Battle of First Manassas. He asked, "Do you know why we Confederates won?"

"I've heard all kinds of reasons given."

"The real reason is because of a spy in Washington, a woman spy."

Laurel stopped, her heart leaping in anxiety. "A spy?"

"Yes. Her name was Rose O'Neal Greenhow. A widow, she lived right in the capital. She learned that the Union General, Irvin McDowell, planned a surprise attack against our General Beauregard's troops near Bull Run Creek. Mrs. Greenhow got word to our generals, even including the Union's plans to cut railroad lines to prevent us from sending reinforcements. So the Federals got a real surprise when we beat them."

Laurel asked cautiously, "You approve of spies?"

"My approval had nothing to do with war. There were countless spies in both the North and the South in the late unpleasantness. I'm convinced that one of them learned of my troop's plans. That led to the ambush where my brother was killed and I got a Yankee minié ball in my leg as a souvenir."

She looked sharply at him as his voice grew cold.

Through clenched teeth he growled, "If I could ever find out who that spy was. . . ."

He didn't finish his thought, but Laurel shrank back from the fierce anger that flared in his eyes and hardened his jaw. She was unable to move, wanting to ask where this ambush had taken place, and yet she was afraid of the answer.

She was saved from further anxiety when Sarah came out of a side dining room door to call, "You two about through? The sheriff is here and wants to question everyone in here."

"We're just finishing," Laurel replied, then turned to look across the table at Ridge. "Thanks for supper, but you'd better go on in. I need a moment alone with Sarah."

"Oh? I hope I didn't do the wrong thing in telling you what she said about returning to her beau."

"No, no! It's not that. Please, give me a minute."

"All right, but don't be long. I have to get back to the express car as soon as possible."

He went on, relaying the message to Sarah that Laurel wanted to see her.

As Laurel pulled Sarah outside, Sarah asked tartly, "What's so important that you have to drag me all the way out here in this weather?"

"I've got to know something. Did you tell Ridge that you're going to return to Chicago and make up with John?"

"Yes, I did. And why not?" Sarah hugged herself against the cold night air. "Ridge isn't interested in me, but John is. I was blind not to see that he and I are much more suited to each other than I thought before. Now, let's get inside—"

"Just a second more. Did you ever say anything to Ridge about my . . . uh . . . work during the war?"

"No, of course not. Why do you ask?"

With a gentle sigh, Laurel replied, "No special reason."

"Nonsense!" Sarah snapped. "Ridge only has eyes for you, but you're blind and can't see it. You're still thinking about that useless Claude Duncan. If you keep that up, you'll lose Ridge!"

"That's not an issue now!"

"Oh, yes it is! Ridge will probably never say anything to you because he's too much of a gentleman, too gallant, knowing that you're looking for your fiancé. And you won't even listen to your own heart! Frankly, Laurel, I'm losing respect for you!"

Sarah whirled about, opened the restaurant door and rushed through it, slamming it hard.

Laurel stood staring after her. *What in the world has gotten into her?*

Laurel spun around at the sound of heavy footsteps behind her on the wooden platform. By the light of the lanterns, she recognized Jacob Lucas approaching.

"Good evening, Miss Wilson," he said, doffing his hat. "I'm glad I found you alone."

"I was just going inside. Sarah says the sheriff is here about the second murder."

"That will wait." He came up and stopped before her. "I just came from the telegrapher's office."

Checking to see if I sent another telegram, Laurel thought. "I'm sure that's interesting to you, Mr. Lucas, but I've got to get inside."

"Wait!" He lightly took her elbow as she started to turn away.

"Everywhere you've gone, you've asked about Claude Duncan—"

She interrupted, "You know where he is?"

"No, but you've also mentioned a friend of his named Ambrose Nevers. I know where he is."

"You do? Where?"

"The telegrapher read me a message he had just received, saying that some men had been jailed on charges of committing that robbery where those women and the child were killed. One of the prisoners is Ambrose Nevers."

Laurel looked hard at the short, big-chested man. "Mr. Lucas, if you're lying to me—"

"No, honestly! Go ask the telegrapher to let you read it for yourself."

"Thank you. I will, because Ambrose may know where Claude is." She started walking very rapidly back toward the telegrapher's office with Lucas half a step behind.

She fought down a sickening feeling when she also remembered what another telegrapher had told her about a man in an earlier raid answering Claude's description.

Moments later, the telegrapher had confirmed Lucas' story. In a rural county seat called Turkey Trot, a few miles away, some men had been caught trying to break into the treasurer's office. In a gunfight, one of the attackers was killed. Four others had been captured, including Ambrose Nevers. No other names were yet known.

The telegrapher waited until Laurel had finished reading before he spoke. "I'm right sorry, Miss. He a friend of yours?"

"I've known him since we were children. I need to see him. He may know where my fiancé is."

A frown creased the telegrapher's brow. "You might need to

be in a hurry to do that."

She raised her eyebrows questioningly.

He squirmed in his seat and lowered his eyes. "Another message came in after that one." He reached for a sheet on the desk near his telegraph key. "I'm not sure you want to know about this, though."

"Please! I must know."

Glancing first at Lucas, who nodded, the telegrapher read aloud from the later dispatch. "There is talk of a vigilance committee planning to seize the prisoners from the jail because of the repeated wanton killing of women and children in recent months—"

"Vigilance committee?" Laurel interrupted in alarm. "You mean mob justice?"

"Call it what you want, Miss. That's what it says here."

She turned to Lucas. "Do you think Ambrose might be hanged without a trial?"

"Some folks say that lawlessness has been going on far too long, so it's possible."

"Excuse me!" Laurel turned toward the door. "I've got to talk to him before . . . before anything happens."

Lucas asked sharply, "Where are you going?"

"To tell Sarah. Oh, we'll need a rig." She looked at the telegrapher. "Is there a livery stable close by where we can rent a horse and buggy?"

"Yes, just down that side street." He pointed. "The owner lives in back, so you can rent a rig anytime."

"Thank you." Laurel opened the door and stepped into the night. She lifted her skirt slightly to take longer strides. Her footsteps were echoed by Lucas' on the wooden platform.

"Miss Wilson, you're surely not thinking of going off alone in the night, just two women in a country filled with lawless men?"

"I have no choice. I must talk to Ambrose before it's too late."

"It's madness!" Lucas caught up with her and placed a restraining hand on her arm. "Don't do it!"

"Let go of me!"

He obeyed, but said, "Then let me go with you!"

"No, thank you! I don't like you, Mr. Lucas! You've followed me and you've frightened me." She broke into a little run toward the restaurant.

"Very well, if you insist. I'll assist by renting a horse and carriage for you and Miss Perkins."

Laurel didn't look back, but hurriedly entered the restaurant. She located Sarah and Ridge standing side-by-side with all the men who were clustered around a uniformed sheriff. Laurel didn't even look at Ridge but roughly grabbed Sarah by the arm and pulled her aside.

"What's the matter with you?" Sarah demanded. "You should be listening—"

"I've found out where Ambrose is. We've got to go to him right now."

"At night in strange country? That's too risky!"

"We must. That's all you need to know for now. Come on, we'll rent a carriage and I'll tell you on the way."

"You've lost your senses! No! I'm not going."

"You've got to!"

"No, I don't! I've made up my mind. As soon as I can get a train heading north, I'm on my way home. And I'm never again going to risk my life as you do yours!"

Laurel suppressed a moan of disappointment. "It may be my only chance to find Claude!"

"My decision is final–no!" Sarah headed back toward the group of men just as Ridge pushed his way through. He stopped and spoke to Sarah.

Laurel spun on her heel. *I don't want to talk to him right now!*

She raced out the door onto the station platform. "Mr. Lucas!" she called as he headed down the side street toward the livery stable. "Wait for me!"

Chapter 16

Laurel sat hunched over on the single seat as the horse's hooves rhythmically rose and fell on the dirt road. Even snuggled under the lap robe for the open four-wheeled runabout that the livery-man had provided, Laurel shivered while struggling to see beyond the pale glow of the vehicle's twin kerosene lamps.

"You still cold?" Lucas asked from where he sat beside her with the reins in his hands. He wore an old Federal sky blue wool kersey overcoat with short cape and stand-up collar that he had retrieved from the train before driving into the moonless night.

"A little," Laurel admitted, but she suspected that excitement and concern were affecting her more than the sharp night air.

Three major thoughts had occupied her on most of the five miles they had covered so far. What would happen when she saw Ambrose? How angry would the sheriff be with her and Lucas for leaving a murder investigation without permission?

Laurel had misgivings about her hasty decision to let Lucas accompany her. In one way, it was comforting to have an armed male escort along. However, he had earlier done some things that bothered her.

She tried not to think about why he had asked the telegrapher at Brookeville about the message she had sent. She didn't know why he had followed her at Trinity until she ordered him to stop. But now he was her only hope of getting to see Ambrose Nevers before the vigilantes hanged him. That was her third and main concern.

Lucas broke into her reveries. "You feel like talking about this Ambrose person?"

Laurel was not inclined to discuss personal matters with a man she didn't really know, but the night was cold, lonely, and foreboding. Her introspection tended to be more gloomy with silence.

Ambrose, like Claude, had always been wild, she reminded herself while the mare plodded steadily along the desolate country road. Yet it had never occurred to her that either might be accused of being in an outlaw band, especially one that killed women and children.

She said to Lucas, "As I told you back there, he and my fiancé were friends. We all grew up together."

"You think Ambrose may know where your beau is?"

Laurel explained how Ambrose had returned to Chicago after the war, saying he and Claude had walked out of Georgia's infamous Anderson prisoner-of-war camp together five months ago. "But," she concluded, "I never saw nor heard from Claude, not a word. Then, Ambrose recently returned from a trip, telling me that he had seen Claude working on a railroad near Trinity."

"So that's why you were running all around back there before the replacement engine arrived?" When she nodded, Lucas added, "But you obviously didn't learn of his whereabouts."

"No, I didn't. That's why it's so important that I talk to Ambrose before . . . I mean, as soon as possible."

"We're almost there." Lucas pointed ahead and to the right of the gently rolling countryside. "I can see lights of the town."

The horse suddenly shied, making Lucas tighten the reins and speak soothingly. "Easy, there! Settle down!"

Laurel tried to see what had spooked the mare, but there was nothing visible except her shadow cast by the twin kerosene lamps on the runabout. "What do you suppose scared her?" Laurel asked quietly.

"Something ahead and off to our left." Lucas motioned with his head. "But it can't be anything really dangerous. This is too close to town, so there won't be any big wild animals or anything like that around."

Straining to see, Laurel asked in a low tone, "Could it be a guerrilla band?"

"I don't think so. Listen! I hear something."

He pulled back on the reins and brought the mare to a stop. She blew noisily, still looking with her ears cocked ahead and to the left.

"Hear it?" Lucas whispered.

"Yes. I can't see anything, but it sounds a little like a train moving slowly, yet I don't see a headlight."

Lucas glanced ahead. "You're right. I can barely make out a railroad crossing just ahead. I remember it from when I was in Turkey Trot before. But why would cars be running without lights or a bell? And why isn't the engineer giving a warning whistles for that crossing?"

Laurel didn't answer as the locomotive slowly became a visible separate entity emerging from the darkness. Enough of a glow from the town's pale lamps outlined the black engine so it was recognizable as it passed the road in front of the runabout. The engine pulled only the tender and two coaches. They moved ominously toward the community with no sound except the clank of wheels on steel rails, the stroke of drive wheels, and the hiss of engine steam.

The moment it passed, Lucas snapped the reins smartly over the horse's back. "I think I know what that is," he declared as the mare leaped ahead. "We've got to get into town fast!"

"Why? What is it?" Laurel asked in alarm.

"Vigilantes!" Instead of crossing the tracks, Lucas turned the horse to the right and drove parallel to them along a faint wagon road. "Let's hope we're not too late!" he cried, pulling the light whip from its socket and snapping it over the running mare.

Ridge had silently fumed since the sheriff, followed by the others from the train, had run out the restaurant door and vainly shouted for Laurel and Lucas to stop. The sound of their carriage heading out of town away from the restaurant had upset the officer. However, he had no deputy or backup with him, so he had let them go and resumed interrogating the others.

When he finished, the tall sheriff closed his notebook and said he now had everyone's statement about the murder except for the two who had fled the scene.

Ridge seized Sarah's arm and pulled her away from the others. "What's going on?" he demanded. "Where did Laurel go with Lucas?"

"She found out where Ambrose is and wanted to go to him right away in hopes he would know where Claude is."

Ridge scowled. "Where is this Ambrose?"

"She didn't say. She wanted us to rent a carriage and said she would tell me on the way, but I wouldn't go. So she went off with Lucas."

"What does she know about this man?" Ridge asked.

"Not much. When Mr. Lucas first got on the cars, he said that his wife was dead, so he was going south to be with his daughter who was expecting her first baby. He also said he felt like a father to us, and he has a pistol."

"Laurel must have been really desperate to see this friend of hers if she went off with a man like Lucas at a time like this," Ridge mused.

He looked out the window at the darkness. "I would like to go find her," he said thoughtfully, his voice thick with concern, "but I'm obliged to guard that coach with George Aiken to the end of the line."

Sarah clearly saw his dilemma and tried to ease his distress. "She'll be all right, so you needn't fret."

"I'm trying." The anguish in his voice touched Sarah. "I recently swore that I would not let myself care about another woman. I've only known Laurel for a few days, but she's done something to me. I feel a little silly, but I can't help myself."

An ache began deep inside Sarah. No man had ever expressed such strong feelings for her, not even John, even though he was a good man. She cautioned Ridge, "You should get to know Laurel better before you get too involved with her."

"I've already learned a lot about her, even in these few days. She is beautiful, headstrong, self-reliant, and has a smile that would melt a stone." He shook his head. "She reminds me of a magnificent unbroken horse I used to own. With gentleness and time, she became the most perfect animal I've ever seen."

He grinned. "If she thought I was comparing her to a horse, Laurel would probably never speak to me again."

Sarah mused thoughtfully, "You're really smitten, aren't you?"

"I've tried to put her out of my mind, but I can't."

"Well, you would be so much better for her than that Claude, even though you and Laurel were on opposite sides of the war. But that's over."

Taking a slow breath, Ridge declared quietly, "For some of us, it may never be over."

"You can't let the past ruin the future! To go on, there comes a time when you have to forgive and forget."

"You sound like that preacher we heard Sunday."

"I'm just being practical. I'm sure you had to do things in the war that you would rather not have done."

When Ridge nodded, Sarah continued, "So did Laurel."

His eyebrows shot up. "What do you mean?"

Still touched by the deep feelings he had just expressed about Laurel, Sarah tried to explain. "You have to understand that when her brother got killed–the only person in her family she felt who really loved her–she felt she had to do something besides make bandages and knit socks for the boys. That's what most women did. But Laurel doesn't think of herself as ever being a spy, more of a courier–"

"What?" Ridge interrupted. "Did you say 'spy'?"

Dismayed at her verbal slip, Sarah hurriedly added, "It wasn't something she wanted to do, but she felt that she could save thousands of Federal soldiers' lives by crossing enemy lines to gather military intelligence."

Ridge stared in disbelief as Sarah plunged ahead.

"She was doing her job, the same as you were doing yours in that war. Why, at Bethel Crossing alone, she has been credited with saving thousands of Union—"

"Bethel Crossing?" Ridge exclaimed so loudly that people in the restaurant turned to stare. "She's responsible for the massacre at Bethel Crossing?"

"Massacre?" Alarmed, Sarah repeated a little lamely, "She was just doing her job."

"Her job killed my brother!"

Sarah's mouth dropped open. "That happened at Bethel Crossing?"

"Yes! He was killed and I got this leg wound that will make me limp the rest of my life!"

"Oh, my!" Sarah whispered in shock. "What have I done?"

⚓

The mare was starting to sweat when Lucas turned her onto the cobblestone main street where the train had halted in front of a few single-story brick buildings. Laurel saw the last of some vigilantes in black hoods pour out of the cars, silently cross the street, and turn right along the boardwalk.

She asked Lucas, "Where are they going?"

"There." He reined in at a hitching rail and pointed to a small, one-story building where another black-hooded man held up a lantern. The word "Jail" showed briefly in the yellow light. About fifty men quietly surrounded the building, leaving half a dozen or so in front.

Laurel started to alight, but a vigilante with a rifle in his arm moved away from the others and blocked her way.

"You can't stop here."

"I must!" she exclaimed. She stepped up onto the boardwalk directly in front of the rifleman while the other masked men turned to stare at her in disapproving silence.

"No woman should see this," the man with the rifle mumbled through his hood. "Driver," he said to Lucas, "get her out of here fast!"

"No, please listen!" Laurel cried, looking beyond the man blocking her way to the others who waited outside the jail door. "I'm a childhood friend of Ambrose Nevers, and I must see him!"

"No, and that's final!" The man with the rifle turned and nodded to the others. One produced a key and opened the door.

"Please, Sir!" Laurel exclaimed, trying to step past the first vigilante. "Give me a few minutes with him."

"No! I told you that you shouldn't see this."

Frightened yells erupted from inside the jail, making Laurel take a step back. About a dozen masked men emerged from the jail, forcibly bringing two prisoners into the lantern light. Laurel didn't recognize them. Still without a word, the vigilantes dragged the shrieking victims toward a nearby tree.

Laurel turned away and opened her mouth to again petition the man with the rifle, but Lucas spoke first.

"Sir," he said, "let this young woman pray with Ambrose Nevers."

"He's not worth your prayers, Miss," the guard told Laurel. "His soul is blacker than most because he killed women and little children."

Lucas said quickly, "All the more reason he needs a prayer before meeting his Maker. You strike me as the kind of man who would understand that."

"Please," Laurel asked softly, her voice breaking.

"All right, but only for a couple of minutes." The vigilante motioned to another hooded man with a rifle. He picked up a lantern and motioned for Laurel to follow him.

Without a word, he led her down a small hallway with a solid wall on one side and a row of four cells on the other. The vigilante's lantern showed one man sitting on a simple iron bunk at the back of the last cell. His chin rested on his chest.

The guide said gruffly, "This lady wants to pray for your black soul, so get over here."

The prisoner didn't even look up.

Laurel called softly, "Ambrose?"

He leaped up. "Laurel! Is that really you?"

She turned to the guide. "Could I be alone with him?"

"Sorry, Miss. No offense, but I can't risk having a gun slipped to him. I'll stand back so I won't hear, but I must watch."

"Thank you." She turned and gripped Ambrose's hands ,which he thrust through the bars.

"You came to get me out?" he asked eagerly.

Slowly, she shook her head. "I'm sorry I can't do that." She hesitated to tell this lifelong friend that she had only come to ask about Claude. But she glanced at the watching vigilante before asking Ambrose, "Would you like to pray?"

"What for?" Bitterness dripped from the words. "I'll die the way I lived."

Laurel was startled to realize that shocked her. "Please don't say that!"

"I thought you'd quit praying a long time ago. So why? . . . Oh, I see! You really came to ask if I could tell you where to find Claude, didn't you?"

"I must find him."

A hoarse laugh exploded from Ambrose, making Laurel release his hands and draw back in surprise.

"You won't have no trouble doin' that, Laurel, that is, if you hurry."

She didn't understand, but there wasn't time to ask for clarification. "Where is he?"

Ambrose's face sobered. "Ask him." He tilted his chin toward the watching vigilante.

Laurel started to, but stopped upon hearing heavy footsteps in the hallway. Half a dozen men in black hoods purposely approached.

The one who had been watching the cell stepped close and said quietly, "You've got to go now, Miss."

Laurel numbly turned to look at Ambrose through the bars. His face had become as blank as the hoods the captors wore.

"I guess I can do one right thing before I die," Ambrose said in a low but controlled tone. "I know why Claude never returned to you after the war."

"You do?"

"Yes. Once he made me really mad, so I got even by boasting of the one thing I knew would hurt him. I lied, telling him that you and I . . . well . . . you know."

The tears that had started to form behind her eyelids stopped cold. "You what?" she exploded.

"I said we did . . . on several occasions."

Stunned by this monstrous lie, Laurel demanded furiously, "You've got to tell him the truth!"

Laconically, Ambrose glanced at his captors. "I don't think they're going to give me time to do that."

"Then tell me where Claude is so I can tell him what a lie you told!"

"We're all liars, aren't we?" Ambrose asked.

Laurel turned to face the approaching prisoner escort. "You've got to give him a few more minutes! He has something terribly important to do!"

One of the newly arrived vigilantes with keys reached for the cell door. "Sorry, Miss, but this man has a previous engagement that must be kept."

Helplessly, she stepped aside while the group of masked men roughly seized Ambrose. As they pulled him away, he called, "If you hurry, you can tell Claude that I made a dying confession: I lied to him about you and me. I'm sorry, Laurel, really, I am."

She turned her face as a man she had known all her life was led away to be lynched. She was too filled with indignation to answer and too numb with shock to cry.

Ambrose did not shriek or resist as the first two men had when they were dragged away. Laurel vaguely heard the many footsteps fade down the hallway.

The guide with the rifle said quietly, "Miss, if you want to see this other prisoner, you'd better hurry."

"Claude Duncan?" She asked. "He's here?"

The vigilante nodded. "He's the gang leader, so we kept him in a special cell to hang last."

"He's the gang leader?" Laurel cried in disbelief.

"He sure is, so we couldn't take a chance on him escaping until he paid for his crimes. Come on."

Reeling from this second unexpected blow, Laurel dully followed the vigilante out of the jail.

She was vaguely aware that her guide waved Lucas back

when he started to approach her. Emotionally paralyzed, Laurel trailed the armed vigilante down the boardwalk. Except for the hooded men and Lucas, the streets were deserted.

At the courthouse, Laurel's guide walked past a saddled horse hitched to a rail. She followed the silent vigilante down some outside courthouse stairs to a moist-smelling basement with a single, double-barred cell. Another vigilante rose from a chair facing the bars and holstered his heavy pistol.

Her rifle-carrying guide said before he left, "She's a friend. Give her a few minutes."

Laurel approached the barred cell door with mixed feelings. She had finally found Claude, but under the circumstances, there was no joy in it. She was also filled with indignation over the horrible crimes Claude and Ambrose had committed, and the terrible lie Ambrose had told Claude about her.

"Laurel?" Claude asked, turning from where he had been standing in a back corner of his small quarters.

She nodded but didn't reply while her torn emotions gripped her. She had decided not to volunteer that she had just talked to Ambrose. She wanted to learn for herself if he had indeed told Claude those lies, and if Claude led a gang that killed innocent women and children.

Unhurriedly, he took the few steps across the cell and reached through to take both her hands. "It is you."

She didn't trust herself to speak, but gazed at him and tried to think how to say what was on her mind. During the search for him, she had rehearsed what it would be like to see him again. Yet in the last several minutes, Ambrose's revelation had smashed those images.

"How did you find me?" he asked, pulling her close to the

bars of the cell.

"I came looking for you." She locked her blue eyes on his gray ones where they were partially hidden by heavy reddish eyebrows. As always, she could not see into him the way she could with other men.

"You shaved your beard," she continued, noticing that he was still handsome and looked fit, although his light blond hair was uncombed. She added, "You look good for having been in a prison camp."

"Prison?" he asked, then laughed. "Oh, that! Well, truth is, neither Ambrose nor I were ever prisoners."

"You weren't?"

"No. We deserted again. But you didn't come here to talk about that."

She wasn't really surprised at his confession. It was just another lie. "No," she said, her voice was low but firm, "I came to see why you never returned to me, and if you really led a gang of outlaws who did such terrible things that caused a vigilance committee to be formed."

"I just did what Quantrill did." Claude dropped her hands and shrugged indifferently. "I had big plans for after the war, and they kept me busy."

"Too busy to visit me even though we were engaged?"

"Engaged? Oh, you mean that time in the buggy when we were joking about how to hurt your old man's feelings. How did he take it when you told him?"

Laurel chose not to answer that. Instead, she asked, "So you never loved me?"

"Love? What gave you that idea?" He saw the stricken look in her eyes and added soberly, "You didn't ever say you loved me, so why should I?"

"Never mind!" She broke in quickly, trying to hold back the feeling of foolishness that swept over her. She wanted to turn and run from her folly, but there was one more thing she had to do. She tried to think of how to say it the way she wanted.

Claude spoke first, "Anyway, I was so angry at you because of what happened with you and Ambrose. You really disappointed me, Laurel."

That broke the dam, and her words exploded. "I disappointed? . . ." She started to sputter in anger, but got control so she spoke rapidly and with great passion.

"You know better than that! No man has touched me, ever!"

Claude shrugged. "If you say so."

"You don't believe me!" Her indignation rose with her tone.

"You were always a pretty good little liar, Laurel. I don't blame Ambrose, so there's no use in your denying what happened."

"Stop!" She gripped the bars in fury and pushed her face close to them. "You don't want to believe me! Well, I may have told a lie now and then, but so help me, I'm telling you the truth now! Nothing ever happened between me and Ambrose!"

She let go of the bars and took a step back and dropped her voice. "I've known you all my life," she said sadly, "and yet I never knew you—not really—not even a little bit. I've been a fool! A very big fool!"

She felt the guard step close and take her elbow to lead her away. She didn't resist, but turned to speak over her shoulder. "It's a terrible thing for me to think at a time like this, but you need to know. I just realized that you're not worth the time I've spent looking for you!"

In great pain, she turned and blindly ran back toward the basement stairs and out into the night.

Still in shock, she was only remotely aware that Lucas helped her back into the runabout, covered her with the lap robe, and then silently backed the horse into the unpaved street.

Even though Lucas took care to drive down a side road, away from the vigilantes silently keeping their vigil outside the jail, Laurel caught one quick glimpse of three bodies hanging from a massive limb of the winter-bare tree growing at the end of the boardwalk.

She knew that Ambrose was among them. Soon Claude would join them.

The carriage passed the locomotive and two coaches that still stood without lights, waiting to return the hooded passengers to wherever they had come from.

Shouting and a volley of shots shattered the night's stillness, making Lucas swivel in the seat and look back, but Laurel did not move. She sat with her head down, dark curls hiding her face.

"Celebrating, I guess," Lucas commented, again facing forward. "Terrible thing to celebrate, though."

Laurel heard his voice as from a great distance, and then shouts and the sound of a galloping horse. But none of that really penetrated her consciousness. She had slipped away into the deep recesses of her mind where she hoped not to feel the emotional pain so keenly.

But she could not escape pondering the great troubles that burst around her. They flared like Fourth of July fireworks. One exploded with an illuminating realization. *Ambrose lied to Claude, but I lied to myself, thinking he really cared.*

In the same instant, another thought streaked up and

flashed brilliantly. *I shouldn't have left Claude to die with my angry words hanging over him. Hanging!* She involuntarily reached up and touched her throat which seemed to constrict painfully.

Her mind leaped again. *I don't want to, but I really do care for Ridge. Yet I can't let a relationship develop. From what he said, he hates spies because one of them got him wounded and his brother killed. So I can't tell him what I've done.*

The rocketing thoughts kept coming, faster and faster, until her whole brain seemed about to burst.

But if I don't tell him, there will be a huge lie between us. That could blow up in my face, and he could storm off and I would never see him again. Not that I could blame him. But if I tell him the truth right after we get back to the train . . .

Another rocket exploded, making her groan inwardly.

There's a killer in those cars, waiting for me and maybe Sarah! If anything happens to her while I'm out here. . . .

"Oh, Lord!" she whispered in great agony of soul, "What am I going to do?"

Lucas asked, "What did you say?"

Startled, Laurel lifted her head. "I . . . I guess I said a little prayer."

"I've been known to do that myself. It helps."

"I haven't prayed since I was about twelve."

"Things like what happened back there are enough to make a body think about what's important."

"That's true. Oh, thanks for saying what you did to that vigilante so he let me in to see Ambrose."

"Did he tell you where to find your beau?"

She paused before answering. "Yes, and I talked to him, too.

Only he's not my beau anymore."

When Lucas didn't reply, she decided he was waiting to see if she wanted to tell him the details. She dropped her head to discourage his interest.

So many things had gone wrong, and were getting worse. She was powerless. The charm and ability she had depended on all her life–and especially during her spying missions–were absolutely worthless now. She had nobody to help.

As a tear slid, unbidden, down her cheek, she realized that she was utterly, helplessly alone.

Then a fragment of a nearly forgotten comment flitted through her mind. Her instructor had said it during training before her first mission into the Confederacy. His words echoed faintly in the distant recesses of her mind.

"There will come a desperate time when all you've learned and all that you are will not be enough. Then there will be nobody but you and God. Call on Him then, because He can do what you cannot."

She had not scoffed at that, but neither had she believed. Now, crushed by circumstances over which she had no control, she sat with head still bowed while tears slid, faster and faster. They dropped noiselessly into the lap robe while she silently did what she had never again expected to do. In the silence of her mind, she formed heartfelt words.

Lord, I cannot undo what I've done, and I'm sorry. Please help me do the right thing, make the right choice.

Slowly, over the passing miles, she felt some comfort. She could not change the past, but she could end her deceit and maybe change the future. *I can be honest with Ridge. I can . . .*

Lucas cleared his throat, breaking into her thoughts. "We're almost back," he announced quietly, "and I can see they've held the train. I guess that's because the sheriff is going to ask some hard questions about why we left the murder scene. Are you able to face him?"

Laurel mouthed a silent "Amen," sat up, and squared her shoulders. She brushed tears from her cheeks with the lap robe's rough edge. "Yes," she whispered. "I am now."

Her thoughts jumped to Ridge. *I hate to tell him the truth about what I did in the war, but I must, regardless of the risk.*

Chapter 17

As the lights of Smartville drew closer, Laurel and Lucas lapsed into silence. She felt a strange mixture of quiet peace–feeling she had taken a step forward in her faith–and shock from having vigilantes hang two lifelong friends moments after they crushed her heart with their words.

She severely castigated herself. *How could I have been so blind as to not see that everything they did was wrong? Neither Claude nor Ambrose ever did a decent thing in his life. But because I wanted to hurt my father the way he hurt me, I remained friends with them just to spite him. Still, I wouldn't want anyone to die as they did, but how could they have killed women and children?*

Ambrose had lied about her, but she had lied to herself about Claude. She could not blame anyone but herself for that, and that made the remorse even worse.

She was not aware of where they were until she heard Lucas' soft command, "whoa" to the horse. Through puffy eyes, Laurel saw that the train still waited on the tracks. The passengers and crew standing inside the restaurant watched Laurel and Lucas' return. A quick double-check showed Laurel that Ridge was not among them. Sarah rushed out the door just ahead of the sheriff, but her long skirt delayed her so that the tall officer's long stride easily outdistanced her.

Lucas whispered, "He looks plenty upset!"

The officer reached the runabout as Laurel got down.

"I'm Sheriff Buell," he said gruffly. "You two better have a mighty good excuse for leaving the scene of a crime."

Lucas said soothingly, "Yes, Sir, and we have. There was no choice. If you'll give me a couple minutes to return this rig, I'm sure we can clear this up to your satisfaction."

"Hold on," Buell commanded sternly. "You're not going anywhere. Tie this horse right here, then both of you march inside where I can question you. But first, Mister, hand over your pistol."

As Lucas complied with the order, Sarah came running up. "Laurel, did you find him?"

"Yes, but I don't want to talk about it right now."

"Bad news, I guess?"

"The worst!"

"I'm not surprised. But I've got to talk to you right away about something else."

Buell snapped, "You'll have to wait, Miss Perkins."

Laurel saw the torment in Sarah's eyes and realized she was extremely distraught. Concerns for Sarah's and her own life snapped back on Laurel in a rush of reality, pushing her misery over Claude and Ambrose into the background.

"What is it, Sarah?" she asked fearfully, reaching out to take her hand.

The sheriff raised his voice. "I'm trying to finish my investigation. I said you two will have to wait."

Laurel reluctantly turned to the officer to ask, "Did you find out who murdered that brakeman?"

"Not yet, but I will." Buell gripped Lucas' and Laurel's arms. "Let's get inside."

That told Laurel that the killer was still unknown and still at large. She made a last desperate effort to learn what was upsetting Sarah. Over her shoulder as she was led away, Laurel called, "Has anyone bothered you?"

"No, it's not that! But we have to talk!"

A frightening thought struck Laurel. She raised her voice. "Is it Ridge?"

Buell answered before Sarah could. "If you mean that express messenger, he's fine. I questioned him and sent him back to his duty."

Laurel sighed with relief.

Sarah blurted, "But he's the only one who has nobody to back up his alibi. He was alone in the express car when that poor man was killed."

Alarmed, Laurel asked the sheriff, "You suspect him?"

"I'll ask the questions, Miss. Now, Miss Perkins, you leave us alone while I finish my investigation."

❧

Ridge paced the express car, wondering if Laurel had returned. There was no way he could see without opening the sliding door or going into the adjacent coach to look out a window, but Aiken had forbidden that.

He called from his usual seat in the tilted-back chair, "Stop that blasted walking and sit down."

Ridge was in no mood to obey. He replied bluntly, "I'm not

hurting anything this way."

"You're getting on my nerves!"

"I've got my own concerns."

"So I heard. That sheriff is going to nail you for not having an alibi of where you were when it happened."

"You know I wouldn't leave this car unguarded while you were away. The sheriff has to believe that, too."

"I know you were supposed to be here, but like the sheriff said, nobody saw you. Yet some people seen me walk toward the restaurant about the time it happened."

"Good for you, George. But I'm not thinking about myself."

"You're not? Oh, her. Well, wearing a hole in the floor won't help, wherever she is. But I can see why you'd be upset over her going off with that Lucas fellow. He strikes me as pretty strange. I wouldn't trust him with my gal."

Ridge pivoted to face the burly guard. "Please do not refer to her as a 'gal.' And keep your opinions to yourself!"

"Don't get all het up. I didn't mean anything. . . ."

He broke off as Sarah appeared at the small rear door.

Ridge hurried toward her.

"They're back," she said, a note of hope in her tone. "The sheriff is talking to them."

Ridge took a slow, deep breath. "Thanks."

Glancing at Aiken, Sarah lowered her voice. "Ridge, I can't tell you how sorry I am about blurting out something I should never have said."

"It doesn't matter," he said so quietly the other man could not overhear. "I've only got one thing to say to her, and then I never want to see her again!"

"Oh, please, don't say that!" Sarah laid her hand on his. "I was trying to help her, to say a good word about her, but I made a terrible mistake. Please don't—"

"Thank you," he interrupted stiffly, "but I am quite capable of making my own decisions." He turned his back on her and walked away.

For a moment, Sarah stood, one hand reached out imploringly, then she spun about and hurried away.

Buell had separated Laurel and Lucas promptly upon reaching the empty waiting room, so Laurel sagged weakly onto a hard bench while Lucas was interrogated in the station agent's office. She could see them through the glass window, but she was unable to hear a word.

Laurel had pleaded to be questioned first so she could go talk to Ridge, but the sheriff had insisted she be last. Lucas' interrogation had taken a good halfhour so far, giving Laurel more time to grapple with the various problems that had been thrust upon her in the last few hours.

I should feel some satisfaction, she told herself, knowing that she had found the conductor's incriminating ledger. *I have accomplished both my goals in coming on this trip. I have proof that Schramm is stealing from the railroad, and I found Claude. But I feel miserable and it's getting worse. Sarah and I are still in danger from Schramm and his killer friend, whoever he is, and now Ridge could be blamed for something I know he didn't do.*

She stood up and looked out the window toward the express car. She realized that in the few short days she had known Ridge, she had come to care about him. If she told him about being a

Union spy in the war, he might walk out on her and she would never see him again.

She tried to convince herself that it was too soon to reveal such a secret. He didn't need to know until or if their relationship developed into something special. She could wait until then, or could she?

But if I'm not honest with him, my secret could someday blow up in my face, and that might be even worse. I've got to risk it, even if it ruins our relationship. My days of deception have to end before something happens to make things even worse. I've got to talk to him.

Her mind flipped over to Schramm and the unknown man she had overheard admit killing the Pinkerton agent. Whoever that murderer was, he was now a threat to her and Sarah.

Well, at least if we can get through the rest of tonight and tomorrow, the trip will be over. So we've just got to be careful until then.

The door behind her opened so fast that she whirled around in sudden alarm, then sighed with relief. The telegrapher looked around the room.

"Where's the sheriff?" he asked excitedly.

"In there." Laurel pointed. "Something wrong?"

"I'll say!" The telegrapher scurried across the floor toward the agent's office. "A wire came in saying that vigilantes broke into the jail and hanged some of those outlaws who've been robbing and killing!"

Laurel hoped her face didn't show that she already knew firsthand about that.

At the depot agent's door, the telegrapher started to knock, then glanced back at Laurel. "Terrible thing, though. Their leader, name of Claude Duncan, escaped."

Laurel's eyes opened wide in surprise. "What?"

"That's what the wire says, Miss. He somehow got hold of the gun his guard had, killed him, and then escaped on horse-back."

Before the sheriff galloped off to the scene of the vigilantes' hanging and Claude's escape, the telegrapher had spread the word through the passengers and crew.

While they waited for a deputy to come finish the investigation, Laurel wanted to go to see Ridge. However, Sarah insisted that Laurel first tell her about finding Claude.

In a quiet corner of the depot, Laurel gave a brief report. She concluded, "I've got to talk to Ridge right away. Can you distract the other guard so he won't overhear me?"

"Yes, of course, but why?"

"I've had enough of deception," Laurel declared. "I'm going to tell him about my wartime activities."

"Laurel, wait!" Sarah licked her lips. "What . . . if I told you that he—"

Lucas threw the door open and interrupted. "Miss Wilson, the deputy is here and wants to talk to you."

"In a minute, Mr. Lucas."

"He told me to bring you in right away."

"I've got something else that I must do first."

"This is a young deputy who's feeling the authority of his badge, Miss Wilson. If I were you, I wouldn't keep him waiting."

Sighing in resignation, Laurel nodded. "All right."

As she stood up, Sarah gripped her hands. "When you finish with him, I've got to talk to you before you see Ridge."

"You'll just have to wait. I've got to tell Ridge before I lose my courage or change my mind."

"No, please! Just give me a couple of minutes first!"

Lucas called impatiently from the door, "Miss Wilson, you've had enough problems tonight without aggravating that deputy."

"Coming." Laurel lowered her voice so only Sarah could hear. "That killer probably won't try anything while we're stopped here, but you be careful. I'll talk to you as soon as possible."

Laurel heard Sarah give a low moan as she walked away with Lucas.

"I've been asking questions," he said as they walked down the depot hallway. "Before the sheriff left, he had followed up every statement made by passengers and crew. He confirmed where each person was at the time the brakeman was murdered. All except Ridge have an alibi that was backed by different witnesses."

"Everyone?"

"That's what I've been told."

Laurel frowned. "How about the conductor?"

"He was breaking up a card game in the smoking car, according to some men who were playing for money."

"I see. Then what about Ridge? If he was alone in the express car, where was the other guard?"

"Some passengers saw George Aiken walking away from the cars and toward the depot at the time of the murder."

"Ridge didn't kill that man."

Lucas turned questioning eyes on Laurel. "I'm inclined to agree, but then the question still remains: who did, and why?"

"I don't know." Laurel had enough things to think about without that. She asked, "I assume the sheriff accepted your story of why we left so suddenly awhile ago?"

"It's too strange a story for it to be made up, and the report from the telegrapher certainly backed it up. I also have witnesses as to where I was when the brakeman was killed." He opened the door for Laurel. "Good luck."

She stepped inside, then turned back to face him. "I want to thank you again for helping me get to see Ambrose after that vigilante refused my request."

"I'm glad I could help." He gave her a quick smile and closed the door.

The young deputy looked up when she approached him where he sat in a corner of the empty waiting room. He did not rise but swept her appreciatively with his eyes. "Nice of you to come," he said sarcastically.

Laurel briefly closed her eyes. *I don't need any more trouble,* she thought, then forced a disarming smile. "I'm sorry to have kept you waiting, but I'm sure an astute young officer like you already knows that."

He scowled, obviously suspicious of flattery, but motioned for her to sit down. "Just don't try to put anything over on me," he warned, but with less menace in his tone. "If you've got nothing to hide, things will go well for you. Now, tell me why you and that little fellow took off so suddenly after the murder?"

Laurel had completely charmed the young deputy before she finished her painful but carefully edited account of the experience with the vigilantes. She described Claude and Ambrose as child-hood friends, and skipped the more personal details. She didn't feel that it was any of the officer's business to know everything. She omitted the great lie that Ambrose had told. She also kept quiet about how humiliated and foolish she felt in thinking she was engaged to Claude.

She concluded, "I knew them all my life, yet I didn't really know them at all. I would never have dreamed they were capable of the terrible things they have done. It hurts to lose people when you've known them so long, in spite of how they turned out."

The deputy reached out a consoling hand to touch hers. "Don't be too hard on yourself, Miss Wilson. You did what you could for that Ambrose. We'll catch the other one. It's just too bad they couldn't have been nice, like you."

The station agent stuck his head in the door. "How long you going to drag this out, Deputy?" he demanded. "The superinten-dent is burning up the wires about when this train can get rolling again."

"I'm finished," the deputy stood and put away his notebook. "We'll continue to investigate this murder and bring the respon-sible person to justice."

"I'm confident you'll do your best." Laurel gave him one of her warmest smiles. "Now, if you'll excuse me, I need to take care of something right away."

Laurel vainly looked around for Sarah. *I wonder why she was so anxious to talk to me? Well, I can't wait. I've got to talk to Ridge before the cars pull out, or I lose my courage.*

News that the train would be allowed to proceed sent relieved crewmen to their stations, aided by a replacement brake-man. All passengers except Laurel went to their seats. She went straight to the express car and stopped at the little rear door. In the dim light of the kerosene lamp, she saw that Ridge was alone.

She called to him across the car, "May I come in?"

"Of course." He placed his shotgun on the seat of Aiken's chair and stood facing her, but without a welcoming smile.

She fought against a feeling of wanting to run and not tell him. Yet the very sight of him excited her and made her eager to say what she felt she must.

At the same time, she warned herself, *Remember, he may just walk out and I'll never see him again. But it's time to put all lies behind me.*

"I've got to talk to you," she said, crossing toward him.

"And I've got something to say to you."

There was something in his tone that made her stop uncertainly in the middle of the car. She tried to see his eyes, but could not. She was aware that he had not come to meet her.

"Very well," she replied, puzzled. "But please let me speak first." She moved quickly to stop in front of him.

"Maybe I can save you the trouble." His voice was cold, his eyes now clearly visible, steel-hard in the lamplight. He spoke softly, yet with words that cut through her soul. "Is it true that you were a Union spy during the war?"

Sarah told him! That's what she wanted to tell me!

"Well?" Ridge demanded brusquely.

"That's what I wanted to talk to you about," Laurel replied, her voice weak with a sense that she was too late. "When my brother was killed—"

"Please answer the question!"

"I'm trying—"

"So it's true!" The fury in his eyes rose with his voice. "Is it also true that you were the spy who brought the Federals information about the planned Confederate cavalry attack at Bethel Crossing?"

She cringed at the dreaded word "spy." "I . . . I . . . ," she floundered, frightened by the ruthless lash of his words.

"Well?" he prompted.

She gained control of her voice and explained. "I pretended to be a displaced Memphis plantation owner's daughter. I flirted with a talkative young lieutenant who tried to impress me by telling of a plan for a secret cavalry strike at a new Federal railroad bridge."

"You were the one who caused my wound and cost the life of my brother and many of our troop!"

She took an involuntary step back. "You were both at Bethel?"

"So it is true!" He thundered while the intensity of his anger seemed to flash like lightning from his eyes. "You're the one! I want to kill you with my bare hands!"

She backed up quickly. "Please let me explain!"

He roared, "No explanation is necessary! Men kill each other in war, but you hid behind your pretty face and never got your little hands bloody! Good men died because of you, and . . ."

He stopped abruptly, glaring at her while all speech fled from him. When he spoke again, his tone was quiet and deadly. "You have been doing the same thing to me that you did to that lieutenant. It's only a game to you, isn't it?"

"Oh, no!"

"You've lied enough for a lifetime! From the moment you saw me on the train and remembered me from that brief meeting in Chicago, you have toyed with me. You have a very sick mind!"

"That's not true! Oh, please listen! I was coming here to tell you everything!"

"I don't believe you! Now, get out of my sight before I forget that you're a Jezebel and do something that will bring me down to your level!"

He whirled around and limped away. Laurel started after him just as the other express messenger returned. She rushed by Aiken without speaking. Tears of frustration and failure scalded her eyes, and her heart thudded so fast against her ribs that she seemed about to explode.

An overpowering urge to lash out at Sarah drove Laurel straight to the coach seat they had shared, but Sarah wasn't there. Laurel slid across and bent forward, burying her face in her hands. A male passenger walking down the aisle asked if she was all right. She ordered him to go away.

In the last couple of hours, she had suffered four severe blows straight to the heart. Ambrose had lied about her; Claude had rejected her; and Sarah had betrayed Laurel's deepest secret. Now Ridge was lost to her. Yet, even in her excruciating emotional pain, Laurel could not believe that Sarah had deliberately told Ridge about Bethel Crossing. It had to have been a slip of the tongue.

It's not her fault, Laurel reminded herself. *I can't blame her. But why does it have to hurt so much to have Ridge hate me?*

In that moment, she knew the answer. It didn't matter that she and Ridge had only known each other for such a short time. There had been something that drew them together like the invisible attraction of a magnet.

Laurel realized how very much she cared for him.

But now he's lost to me, and I can't blame him.

The incongruity of war hit her hard. Up to now, what she had done had not really been personal, except for trying to avenge her brother. He was barely more than a boy who had died like a man in battlefield hand-to-hand combat, but she had deceived a young officer who might have also died at Bethel Crossing along with Ridge's brother.

I'm responsible for his death, and all those others, both North and South, just as I'm responsible for Ridge's wound. I killed them just as surely as if I stood on that battlefield and shot them down myself.

She felt Sarah slide into the seat beside her. "Laurel," she whispered urgently, "I've been looking all over for you. I've got to tell you . . ." She interrupted herself as Laurel lifted her grief-stricken face.

"Oh!" Sarah cried, "You've already talked to him!"

Laurel stared dully out of red and swollen eyes, then slowly nodded.

Sarah exclaimed, "I slipped! I didn't mean to, but I said the wrong thing—"

"It's all right," Laurel broke in. "I knew it had to have been an accident. I don't blame you."

"But I can see by your face that things went wrong."

"Everything has gone wrong today," Laurel said in a dull, lifeless manner. "Every time I think I've made some progress, things blow up in my face."

"Well," Sarah began, glancing around to make sure nobody could overhear, "I don't want to heap any more troubles on you, but whoever killed those two men is still on these cars, and we could be next."

Impulsively, she gripped Laurel's arm. "Let's get off right

now and wait for the next train going home!"

"I can't. Someone will be waiting at the end of the line to take this ledger off my hands." Laurel lightly touched her reticule where she kept the evidence she had taken from the conductor's office.

Sarah protested, "But we've been delayed so much, how do you know your contact is still going to be waiting?"

"The telegraphers will have kept the station agent informed of our schedule change, and I'm sure the agent will post the changes for people waiting for the train, so my contact will know to be on hand when we arrive."

"It's not worth risking your life for, Laurel! Don't you see? If the murderer is going to try killing either or both of us, it has to be before our trip ends tomorrow. Please! Let's get off now and wait for the next train back to Chicago!"

With a low sigh, Laurel confessed, "Right now, I hurt so much that I don't care about what happens to me."

"Don't say that! You're not the only one in danger."

Laurel still struggled to bring her mind back from the torment of what had happened that day. "You're right. Right now I just want to go off somewhere all alone and curl up in my misery, but I can't."

"I'm glad you see it that way. I want to live to return to John, and hope he'll take me back. I don't think I can get through this alone. You've got to help us both stay alive."

With great effort, Laurel nodded. "I got you into this through no fault of yours. I'll get you out."

Laurel glanced out the window as the train jerked and started to slowly move away from the depot's lights. At the same time, she heard Lucas approaching.

"Well, ladies," he said, "I almost missed getting to ride with you. The telegraph operator asked me to deliver a message to the conductor." Lucas threw his overcoat on the seat, but didn't sit. "That telegraph just came in, so I'd better find the conductor right away."

As Lucas walked down the aisle, Sarah asked, "Do you feel like talking about your ride to see Claude?"

"Maybe we were wrong about Lucas." Laurel turned to see that he had stepped across the back platform onto the last coach. "He was very helpful to me tonight."

A male passenger entered the car and started down the aisle, but stooped and picked up something. Turning to the women he asked, "Did one of you drop this?" He held an unsealed envelope toward them.

Sarah started to shake her head, but Laurel saw the conductor's name on the envelope. "Wait!" she exclaimed. "I'll take that. Thank you, Sir."

He nodded and walked on.

Sarah protested, "That's the telegram Mr. Lucas was supposed to deliver–"

"Yes, I know," Laurel interrupted.

"You're not going to open it?"

"It's not sealed, and besides, I have a good reason to read it." Laurel pulled the sheet out and glanced at it. "Listen to this!" Laurel lowered her voice and read in a whisper.

" 'Plans firm for tomorrow morning. Finish the job.' " It was unsigned.

Sarah said reprovingly, "You shouldn't have read that."

"It's a good thing I did." Excitement showed in Laurel's face. "Here, put this back on the floor by Mr. Lucas' seat. When he returns, he'll think he dropped it there."

Sarah did as requested, then asked, "What do you think it means?"

"I'm not sure, but I have a feeling that 'finish the job' has something to do with you and me."

"You're starting to frighten me again, Laurel!"

"Save that for tomorrow." Laurel glanced out the window at the open countryside, now in total darkness without a single light showing anywhere. Laurel shivered with mixed fear and anticipation at what the morrow would bring.

Chapter 18

Ridge swayed with the motion of the express car, staring toward the strongboxes stacked against the wall, yet he was not conscious of them.

He was so deep in troubled thought that he didn't see the conductor come to the rear door and motion for the other express messenger to come to him. When Aiken nodded, Schramm promptly stepped back where Ridge could not see him.

Aiken brought the front chair legs down and stood up. "I got to go see a man about a horse," he told Ridge.

Ridge nodded without turning, understanding that Aiken had a call of nature.

When Aiken squeezed through the narrow door, Schramm showed him the telegram Lucas had just delivered.

"Good!" the guard exclaimed softly. "I'm ready."

The conductor asked under his breath, "Did you go through her trunk?"

"Yes, while she and Lucas were gone in that rented carriage, but it's not there. It wasn't in her friend's trunk, either."

"You sure?"

"Positive."

"Then she's got it on her, probably in that drawstring bag she carries everywhere. I've got to get that ledger back before she can turn it over to the Pinkertons." Schramm used the common term for all the agents who worked for the nation's most famous detective, Allan Pinkerton.

"You'd better," Aiken warned, "otherwise, your days of stealing from the railroad are over."

"So's the share you've been getting," Schramm reminded him.

"We can't let that happen. So what are we going to do about it?"

"When the robbery comes off, it would be too obvious if we just took the ledger. We've got to take her bag so she doesn't get suspicious, not that she's going to be able to tell anyone afterward."

"You'll have to do that because I'll be in the express car taking care of that Reb."

"I've got to look innocent. One of the riders who goes through the cars robbing passengers will have to get it from her."

"That makes sense, but what about the woman traveling with her?"

"Leave that to me. When we stop for breakfast at Harley's Station, I'll wire ahead to make sure everything is done exactly as I planned."

Laurel didn't think she could sleep because her misery was so intense, so she was startled to realize she had been asleep when the car jerked to a stop. Her eyes popped open. Through the coach window, she noticed that it was already full daylight. Black clouds in a dark and gloomy sky hovered over another depot and restaurant.

"Breakfast stop," Sarah volunteered. "You hungry?"

Laurel glanced around the car where the passengers were rousing themselves from a night of trying to sleep sitting in coach seats. Jacob Lucas was already gone from his place across the aisle. "No, Sarah, you go ahead."

"And leave you alone where somebody might sneak up on you and leave you under the wheels like that brakeman?" Sarah shook her head. "We're going to stay together until we get to the end of the line."

"But I don't want anything."

"At least you could have some coffee and keep me company."

"Thanks, but I don't think my stomach would even handle that. It feels as if it's been tied in knots and kicked across the whole of creation."

"Then at least go fix your face. You look awful."

"I don't care."

"Well, I do, and I don't want to be seen with you looking like this." Sarah stood up, took Laurel's left arm, and began pulling her toward the aisle.

"I've never seen you this way," Sarah commented as Laurel slowly yielded and got to her feet. "What would have happened to you during the war if you let your feelings get you down?"

Laurel let Sarah tow her down the aisle toward the rear platform. "I've never felt like this before."

"Well, sitting around moping won't help. Stop feeling miserable about Ridge. Think of something else."

Laurel asked a little sharply, "Who said I was thinking about him?"

Sarah stepped onto the platform at the rear of the coach before turning to smile at Laurel. "You'd be wasting your time thinking about Claude, even if he has escaped. So I know you're stewing about Ridge. Right?"

"Well, yes," Laurel admitted, stepping down to the graveled roadbed. "But I've also pondered all that's happened on this trip. Everything was bad."

"That's not true." Sarah dropped her voice. "Your goal of finding Claude has been reached. When you told me what happened, I know it was a harsh blow to your pride. But that's over and done with. Ridge needn't be, though. He's worth fighting for."

"He made it plain that he would have killed me if I had been a man."

"But you're not, so don't give up on him."

"There's no use talking about that, Sarah."

Sarah shrugged. "Suit yourself. Everyone's entitled to cry awhile when they've fallen down." Sarah started across the double set of tracks toward the restaurant, then stopped and added firmly, "You've had all night to wallow in your misery, and that's enough. So get up and go on. Think of something else."

"Like what?" Laurel asked dully.

"Well, for one thing, on this trip I've thought about how good it will be when George Pullman's sleeping cars are on all railroads. Then we can lie down at night instead of sitting up in a torture rack."

Laurel understood that her friend was trying to cheer her up, so she tried to be more cooperative. "I've heard about those. The first one was put in service last year, but rail lines are having to strengthen certain bridges and widen some tunnels to accommodate the Pullman cars."

"That's better! Now if you want to do something else really good for your fellow man, why not invent a car with meals so we don't have to keep stopping at terrible little restaurants like this?"

"Seems to me that I heard a dining car is already being planned for use in a couple of years."

"We should have postponed this trip until then," Sarah joked, reaching for the restaurant door.

Laurel held back. "What if he's already inside?"

"Even if he isn't, before this trip is over you'll probably run into Ridge, so you had better be ready."

Laurel groaned inwardly. *I'll never be able to do that, she told herself. I couldn't stand to see his hurt, anger, and hate again, the way I did last night.*

Sarah added, "You run around in back and use the facilities. I'll go get us a table until you're presentable again."

Laurel nodded and started around the building. "All right, but get us a small one in the back someplace."

In the tiny house out back, Laurel found a blue-and-white metal pitcher and chipped wash basin with fresh water. She poured some water from the pitcher and surveyed herself in the broken mirror.

You do look frightful! Her eyes were puffy and red-rimmed, her hair was in disarray, and her clothes wrinkled from sleeping upright in them. In spite of her crushed feelings, she removed a comb and brush from her reticule and began repairing the damage to her person.

It would never have worked out with Ridge anyway, she silently told the mirror image. *We're from different worlds: North and South, country man and city woman, and both strong-willed. Besides, we have only known each other a few days.*

She paused, the comb in her hand, and sighed. *Claude hurt me terribly, but I'm not thinking about him. Why do I care so much about Ridge?* She saw the answer reflected in her eyes. *You're mightily attracted to him, but it's too late, she told herself, so concentrate on saving yourself and Sarah if Schramm and his unknown murdering friend try to hurt you. I'd better get back to her.*

Sarah had found a small table in the far corner, facing the restaurant's front door. Laurel rejoined her, deliberately moving her chair so that her back was toward that door, the other passengers, and the crew. She didn't want to see Ridge if he came in.

Sarah glanced over the top of her bill of fare to make a visual inspection of Laurel. "That's better," Sarah said approvingly.

"Thanks." Laurel started to put the napkin in her lap, but stopped suddenly.

Sarah asked, "What's the matter?"

Laurel leaned forward to whisper across the table. "That voice behind us! It sounds like Harkins."

"He's dead, remember?"

"I know. I don't want to turn around, but tell me who it is."

Sarah seemed to glance around casually before reporting. "That's the other express messenger. He's eating with the conductor and some other crew—"

"Aiken!" Laurel exclaimed. "Of course!"

"What about him?"

"Sh! Keep your voice down," Laurel warned. She leaned back and took a quick, deep breath.

I wrongly suspected that Harkins killed the agent Woods, but

Schramm and Aiken must have wrongly thought that poor brake-man was also an agent, so they killed him.

Sarah said, "Don't just sit there; tell me what you're thinking."

"I can't right now, but I will when we're alone."

"I don't like being kept in the dark . . . oh, look who's coming this way."

Ridge! Laurel thought, wanting to jump up and run away. But she relaxed upon realizing that he couldn't leave the express car while Aiken was gone. It was Jacob Lucas whom she saw heading for their table.

"Good morning, ladies," he said cheerfully, stopping beside them while they returned his greeting. He said somberly, "If you don't mind, I'd like to join both of you to share some confidential news."

He was still too pushy to suit Laurel, and he seemed to have his nose in everyone else's business. But she reminded herself of his kindness last night in driving her to find Claude and getting the vigilantes to let her see him. She replied, "Please sit down and tell us."

He pulled a chair from the adjacent empty table and sat down quickly. He glanced around before lowering his voice and leaning forward across the table. "I was in the telegraph office moments ago when a message came in from the sheriff. The operator was so excited he read part of it to me."

Both women bent expectantly toward him.

He paused for another quick look around, then whispered, "Our train is to be robbed today."

"No!" Sarah exclaimed. "There's never been a train robbery in history!"

"True," he admitted, "but there's been speculation about one for some time."

"Yes," Laurel said, "I've heard such talk. But how do you know this train is going to be attacked today?"

Lucas took another look around. "It seems that one member in the outlaw band got frightened because of the vigilantes' action last night, so he went to the sheriff. The turncoat claims he doesn't know when or where the robbery is to take place, except that it's sometime today."

Sarah exclaimed in dismay, "We could all be killed."

Laurel remembered last night's dropped message intended for the conductor. "You may be right, Sarah."

"You think so?"

"What better time would there be to kill someone than when there's a robbery. A stray ball fired—"

"Then we won't go on!" Sarah broke in. "We'll just stay here and catch the next train back to Chicago."

Laurel had a terrifying thought. *Aiken won't defend the car because he's in on the plan. He'll betray Ridge!*

Laurel told Sarah, "You can go if you wish. In fact, I think you should, but I'm going on south."

"And risk being killed when it's not necessary?" Sarah demanded in disbelief.

Lucas said, "With all due respect to your courage, Miss Wilson, I think you should both return to Chicago from here."

"No." Laurel said firmly. "Now that we've been alerted, we can be on guard. I must go on to the end of the line for reasons I can't say." She turned to Sarah, "But you could catch a north-bound train right here at Harley's Station."

"Would you go with me?" Sarah asked, but quickly shook her

head. "No, I already have the answer to that. You gave me one reason, but now I see another: Ridge. The robbers will target the express car because that's where the treasure is. Ridge is going to be back there with nobody but that other guard to hold them off!"

Laurel nodded briefly to acknowledge the truth of Sarah's remark. Laurel quickly stood. "Thank you for bringing that information, Mr. Lucas."

He also rose to his feet. "Where are you going?"

"To do some thinking."

"About what?" Sarah demanded.

"About a mistake I made in believing that dead brakeman was the other person I overheard . . . ," she broke off, her eyes flickering to Lucas. "I hope you'll forget what I just said."

"Overheard what?" he asked. "Do you know something that can help stop this robbery?"

"No, not stop it." Laurel scanned his face, trying to make up her mind if it would be an error to tell what she suspected to this man with the inquisitive nature.

He reminded her, "What would have happened last night if you hadn't trusted me enough to ride with me?"

"I'm remembering that, Mr. Lucas. Give me a few minutes, please, and I'll get back to you. Sarah, come help me think something through real fast."

The two young women walked around the depot, unmindful of the cloudy skies and light wind that seemed to herald a coming storm. They stayed close to the buildings for safety from any human attack, but far enough away from anyone who might overhear them. Laurel briefly revealed what she knew about Schramm and Aiken.

"You see," she concluded, "it wasn't Harkins, the brakeman, I heard admitting he had killed the Pinkerton agent. It was Aiken. I know Schramm is in on the plan. The logical other person has to be one who can open the express car from inside and let them take the treasure boxes of gold or whatever is in them."

"Ridge would not allow that, unless . . . Oh!" Sarah hesitated, her eyes open in surprised understanding.

"That's why they won't give him the chance," Laurel mused. "Aiken is probably going to prevent Ridge from defending whatever they're guarding."

"You mean . . . kill him?"

Laurel swallowed hard. "He won't expect Aiken to turn on him."

"But you can't help because Ridge will be up there in the express car with Aiken, and you'll be in the coach."

"I've thought of trying to be there, but Aiken might not let me, and I don't know when it's going to happen."

"Besides, he might shoot you, too."

"That's possible. Anyway, Ridge needs to be warned, but he may not believe me."

"You want me to tell him?"

"He'll have no reason to doubt you. We just saw Aiken at breakfast. Now's your chance to tell Ridge while he's alone."

"All right. But what about Lucas?"

Laurel considered that. In spite of her rebuff by Ridge, she had made a decision. She told Sarah, "I'm going to tell Mr. Lucas all I know and what I suspect. Then I hope he can help keep us—and Ridge—alive."

"But you don't know much about Mr. Lucas! Suppose he's part of the gang?"

"I don't think he is. He's strange, but I believe he's trustworthy." Laurel gave Sarah a gentle push. "Go to Ridge before Aiken returns."

Sarah hesitated a moment, her eyes softening as she looked into Laurel's. "Now you're acting like the person I've always known."

"Thanks. Now please go!"

"I'm on my way, but first, you should know that I'm going to stay with you for the rest of the trip, no matter what happens." Sarah lifted her skirts and started walking rapidly toward the express car.

Laurel headed back to meet Lucas.

🐾

Laurel met Lucas coming out of the telegrapher's office. She said bluntly, "I'm going to risk my life on the belief that you are a man of integrity and tell you what I mentioned overhearing."

"I appreciate that, but to bolster your faith, I'll first give you another reason to trust me."

"Oh?"

"Telegraphers lead a rather lonely life," he said. "They sit alone for hours with nothing but a little key and some sounds to keep them company, so I've learned to cultivate their friendship. This one," Lucas jerked a thumb toward the depot with its small adjoining telegrapher's room, "is the talkative type."

Laurel waited without comment.

Lucas continued, "He told me that the conductor, Schramm,

has some idea that a pretty young woman on his train has sent coded messages to Allan Pinkerton."

Laurel hadn't sent anything from Harley's Station, but she involuntarily licked her lips at what Schramm had to be thinking.

"I know it sounds ridiculous," Lucas went on, "but Schramm is convinced that the famous detective has assigned you to spy on him."

"Me?" Laurel tried to sound incredulous.

"I know you're not an operative, but you're in just as much danger from Schramm as if you were."

Laurel felt she must give Jacob some explanation for the telegrams she had sent earlier. "The Pinkerton agency was trying to help me locate Claude." It was misleading, but partly true, she told herself, and wasn't a real lie.

Lucas' eyes narrowed very briefly as though he knew the Pinkerton agency didn't take missing person cases, but he quickly nodded. "I can accept that, but it won't make any difference to Schramm because he's convinced you are an agent. He is afraid that you found out he's been stealing from passengers' cash fares, and you even have some kind of proof."

Laurel was startled by Lucas' knowledge. She asked a little sharply, "What makes you say that?"

Lucas smiled knowingly. "I have a bad habit of sometimes eavesdropping on people."

"Like Schramm?"

Lucas smiled. "Among others. So you be careful."

Laurel admitted, "I don't know what to say."

"There's nothing to say except that I'll look out for you and Sarah as much as possible. Now, what were you going to tell me?"

Laurel took a deep breath and told him what she had overheard Schramm and Aiken say.

Lucas listened without interruption until she had finished. "All right," he said, "we can't stop the attempted robbery, but we can be ready when it happens."

"How can we do that when we don't have any idea of how the train is to be attacked?"

"Their primary target has to be the express car. They may also try to rob passengers, or maybe they'll just shoot up the cars before breaking into the express coach. We'll have to play whatever hand is dealt us. Until then, we wait and try to be as ready as possible."

Back in their seats, while the train continued south, Sarah reported that Ridge had thanked her for alerting him to the planned attack. He assured her he would watch so that Aiken would not catch him off guard.

The hours dragged on while heavy black smoke from the wood-burning locomotive, pushed low because of the threatening storm, billowed past the car windows and sifted inside.

Countless thoughts rolled and tumbled in Laurel's mind. She briefly wondered where Claude had gone after escaping the vigilantes, but she quickly put that thought aside. She tried to concentrate on what to do when the cars were attacked, and she fervently hoped that Ridge would not be killed.

Across the aisle, Lucas seemed to be sleeping with his hat low across his forehead. But she caught quick eye movements and knew he was watching. He had pulled his heavy overcoat over his knees and up to his waist. His hands were covered, so she was sure that was to hide the heavy revolver the sheriff had returned after questioning him about encountering the vigilantes.

The conductor entered the car from the front and made his way down the aisle just as the train began to slow. Laurel peered out the window and saw that they were in a wooded area. Except for the railroad tracks, it was lonely and desolate, with no sign of human habitation. Sarah guessed, "Must be stopping for water or wood."

Laurel glanced out of the window on her side where the ever-present telegraph poles followed the tracks. She shifted her gaze to the window on Lucas' side and sighed with relief as the engine rounded a slight curve and a water tower came into view.

Then she frowned at the sight of some saddled horses tied behind the tower. She mused, "Sarah, what do you suppose those . . ." her thought left unfinished as the train stopped and she noticed the single strand of wire hanging down beside the nearest telegraph pole.

"It's been cut!" she exclaimed, tensing.

"What has?" Sarah asked.

Laurel lowered her voice. "Riders cut the telegraph wire! This must be where the robbery—"

She didn't finish because shots sounded from outside and to the rear. She glanced out the window and saw about half a dozen riders with drawn pistols spurring out of the sheltering trees, riding hard toward the train. Out of the corner of her eye, she saw the conductor throw himself flat on the aisle floor between the women's seat and Lucas'.

He yelled, "Outlaws! Ladies, get down! Everyone!"

Laurel dropped into the space between her seat and the one in front of them, pulling Sarah down with her. They crouched low where their feet had been.

There were the hoarse cries of surprised male passengers diving into the aisles. Another pistol ball thudded into the ceiling, breaking a kerosene lamp.

A second later, the glass exploded around Lucas from a ball fired from outside. Laurel saw that Lucas had shoved his overcoat aside and brought his heavy revolver up to aim out the broken window.

Laurel's arm was thrown protectively across Sarah's shoulders while Lucas fired. The conductor crouched in the aisle between Lucas and the two women.

Laurel sucked in her breath when she heard boots suddenly thump on the rear platform and a pistol hammer brought back to full cock position. Peering down the aisle, she glimpsed a man with a red bandanna over his face shove a pistol against the back of Lucas' head.

The masked man ordered harshly, "Drop your gun, Mister, or you'll wake up dead!"

Lucas' revolver clattered to the floor. The bandit, who obviously had ridden horseback to the platform and swung on board the train, aimed a second revolver at Schramm. "Don't move, Conductor!" the outlaw growled as all firing from outside the coaches suddenly stopped.

"Now," the robber ordered Lucas, "Kick your pistol into the aisle. You, Conductor, and the rest of you people, stand up slowly and keep your hands where I can see them. Anyone with a gun is dead!"

Rising with Sarah, Laurel saw a rider outside Lucas' window who wore a blue bandanna over his face, but he did not fire again. Another outlaw jumped through the coach's forward door with a shotgun. He wore a black hood over his head with holes cut in it so he could see. He swung the gun menacingly over the car as the first robber removed the gun from Schramm's ribs, holstered it, then put Lucas' weapon in his waistband.

The first man produced a sack from under his long coat. "You," he loudly said to Lucas, "take this up the aisle. All of you—drop your valuables into the sack: guns, jewelry, money, everything! Do it fast!"

With obvious reluctance, Lucas stepped into the aisle with his hands raised and took the sack.

"You ladies first," the gunman ordered.

Laurel protested, "Let us keep—"

"No, you keep nothing! Put those drawstring things in the sack, and do it quick!"

Lucas approached with downcast eyes. "I'm sorry," he whispered, "I didn't expect them to come in from behind."

"No talking!" the outlaw ordered. "Get on with it!"

As Laurel released her reticule into the sack, Sarah whispered, "The ledger!"

"Sh!" Laurel cautioned, glancing at the conductor, who stood with his hands high. She thought she saw a triumphant gleam in his eye. That infuriated her because she realized he was trying to look as if he were an innocent victim along with the passengers.

The bandit snapped, "That's better. Now, you women follow your short friend toward the front of the car. Conductor, you'd better join them."

Laurel glanced at Sarah, who was trembling. Laurel protested to the robber, "We need to sit down—"

"Do what I told you!" he interrupted, wagging his weapon. "Now shut up and move forward! All four of you!"

As she stepped into the aisle, Laurel remembered Ridge and Aiken in the express car.

The moment the train stopped, Aiken lowered the front legs on his chair and stood up. He ordered Ridge, "Take a look inside that coach and see what's going on."

Ridge casually shifted the Henry repeating rifle in his hand. "Probably just stopping for water," he said, trying to sound at ease.

"Better make sure, anyway."

Ridge shrugged and started to turn his back as if to obey. He heard Aiken's quick step behind him and whirled just as a pistol barrel slammed down toward him. Ridge jerked his head aside so the blow clipped his ear and thudded into his shoulder. He ignored the pain and jabbed the barrel of his rifle hard into the other man's midsection.

Aiken groaned in pain and instantly doubled up, dropping his revolver. Ridge retrieved it and shoved it into his waistband while the sound of galloping horses and shots came from the coaches behind him.

"Don't move!" Ridge said through clenched teeth to the man writhing on the floor. "I'll take it from here."

He backed up to the wall and leaned the rifle against it, but he kept the revolver on the groaning Aiken. Going to the far end of the strongboxes, Ridge threw off the canvas cover. Quickly, he dragged some of the boxes with his free hand. He heard the clink of heavy gold coins as he constructed a small barricade in front and on both sides of himself. He left some boxes stacked against the car wall to act as protection from shots fired from the outside.

Aiken swore mightily between groans. "Looks good, Reb, but you still don't have a chance!"

"Maybe not," Ridge admitted, "but mine are better than yours."

He retrieved the rifle, placing it and the shotgun on top of the boxes. With the pistol in hand, Ridge turned down the wall lamp so the car was nearly dark. He glanced at both large sliding doors and the two small ones at either end of the coach. No matter which way the robbers tried to come at him, he would be hard to see, but they would be outlined against the outside light.

Satisfied, with all his weapons at hand, Ridge crouched behind his four-way shelter.

Then he waited.

Chapter 19

Laurel and Sarah followed Lucas down the narrow aisle toward the front of the first coach. Schramm followed them with the first armed bandit bringing up the rear. The second outlaw stood at the front door with his shotgun at the ready.

"Hurry it up!" the first man ordered Lucas as he neared the front of the car. "Hold that bag out so those other passengers can drop their valuables in it—fast!"

When the last man had been robbed, Lucas stopped uncertainly before the second outlaw, forcing the women and the conductor to also halt. The shotgun-wielding bandit shifted the weapon to his right hand. With his left, he snatched Lucas' sack.

"Much obliged," the bandit said sarcastically. "Now, Mister, get down on your belly in the aisle and don't move!" He glanced at Sarah, who was sobbing and also starting to get down. "Not you, Miss; just him!"

As Lucas obeyed, the outlaw with the filled sack backed onto the front platform. The horseman with the blue bandanna rode up, leading a saddled but riderless mount. The robber handed him the sack, then leaped from the platform onto the spare horse. Both men galloped toward the sheltering woods while two other horses galloped up. Again, one was riderless.

Laurel started to turn toward the remaining man behind her, but he stopped her with a curt command. "Don't look at me!" As she shifted her gaze away, he spoke roughly to Schramm standing in front of him with his hands raised.

"All right, Mister Conductor, you're our hostage. Get on the horse. Just remember I've got this gun on you."

Schramm nodded and started forward, then suddenly knocked the weapon away with his elbow. The gun fired, sending the ball into the coach wall behind Laurel. At the same instant, the conductor palmed a small hideout derringer. The outlaw struck out at it, knocking the barrel toward Laurel.

She had involuntarily ducked as the robber's weapon fired, so she was moving when there was a second shot from Schramm's hideout gun. The heavy ball angrily buzzed by her head. Instantly, she cried out and crumpled to the floor at Sarah's feet.

"Laurel!" Sarah screamed, and hastily crouched over the still figure in the aisle.

The bandit ordered Schramm, "Drop it!" The conductor slowly opened his hand and let the single-shot pistol fall on an empty seat.

The outlaw warned Schramm, "You try anything like that again, and I'll blow you into kingdom come! Now get on that horse! The rest of you, don't move until we're out of sight, or he dies!"

Sarah sobbed brokenly, "Laurel! Laurel!"

Before the last outlaw stepped outside the car, he reached up over his head with a knife. With one swift stroke, he severed the signal cord that linked the cars together. At the same time, Schramm stepped from the platform into the saddle of the nearest horse, which was held by the third bandit.

The first outlaw slid his knife into its belt sheath and leaped onto the second horse. All three raced toward the woods, leaving only the passengers in the coach.

Sarah frantically searched Laurel's still form for signs of blood or a wound.

Lucas bent over them. "Where's she hit?"

Laurel cautiously opened her eyes and looked up at them. "I'm not! I'm all right."

Sarah jerked backward in disbelief.

"I'm fine!" Laurel cried, reaching up to seize both of Sarah's hands. "He missed me, and I played dead so he wouldn't shoot again!"

There were relieved exclamations from the passengers as they crowded around. Laurel glanced toward the coach walls. "See? There's where both balls struck."

Releasing Sarah's hands, Laurel pointed to where one bullet had splintered the wooden coach wall behind the seats. The other had struck the row of birds painted just below the ceiling.

Sarah moaned with mixed relief and anger, then suddenly leaned close to whisper in Laurel's ear. "The ledger! They got your ledger!"

"No, they didn't," Laurel whispered back. "I slid it under the seat when the first robber entered the car. It's safe."

A male passenger standing in the open front doorway shouted, "Another outlaw is riding this way!"

There was a general excited scramble to duck behind seats as the rider passed the tender and express cars.

The frightened male passenger exclaimed, "He's going to kill us all!"

"No, I don't think so," Lucas replied calmly. "They robbed us of everything. He's after something else."

Lucas sounded so positive that Laurel raised up to where she could better see through the open front door.

The outlaw dismounted between the coach and express car, and bent quickly over the rails between the two cars.

"What's he doing?" Laurel asked Lucas.

"I think he's stealing part of this train."

"What?" she cried in disbelief.

"Watch!" Lucas instructed.

Laurel saw the outlaw reach down from the saddle, make a pulling motion, then quickly back his horse away from between the coach and the express car. Facing the engine, he triumphantly waved a long metal pin aloft.

Lucas quietly explained, "He's showing one of his outlaw friends in the locomotive that he's pulled the link-pin coupling this passenger coach and the rest of the train to the express car."

Laurel shook her head as the outlaw galloped toward the trees and two short blasts of the locomotive's whistle sounded. This was followed by the sound of drive wheels slipping on the tracks. The wood-burning engine poured heavy black smoke out of the diamond stack. Railroad tracks and ties began to show as the express car, tender, and locomotive pulled away, putting distance between them and the rest of the train.

Sarah cried in alarm, "They're moving, but our car isn't!"

"Right," Lucas agreed. "They're taking only the engine, tender, and express car, and leaving us behind."

Laurel's hand flew to her throat. She cried in a hoarse whisper, "The express car? Ridge is in there!"

Ridge was surprised when he heard the locomotive's drive wheels begin turning and his car started to move. Light from outside filled the small side door facing the first passenger car.

"What in the world? . . ." Ridge muttered in surprise. He raised up from behind the strongbox barricade he had erected to defend himself and the gold.

Aiken laughed nastily from where he still lay on the floor, holding his stomach. "You didn't figure on us stealing part of the train, did you, Reb? Well, as soon as they get down the tracks where nobody will disturb us, they'll bust this car open. You'll be very dead!"

Laurel watched the distance rapidly widen between the passenger coach and the stolen part of the train.

She fearfully asked Lucas, "What's going to happen?"

"My guess is that they'll take it down the tracks where it's safe to rob at their leisure."

Laurel's eyes opened wide in fright. "We can't just stand here! If Aiken didn't surprise him, Ridge won't give up without a fight! We've got to help him!"

"There's nothing anybody can do," Lucas gently pointed out. "We're stranded here without any weapons or form of transportation!"

Laurel declared, "Well, I'm going to do something, even if I have to walk!"

"I understand your concern," he assured her, "but your emotions are overrunning your mind. You'll never catch up to both horses and a locomotive. We can't even call for help with the telegraph wire cut."

"There must be something we can do!" She stepped out onto the front platform, desperately looking at the engine, tender, and express car moving away.

She stepped down to the tracks and hurriedly glanced in all directions. Except for the water tower, there was no sign of a structure or human activity.

Stricken with greater feelings than she had ever known, Laurel desperately longed to help Ridge.

The knowledge of his great danger made her realize her deep feelings for him. At the same time, all the logical reasons she had earlier considered for not getting involved with him came flooding back.

He's too arrogant. Too self-reliant. We're from two different worlds. Besides, he hates me because my spying caused the death of his brother and his own wound. He said if I were a man, he would kill me. I can't change that, but I care too much for him to let him get killed. I've got to help him—but how?

Sarah called from the platform, "What are you doing?"

"Looking!" Laurel moved toward the wooden water tower, the graveled roadbed hurting her feet.

"Looking for what?" Sarah wanted to know.

"A horse, a mule!" Laurel stopped and surveyed the woods. They seemed dark and ominous from the threatening storm hovering above them. She added, "Anything."

"You're talking foolishly!" Sarah left the platform and hurried forward. "I knew you were losing your heart over Ridge, but use your head! You had me warn him! He's intelligent. He won't let that other guard fool him."

"It isn't just Aiken, but all those other men!" Laurel stopped and waited for Sarah to catch up. "I killed his brother, but maybe I can help save Ridge." Her voice broke. "Oh, I know he hates me, but I couldn't live with myself if I didn't try to make up for what I did to his brother and those other men in Ridge's command."

"That was war, and you did what your country needed you to do," Sarah replied, slipping her arms around Laurel's shoulders. "Trying to help Ridge now won't bring those men back, no matter which color uniform they wore."

It was obvious that was true, Laurel realized as she and Sarah clung to each other while the other passengers spilled out of the two coaches and gathered around Lucas in excited conversations.

"I know all that," Laurel said quietly to Sarah. "But I've got to try to help Ridge."

Sarah shook her head. "Whether it's to ease your conscience, or to help heal your shattered heart, be realistic. There's no way you, I, or anyone else can help him. He's on his own."

Laurel raised her head. She watched helplessly as all the horsemen reappeared. They followed the stolen section of train around a curve. The express car with Ridge inside was the last to disappear from sight.

Off to the right, lightening flashed, reflecting briefly off the cut and dangling telegraph wire. A moment later, heavy thunder rolled out of the dark sky.

Sarah said softly, "We'd better get back inside the car before it starts to rain."

In a daze, Laurel murmured, "I don't care. I'm going to follow the rest of that train."

"No, you're not! Now come on back inside, or do I have to call some of these men to help me?"

The helplessness of the situation made Laurel turn away to hide the anguish that leaped to her face. "In a minute," she said hoarsely. She hurried to the water tower and stumbled around it to where nobody could see her yield to her heartrending fear and grief.

Tears already filming her vision made her bump into something. Glancing down, she saw a small, four-wheeled vehicle. For a moment, she didn't know what it was. Then she saw an upright portion with a handle sticking out on both sides above the flat platform.

"A railroad handcar!" she exclaimed aloud.

Whirling around, she rushed to the front of the water tower yelling, "I found something! I need help!"

The men, led by Sarah and Lucas, gathered around her discovery.

She cried excitedly, "We can use that to follow the train. Let's get it on the tracks."

Willing hands did that, but when she started to step on the vehicle, Sarah yelled in alarm, "You can't go! You don't know how to make that thing work!"

"I've seen it done," Laurel replied, her eyes filled with sudden hope, sweeping the crowd. "Who will go with me?"

All except Lucas shifted nervously and looked away, refusing to meet her eyes. "I'll go," he said, "but not with you. I need another man."

Someone called from the protection of the crowd's middle, "Not me! You would both get killed!"

There was a low murmur of agreement from the men before Laurel's temper flared. "Then stay here and be safe! I'm going!" She lifted her long skirt, scrambled up onto the handcar and took a firm grip with both hands on the rough handle nearest her.

When Lucas started to protest, Laurel snapped, "Then I'll go by myself!" She pushed down on the handle and the vehicle started the wrong way, toward the spectators.

Lucas leaped upon the car, grabbed the other handle and forcibly stopped the vehicle while the men scattered with startled yells.

"I'd better help you," he said with frank admiration in his eyes. "But they took my pistol, so going after them unarmed will be taking an awful risk."

"Then why are you doing it?" she demanded. "This is not your fight!"

"I've got my reasons," he assured her. Glancing at the glowering skies, then at the tracks where the stolen part of the train had disappeared, he asked, "You ready?"

"Let's go!"

"Wait!" a male passenger called, stepping forward. "I'll not be shamed by letting a little woman like you go while I stand and watch. Step down, Miss, and I'll go with this other man."

"No!" Laurel spoke sharply, then softened her tone. "I thank you from the bottom of my heart, but I need to do this."

Other embarrassed men crowded around, offering to go, but Laurel steadfastly refused. "There's only room for two on this thing, so I'm going, and that's final." She looked at Lucas. "Let's get started."

He nodded and reached for the other handle as a uniformed crewman ran up.

"I remembered this was in the baggage car," he said, handing a shotgun up to Lucas. "It's loaded, but there's only one shot, and I didn't see any other cartridges."

Lucas took the weapon, checked it quickly, then laid it down on the car by his feet. "Thanks. Now, Laurel, let me tell you how this vehicle operates."

He quickly explained that they stand facing each other, with him riding backward. Each took hold of the handle in front. Using both hands, Lucas demonstrated how when he pushed down, Laurel's handle came up, and the car moved down the tracks. When she pushed down, the car gained momentum and rolled tracks in the direction the stolen train section had taken.

They pumped hard, urged on by the approaching storm.

A few miles down the track, Ridge crouched behind his breastwork of treasure chests while the express car slowly rolled to a stop. It was dark inside with the coal oil lamp unlit, but Ridge's eyes had adjusted well. He rechecked the loads in the repeating Henry rifle, the shotgun, and the revolver he had taken from Aiken.

Ridge sat on the floor, his back against the side where padlocked strongboxes were stacked higher than his head against the wall. The boxes on both sides and in front were not as high, but they offered some protection.

Ridge heard crunching gravel as footsteps approached the car. Aiken announced with obvious glee, "They're coming, Reb." He still held his stomach where he had been struck with the rifle barrel. "You're as good as dead!"

"Not yet. If they shoot in here, you're more likely to get hit than I am."

"The odds are ten to twelve against you, Reb, so open one of those sliding doors."

"Sorry, but I plan to finish what I was hired to do."

The graveled footsteps halted outside the far sliding door, and a man's voice ordered, "Open this door!"

"Can't do that," Ridge called out in reply.

"Aiken?" the outside voice called, "is that you?"

"No. That's the Rebel! He took my gun."

Ridge shouted, "My orders are not to open this car for anyone until we get to our destination."

The outside voice called angrily, "I don't care who you are or what your orders are! Open this car right now or we'll shoot it to pieces."

"Claude?" Aiken called. "Is that you?"

"Who else would it be?" the voice replied.

Claude? Ridge silently repeated.

Aiken triumphantly told him, "He's the leader, and you've made a big mistake crossing him."

"We'll see," Ridge replied.

"Aiken," Claude called, "get out of the way as best you can. We're going to start firing."

He cursed vehemently, then howled, "Don't shoot! You'll hit me! This Rebel knocked me down with his rifle and made himself a safe place behind the strongboxes. I'm out in the open without any protection."

Ridge said approvingly, "Good thinking, Aiken."

Claude could be heard speaking to others outside the car, but Ridge couldn't understand them. He waited.

Soon Claude announced, "We're going to use black powder and blow this car wide open."

"What?" Aiken roared in surprise. "You'll kill me for sure if you do that!"

"You knew there was a risk," Claude replied casually. He lowered his voice and said something to those outside with him.

Aiken cursed Ridge. "I know you don't care if I get killed, but is it worth defending this car and leaving that pretty little gal alive for some other man?"

The words hit Ridge like a fist to the stomach. He was furious with Laurel for causing the death of his brother and other Confederates. But there was something else about her that kept muffling his anger so it was not as loudly insistent as the emotions that drew him to her.

He forced those thoughts aside upon hearing a clink of metal to his left, toward the engine.

Aiken explained, "They've pulled the link-pin coupling this car to the tender. In a minute, the locomotive and the tender will go on down the tracks, leaving this car all alone so they can blow it up. You'll die, Reb, and you'll never see that woman again."

Ridge didn't answer, but listened to the sound of the engine and tender moving away, leaving the express car behind. The engine puffed away into the distance before there was again the crunch of gravel.

"You're surrounded," Claude called from outside. "This is your last chance to open this sliding door."

Ridge aimed the rifle in the general direction of the voice. "No! I'm about to start shooting."

"Enough talk!" Claude shouted. "Set the charge!"

Ridge ducked low behind the strongboxes and fired two rounds through the wooden door. Those surrounding the car outside returned fire.

Ridge snapped off three more quick rounds from the Henry

in the direction of the men shooting at him. He laid the rifle on a box beside him and picked up the pistol. He spun around at the sight of someone trying to slip through the small left side door.

He fired quickly, then shifted to snap off another shot at the rear sliding door. A ball smashed into the padlock of the strongbox at his left, sending a shower of splintered metal flying. Ridge realized he had been hit, and glanced down to see how serious it was.

He sensed more than heard Aiken rush toward him from behind. Ridge pivoted to meet that threat, but Aiken had already snatched up the rifle. Ridge tried to dodge, but the glancing blow from the weapon caught him on the temple. He sank to the floor, vaguely hearing Aiken's frantic cries.

"Don't shoot! I got him! I got that crazy Rebel!"

Ridge heard no more.

Laurel and Lucas pumped the little railroad handcar along the rails that occasionally glistened with the frequent lightening flashes. The tracks led into a wooded area that made the whole world seem darker.

Her hands felt as though they were beginning to blister, but she doggedly kept shoving down on her handle each time Lucas forced it up.

He puffed, "They surprised me back there. I didn't expect them to come through the cars like they did. I thought they would just take the express car with its gold shipment and not bother the passengers."

Laurel had always resented Lucas' tendency to be curious

about everything, but since he had helped her get to Claude, she had felt differently about him. Talking with him helped take her concern off Ridge.

"It's not your fault," she assured Lucas while the curls fell in disarray around her face. "There's never been a train robbery, so how could anyone know the way it would be done?"

"Thanks, but at least I now know how this gang did it. Others will surely do it even more efficiently. I figure there were about ten or twelve men. Some were hiding behind the water tower when the train stopped.

"One witness told me he saw two men swing onto the rear of the tender and start climbing over the wood toward the cab. Nobody saw what happened next, but it's logical that those bandits dropped down into the cab and forced the engineer and firemen to stop the train at gunpoint.

"Four others split up into pairs. Each of those entered the coaches, one from the back platform, one from the front. They robbed the passengers. The remaining gang members were on horseback, hiding in the woods. When the passengers were robbed, the horsemen rode up with extra mounts for the robbers in the cars, plus one for the conductor. The other outlaws stayed with the locomotive, forcing the engineer and firemen to pull away with the express car and whatever treasure it's carrying."

"Schramm wasn't really a hostage," Laurel said. "He was part of the gang. They just tried to make it look as though he was forced to be a hostage."

"I'm not surprised. You were mighty lucky when they both fired in your direction."

"Thanks to your timely warning, I was ready with a plan to play possum."

"You tired?" Lucas asked. "Want to rest a minute?"

"No, I want to keep going." She raised her head and looked down the tracks. "There it is!"

The stolen express car stood abandoned on the rails. There was no sign of the engine or tender.

Weary as she was, Laurel pumped faster, driving the handcar forward. As it neared the express car, they stopped the handcar. Laurel lifted her long skirts, leaped off, and ran along the cross ties toward the coach. It was ominously quiet.

"Careful!" Lucas called, leaping off with the shotgun and trying to catch up with her.

Lightening flickered, filling Laurel with fear at the sight of all the bullet holes in the car's side. She dashed around the front to find the sliding door open.

Another jagged streak of light from the sky momentarily illuminated the interior of the express car. In a glance, Laurel saw a body sprawled unnaturally on the floor.

"Ridge!" she screamed, and started trying to climb into the car, but there was no step and her long skirt prevented her from swinging her legs high enough.

"You'd better stay back," Lucas said. He laid the shotgun on the doorway entrance and hoisted himself into the darkened interior.

Laurel stood, trembling with fear, while Lucas bent over the still form inside.

"It's Aiken," he called. "He's dead."

"Ridge?" Laurel whispered.

"I'm looking." He moved toward the scattered strongboxes. "The treasure boxes have all been broken into. They must have been full of twenty-dollar double eagle gold pieces because there are still a few scattered around on the floor."

"What about Ridge?"

"No sign of him."

"Where do you think he is?"

Lucas returned to the doorway, his face sober. "I hate to say this, but, well, there's blood all over."

Sick with fear, Laurel asked, "Do you think?"

"I don't know," he interrupted. "Could be Ridge's."

"He must be alive!" Hope drove her voice high. "Maybe he's a prisoner."

"Maybe, but, well, I hate to say this, but they could have dumped him off along the tracks. I'll take a look. You'd better get inside before the rain starts."

"I can't rest until I find Ridge!"

"Very well. You can help me look, but you're likely to get soaked if the rains begin."

The search took several minutes while they split up and walked along both sides of the tracks the way they had come. Then, after a fruitless trek, they searched the same way up the track where the engine and tender must have gone.

"Nothing," Lucas mused, "just horse tracks and a few more scattered coins. These were probably dropped when being loaded into saddle bags."

"Where did they go?" Laurel looked quickly in all directions. "They must have stopped the car here for some special reason."

"Yes. They probably have a hideout close by."

"There!" Laurel pointed. "Beyond that little rise. There's a chimney with smoke coming from it. Probably a farmhouse. They've got to be there!"

"I checked Aiken's body, but they had taken his gun, if he

had one. So that's about ten men against this shotgun," Lucas mused. He jumped down from the car and picked up the shotgun with a single shell that the crew member had given him.

"Maybe they've split up," Laurel said hopefully. "They've had time to divide the money and ride off, at least, some of them have. But somebody's still there because they've built a fire. Maybe that's where Ridge is. Let's go take a look."

"We can go closer," Lucas agreed, "but keep out of sight. The storm will help. If he is in there, and we get caught or make a mistake—"

"I know," she interrupted, "but there's no use standing here. Let's see what we can do."

She started toward the farmhouse as the first drops of rain fell.

Chapter 20

Some time earlier, Ridge opened his eyes in the express coach and groaned with pain. He touched his temple, felt the stickiness of blood, and then remembered what had happened. He thought of Laurel in the abandoned part of the train, and flinched in recalling how brutally he had spoken to her before ordering her out of his life.

Can't think about her now. With effort, he sat up. Through the gloom of late afternoon and the approaching storm, he saw that the sliding front door was open. The strongboxes had been broken into and were empty. Some gold double eagle coins were scattered about. Forcing himself to his feet, he stood, swaying while the drumbeat of pain in his head made him fearful of passing out again. By force of will, he remained upright and started to search for his weapons. At first, he didn't see anything. He took a stumbling step toward something on the floor and realized it was George Aiken's body. A quick check for pulse showed he was dead.

Ridge reeled uncertainly toward the open sliding door and looked out. Sheet lightning revealed many fresh hoof prints and the deep ruts of wagon wheels, but not a horse or living person was in sight. *They might come back,* he told himself. *I've got to get out of sight.*

He slid wearily to the graveled roadbed and steadied himself against the side of the express car. *I smell smoke.* He slowly turned, sniffing to find the source. *That way. They've gone to a house that way.*

He staggered forward, nearly tripping over a dropped rifle beside the tracks. He picked it up and checked the load. The gun was empty. *Not much good this way,* he told himself, but he still held onto the weapon out of habit. He had only gone a few steps when the blackness again threatened him. *Can't let them find me.* He looked around and slid down into a weed-filled ditch. In spite of his best efforts to remain conscious, he collapsed and let the blackness claim him again.

Hannibal Schramm adjusted the conductor's small-billed cap on his head and stood up from the farmhouse's long kitchen table. From its center, a kerosene lamp cast a pale yellow light over the group.

"Everyone satisfied?" the conductor asked, glancing at the men sitting around with saddlebags of gold coins in front of them.

The murmur of agreement was drowned out by the crash of thunder. Schramm glanced at the window where the first small drops of rain were starting to make little cat footprints on the dusty glass. "All right, then," he said with finality. "You can all either saddle up and scatter, or stay here and wait out the storm."

One prematurely bald outlaw laughed and swung the heavy saddlebags over his shoulder. "Wait here for the posse that'll come when that engineer spreads the word? No, thanks, Hannibal. I'll chance the storm."

The others agreed, and quickly exited the kitchen's side door with their leather pouches filled with clinking gold coins. A moment later, Schramm stood alone, staring thoughtfully out the window. He heard only the fast drumming of galloping horses and crackling of fire in the wood-burning stove.

Lightning zigzagged across the sky, briefly illuminating the outside trees, the barn, and the other outbuildings. There was something else, too.

"What the? . . ." he exclaimed, reaching for the revolver he had laid on the table by his saddlebags.

A voice from the foot of the stairs in the front parlor asked, "What did you say?"

"I just saw that Rebel out there!"

Claude Duncan chuckled and clumped noisily into the kitchen with a holstered revolver at his belt. "You *thought* you saw him, Hannibal. I didn't think you could have a guilty conscience."

The conductor took a few quick steps and stepped to the side of the window, pistol in hand. "I tell you, he's out there!"

"Couldn't be." Claude's gray eyes rested on Schramm's saddlebags. "He's dead. Remember?"

Another flash of lightning made Schramm anxiously peer outside. After the peal of thunder, he turned away from the window. "Well, it may not have been him, but I sure as blazes saw somebody out there."

"You probably saw one of the riders getting away late." Claude motioned for Schramm to sit down. "Let's get on with plans for the next job."

"I think I'll look around outside first."

"Why waste time? Aiken smashed his skull just before trigger-happy Rufus started shooting up the car and killed Aiken. I don't want Rufus on the next raid."

Schramm slowly lowered himself into the chair he had previously occupied. "Then why wasn't that Rebel's body there when I sent the wagon back to get those gold bars?"

"Maybe he fell out of the door when the car went around that last curve. Even if he was alive, he would be unarmed. You said that you took all the guns from the car yourself. Now shut up, and let's get on with this."

Schramm stole glances at the other kitchen windows.

"Doesn't it bother you that your lady friend is dead?"

Claude shrugged. "Of course, at least in one way. But when she started getting in the way of what we were trying to do, there was no choice. That's why I sent word for you and that other man so you could make it look like she died from an accidental stray ball from your derringer."

Schramm shook his head. "Somehow, even with her dead, she bested me. Without that ledger, I can't even go back and claim that I was a hostage who escaped. She could have ruined me."

"She *did* ruin you, Hannibal," Claude said bluntly. "She probably gave it to her friend Sarah, who will turn it over to Pinkerton. They'll figure out that you shot her on purpose instead of accidentally. Vigilantes don't take kindly to women getting killed. If they catch you, they'll stretch your neck real quick, like they almost did me. Anyway, you're through as a conductor."

"This whole thing didn't turn out right," Schramm complained.

"Not for you, anyway." Claude's eyes narrowed as he studied the conductor. "You thought that when the vigilantes finished with me, you'd take over as leader of this gang."

"No, I didn't! I'm satisfied to be second in command."

"The blazes you are, Schramm! You figured you would split the double eagles with the others, and then take my share of the gold bars along with yours. It would have been easy because the men didn't know about the bullion hidden under the stack of firewood for the stove. Only you and I knew that."

"I swear to you, Claude. . . ."

"Don't lie, Hannibal! You can't fool me. In fact, you couldn't even fool Laurel, even after I warned you that she was smart."

Claude began feeling in his pockets. "Once Pinkerton has your book, they'll not only have proof that you were stealing from the railroad, but they'll figure out that you're a part of this gang." Claude stopped and stood up.

Schramm asked, "What's the matter?"

"I must have left the new plans upstairs. I'll be right back." He started through the door toward the parlor. Over his shoulder, he said, "If Pinkerton ever finds out that you and Aiken cooperated to have that agent and the brakeman killed, you'll be on the run the rest of your life. Now, just sit there and don't go shooting at shadows."

Laurel and Jacob had approached close enough to see that the old, two-story farmhouse had a porch that ran from the front around the sides to the back. It wasn't quite dark, so they slipped up close to the dilapidated frame structure and moved cautiously toward several horses tied in back by what appeared to be the kitchen.

Laurel hoped with all her aching heart that Ridge would be in there, perhaps a prisoner, but alive. She brushed the first drops of rain from her face just as the back door opened. She and Lucas stooped low and squeezed up against the building while several men hurriedly crossed the porch, secured heavy saddlebags over their horses' backs, and rode away. Only two animals remained.

Laurel whispered, "Two men must still be inside."

"Stay here. I'll slip up and peek into a window."

She waited impatiently until lightning flickered again and Lucas hurried back.

"I saw Schramm, the conductor. He's alone, counting the stolen gold coins. Unfortunately, I think he saw me."

Lucas grabbed Laurel's hand. "Come on. Let's get back a ways in case he comes out to check."

"Ridge must be in there with him."

Crouching and moving along the outside of the house, Lucas said, "I don't think so. Anyway, I didn't see him.

"I've got to be sure," Laurel whispered.

"No! That's too risky!"

"I'm not going until I make sure. I have an idea."

After she quickly outlined it, Lucas nodded. They separated, with Laurel stepping up on the long porch to approach the front door. Lucas headed toward the back.

She waited, breathing hard with fear, excitement, and worry, until she heard a horse whinny. She flinched, guessing that the animal had seen Lucas. That meant he had time to be in place, so she cautiously grasped the knob on the front door.

It opened, the sound drowned by a thunderclap. She boldly stepped inside the empty parlor and hurried past the stairwell. Quietly, she pushed the pocket doors aside that separated the parlor from the dining room. She glided on tiptoes to the open kitchen door. There she saw Schramm fingering some gold coins from the open saddlebags on the table before him.

He leaped up at the sight of her and snatched at the revolver on the table, but Jacob burst into the room behind him. "Drop it, Schramm!" he ordered, "or this scattergun will blow you apart!"

For a long moment, Laurel froze, unsure if the conductor were going to obey or fire his weapon at her.

He stared at her and slowly released the pistol. "I thought you were dead!" His voice was a hoarse croak.

"You missed, but I pretended to be hit," she said with great relief while Lucas shoved the shotgun barrel against Schramm's back and took his revolver.

Lucas asked, "Laurel, can you use a shotgun?"

"I used to go hunting with my brother," she assured him, walking around and taking that gun while Lucas held the pistol on Schramm.

"Good!" Lucas ordered the conductor, "Face her and put your hands behind your back. You're under arrest for robbery and murder!"

Laurel blinked in astonishment as Lucas produced a pair of handcuffs and secured them around Schramm's wrists.

"Arrest?" he asked over his shoulder, but with his eyes on Laurel's level gun. "You can't arrest me!"

"I just did," Lucas announced with obvious satisfaction. "I'm a Pinkerton operative, with broad arrest powers without regard to local jurisdictions."

Laurel made a startled sound, causing Lucas to glance at her. "It's true," he assured her. "Besides the train robbery, I'm charging him for attempting to murder you, plus killing Ridge."

Laurel cringed at the blunt statement. She didn't want to believe he was dead. She glanced around the room before asking

Schramm, "Where is Ridge?"

"I'm not sure," he replied, looking in bewilderment from Laurel to Lucas. "I heard that Aiken cracked him over the head before one of our own men accidentally shot Aiken. I guess your friend got shot, too, but we couldn't find his body."

Laurel stifled a low moan and closed her eyes.

Lucas motioned with the revolver. "Sit down, then tell me how much the gang stole, and how much is in here." He shoved the saddlebags of gold out of the other man's reach.

Laurel glanced around as thunder boomed and the rain fell harder. "Who's that second horse for?"

Schramm's expression changed ever so slightly, but Laurel caught it.

"That horse?" the conductor paused. "Oh, it was for Aiken, but he won't need it."

"I think you're lying." Laurel felt hope stir that Ridge was somewhere in the house. "Mr. Lucas, if you can keep an eye on this man, I'm going to look around."

Lucas sighed. "Don't get your hopes up too high, Laurel. Besides, it's getting too dark to go wandering around, and I don't see another lamp besides this one."

"There's a candle on that little shelf by the stove, and another lamp upstairs," Schramm said smoothly. "Light that candle and go look around for yourself."

Laurel frowned, looking suspiciously at him.

Schramm quickly turned to Lucas. "You two really had me fooled. I thought she was the Pinkerton, but now I understand. You had her telegraph the reports back to Allan Pinkerton so that I would be thrown off the track. Well, it worked."

Laurel's powerful urge to find Ridge made her ignore suspicions about Schramm. She walked around to the shelf and retrieved a three-inch candle stub.

Jacob said with pride, "That was the idea, Schramm. I was assigned by Allan Pinkerton himself to watch her."

Laurel whirled with the candle in her hands. "Me?"

"Yes," Lucas admitted. "I had been working on rumors that there was a train robbery planned. Mr. Pinkerton said it was possible that the outlaws were using a woman to help them gather inside information. Naturally, a woman like you wouldn't be suspected."

Laurel's first reaction was to lash out verbally at Allan Pinkerton, but instead, she laughed lightly.

So what I've heard is true, she thought. *He doesn't trust any of his operatives, so he gets them to spy on each other. When I get to Chicago, I'm going to tell Pinkerton what I think of his sneaky ways! Meanwhile, I've fooled both these men; neither knows I'm also a Pinkerton.*

Lucas asked, "What's so funny?"

"Oh, nothing." She carried the candle to the lamp, carefully lifted the glass chimney by its base where it wasn't too hot, and touched the candlewick to the flame.

"I was just intrigued by the fact that I was innocent and Mr. Schramm here is guilty. Men's minds work strangely."

Laurel's moment of lightheartedness passed, and the pain of what had happened to Ridge swept back over her. She replaced the lamp chimney and straightened up with the lighted candle. "I'm going upstairs to look for Ridge."

Lucas urged, "Better take the shotgun, just in case there's another one of these robbers hiding out here."

Schramm said, "I'm alone. That horse was for—"

"I know," Laurel interrupted. "But I'm going to find out what happened to Ridge, starting right here." She shifted the candle to her left hand, picked up the shotgun with her right hand, and started back into the dining room.

Lightning flashed and thunder crashed as the storm broke over the farmhouse. Laurel moved toward the stairwell, remembering the strange expression she had glimpsed in Schramm's eyes.

Ridge didn't know how long he had lain unconscious in the ditch. Rain falling on his face made him stir. For a moment, he lay still, shivering with the cold. Again, he remembered how he had parted from Laurel. That hurt more than his injured head, but at least she was safe back in the cars.

He sat up, still holding the empty rifle. He felt somewhat better. He hoped he wouldn't pass out any more. He crawled out of the ditch as the sky lit up again. The express car was momentarily silhouetted. On the tracks near it, light reflected from metal. Ridge waited for another lightning flash.

"Railroad handcar," he muttered to himself. "Wonder where that came from." Shrugging, he turned, sniffing the fragrance of wood smoke. *I've got to find some shelter.*

He threw himself onto the ground when several horsemen galloped by. They shouted gleefully and disappeared into the darkness. Ridge went on and soon saw the farmhouse. The riders must have come from there, so others might still be inside.

Ridge slipped up on the front porch while the thunder and lightning storm unleashed its fury. He momentarily closed his eyes against the throbbing pain where Aiken had struck him on the head.

When he opened his eyes again, through the window he saw a tall man walking from the back of the house toward the front door. Ridge froze, swinging the rifle around to use as a club. But the man turned at the foot of the stairs and took them two at a time.

That's got to be one of the gang, but how many others are still inside? Ridge was tempted to slip along the long sheltered porch to peer into every window and find out, but he decided to wait until the first man came back downstairs.

Ridge saw a candle moving through the house from the back. *Here comes another one. . . . Laurel? No! It can't be!* He blinked, quickly rubbed his eyes, and looked again.

In another few seconds, the candle light fell fully on her face, and he nearly shouted in surprise. *It is Laurel! How did she get here?*

He watched her cautiously start up the stairs with the candle in her left hand, and the shotgun in her right. The weapon alerted him that she was not a prisoner, but was she trying to find the man who had gone upstairs, or was she checking out the house for intruders? Either way, Ridge realized that she was in jeopardy.

Even though he was still irate because her spying had caused the tragedy at Bethel Crossing, the sight of Laurel heading into danger stirred him deeply.

"No! Laurel!" he whispered in alarm. "Don't go up there!"

He started toward the front door, but the sudden movement sent waves of weakness sweeping over him. He had to wait until it passed while his mind raced.

Gripping the rifle firmly, Ridge rose and quietly crossed to the front door while lightning flickered again. He waited for the thunder to cover his sound, then quickly opened the door, slipped inside, closed it, and limped toward bottom of the stairs.

He saw that Laurel had reached the second floor. She moved the candle around to better see what was in the shadows that darted and dodged as the light shifted.

Ridge cupped his left hand to his mouth, ready to call her, then shook his head. *No! that man might hear me, or she could be so startled that she turns and fires at me without seeing who it is.*

Ridge continued silently to the first landing where the steps turned left before continuing up.

He heard her call softly, "Ridge? Are you up here?"

He began ascending the second level of stairs, which gave him enough elevation to see her upper body and both hands. She stopped at a closed door, held the shotgun against her body with her right arm, and used her free hand to turn the knob.

Ridge saw the shadows slip away, revealing a large closet. Laurel quickly passed the candle back and forth, making sure the room was empty. She started to step back and close the door.

A streak of lightning showed Ridge another door open behind Laurel.

"Laurel, look out!" Ridge shouted, but a clap of thunder drowned his voice.

As the rumble faded, he heard her muffled cry and saw the candle sail through the air. It fell, revealing the man's left hand clamped over Laurel's mouth. Then the candle went out and the shotgun landed with a muffled sound on the carpeted hallway runner.

Then there was nothing. No sight. No sound. Just an upstairs hallway swathed in ominous dark silence.

Ridge fought an urge to rush up the last few stairs and attack with all the pent-up anger boiling inside of him. But four years of war had taught him to wait, to learn what he faced, before acting.

The next electric flash showed him clearly what was happening, bringing a raging roar from his throat.

Laurel's mouth was still covered by her attacker's left hand. She struggled, frantically striking with her hands and feet, but her assailant only laughed and used his right arm to swoop her up. He carried her toward the room where he had been hiding.

As fast as his injured leg would permit, Ridge scurried down the hall, grateful that the almost continuous peals of thunder hid his sound. He reached the open door where another lightning flash showed him a bed chamber with an old mattress thrown on the floor.

Laurel's attacker roughly dropped her and started to unstrap his gunbelt when he suddenly tensed and whirled to face the door.

Ridge's rage carried him across the carpeted floor, the empty rifle gripped by the barrel. He started to swing it while the man clawed at his holstered pistol.

Ridge's throat burned from the roar that erupted there. All the primitive emotions inside him exploded into uncontrollable outrage. He swung the rifle butt toward her attacker's head. The blow staggered him, but he kept his feet and tried to pull his revolver.

Ridge's raw savagery took over. He knocked the pistol away and leaped upon the adversary. They fell to the floor, both struggling in the darkness, puffing hard, screaming in the way men do in terrible fights. Dimly, by periodic streaks of lightning, Ridge realized that Laurel had crawled out of the way. Then he was aware that she was coming toward him.

"Ridge!" she cried, pulling vainly on his shoulders which rose and fell as he drove his blows down. "Stop! Stop! You're killing him!"

Slowly, through the red fog of hatred that nearly blinded him, Ridge realized he had straddled the other man and was striking him repeatedly although he had stopped resisting.

"Please, Ridge!" Laurel begged, grabbing his right arm as it drew back for another blow. "Stop! Oh, please stop!"

She felt him hesitate, the right fist still upraised. Then, very slowly, he relaxed and looked up at her bending over him.

"Laurel," he said through bleeding lips, "are you all right?"

"Yes, but that's Claude! Please, stop hitting him!"

Ridge stared at her as though he didn't understand. "Claude?" he asked in bewilderment.

When she nodded, Ridge jerked backward in horror at what he had done.

Laurel quickly knelt and felt for a pulse in the limp wrist. "It's all right, Ridge," Laurel said with relief. She turned from Claude to help Ridge to his feet. "He's just unconscious."

Getting to his feet with difficulty, Ridge nodded and looked down at Laurel with eyes that lost their ire. Instead, a softness seeped into them.

He held out his hands with the skinned knuckles and she started to come into the circle of his arms.

They both stopped as Lucas burst into room with the coal oil lamp in one hand and a gun in the other. He looked from the couple to the prone man on the floor.

Whistling in surprise, Lucas said, "At first I thought I was just hearing the thunder. When I realized something was . . . Ridge! I thought you were dead!"

"They tried hard enough to kill me," he replied.

Lucas asked anxiously, "Are you both all right?"

When they silently nodded, Lucas sighed. "I guess I didn't really need to ask." He set the lamp and gun on the floor and bent over Claude. "I'll get him out of here. You two come down when you're ready."

Laurel and Ridge looked at each other, each seeing something had changed in the other.

"Thanks," Ridge said through puffy lips, "but we'll help you down with him." He glanced at Laurel. "Later, you and I have to talk privately."

She studied his face, hoping for some sign that he meant it would be a pleasant conversation. But when she could not discern that, she apprehensively licked her lips. Hiding her concern, she nodded. "Yes."

Chapter 21

The wind blew across Lake Michigan, blasting through Chicago's streets and shaking window panes above the famous sign of *The Eye That Never Sleeps*. Inside his office, America's best-known detective thoughtfully stroked his beard and looked across his desk at Laurel.

"So," he summarized, "Schramm is sure to be convicted because you recovered the ledger that Sarah kept for you until you got back after the train robbery."

"She's certainly happy to be home. She and her beau patched things up and plan to be married soon."

Pinkerton nodded without interest, then continued. "Schramm also faces murder charges for plotting with Aiken to kill my agent, Woods, plus Harkins. Schramm admitted that he and Aiken mistakenly thought the brakeman was also one of my operatives."

When Laurel nodded, Pinkerton continued. "Aiken was apparently killed by his own gang, maybe accidentally. Their leader and your former fiancé is recovering from the beating your friend Ridge gave him."

Laurel lowered her eyes to hide the embarrassment over Claude, but Pinkerton didn't seem to notice.

He continued, "Claude will be tried for murder and train robbery, plus the old charges for which the vigilantes almost hanged him. He might have been better off if they had succeeded."

"It's hard," Laurel admitted. "I knew him all my life, but in some ways, I didn't really know him at all."

"I understand." Pinkerton made a tepee of his fingers. "What did you tell Jacob Lucas when he asked you how you knew Woods was an agent?"

Hesitating, Laurel considered that her first step toward spiritual reconciliation had been followed by a test she had failed. That left a nagging sense of guilt. But she had done it, and she planned to do better in the future.

She told Pinkerton, "I let him think that a reporter for the *Chicago Globe* had wired that information to me."

Pinkerton nodded in approval. "You did a good job on this one, Laurel. You even managed to keep Sarah from knowing that you were working for me."

Laurel shifted uneasily, wondering if Pinkerton were testing her honesty. Had he somehow learned that Sarah had guessed the truth? No, Laurel decided; he was sincere. For once, the great detective didn't know everything, and Laurel didn't feel she should tell him differently.

She relaxed and smiled at Pinkerton. "Thank you." She also decided not to say that she believed he had sent Lucas to protect her, not just to spy on her.

Pinkerton tapped the newspaper spread out on his desk. "The *Globe's* first-person story is almost as detailed as your report to me. Well, except there's nothing here about your working as an operative."

Returning the smile, Laurel replied, "I made sure of that.

After I turned the conductor's ledger over to your agent at the end of the line, I knew the transcontinental railroad material I'd gotten from Schramm wasn't very exciting. So I wrote the first-person account of the murders and train robbery. That's what I wired to the editor before our train started back to Chicago."

Pinkerton's smiled broadened. "I hear the *Globe* liked it so much that they offered you a regular paid staff position as a correspondent."

During the war, Laurel had become used to Pinkerton's uncanny way of seeming to know about all sorts of supposedly confidential matters. "Yes," she said. "They did. That's why I came to see you."

"You want to know if I'm going to propose a detective job that's better than the *Globe's* offer."

She started to shake her head. She had come to give him her final report and to say she no longer wanted to be an agent. But she could not bring herself to tell him why: since the events of the last several days, she had changed and didn't want any more lies and deception. Yet the excitement of secret detective work was intoxicating and even habit-forming. It intrigued her almost as much as when she had been a Union agent in the war.

When she didn't answer, Pinkerton continued. "If you want the adventure of your life, you can have it by going undercover for me on the new transcontinental railroad being built west out of Omaha toward California. Are you interested?"

Laurel hadn't expected that, especially since she had met Ridge Granger. Still, she had to know more. "Tempt me," she said.

"I'll pay the same money as the *Globe* offered you, but you can write freelance or part time for them. They'll pay you by the column inch for published copy; I'll pay you a regular operative's undercover salary. You can't beat that, so how about it?"

That was something else she hadn't expected. "What would be my assignment?"

"As you know, this agency does a lot of work for railroads. They've started building the transcontinental line from Omaha to Sacramento, but already they're having a lot of problems besides the usual ones associated with any rail line construction. Those include one mysterious disappearance of a railroad official, plus two deaths. My agency was retained to send an undercover operative to infiltrate the inner railroad circles to discover if there's a connection between the disappearance, murders, and unusual problems."

Laurel felt the old thrill of flirting with danger rush over her. "What kind of problems?"

"I'll tell you only if you take the assignment." Pinkerton paused and thoughtfully regarded Laurel across the desk. "Naturally, there will be some risk to the agent," he continued soberly. "But a woman correspondent may ask seemingly innocent questions without arousing as much suspicion as a male agent would. You want to do it?"

The adventure appealed to Laurel, but she held back, thinking of Ridge. It was too soon to know if a meaningful relationship would develop between them. Yet being separated for a long period without knowing the answer troubled her.

Shaking her head, Laurel confessed, "I don't know."

The famous detective leaned back and laced his fingers behind his head. "Then think about this: Wouldn't it be exciting to not only write about building a railroad across two thousand miles of wilderness, but to eventually be the first woman ever to ride the rails all the way to the Pacific? That could be historic."

It was intriguing, but Laurel still stalled. "I'll have to think about it."

"You mean, you'll have to talk to your new beau?"

That flustered her. "Ridge isn't my beau. We only met a few days ago."

"But you're obviously interested." Pinkerton leaned forward again. "I did some checking, Laurel, and I hear he's a good man. In fact, the railroad was so pleased with his work on that trip that they've offered him a job as a regular crewman."

Laurel's eyes opened wide at that surprising news.

Pinkerton said, "I see you didn't know that. I'm sorry if I spoke out of turn. He probably wants to tell you himself. Maybe that will make a difference in whether you accept my offer or not."

Pinkerton stood, indicating the interview was over. "You'll make a fine operative, Laurel, but I will understand if you don't accept. However, the railroad is pushing me to act, so I need your answer in twenty-four hours."

❦

Laurel knew she couldn't make a decision until after her dinner engagement with Ridge. That evening, she put Pinkerton's newest deadline at the back of her mind. She sat across from Ridge at a small restaurant overlooking the lake. Outside lanterns reflected off the whitecaps where the stiff wind dashed them against the shore. Only candles softly illuminated the dining area where muted violins played in the background. Waiters in dark suits moved discreetly among the linen-covered tables.

Laurel wondered where Ridge had gotten money for such an expensive evening. Then she remembered that he had not worn his overcoat this cool evening. *Probably sold it,* she thought, *and maybe his gun, too.* Such sacrifices warmed her feelings toward him.

Through their window table for two, Laurel watched the waves. "They're beautiful," she said softly.

"You're more beautiful." Ridge's voice was husky. "The most beautiful woman I've ever seen."

She flushed and turned to meet his eyes. The candlelight danced in their depths, stirring her. She quickly glanced down at the corsage of pink rosebuds pinned to her white gown. "Thank you again for these."

"I tried to get real flowers, but this late in the year and so soon after the war made that impossible. I got these from an old woman who makes them to sell on the street. You deserve better, but—"

Laurel interrupted. "I'd rather have these." She smiled at him across the table. "I will keep them forever."

The waiter came for their order, but Ridge asked him to give them a little longer. As the waiter left, Ridge said to Laurel, "I hope I'm not too presumptuous, but I want to say something to you."

He reached across the linen cloth and took both her hands in his. "Laurel, there's something so special about you that I don't want to lose you. I'd like to know you better, so every moment with you is . . . well, precious."

It wasn't a word she would have expected from him, but it sounded just right to her. "I would like to know you better, too," she said softly.

They fell silent, hands gently touching. It seemed impossible to Laurel that only a few days had passed since they had first met. She was beginning to feel comfortable with him, yet earlier that evening when he had called for her in a hired hackney, she inwardly fretted because of their past tensions.

She had made an effort to be reconciled with her father, and had asked Ridge to call for her there. She was surprised that her father was not his usual brusque self with Ridge. The two men had talked freely, although Laurel sensed that her strong-minded parent didn't really expect a former Rebel to court his youngest daughter.

On the drive to dinner, Laurel and Ridge's conversation had been a bit strained. It was the first time they had been alone since the stormy night at the farmhouse.

Confessing to Ridge about Laurel's wartime spying activity had almost lost him, yet she still kept secret her work as a lady Pinkerton detective. She tried to tell herself that it was too early to admit that, and besides, Pinkerton didn't want it known.

However, if her relationship with Ridge developed, she would someday have to tell him. By then, he might not trust her at all. But she could not tell him everything, not yet, anyway. Still, she had to make a start. She wished she could read his thoughts.

In the hackney, Ridge had also been reflective. It had started on the train following her confession of being a Union spy and her part in the tragedy at Bethel Crossing. At first, his anger had been so great that a black mood engulfed him.

Since then, his mind had cleared enough that he realized he should have suspected she was an operative. The day they had met, he had seen her enter Pinkerton's office and wondered why a pretty young woman would go there. At the same time, he had recalled that Pinkerton had formed the North's Secret Service for General George McClellan to spy on the South early in the war.

I should have guessed, he told himself. Her spying had obviously ended with the war, but was she still a detective? Was she still keeping secrets from him? Could he trust her? He wasn't sure, but one thing was certain: he was so greatly attracted to her that he had to keep seeing her, at least for a while.

His mind leaped form the hackney back to when they had ridden the train north to Chicago. She had told him about her experience with the vigilantes, and confronting Claude Duncan over the shameful lies Ambrose had told about her. She delicately avoided the detailed charge.

Ridge understood because he had said through clenched teeth, "If I had known that, I would have probably killed him before you could stop me. As it was, tangling with him was cathartic. After the war, everything I had fought for was lost. I was filled with anger and wanted revenge on someone, anyone. I was really spoiling for a fight. Now, that feeling is gone, and I'm grateful. I can face the future without those terrible negative emotions."

"The future?" Laurel asked softly.

"Yes. I originally came to Chicago figuring that I would deliver that letter and then return to Virginia with answers to the questions I needed to think through."

"And do you have the answers?"

"Not yet," he admitted, but when you're home again, I would like to call on you. Over dinner, I'd like to get to know you better, learn what your future plans are."

"Dinner? Sounds wonderful. I accept, if you'll tell me what you're thinking."

"Let's save that for our dinner together."

They had left it there. Now, holding hands across the table while the candlelight played on Ridge's handsome features, Laurel was comfortable, and yet she felt some trepidation. Unable to stand it any longer, she asked a question in hopes she would like the answer. But she couldn't be sure.

"You were going to tell me about your future," she prompted.

"Yes, but first I would rather hear about your plans."

She paused, fully aware that Allan Pinkerton would not want her to tell anyone that he had offered her a new assignment.

Ridge prompted, "When I first saw you entering Pinkerton's office, I should have suspected you worked for him."

It wasn't a question, but Laurel knew that's how Ridge intended it: Was she still a Pinkerton operative?

She said evasively, "That was a one-time assignment to help me find Claude."

"I see." Ridge seemed to give a quiet sigh of relief. He fixed her with steady eyes. "Now what are you going to do?"

She squirmed uneasily and lowered her eyes, unwilling to tell him a lie. She hedged, saying, "I have been offered a correspondent's job with the *Chicago Globe*."

She thought a shadow of disapproval flickered across his face.

"I can understand because I read what you wrote about the experiences on our train ride. You're a good writer."

"Thanks." She took a deep breath. "What do you think about that as a job?"

"There certainly aren't many women correspondents in this country."

"Does that mean you disapprove?"

"No. We fought a war because of what people thought. I believe in your right to choose, even if it is an unusual occupation for a woman."

She freed her hands and sipped from the water glass, feeling her heart speed up. Would he guess her next words were to learn how he felt about their possibly being apart for an extended time? How would he feel about that? But she couldn't say all of it because Allan Pinkerton had forbidden that.

She announced, "I also have a second offer."

"Oh? What's that?"

She said softly, "My work could take me west with the transcontinental railroad that's being built."

"Really?" Ridge reclaimed her hand. "That's a very interesting coincidence, because I have an offer to join train work crews building west out of Omaha."

She caught her breath before asking, "Are you going to take it?"

He shrugged. "I don't know. I still feel somewhat restless, and don't really know what I want to do with my life right now. So building the transcontinental railroad might be interesting."

"You once mentioned having a plantation in Virginia. I would think that would have strong ties to draw you back there."

"It's been in the family for three generations, and naturally it means a lot to me. But the carpetbaggers manipulated it out from under me under the Federal Confiscation Acts."

"I don't know much about them."

"Basically, confiscation allowed Northerners to seize property of Southerners like me. So when the Union began their so-called Reconstruction after the war, some Northern opportunists crammed their belongings in carpetbags and descended on the

South to legally steal what little of value was left."

Laurel believed that most carpetbaggers had gone south to build schools and do other good works, but the sudden harsh edge to Ridge's tone warned her that this was no time to mention that. She remained silent.

Ridge took a slow, deep breath before adding, "There's nothing left except the land, and I'm not financially able to fight the legal battles it will take to possibly regain it."

"Do you want it back?"

"In some ways, yes. But a plantation with just myself would be a lonely place."

She lowered her eyes, knowing it was too soon for either of them to talk of such things. She said quickly, "Do you have a third choice?"

He grinned. "Well, we had some Texas men in the cavalry. After the war, with absolutely nothing on their backs except what was left of their uniforms, they told me they were going to steal Yankee horses and go home. After all, a Texas man can't be expected to walk all that way. They wanted me to go with them."

"To do what?"

"It seems that people in the East are getting tired of eating pork, so some Texas men plan to round up great herds of wild longhorn cattle. They will be driven north toward Kansas where the railroad should be arriving pretty soon. The cattle will be shipped east on cars. The idea has a certain appeal to me."

"That sounds like a very difficult and lonely job, Ridge."

"It probably is, but if a man is single and has nothing to his name except the clothes on his back, well, that's a way to have time to think through many things."

Laurel's heart sank at the thought of what such a separation might mean to them. But she said, "You have some hard choices."

"Yes, but at least I made one decision while riding the cars back to Chicago."

That piqued her interest. "That's also a curious coincidence because I also made one then."

She freed her hand and took another sip of water while her pulse pounded with anxiety over how he would react to what she was about to say.

"Ridge," she began, looking directly into his eyes, "I regret with all my heart the part I had in the Bethel Crossing action. I beg your forgiveness for causing your wound, and the death of your brother and all the others."

His fingers closed so hard around hers that she flinched, but he didn't seem to notice. "When I first learned that, I was so enraged that I couldn't think straight. But on the ride back here, I realized that neither you nor I can change what's past. We each did what seemed right during the war, and people died, people we loved."

He swallowed hard before continuing in a low tone, "But now, as General Lee and the late President Lincoln said, it's time to bind up the nation's wounds. That has to start with individuals. So I did something I never expected to do."

He paused, then explained, "I asked God to forgive me for the wrong I've done, then I remembered that the Lord won't forgive us unless we first forgive our brother. So, to answer your question, I have already forgiven you. Can you do the same for me?"

Laurel couldn't keep the sudden tears from flooding her eyes. "I do that, with all my heart."

He lifted her fingers and brought them to his lips. "Thank you, Laurel." He gently replaced her hand on the table under his and sighed heavily. "Well," he said with great relief, "that's a tremendous load off my mind."

"Mine, too."

"Laurel," he added in a throaty tone, "whatever happens, I don't want to lose track of you."

Their eyes melded in unspoken understanding. Then Ridge sighed again. "I have a feeling, though, that you like adventure and excitement."

"It's true. I like to do things that other women my age do not. Do you disapprove?"

"You have every right to do as you wish, but what if that someday clashes with what someone else wants?"

Laurel hesitated, trying to carefully phrase her words so that she was honest and yet left room for her own personal fulfillment someday. "I don't expect to do such things *all* my life."

That seemed to satisfy Ridge, for a hint of pleased smile touched his lips. He continued, "In the meantime, if you choose to accept the journalism offer, and I take that railroad job, we might run into each other out there. I feel it's meant to be."

She didn't want to leave their lives to such an uncertain future, but she forced herself to answer quietly, "It's possible, I suppose."

"I'm glad, because in spite of what you have told me in the past, I think you need someone to look after you."

She teased, "Are you interested in doing that?"

"Why don't we meet tomorrow and talk about it?"

Smiling warmly, Laurel said, "I would like that very much."

If you enjoyed *Days of Deception*, watch for another book about Laurel and Ridge—the second of the Pinkerton Lady Chronicles— coming in 1999 from Victor Books.

**If you liked this book from
ChariotVictor Publishing,
check out this great title . . .**

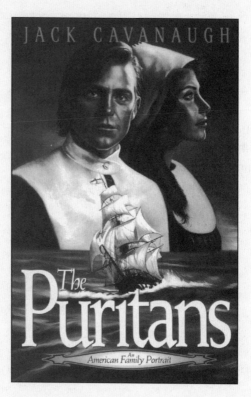

The stirring epic of faith, love, and sacrifice traces the
adventures of one of America's first families of faith. As Book 1
in the series, this compelling novel sets the stage for the spiritual
saga of the Morgans. Here we meet Drew Morgan, a young
Englishman who dreams of being a knight, but finds love and
faith in the New World.

The Puritans - Book #1
by Jack Cavanaugh
ISBN: 1-56476-440-0
Retail: $11.99

If you liked this book from
ChariotVictor Publishing,
check out this great title . . .

A contemporary mystery/suspense novel exploring the current
topic of assisted suicide. Dr. Gates McClure uses all her training
and wiles to solve the mystery surrounding the death of a doctor
who is protesting assisted suicides. As she searches for answers,
she comes to grips with her own views of medically induced
death and her faith. The first book in the new *Ridgeline*
Mystery series.

Marked for Mercy
by Alton Gansky
ISBN: 1-56476-678-0
Retail: $10.99